FEAR RUNNER

DALE BRANDON

DISCLAIMER

This novel, which is set in 1991, is a work of fiction. Any resemblance to actual persons, living or dead, or actual events is purely coincidental. Any real names appearing in the novel have been used to produce a sense of realism in the story. The author in no way suggests that the governments, companies, persons, or institutions have, or will, act in the manner described in the novel. The events described herein are a product of the author's imagination and are used fictitiously. The sole purpose of the book is to entertain the reader.

For my family:

Kittie, Carie, Dale Jr., Kathleen, Aaron,
Devynn, Kelsey, Tyler, and Mason

ACKNOWLEDGMENT

I want to give special thanks to Joan Steiger for editing and proof reading the manuscript, and for her enthusiasm for this project. Her input is sincerely appreciated.

By the same author

Dead Fall
Death Mountain

CHAPTER 1

Spring, 1991

The trading floor of the Chicago Board of Trade marked the center of Scott Quinn's world—a world racing toward meltdown. Recent losses had already dealt his career a severe blow, but his ultimate fate depended on decisions he would make during the next fifty minutes. He hoped to survive the day, but he knew markets rarely accommodated scared money.

Scott stood in a boisterous trading pit, surrounded by a throng of organized chaos. Traders with strained necks and reddened faces exchanged hand signals and shouted at one another. Scraps of paper covered the floor. Along the fringes, runners clad in brightly colored jackets fanned out like spokes in a wheel, rushing between phone banks and brokers, their faces expressing urgency. Scott likened the scene to that of a bustling beehive whose inhabitants scurried about on some desperate mission only they understood.

Scott usually balanced his trading activities between the Dow Jones and grain futures trading pits, but he had temporarily changed his tactics and he now held an unusually large position in soybean futures. Five days ago, a surprise news flash announced the collapse of negotiations with Russia for a contract to purchase large amounts of various grains. Stunned traders at the CBOT drove prices limit down within seconds. Prices locked limit down for the next four days, creating an avalanche of margin calls. Large numbers of traders tried to sell to meet capital demands, but a dearth of buyers brought trading to a standstill. Those who wanted out were trapped—they could only wait and hope. Fear and urgency produced an air of panic that hung over the pit like dirty smoke.

Traders had anticipated the Russian purchase, and the uptrend of the last three weeks reflected their expectations. Driven by optimism, Scott increased the size of his holdings ten days ago. His current position of 600 contracts meant that each daily limit move of just thirty cents a bushel resulted in a loss of $900,000. If the market locked limit down again, he would have to liquidate most of his other holdings to meet the expected margin call. He reflected on the old trader's axiom—leverage kills.

Trading had been brutal since the opening bell. Soybeans futures dropped precipitously in the first minutes but did not fall the limit as expected. The market held just above the critical point then rallied sharply only to fall again. Prices fluctuated wildly as waves of panic knifed through the pit. Countless micro-trends sprang up and faded amid flurries of shouts and hand signals.

Because soybeans did not fall the daily limit, Scott had the opportunity to liquidate his position for the first time in five days, but he held back. If he sold now, he would lose most of his capital, although he still held small positions in Dow Jones and gold futures. Thoughts and strategies spinning through his mind converged and formed a desperate theory. He believed traders holding short positions were overdue to take profits, and he hoped their buying pressure would cause a temporary rally. He knew rapid price movements often led to periods of consolidation highlighted by violent swings. Using a risky strategy, Scott attempted to add to his position on weakness and sell on strength, but he was careful to trade nimbly. A sudden change in sentiment could easily drive the market down the limit once again.

After liquidating part of his position during a rally, he watched as a new wave of selling drove the price down the limit. A current of fear stabbed at his inner core as he considered the implications of another limit move. A few minutes later, prices bounced off the limit and traded violently near the lows. He watched the action, and then bought more contracts. A dangerous strategy, which he equated to that of dancing on the edge of a sword. One slip . . .

After a surge of volatile action, short covering sent soybeans substantially higher. He noticed the trend weakening toward the close, and he began to doubt the longevity of the move. It did not feel right.

Jason McDonald, Scott's friend and trading partner, maneuvered through the crowd and yelled over the din, "What do you think?"

Scott leaned toward his friend. "This rally won't hold. I think it'll hit a vacuum when the shorts stop buying."

"But there are buy-stops around 840 on November."

Scott glanced at the wallboard while considering the risk of not liquidating. Another price collapse to limit down would be catastrophic. "If the market hits them, I think we should get out. Sell into strength—salvage what we can."

"I'm not so sure," Jason said. "It looks like a potential key reversal day."

"Not a chance. It's a dead-cat bounce, a sucker move."

Soybeans churned until a broker with large commercial interests bought nearly two million bushels, forcing the price of November beans to 839.

Scott focused on 840, his mind in a state of heightened alertness. He felt as though he was wrestling with the devil himself, but he had to maintain control. He took a deep breath and concentrated on the action. Three minutes later, soybeans went through the critical price and hit a series of buy-stops.

"Now!" Scott yelled. He flashed hand signals and sold his entire position within a few seconds. He usually traded Dow futures after he finished with the grains, but he had taken a serious financial hit, and he felt emotionally spent. He motioned toward the edge of the pit. "Let's get the hell out of here."

They pushed their way through the crowd and left the trading floor. They took the elevator to their office, walked in, and slumped into chairs. Neither spoke. Scott stared at the wall, listening to the incessant hum from the fluorescent lights. There were still five minutes of trading left when he finally checked his quote machine. He punched several keys and said, "Soybeans tanked. Down the limit."

Jason shook his head and muttered something unintelligible.

They grew quiet while reviewing their trades.

Scott punched several keys on his calculator and then penciled numbers on a scratch pad. The loss was not as bad as he had expected, but he still felt devastated. In five days, he had lost just under $3 million, and there was no one to fault but himself. He had violated his own rules by allowing his position to become seriously overextended—an amateurish mistake. Thankfully, today's frantic trading had reduced his loss by over thirty percent.

He leaned back and stared at the wall. Deep within, in some fragile part of his psyche, he struggled with his intense fear of failing in the market. Failing as his father had nearly twenty years earlier. He felt as if he had lost several years of his life in a few days.

Scott ran his fingers through his hair as his mind searched for something positive. His thoughts shifted to his ultimate goal of founding and managing his own futures fund. Though he had suffered a severe setback, he believed he could still attain his dream with a carefully orchestrated strategy. An important component of his plan centered on an upcoming issue of *Stocks & Futures Magazine*. Scott's growing stature at the CBOT, coupled with his friendship with the editor of the magazine, created an important opportunity. He had agreed to write a cover story in a forthcoming issue of the prestigious magazine. His article would be a major, multi-page commentary outlining a trading strategy that combined fundamental and technical analysis.

To complete his research, Scott had previously scheduled two appointments with officials at the Department of Agriculture for the following Tuesday in Washington, D. C. He elevated his trip to critical status.

He checked entries on his calendar and turned to Jason. "The crop production report comes out next Tuesday, but I'll be out of town."

Jason leaned back and laced his hands together behind his head. "That's as good a place as any. I sure as hell don't want any positions going into the report." Both traders knew the report could have a dramatic impact on futures prices, which would ultimately affect the cost of a wide variety of products in the global marketplace.

After a moment of silence, Jason shoved his calculator aside. "I have enough left to buy lunch."

"You're on. Give me ten minutes."

They left the office, passing several colleagues returning from the floor. They saw a startling range of emotions on the trader's faces. Some had made large profits, but others had suffered devastating losses. Scott marveled at the ability of the human face to reveal complex emotions so graphically. Pain, joy, agony, greed, confusion, and desperation—they were all there.

———

Unable to sleep, Scott rolled over and glanced at the clock—four-thirty. After dinner, he had spent the evening seated at his desk, drinking red wine, and agonizing over his recent losses. He went to bed a little before midnight. He tossed for hours, his mind churning, until frustration caused him to give up his struggle with insomnia.

He swung his legs over the edge of the bed and sat motion-less, burdened with concern, until a flash of lighting caused him to look out the window toward an approaching storm. At the next flash of light, he rose and turned off his alarm. Clad in white pa-jama bottoms, he went to the kitchen and made coffee. He took the pot and a cup to his bedroom, turned out the light, and seated himself in front of the window. His twelfth-floor apartment of-fered an excellent view of the fast-moving storm as it swept across the Chicago skyline. Scott enjoyed the spectacle of intense storms, and he hoped the panorama would provide a necessary respite from his distress.

He tried to concentrate on the jagged bolts hurtling earth-ward, but his thoughts kept returning to recent market action. He had lost a substantial amount of trading capital in what seemed like an eye blink of time, and the grip of despair that seized him had an overwhelming depth that stunned him. He could think of nothing else. With his heavy losses, he faced a daunting task in the days and weeks ahead. Whatever it took, he had to overcome the challenge.

When a series flashes brightened the room, Scott shifted his gaze to a small black and white picture of his mother and father resting on a nearby table. He picked up the frame and pulled it closer. He waited for the next flash; then, he focused on the male figure in the photo. Scott had just celebrated his seventeenth birthday when his father committed suicide. After losing everything during the unrelenting stock market decline of 1974, Richard Quinn had been unable to bear the pain and had ended his life by driving his car into a large oak tree at ninety-five miles an hour. Scott had never forgiven his father for an act he considered cowardly. Now, for the first time, he shared a similar burden.

As the room alternated between light and darkness, Scott's gaze remained on the picture. When the room brightened again, he stared at the photo as if he were trying to see inside the person. Though the physical image in the picture remained unchanged, he began to feel differently about his father. As he contemplated the powerful despair that had driven his father to commit suicide, a surge of emotions swept over Scott. Confused by a sudden feeling of guilt, he stared out the window in a moment of reflection.

He sat motionless, staring into the night, seeing nothing. Time slipped into slow motion, and he became immersed in an internal world of reflection. His mind sifted through a jumble of thoughts—linking, shuffling, isolating, and then casting them aimlessly aside. He closed his eyes shielding himself from the lonely night. A siren wailed in the distance and then faded into nothing.

———

The next morning, Scott awoke with a slight hangover and a queasy stomach. He washed down a Zantac with his favorite Kona coffee and made a mental note to pack the medication for his trip to D. C., a destination that was far more important now than a week ago.

He flew to Washington on Monday and checked into the Jordan Colonial Hotel. Tuesday morning, he drove to the Department of Agriculture, arriving early enough to familiarize himself with the complex and have coffee. He signed in and then went to a cafeteria in the basement of the Administration Building where he bought coffee and a newspaper. He had thirty-five minutes before his first meeting. His second appointment was set for one o'clock.

A man seated at the table next to him inadvertently knocked a folder to the floor. When Scott noticed that the man used a cane, he immediately rose from his chair, picked up the papers, and handed them to the man.

The elderly man smiled. "You're a gentleman. Thank you."

Scott acknowledged the compliment and turned toward his table. Laughter from a group of women across the room caused him to look in their direction.

At that moment, he saw her.

Though he had previously heard the group of women, a pillar had blocked his view of the brunette that suddenly captured his attention. The noise in the crowded room seemed to vanish as he observed her. He stood motionless for a moment, his gaze locked on her; then, he returned to his table. The pillar, again, blocked his view. He eased to his left and caught a glimpse of her hair. She suddenly tilted her head and looked across the room at Scott.

He smiled.

She disappeared behind the pillar.

He shifted his chair so he could see most of her face.

She glanced toward Scott and smiled. He thought she had the prettiest smile he had ever seen. A smile that made a person want more.

As he watched, members of her group rose and began to exit toward the busy hallway. Scott now had an unobstructed view of the brunette. She wore a classic, navy blue suit with a contrasting white, silky blouse. A tiny pendant attached to a gold chain hung from her neck. She was attractive and well groomed, but something else intrigued Scott; nature had blessed her with a fresh, natural glow. He thought she was pretty but not beautiful—perfect.

She held eye contact for a moment; then, she turned to join her group as they began to exit the cafeteria. As she left the room, she turned and looked at Scott. He felt a frisson of excitement as he watched her. Something had happened during that look; something he could not define, but he wanted to hold onto the feeling.

He had to talk to her.

Six people in another group blocked his view as they began to file out of the cafeteria. He grabbed his briefcase and hurried across the room. He entered the crowded hallway and maneuvered past several people only to find himself blocked by others attempting to enter the elevator. Where was the brunette? He inched along just as the elevator door began to close. Unable to locate her, he leaned to one side and saw her in the back of the elevator. She turned to face the front and made eye contact. He attempted to inch forward but found his access completely blocked. He watched, helplessly, as the door closed. He felt a surprising sense of loss.

He watched the indicator lights, noting that the elevator stopped at each level during its ascent. He took the next elevator, exited on the third floor, and looked down the hallway, but there was no brunette in a navy blue suit.

There was something about her that attracted him, something besides her face and her smile, something stronger. His thoughts, fueled by disappointment, gave him a sense of urgency to find her. But how? He continued to think about the woman for several minutes and then, reluctantly, turned his attention to the reason he had flown from his home in Chicago to visit the Agriculture Department. Even though he was on a critical mission, and his first appointment was minutes away, his thoughts returned to the brunette and her captivating smile. He felt certain she had gone to a nearby office. He pondered the thought for a moment and then checked his watch. Ten twenty-five. He looked down the hallway one last time, but there was no sign of her.

Scott's first appointment went reasonably well considering his state of mind. Though he tried, he simply could not stop thinking about the woman in the cafeteria. His meeting ended at eleven-fifteen, and he headed toward the elevator. The official had given him a list of germane publications available at the Information and Publications Office on the first floor.

He left the elevator and scanned the hallway. Again, no sign of the woman. Scott obtained the material he needed and was leaving the Information Office when he thought about the cafeteria. It seemed reasonable he might see her again during the lunch hour. It was worth a try. He arrived at the cafeteria before noon and found a small table with a good view of the room.

He put down his tray and heard a voice from behind.

"Excuse me. I was at the table next to you this morning."

Scott turned and recognized the man with the cane he had helped earlier.

The man smiled. "You rushed out of here so fast you left a very nice pen on the table. It was engraved so I took it to lost and found. You can pick it up there."

Scott extended his hand. "That was very thoughtful. Thank you."

The man shook his hand. "No problem."

Scott hesitated, and then said. "Did you notice that attractive woman in the blue suit this morning? Over by the pillar."

"It would've been hard to have missed her."

"Do you happen to know her?"

"No. I've seen her a few times, but there are an awful lot of folks in this complex."

Scott nodded his agreement.

He waited until twelve-forty but there was no sign of the brunette. Reluctantly, he left the cafeteria and walked to the room number for his second appointment. A secretary told him that Mr. Connelly was on a conference call but would be available shortly. Scott took a seat and picked up a copy of *Forbes*.

He occasionally looked up and watched the secretary struggle with her computer. Several times the woman pecked at the keyboard, frowned at the screen, and then threw up her hands in disgust.

Scott lowered his magazine. "Having a problem this morning?"

"It's these spreadsheets. I always have trouble with them."

"They can be tricky." He resumed reading while she made a phone call. A few minutes later, a young woman entered the room. Scott felt a surge of energy as he found himself looking at the brunette in the navy blue suit.

CHAPTER 2

The brunette closed the door and took a few steps. Scott stood, hesitated, and then said, "I didn't expect to see you again."

She stopped and turned as if caught off-guard. She smoothed the hair on the left side of her head. "Good morning."

"I suppose you noticed I was trying to get on the elevator with you."

"Yes, I picked up on that."

Scott took a step closer. Her nearness offered him a good look at her eyes. They were hazel with flecks of green, fringed with long curving lashes. Unusual and beautiful. His gaze swept over her face and neck, noticing a skin tone that promised a delicate consistency over her entire body. Scott felt his world change in the span of a single heartbeat.

He caught her scent for the first time. Shalimar, one of his three favorite perfumes. Shalimar vaulted into first place, and Scott felt himself sliding over the edge.

The brunette turned toward the woman at the computer and then looked back at Scott. "You'll have to excuse me. I have a presentation Wednesday, and Marianne is having a problem with my data." She walked across the room and slid a chair next to the other woman.

Scott took a seat and attempted to read, but his mind had already locked on the nearby conversation. The brunette had the situation under control within a few minutes, and she had calmed the other woman in a way that seemed to change her attitude toward the computer. The brunette seemed dedicated and she was obviously compassionate.

Twice, she glanced at Scott.

He noticed the way she raised her eyebrows when she looked toward him, the way her hair moved when she turned her head, and the enchanting smile that had captivated him at first sight. A door opened and a heavyset man motioned him in. Scott sensed the brunette watching him as he went through the door.

Franklin Connelly had an average-sized office for a man of his position, but he had an unusually large and cluttered desk. Dozens of folders covered the working area, allowing the wood to peek out from only a few narrow strips. After exchanging pleasantries, Scott consulted his notes and began a series of questions. Usually, he would have considered Connelly's verbose responses an important part of the interview, but he became impatient and covertly checked his watch. After twenty minutes, he had finished only half of his questions. His mind strayed, and he wondered if the brunette had already left the outer office. He had to find out. He asked a final question, thanked Connelly, and got up to leave. He stepped into the next office and caught a glimpse of the brunette leaving the room. He hurried across the office and stepped into the hallway.

"Miss."

She stopped and turned.

He smiled and walked toward her. "I hope you don't think this is too forward, but I wonder if you would have dinner with me?"

"I don't make a habit of arranging dates in the hallway with strangers. I'm sorry; it's nothing personal."

"I understand, but I guarantee I'm a gentleman."

She smiled. "I believe you, but I don't want to break my rules." She glanced at her watch. "I have to get back to my project." She started down the hallway.

Another approach, *quick*. "A drink after work? No date, just a friendly drink."

She continued walking, but at a slower pace.

Scott took several steps. "If you say no, we'll never see each other again. I don't want that to happen."

She stopped, hesitated, and then turned. "Henry's. Five-thirty."

"My name is Scott Quinn. Yours?"

"Lauren."

He felt a surge of energy as he watched her walk away.

———

Lauren Chandler walked toward her office, but her thoughts were not on her upcoming presentation. She found herself thinking about another man for the first time since the death of her fiancé. She found Scott's casual good looks and lithe appearance appealing, and she noticed a smooth, almost sensual rhythm in his movements in the hallway. In Marianne's office, she had noticed something else. He had a pleasant, accessible personality.

Lauren reached her desk and felt a pang of guilt as her thoughts turned to her deceased fiancé, Paul Lambert. Adjusting to his loss had been difficult. The pain that had overwhelmed her had been slow to ease, but, gradually, time had done what nothing else could. It had been an agonizing experience, but the burden she carried had slowly subsided and her day-to-day routine had become easier.

Shortly after the tragedy, Lauren knew she needed a change and was pleased she'd had the courage to start over in new surroundings. Seven months had passed since she had accepted a promotion that required her to transfer to the Agriculture Department's Washington, D.C. office. Her new position, with the National Agriculture Statistics Service, required her to make presentations to various department heads on a regular basis. Her abilities with numbers were obvious, but she had worried about her skills as a speaker. Though she had stumbled at first, she quickly gained confidence and began to enjoy the challenge.

She had mostly kept to herself the first few months in Washington, although she did form a quick friendship with a co-worker, Marilyn Shepard. They had gotten along so well they decided to share an apartment in Alexandria. Lauren was adjusting to her new life in a slow, methodical manner. She had postponed dating because she feared involvement with other men might cause her to be hurt again. She felt she needed the presence of a man in her life, but she was determined that the choice and timing would be on her terms.

She had gotten so good at saying no to men she wondered why she had said yes to Scott Quinn. She began to worry she was still not ready to see another man. She had tried to bury her fear, but it was still there, lurking underneath, waiting to rise to the surface with its baggage of pain. She pictured Scott in her mind and realized that meeting for drinks was hardly a major commitment.

A noise in the office snapped her out of her reverie. She turned her attention to the folders stacked on her desk and resumed work on her presentation. She glanced at a checklist and noticed she had a few items that needed further research. She grabbed a folder and headed for a small library on the fourth floor. She opened the library door and wondered why she had not passed more people on her way over. Then, she remembered the monthly USDA crop report would be released today, and many staff members were sequestered inside the lockup facility. Because the report affected prices around the globe, protection of the pre-release data was critical.

Lauren went to the rear of the library and began selecting pertinent volumes. She heard the door close. She was behind a row of books and could not see the person who had entered but paid little attention because many employees routinely used the facility. She continued working, but she could not help overhearing the person talking on the phone. It was Hayden Benson, the Deputy Secretary. She had done research for his office on several occasions. Lauren gathered an armful of books and turned toward a desk but something about the person's conversation bothered her. She stopped, tilted her head, and listened.

"I'm positive," Benson said. "The report has a minus five rating. There's a huge increase in soybean acreage." He said something else and then hung up.

The crop report? Lauren stood motionless, doubting her senses. It wasn't possible; the lockup was sealed. Yet, the Deputy Secretary of Agriculture had just given someone priceless information *before* the official release to the financial press. She knew that anyone receiving pre-release data could make a fortune in the futures market.

Stunned by what she heard, Lauren failed to see a manual on top of her stack begin to slip. She felt her load shift and made a desperate attempt to catch the falling book but her swift movements only made matters worse; her entire load crashed to the floor.

She froze. She had no idea what to do. She stood still, her feet anchored to the floor, hoping it was all a terrible mistake.

A voice jolted her back to reality. "Who's there?"

A tense, expectant silence gripped the room.

She heard footsteps.

CHAPTER 3

Victor Merrick hung up the phone and checked the clock; the futures market closed in seventy seconds. Immediately after receiving Hayden Benson's phone call, Merrick instructed his floor broker to short the market by placing a large sell order in soybeans. It would be close, but he expected most of his order to be filled. Still, he intended to issue a stern warning to Benson about his last-minute phone call.

Merrick lit a cigar, leaned back in his chair, put his feet on his desk, and reflected on his recent success. His scheme to reverse the fortunes of the Burgess Corporation was creative, but Merrick preferred another word: brilliant. His plan was far more profitable than his illegal takeover of Burgess two years earlier, and it was equally undetectable.

When he had first entered the business, Merrick considered commodity trading to be a mundane subject. Why would anyone get excited about trading futures contracts? After further review, he discovered the true power of leverage. The typical commodity was leveraged at about fifteen times the initial margin. This meant that he could control tens of thousands of dollars of a commodity, or financial instrument, with a few thousand dollars in margin for a single contract. If the underlying commodity moved approximately eight percent, he would double his investment. When a trader held a large number of contracts, he entered a world of extreme profits and losses.

Merrick opened a folder and reviewed a summary of his recent commodity transactions; then, he removed an old statement and compared the two. He saw a startling difference. The earlier report summarized trading results shortly after he had taken control of Burgess. His initial decision to forego standard hedging practices had caused near catastrophic losses in the futures market. He looked at his most recent statement. The trades placed after implementation of his scheme showed substantial profits. A thin smile formed on his lips as he remembered how the idea had come to him over a year ago. It had happened the very day he had suffered heavy trading losses after guessing wrong on the monthly USDA Crop Production Report. From the depths of gloom came a flash of brilliance. He would attain wealth by using the very reporting mechanism that had caused his heavy losses.

The Department of Agriculture uses a protected lockup facility to decrypt and compile data from forty-five state offices. The release of the final figures came after the markets closed, but Merrick knew the information was worth a fortune if he could obtain the data before trading ended. But how?

He studied USDA procedures until the various components of his plan fell into place, one item at a time, like tumblers in a lock. First, he needed a weak link inside the Agriculture Department. He compiled a list of key officials; then, he had his men follow those individuals and report on their outside activities. It took weeks, but Merrick finally narrowed his list to two candidates. His highest priority had been Hayden Benson, the fifty-four year-old Deputy Secretary of Agriculture. Early reports portrayed a man of flawless character, but surveillance eventually discovered an exploitable weakness. Benson frequently stopped on the way to his home and had a few drinks. There was nothing wrong with that, but after he had a few cocktails he invariably approached young, attractive women but with little success. They had found his weak spot.

Merrick had several women at his disposal, but he needed someone special for his plan. He decided on Shannon Peterson, a striking woman in her early thirties. Her most impressive attributes included blonde hair that cascaded over her shoulders and a stunning figure. Moreover, Shannon had another essential element: a sense of style that made her ideal for a government official. Merrick knew Shannon's ambition was to make as much money as possible with the least amount of effort. Thus, his approach had been straightforward. What could be easier than servicing an older man, twice a week, in a new, rent-free apartment? She would receive $5,000 a month, and, if the plan worked as well as expected, there would be large bonuses. The total package could easily exceed $200,000 a year, tax-free. His offer had been generous, because she was the key. The plan would fail without Benson's involvement. It had been an easy decision for Shannon.

To set the trap, Shannon waited at Benson's favorite lounge every day until he came in. She made contact on the fourth day and quickly developed a relationship that led to sexual encounters in her apartment. Two weeks later, Merrick had what he wanted. When Hayden Benson made his next visit to Shannon's apartment, Merrick was waiting.

Benson entered the room, glanced at the stranger, then at the television. Vivid scenes of the Deputy Secretary of Agriculture having sex with a young blonde flashed on the screen. Benson's face turned ashen. He froze for a moment, then sank in a chair, leaned forward, and buried his face in both hands.

Shannon extended a shot glass to the shaken man.

Benson looked up, took the drink, downed the vodka, and then stared forlornly at the floor. "How much do you want?"

Merrick felt a sense of power and control as he walked to the bar and poured a drink. "You've got it all wrong, Hayden. Is it all right if I call you Hayden?"

No answer.

"It's not going to cost you a cent. In fact, you're going to make a profit." Merrick gave his demands and reminded Benson that the indiscretion had already been committed. Either it would be the end of his career and public disgrace, or he consented to the scheme. Merrick told Benson he could still see Shannon every week—nothing would change. With shame and humiliation a mailbox away, Benson had agreed.

Because Benson was not inside the lockup facility during report compilation, a second person had to be recruited. Benson supplied a list of clerks and other participants to Merrick. Kenneth Lindsay, a statistics technician, who indulged himself with an expensive cocaine habit stood apart from the others on the list. After Lindsay's drug use escalated, he had lost his wife and he was on the verge of filing bankruptcy. Lindsay was told he would be supplied with modest amounts of cocaine and most of his debts would be paid. The last component was an unmasked threat of violence. However, Lindsay did not make the expected decision. He said it was wrong, and he wanted no part of the operation.

After learning the depth of Lindsay's resolve, Merrick sent in Ray Lisowski, a huge man ideally suited for the job. Lisowski had once been a professional wrestler whose career had ended abruptly after he attacked a small-time promoter in Texas. After Lisowski gave Lindsay a vicious beating, the victim quickly agreed to supply the information.

Two parts of the plan were in place, but the last element proved more difficult than expected. The key to Merrick's plan was his method of getting data out of the high-security lockup facility. He spent weeks investigating various ideas, but each had an inherent flaw. The USDA had done a masterful job of protecting the report until its official release at three o'clock.

Merrick's research uncovered a myriad of security measures: armed guards, double doors, encrypted files, disabled voice and data communications lines, and sealed elevators. He was particularly upset about the special window shades that prevented electronic transmission.

Awash in a feeling of superiority, Merrick recalled the unusual catalyst that led to a solution. He had been sitting on the toilet, thinking about the problem when the idea took form. He had been searching for a high-tech method to steal the data, and he suddenly realized his mistake. The USDA had obviously utilized every resource to prevent a high-tech theft. Low-tech was the answer, and he was sitting on the ideal device. He lifted his head and whispered, "The plumbing." With his pants still curled around his ankles, he jumped up. "That's it. The pipes! The fucking pipes."

He turned and stared at the wall, his mind processing, visualizing. He saw the men's rest room in the USDA lockup facility, he saw a special pipe installed behind the wall that connected to the floor below, he saw the pre-release crop report numbers secretly being fed into the pipe, he saw a phone call to the trading floor, and he saw riches.

Though Merrick had a clever idea, getting even a minor plumbing job done to his specifications inside a government building proved extremely difficult. It took three months and a substantial sum of money to get the right man into the building to repair a sabotaged commode on the fifth floor. The plumber repaired the toilet; then, he started on the important work. He installed the new pipe and cut it to a precise length. The other end stopped directly behind a toilet on the floor below and could be accessed by removing a single wall tile.

This method allowed Lindsay to obtain the crop data and secretly drop a coded message into the pipe. On the floor below, Benson would retrieve the message and then proceed to his private phone and relay the information. Merrick would buy or sell a specific commodity before the market closed, then simply wait until the next morning to review his huge profits.

The plan seemed perfect until Lindsay wanted to know how to send the message down the narrow pipe. Merrick had assumed paper would work, but the initial test showed that it hung up and never reached the bottom. A metal object would be too noisy. While struggling with the problem, Merrick noticed a large eraser on his desk. He first thought it too primitive but, upon reflection, he knew he had found the ideal instrument. An eraser was accessible, it was heavy, it was quiet, and it could be written on—it was perfect.

He devised a code to send a simple message. They would use a single number between plus five and minus five with zero being considered a neutral report. A positive number was an instruction to buy—a minus number meant to sell short. Short selling allows a trader to make profits when prices decline. The strength of the number indicated the degree of surprise the report showed. To avoid confusion, a single, volatile commodity had been selected—soybeans.

Merrick put away his trading summaries and felt a sense of great pleasure. He saw his creativity as brilliance. He opened a desk drawer and took out the first eraser they had used. That simple piece of rubber had made him $2,742,000 in three days, and that was just the beginning. He had set a goal of $200 million for his scheme, and he had no doubts about attaining that number. He rose from his chair, walked to the far corner of his office, and stopped in front of a richly textured door made of solid walnut. The entryway provided access to a private world forbidden to everyone but himself. He knew his staff would not understand. He removed a key from his pocket, unlocked the door, and stepped inside. Merrick repeatedly flipped the eraser into the air as he moved across the large room.

CHAPTER 4

The sound of approaching footsteps sent Lauren's pulse spinning free. She stepped back and nearly tripped over the books strewn about the floor. Her instincts told her to run, but there was only one way out of the library and Hayden Benson stood between her and the door.

He came around a desk. "Lauren? What are—"

A surge of adrenalin kicked in. She picked up a large book and flung it at him.

Benson raised his arms, but the book sailed between them and struck him in the face. He lost his balance and slammed against a wall.

Lauren bolted for the door.

Her mind raced as she ran down the hall toward her office. What should she do? She stopped in front of her office door and tried to focus on her options when the obvious jolted her. Benson would never admit what he did. It would be her word against his. Panic caused her thoughts to form in confused jumbles. She realized she could not function objectively and decided to leave the building; she needed time to consider her next step. Lauren took a deep breath and entered her office. She grabbed her purse, went to the adjacent office, opened the door, and stuck her head in. "Linda, I—I'm feeling ill. I think I'd better go home."

"Oh, Lauren, you don't look well. Is there anything I can do?"

"No, I'll be fine, thanks." She worried her tone had failed to conceal the collision of emotions that had been unleashed in her mind. She went to the other door and peered into the hallway. All clear. She hurried to the first floor and left the building. Struggling to control her confusion, she stopped after a few steps to concentrate on finding a car she parked in nearly the same location every day. How could she forget? After a frantic search, she reached her car and drove onto the street, but she had no idea where to go. She knew only that she had to get away—to sort things out.

Lauren turned onto Fifteenth Street and drove past the Jefferson Memorial. She turned south onto Ohio Drive and followed the Potomac for about half a mile before stopping near a row of cherry trees. She sat in the car for several minutes considering her options, but her mind offered only a chaotic web of thoughts. She got out and paced back and forth under the trees. It began to drizzle, but she barely noticed the moisture. Lauren knew she should call the authorities and report what she had heard, but something stopped her. Her mind kept going back to the same thing; there were no other witnesses—it was her word against that of a high-level government official. They would never believe her, not for a second.

———

After Lauren had fled from the library, Hayden Benson got up and hurried across the room. He clasped the doorknob, hesitated, then released his grip. The sight of the Deputy Secretary of Agriculture chasing a female employee down the hallway would require an immediate explanation. That was the last thing he wanted. Benson had no idea what to do, but he knew he could think better in his office. Before opening the door, he rubbed his hand over his face.

No blood. He headed up the hallway and tried to walk in a slow, calm manner, but each step seemed quicker than the one before.

He stopped in front of his secretary's door, straightened his tie, took a deep breath, went in, and felt relieved she was away from her desk. He wrote a brief note instructing her to hold his calls and then entered his office. He stood with his back against the door and shut his eyes. A vision of Victor Merrick flashed through his mind. Everything about the strange, irascible man with the long, black hair scared him, but Merrick's eyes disturbed the most. They were cold, alert, and utterly intense. Benson likened them to deep-set holes of darkness. The image sent a shudder through his body.

His eyelids blinked open, and he began pacing about his office. He knew he should immediately call Merrick and tell him what happened, but he was not ready. He needed time to think, to prepare himself. Benson stopped in front of a large window, gazed out over the grounds, and wondered what he should tell Merrick. Nothing he could have done would have prevented the crisis. Time had been the problem.

Report compilation varied each month, but he usually obtained the information about an hour and a half before the market closed. That gave him more than enough time to go to the privacy of his office and phone Merrick. There was no risk if he called Merrick promptly, but he knew better than to be late. He had missed one report, two months earlier, because he had attended a mandatory meeting. Merrick had been furious and reminded Benson of the two men staying in Shannon's apartment complex. Merrick had even threatened to issue a "margin call" on Benson, or anyone else who threatened his scheme, and he made it brutally clear that he was not talking about a financial obligation—they were code words for a death contract.

Benson replayed his movements before the eraser had finally come down the pipe. He had continually checked the men's room, and he remembered how nervous he had been when there were only thirty-five minutes left before the market closed. He had been so worried he had gone into the bathroom and locked himself in the stall. He sat on the toilet seat, breathing the heavy smell of disinfectant and waited.

He must have looked at his watch twenty times while waiting, and with less than ten minutes left, he had been in full panic. He feared Merrick might kill him or harm a family member if he failed again. When the eraser had finally arrived there was a large minus five written on the surface—a maximum signal. He ran out of the bathroom and checked his watch, but there was not enough time to get to his office. He had to find a phone. He rushed down the corridor searching for a vacant office. When he found the library, he had looked in and thought the room was empty. With the clock ticking, what else could he have done?

Benson turned and strode across the room, thinking about the threat he now lived with. Passing illegal data to Merrick had certainly gone against his principles, but fear and self-preservation were strong motivations. He had been caught in a perfect trap. Shannon had been in on the setup, but it did not matter. He was obsessed with the woman's beauty and attentive manner, and he could not imagine losing her.

Benson glanced at the clock and shook his head. He was considering what to tell Merrick when another thought jolted him. What if Lauren called the authorities? He had delayed too long. He had to call Merrick, and he had to do it now. With trembling hands, he picked up the phone and dialed Merrick's number.

CHAPTER 5

Victor Merrick was checking futures prices when his private line rang. He picked up. A voice on the other end mumbled something incoherent.

"Benson?"

"My God, Victor. She . . . she heard me."

"Hayden, you're not making sense."

"A woman heard me give you the report data."

Merrick's body stiffened. "What the hell are you talking about?"

Benson went into a stuttering explanation about how the late report had made it impossible for him to get to his private phone.

Merrick interrupted in a harsh tone. "Shut up and listen. Do you know the woman?"

"Y—yes. She—"

"Dammit, Hayden, get hold of yourself."

"What am I going to do?"

"What's her name?"

"Lauren something. I think it starts with a C or a K."

"I'm going to give you one minute to come up with her fucking name."

After a pause, an obviously frightened Hayden Benson blurted out a name. "Chandler. That's it. Lauren Chandler. She works down the hall."

Merrick's mind worked swiftly—processing, analyzing, projecting forward.

Receiving no reply, Benson spoke nervously, "What if she turns me in?"

Merrick had thought of that possibility and was already considering others. His scheme was just beginning to pay off, and he realized his top priority was to shield Benson—his golden goose. "Hayden, listen carefully. You have to protect yourself, and the only way to do that is to beat her to the punch. Call security and tell them you heard her giving out information on the report. They're going to believe you over her."

"But what if they don't?"

"Jesus, Hayden, think about it. They can't prove a goddamn thing. If she tries to accuse you after you've turned her in they'll just think she's trying to wiggle out of her own mess."

"B—but I can't do that."

"There was nobody in the room but you and her. Right?"

"Yes, but—"

"It's your word against hers," Merrick snapped. "You have nothing to worry about if you act first." He paused, sensing a need to switch tactics. "Think about what would happen if you don't do anything. You'll lose everything. Your career, your family, Shannon."

Silence.

Merrick knew his words had struck Benson like a club. He pressed the issue, hoping that self-preservation would take control of Benson's mind. "Think this through. You'll be disgraced and probably wind up in jail."

Silence.

"Benson?"

"Okay, okay. I'll do it."

"Good. She may have left the building; so there's one more thing I need you to do, and I mean right away. You got that?"

"Yes."

"I don't care how you do it, but get her home address. I'm going to wait by this phone and I expect you to call me within twenty minutes with that address."

"Why do you need that?"

"I just want to keep tabs on her." Merrick's voice notched up. "You're wasting time."

He hung up and thought about the threat created by the Chandler woman. A quick review corroborated a decision he had made while still on the phone. She had to be killed, and it had to be done today. If his men could get to her before she told anyone, Benson would come out unscathed. Protecting the information source meant tens of millions of dollars in future profits. Nothing else mattered.

Merrick picked up the handset and dialed the apartment where two of his men were staying. He felt pleased with his earlier decision to send his best man, Billy Barker, to watch over things in Washington. Billy was not a big man but he was tough, and more importantly, he had no conscience. He had helped Merrick kill two men in recent years.

Billy answered on the third ring.

Merrick spoke swiftly. "We've got a problem. I'm putting out a margin call on a woman and I want it taken care of today."

"Sure, but I've gotta have certain information."

"I'll get back to you in a few minutes with the details. I want you to leave the instant you hear from me."

"Is this local?"

"Yeah."

"We'll be ready in ten minutes."

Merrick hung up and looked at his watch. It had been only a few minutes since he had talked to Benson. He got up, walked to the window, and stood motionless for several minutes, his mind searching for any missed details. He was proud of his ability to process information and make decisions at moments like this. He prioritized the raw data, analyzed it, and then made the appropriate decision. There was no place for emotion in his formula. It was a simple matter of shrewd, predatory logic. A few minutes later, his private line rang. He hurried to his desk and picked up the phone.

"I've got the address."

"Let's have it." He wrote down the number and street, repeated it for verification and then asked for a description of the woman. He jotted down the details. "Has anything happened?"

"Nothing yet. If she had told someone, I'd have known by now." Benson's voice was still a bit shaky but he seemed calmer. After a pause he asked, "What do I do next?"

"Two things. First, I want you to go to her office and see if you can find anything."

"What am I looking for?"

"Look for her purse. I want to know if she's still in the building. Try to find an address book or anything with personal information; then, call security and turn her in. Call me back and let me know what you find."

Merrick immediately called Billy. He spoke slowly, "Her name is Lauren Chandler. She's about thirty, attractive, shoulder-length brown hair. The address is 3846 Chester Avenue in Alexandria."

"What's that? A house or an apartment?"

"Apartment 12A," Merrick said. "I want this done right away. No slip-ups."

"I'll take care of it."

"If she's not there, wait in her apartment until she shows up." Merrick held down the switch hook, and then released it for a dial tone. He pushed a memory button that automatically dialed the trading floor. "You got my fill?"

"Got part of it, Victor. The market closed before the floor broker could complete the order."

"Yeah, I figured that. What'd we get?"

"We got about two-thirds of your order filled. I'll give you the details later."

"Make sure you allocate the fills to the account numbers I gave you earlier." He hung up.

Merrick felt disappointed that his entire order had not been filled, but he had gotten about what he had expected, and he now had a sizable short position in soybeans. After the report came out, his profit would be substantial. He glanced at his watch. The crop report should be on the wire by now. He punched several keys on his quote machine and read the headline:

HUGE INCREASE IN SOYBEAN PLANTING INTENTIONS.
Limit down expected tomorrow.

He looked at the numbers, jumped to his feet, and slammed his fist on the desk. "Yes! . . . Yes! I've got 'em by the balls." He looked out the window and gazed at the skyline for a moment, then spoke aloud, "I'm gonna make a fucking killing tomorrow." He reached for the phone. "And one tonight."

CHAPTER 6

Scott entered his hotel room, his mind awash with a jumble of thoughts. The importance of his trip to Washington was still intact, and he had enough information to aid in the preparation of his magazine article, but meeting Lauren had altered his thought process and his plans. The first thing he had to do was change his return flight so he could see her again. He called the airline and delayed his departure one day. He phoned Jason McDonald in Chicago and received a market update. He informed Jason that he would return a day later than expected, but he did not mention Lauren.

Scott's normal pattern would have been to consult his charts and study the day's results based on Jason's input, but after hanging up, he realized his usual fire was not there. Instead of focusing on the market, he found himself thinking about his date with Lauren.

After several moments, he moved to the desk and tried to balance the myriad of thoughts spinning through his mind. When he was on the trading floor, he maintained complete focus on the task at hand. Away from the CBOT, time seemed to operate at different speeds, and he frequently found his mind jumping between subjects in rapid succession. He often had too many layers of thoughts rotating through his mind. He needed to work on that.

He opened his briefcase to review his current financial positon. He had been through a rough ten days. Thoughts of failing in the market evoked memories of the day his father had committed suicide. His father had always been quiet and introspective, but during his last years, the elder Quinn had taken on the habits of a recluse, seldom speaking to Scott or his mother. He had withdrawn into his own private world, one that eventually drove him into an intense depression.

Scott thought back to the funeral and visualized a conversation he had overheard between a friend of the family and another man. He pictured the man and heard his words again, "Quinn took the easy way out. It's too bad, really. His wife has emphysema and the boy is only sixteen or seventeen. It's going to be hard on them." The impact on Scott had been immediate and, among other things, his first encounters with insomnia were set in motion. He took on increased responsibilities and became very protective of his mother.

Somehow, he had to overcome the odds, he had to dispel his father's ghost, and he had to succeed. Though he had taken a serious loss, the positive results from his trading on Friday had saved him from a complete disaster. He had enough capital to continue trading, and he felt good about his upcoming article, which he now considered more important than ever. He still clung to his goal of starting his own futures fund, although he realized it would take longer than originally planned.

His rose and walked toward the window, his mind shifting again. He looked out, reflecting on the women in his life and shook his head. He hadn't had a decent relationship in more than five years. There had been several sex-driven infatuations but nothing lasting. He thought of Lauren, her engaging manner, her feminine grace, her incredible eyes, and her smile. Scott recalled the moment he had first seen her in the cafeteria. The memory was exciting, and he held on to it, not wanting to let go.

———

Lauren had spent nearly an hour vacillating, but she held to her initial decision to delay contact with the authorities. A nagging sense of danger influenced her judgment. She could not see it, define it, or understand it, but it was there. She still had no idea what to do and wondered to whom she could turn. She then remembered that her roommate had just started her vacation and was home preparing for a trip. Marilyn Shepard had been an employee of the Agriculture Department for twelve years. Someone with her extensive knowledge of procedures and personnel might be able to help. At least she was someone to talk to, and that was something Lauren desperately needed.

She returned to her car and headed north on Ohio Drive. Lauren had driven only a few blocks when her thoughts turned to Angela Williams, a supervisor on the building security staff. The two women had become friends during Lauren's first lonely weeks on her new job. Because of her position, Angela could offer guidance.

Lauren stopped at a phone booth and dialed the security desk. "Angela, this is Lauren Chan—"

"My God, Lauren. Where are you?"

"I had to leave the building. Something happened and I need your advice."

"I've been worried sick. We just got orders to search all facilities for you."

"What?"

"You're to be arrested on sight."

"Arrested! Why?"

"Hayden Benson said he caught you giving someone pre-release data over the phone. I can't imagine you'd ever do something like that, but I have to ask you straight out. Do you know anything about this?"

"Of course not. I didn't tell anyone anything."

"I didn't think so but we've got a prob—" Angela was interrupted by someone. "Hold on a sec."

Lauren heard part of a muffled conversation, then Angela came back on the line and said, "I've got to go but I want you to call me at home tonight. Promise?"

"Yes, but remember, I didn't do it."

A terrifying urgency engulfed Lauren. Jaywalking was about the only illegal act she had ever committed. Suddenly, without warning, she had been hurled into uncharted waters, and she was simply not prepared for this type of crisis. Her mind raced from one thought to another until a single emotion took control—fear.

She leaned against the side of the phone booth and shut her eyes, searching for something to ease her distress. For a brief moment, she imagined herself at home, a young child alone in her room, drawing pictures on a roll of butcher paper, as was her habit. She wanted to go back in time—to be safe.

Noise from a group of tourists snapped her back. She hurried to her car, got in, and pulled onto the road. She decided against using the Fourteenth Street Bridge because the entry was near the Department of Agriculture complex. Instead, she continued north and took the Memorial Bridge across the Potomac, then drove south on the Jefferson Davis Highway being careful to observe the speed limit. It would take about twenty minutes to get to her apartment in Alexandria.

CHAPTER 7

Billy Barker knew this was an important mark; he had heard it in Merrick's voice. Billy checked his gun while Lisowski changed the license plate on the car; then, they drove to the freeway and headed for Lauren's apartment. Ray Lisowski drove while Billy thought about the hit. Because killing a single, defenseless woman was an easy assignment, he let his mind shift to something far more appealing. His recent bonus from Merrick had allowed him to do something he always wanted to do. Most people probably would have bought a new car but not Billy Barker—he bought a racehorse. Specifically, a $20,000 claimer named Purple Sage, which he had stabled at Hawthorne Park.

He had tried other ways to make money at the track, but betting on horses proved problematic. After the state and the track pocketed their take, there wasn't much left for the betting public. Moreover, horses did not always run true to form—too many variables entered the picture, which made handicapping an unreliable science. So he had acquired Purple Sage, and the horse showed promise, finishing a fast closing second in the six-furlong race that Billy used to claim the horse. Billy had conferred with his trainer, and they decided to enter Purple Sage in a mile race for $30,000 claimers. Although it was a step up in class, the horse showed that he wanted more distance. Billy felt exhilarated as he visualized his horse running down the leaders in an upcoming race. He couldn't wait.

He shifted in his seat. "I'm going to have a whole stable of horses, Ray. You ought to put some money into this."

"Don't you think we should pay a little more attention to this job than your horse?"

"Hell, Ray, this is routine. Nothing more."

"Yeah, but—"

"We've got some big bonuses coming. Why don't you put up some cash for a percentage? I'll handle all the details."

"I don't know. Let me think about it."

"Think hard, Ray. Think hard."

Though Billy would soon put a gun to a woman's head, he could not help but visualize Purple Sage galloping to victory as they drove along the Parkway. The thought painted a beautiful picture in his mind.

When they reached Alexandria, Billy turned his attention to a map. He told Lisowski to turn off the Parkway onto Duke Street. After about a mile, they came to Chester, turned right and easily found the apartment complex. They parked and walked across the street. Because Billy was short and thin, he was glad to have Ray Lisowski along for a job like this. Lisowski was 6'6"and weighed 260. He was big and crude and had an oddly shaped head. The ear on the right side of his head was higher than the opposite ear, making his appearance look oddly unbalanced, but he was also a lot smarter than he looked, and Billy knew his value in tight situations. When they worked together, their teamwork bred success. Billy chalked it up to karma. Hell, everything depended on karma.

Billy knew several ways to get into a secured apartment complex, but today, he did not need them. A large moving van had parked directly in front of the apartment, and furniture was being unloaded and carried through the main entrance.

They walked in and checked the layout. Apartment 12A was on their left, but Billy purposely headed toward the opposite wing. When they were out of sight of the movers, they turned and approached Lauren's building from the side. They scanned the area while putting on gloves, then moved swiftly along the corridor. They reached 12A, stood on each side of the door, and rang the bell.

No answer.

Billy pushed the button again.

He heard a feminine voice. "Just a minute." A few seconds later, a young woman holding a towel around her wet hair opened the door. "Sorry, I was just—"

Billy shoved his way inside and crashed his gun against the woman's head, collapsing her to the floor like a stringless puppet. "Drag her into a back bedroom while I check the place." Billy took a quick look around before going down the hall to the bedroom.

Lisowski was behind the woman, his arms hooked under hers. "You want her on the bed?"

"Yeah."

After his partner had stepped away, Billy grabbed two pillows and placed them over the woman's head. He had followed this routine before and went about his business as though nothing unusual was about to happen. He reached under the pillow, placed the gun against the woman's head, and fired one shot into her temple.

He turned to leave and saw Lisowski going through a purse. "Dammit, Ray. We're not here for that. Let's go."

Lisowski handed him a wallet. "You'd better look at this."

Billy grabbed the open wallet and glared at the name and photo on the driver's license. "Shit!" He ran into the other bedroom, looked around, then went to the dresser and picked up a picture frame. The photo showed two women laughing together in a park. They were about the same age, both brunettes, but one had much longer hair than the other did. He remembered what Merrick had said about the woman having shoulder length hair.

Billy ran back to the bedroom and removed the pillows covering the woman's head. He had earlier shoved the towel to one side but had not removed it. He yanked the towel aside and unraveled the wet hair. It was soaked with water and blood, and it was long, very long. It nearly reached the middle of the woman's back.

Billy turned. "Sonofabitch. We killed the wrong woman."

"Merrick's gonna be pissed. Whatta we do now?"

"I don't know, but one thing's for sure. We're getting the fuck out of here."

———

Lauren Chandler struggled with a chaotic web of confused and frightened thoughts as she pulled into her apartment complex. She was still trying to decide whether she should go to the authorities, or find a safe place where she could take time to decide the proper course of action, perhaps find an attorney. She hoped Marilyn could help her find the right decision.

Lauren parked in the back lot and hurried toward her building. She went up the walkway and was halfway around the corner when she stopped suddenly at the sight of two men coming out of her apartment. She stepped out of view, ran to the rear parking lot and hid behind a car.

Who were they? The only men Marilyn ever had in the apartment were her boyfriend or her brother. These two were strangers, and they had a decidedly rough appearance. Something was wrong. Lauren thought of her roommate and a surge of fear flooded her mind. She rushed back up the sidewalk and peeked around the corner. Seeing no sign of anyone, she hurried up the walkway and attempted to stick her key in the lock, but her hand trembled so much she could not manage the fit. She took a deep breath and tried again. She turned the key, opened the door, and looked inside.

Not a sound.

She entered the front room, looked around and saw a stain on the carpet near the door. The spot was not large, but it contrasted vividly with the beige carpet. She kneeled down and ran her finger over the stain.

Blood!

Lauren's stomach sank. She rushed down the hallway to her bedroom and glanced in. Everything looked normal. Then she noticed an empty picture frame on the bed. Someone had removed the photo. She hurried into the hall but stopped short when she found Marilyn's door closed. She bit her bottom lip and then slowly opened the door. Marilyn Shepard lay across blood-splattered, white sheets.

Lauren expelled a gasp of air and brought a hand to her mouth. The gruesome sight sent a shockwave of horror through her body. She choked and nearly threw up. She turned away and leaned against the wall for a moment, grasping for some sense of equilibrium.

As she attempted to regain her focus, a single thought took hold. What if the killers came back? Instinct turned shock into fear and a force deep inside yelled at her to run. Her heart pounded as she headed up the hallway. Lauren ran toward the front door but stopped abruptly and turned back toward the bedroom. Though she believed Marilyn was dead, she had to be sure. She ran back to the bed, reached for Marilyn's arm, hesitated, and then took hold of the limp wrist.

No pulse.

She felt the carotid artery in the neck. Again, no pulse. She lifted the blanket, covered Marilyn's body, and walked back to the living room, her mind trying to comprehend a mixture of terrible, complex thoughts. She wiped moisture from her eyes before grasping the doorknob. She eased the door open, stuck her head out, and was relieved she saw no one. She left the apartment and headed toward her car. Just as she approached the end of the building, a man opened a door and stepped in front of her. She had been moving so rapidly she collided with the man. She thought it was one of the killers and started to scream, but then she realized he was a new tenant she had seen only once before.

Neither fell, but the man seemed concerned for her. "Are you all right?"

Lauren brought a hand to her breast. "I—I'm fine. You just scared me." She uttered a weak apology, then hurried down the walkway, and turned the corner.

Distress overwhelmed her as she ran to her car. She struggled with the key, got in, locked the door, and lay across the seat. She pressed her face against the fabric and tried to control her shaking body. Her whole life had been turned upside down by a rapid series of events that had spiraled out of control. After a few minutes, Lauren sat up and looked around. She grabbed the steering wheel with both hands, her knuckles turning white from the pressure. She took a deep breath and tried to curb her emotions.

She looked around, then started the car, and pulled into the driveway. Lauren was still shaking when she looked at her watch— it was five minutes before five. She decided to drive somewhere safe until Angela got home and then call her. She desperately needed help. She had barely started up the drive when she saw a police car go by that appeared to be stopping. Had the authorities asked the local police to go to her home?

Panic took hold—she had run.

She backed her car to the end of the drive, turned toward the next apartment building and drove along a space between the buildings used by garbage trucks. A stack of boxes caused the lane to narrow abruptly and the side of her car scraped a Dumpster. She sucked in air, tightened her grip on the wheel, and kept going. She reached the next complex, then she turned and drove to the street. Lauren glanced to her right and saw two police cars, one on each side of the street. She turned in the opposite direction and went up Chester toward Duke, repeatedly checking the rear view mirror, but there was no sign of pursuit. An image of Marilyn Shepard flashed into Lauren's mind as she drove. She saw the limp body and blood-covered sheets in vivid detail, and she knew the memory would be etched into her soul forever.

She turned north onto the Jefferson Davis Highway and drove several blocks, but she had no idea where she was going. She checked her watch. It was a few minutes after five, but Angela had said she might not be home until six. Lauren had no one else to turn to because she had not been in Washington long enough to have many friends she could trust. She decided to park somewhere and wait for Angela to get home. She would use the time to think.

At a quarter past five, she pulled into a large parking area adjacent to a mall. She thought it would be safest to park in a public area. Lauren stopped the car and put her head against the steering wheel. She shut her eyes, trying to calm herself, but the combination of shock and fear proved overwhelming.

After a moment, she looked around to make sure it was safe and saw the sign: Henry's Restaurant. Events had caused her to forget her date in the bar at five-thirty but that was unimportant now. She then wondered if Angela might still be at work and decided to use the restaurant pay phone to try to reach her friend. Feeling desperate, she got out of the car and walked through a light drizzle toward Henry's. Lauren asked the maître d' to direct her to the phone booth. He pointed toward the bar. The restaurant had only a few diners at this hour, but the cocktail lounge was full of patrons celebrating the end of the workday.

She made her way through the crowd and found two phones in a narrow walkway that led to the rest rooms. A businessman was using one but the phone nearest her was available. She dialed security at the South Building and was transferred to Angela's desk. She heard a man's voice and hung up. Angela had obviously left.

Lauren made her way through the crowd, possessed by a feeling of helplessness.

CHAPTER 8

Victor Merrick had just entered his office when his private phone rang. He walked to his desk and picked up the handset.

"I did what you told me." Hayden Benson's voice seemed calmer.

"And?"

"Her purse is gone. She must have left the building right after she saw me."

"Did you find anything?"

"There was a small address book in her desk."

"What else?"

"Not much. Just the usual stuff. Oh, one other thing. I tore out today's page from her desk calendar. There are two appointments listed. One this morning with a staff member, and the other at five-thirty. She wrote in the name Scott Q. next to the time. Below that, it says Henry's. That's a restaurant across the bridge near the mall."

Merrick jotted down the information. "Do you know someone with that name and initial?"

"Never heard of him."

"Did you report her to security?"

"Yes. It went better than I expected."

"Why wouldn't it? You're the Deputy Secretary of Agriculture. I told you not to worry about this."

"I know, but—"

"I'm expecting another call. I want you to give the address book and the calendar page to Shannon. She'll get them to me."

He hung up, reached for a walnut box, and withdrew a cigar. Even though Benson had nearly committed a disastrous blunder, Merrick believed the situation would return to normal as soon as he eliminated the Chandler woman. He might have to skip a report or two, but after tomorrow's expected profits, he needn't be concerned.

Merrick lit the cigar, leaned back in his chair, then tilted his head back and blew smoke rings toward the ceiling. He watched the last ringlet as it drifted higher, wobbling, expanding. In his mind, he pictured the soybean pit floating inside the circle of smoke. He thought about tomorrow's trading action. His position in beans was a sure thing, a dead fucking lead-pipe cinch.

He got up, walked to the window, and stared at the skyline. He stood for several minutes, thoughtful, reflective. It had been a long struggle, but he was now on the verge of attaining substantial wealth, and with wealth came power. He silently vowed to destroy anyone who threatened his mission.

Though buildings obscured his view, he could easily visualize his boyhood home that lay just beyond the skyline. Thoughts of his childhood engendered a profusion of disturbing memories of his father. It had been standard procedure for the drunken old man to beat him and his mother. Merrick touched his right ear and rubbed a scar that acted as a constant reminder of his father's violent outbursts. He wondered how many times he had fled to the dilapidated fire escape outside his room to hide from his father's rage. Safe, huddled on the corner of the landing, he would spend hours staring at the tall buildings, wondering about the people residing there. Surely, they were all rich. His favorite viewing hours were at night when he likened the shimmering lights to beads of brilliant diamonds dangling from the sky. Someday, he would claim those precious jewels for himself.

He had used the fire escape for several months until his father found him and delivered a severe beating. Bleeding from several lacerations, Merrick retreated to the rail yards where he stayed for eight days. He remained in hiding the first day; then, he began to venture into the surrounding area long enough to steal food, which he took back to the boxcar. Merrick watched the daily activities in the yards and developed a fondness for everything associated with trains. He particularly liked the noise and vibrations his body absorbed from passing engines. He received a strange reassurance from the puissant energy of the huge machines.

He had even lost his virginity in a boxcar. He remembered flopping around on a dirty, cardboard covered floor with a redhead named Rhonda. She was two years older, adventurous, demanding, and insatiable.

He had also witnessed the death of an eccentric wanderer struck by a train that mangled the man's body beyond recognition. The man, who called himself Rickets, had shown Merrick where he could safely hide. Hidden in the dark boxcar, he had plenty of time to think, and that was when he decided that life was not fair. Rickets had told him that life was a three-link chain. You were alive once, but you will be dead twice, and the finality of the last event in the chain sent Merrick a chilling message. Make the most of life while you can, and do whatever it takes to get what you want. He formed a philosophy that it was okay to break the law as long as he used his brains and planned everything in great detail. Leave nothing to chance.

A year later, his father deserted the family, leaving them desperately poor, and Merrick learned that day-to-day survival was more important than dreams. He responded quickly to the challenges of the streets, and as he grew bigger and stronger, he began to cultivate his most effective ability—intimidation.

As a young man, he had moved from one job to another until he found a favorable opportunity in a Burgess Grain Company warehouse. Merrick was tough, but he was also smart, and after two years, he began to move up with startling speed. His advancement into management had not been caused by his business skills, though he did possess a propensity for strategic planning. Coercion and violence were his primary vehicles. Over a period of several years, two men had impeded his advancement, but he made sure they did not live long enough to cause further trouble. One death was made to look accidental; the other man simply disappeared.

He moved into management about the same time Martin Burgess' health began to deteriorate. Merrick saw this as one of those strokes of luck that life occasionally offers. After careful preparations, Merrick bribed Burgess' lawyer, then tricked the weakened founder into signing over the company for a fraction of its worth. With no family to oversee his affairs, Burgess had been an easy target. Two weeks after the transfer of ownership, the old man had died without the slightest awareness he had been cheated.

Merrick walked back to his desk, his thoughts shifting to Lauren Chandler. She could have ruined everything, but she was probably dead by now. He was enjoying a cigar when his private line rang. He assumed it was Billy calling to confirm the hit. "What've you got?" His tone expectant.

There was a slight pause. "Victor, I'm afraid I've got some bad news."

Merrick sat up and put his cigar in the ashtray. "What kind of bad news?"

"We delivered the margin call to the wrong woman."

The muscles in Merrick's neck tightened as he sprang out of his chair. "What? What the hell are you talking about?"

"Well . . . it seems she had a roommate, and—"

Merrick screamed into the phone. "You idiot! Can't you handle a simple fucking job like that?"

"We didn't know. She was about the same age and had almost the same color hair."

Merrick was silent for a moment, his mind focusing on the need for control. "Where are you?"

"In a phone booth about two miles from her house. We were gonna drive by her apartment again, but the police are all over the place. Bad karma, man."

"Don't give me that karma shit. Hold on a minute while I think this out." Merrick considered the situation, and one thing remained clear: no matter how they did it, they had to find Lauren Chandler and silence her forever. Everything depended on it.

He decided to use more resources, but there were only three other men on his payroll he could trust for this kind of work, and he always kept one available for personal use. "All right, I'm sending Hammitt and Navarro down there in the morning. If that's not enough, we'll bring in some outside help. What else will you need?"

"We've got a picture but we could use more information on her."

"I'll see what I can do, but I want you to understand one thing. Nothing you've ever done for me is as important as this."

"Okay, okay. We'll find her."

"You'd better, Billy. You'd better."

"We'll get her, but, like I said, we need more information."

Merrick glanced at the note pad on his desk. He grabbed it and spoke rapidly, "I almost forgot. Her calendar shows a five-thirty appointment at a restaurant called Henry's. That's only five minutes from now. I want you to get over there right away."

"Do you have an address?"

"It's next to a big shopping mall right across the bridge from the Department of Agriculture."

"I know where that is. We passed it on the way here."

"Get going. And, Billy."

"Yeah."

"Don't forget what I said. I want her stone cold dead."

CHAPTER 9

Scott freshened up and left the hotel, feeling uplifted by a great sense of anticipation. On the way to Henry's, he saw a flower shop and pulled to the curb. He inhaled a layered mixture of pleasant scents as he entered the small shop. A petite, grey-haired woman with a slightly stooped back greeted him with a smile. He told her what he wanted and then watched her gentle movements as she enclosed the end of a single long-stemmed, red rose in a small water vial, added fern leaves and a sprig of baby's breath. He paid for the flower and left the shop.

The patchy cloudiness and occasional mist of the last two days had given way to a more menacing sky, but a little rain did not bother Scott. His thoughts were on Lauren Chandler. He drove across the Fourteenth Street Bridge, following the directions given him by the hotel bellhop. After a short drive, he pulled into the lot next to Henry's Restaurant, parked next to a blue van and stepped into the moist air.

Scott had temporarily pushed his financial worries to some back corner of his mind, and he walked toward the restaurant with a spring in his step. He opened the door and held it for an elderly couple who were leaving, then stepped into the large foyer. Narrow strips of wood paneling gave the room a feeling of warmth, which was made even more inviting by the addition of several large plants, anchored in ceramic pots, scattered along the walls.

While the maître d' attended to another man, Scott glanced into the dining room and noticed that only a few tables were occupied. It was early. He turned toward the noisy bar. He didn't expect to see Lauren, because he knew women often arrived a few minutes late to avoid waiting alone, but he thought he should check the cocktail lounge just in case. He walked to the entryway and saw Lauren maneuvering through the crowd. He assumed she was coming to greet him, but as she drew closer, he saw an unmistakable look of distress in her eyes; something was wrong. He wondered if someone had insulted her in the bar, but as he continued to watch her he began to sense something far more serious had happened. He had no idea what was wrong, but one thing was obvious; there had been a startling change in Lauren's demeanor in just a few hours.

Because it was crowded and noisy in the bar, Scott decided to wait where he was. She was only a few steps away when he realized she had not recognized him. She glanced in his direction, but she looked from side to side as if he were not there. She went past him, head down, moving toward the door.

"Lauren?"

She froze for a moment and then turned toward the voice.

"Lauren, it's me. Scott Quinn." He extended his arm and handed her the rose. "This for you." He sensed a touch of awkwardness in his voice.

There was a brief hint of recognition as she halfheartedly took the flower, but Scott saw something else—fear. A compassionate reflex took hold as he stepped closer. "Are you all right?"

"O—Oh, Scott . . . I forgot." She broke eye contact, shifting her gaze to the floor. "I—I'm all right." In little more than a whisper, she added, "I have to leave."

Scott saw a moist film glaze over her eyes just before she had looked down. He moved his arm around her shoulder and turned toward the maître d'. "The lady isn't feeling well. Could we use a table in your dining room—and maybe get a glass of water?"

The maître d' put down his pen and came around the podium. "Of course, sir. Follow me." He led them to a quiet booth in the rear of the dining room. "I'll have a waiter bring some water right away."

"Thank you." Scott turned his attention to Lauren. "What's wrong? Is there something I can do?"

She gazed nervously across the room but did not answer.

Scott noticed her vigilance and turned to look. He saw the waiter coming and realized she would wait for him to pour the water and leave before answering. When the waiter had finished, Scott looked expectantly at Lauren, but she lowered her eyes and remained silent.

He spoke in a soft voice. "I'd like to help you, but I can't if you don't tell me what's wrong."

"Some—something terrible has happened . . . but I can't talk about it."

"Is it someone in your family? An illness?"

"No, nothing like that."

"Lauren, you can trust me. I want to help."

She started to speak but began to sob instead.

Scott pulled out a handkerchief and handed it across the table.

She dabbed at her eyes. "Someone. . . ." She shook her head and fell silent.

"Someone what?"

After a long moment, she said, "Someone tried to kill me; b—but they killed my roommate instead. I'm scared to death." The words came in a jerky, choked voice.

A wave of disbelief flooded Scott's mind. How could this woman possibly be mixed up in anything dangerous? Shaken, he was too stunned to speak for a moment as a wild assortment of thoughts flashed through his mind as he sought to put her words into some sort of perspective. It just didn't make sense.

Before he could speak, she continued, "I know that sounds bizarre . . . and it is. I don't know why all of this is happening to me but I'm frightened."

"Did you call the police?"

"Not yet. I need more time to think." She glanced around nervously, and then spoke in a strained voice. "I overheard something at work that I wasn't supposed to hear, and now, they're trying to kill me."

"I don't understand."

"I can't explain everything. All I can say is that I went home and saw two men coming out of my apartment. After they left, I went in and—" Lauren paused, a look of agony swept over her face. "I found my roommate on the bed. She'd been shot."

"Good Lord, you've got to call the police."

"I know, but I'm scared." She frowned and bit her lower lip. "I need to call a friend of mine before I do anything else. She'll be home at six-thirty."

Scott was about to plead with Lauren to call the police when he saw alarm flash across her face. He touched her arm. "What?"

"It's them!"

He looked toward the entrance to the dining room but saw no one. "Who?"

"The two men I saw coming out of my apartment. They just came in and walked toward the bar." Lauren grabbed her purse." I've got to get out of here."

He glanced back across the dining room just as two men came through the doorway.

They saw Lauren.

To his astonishment, the smaller man pulled out a gun and pointed it toward Lauren. Scott jumped up and pulled her to one side. As he searched for a safe exit, the boom from a pistol exploded across the room. The bullet crashed into the wall where Lauren had stood a split second before.

Scott pushed Lauren, guiding her toward the swinging doors that led into the kitchen.

"Run!"

He shoved her toward the doors, then grabbed a small lamp and threw it across the room at the gunman. The roar or two shots overwhelmed the screams of patrons. One bullet tore a hole in the shoulder pad of Scott's sport coat, the other ripped into the back wall. He pulled over a table to block the doors and then ran into the kitchen in time to see Lauren look back as she headed toward the rear of the busy kitchen. "Keep going. Run."

Pots and pans crashed to the floor as excited employees shouted and scurried about.

He slipped on water that had spilled and slammed into one of the workers, sending the man sprawling. Scott barely managed to keep his own footing. He looked over his shoulder as he ran toward the rear of the kitchen.

Lauren stopped just inside a storeroom and looked back with terror-filled eyes.

He reached her and pointed toward one end of the room and yelled, "Go through those doors and keep running. I'll be right there." When she hesitated, he shoved her hard. "Go. Go!"

When Scott entered the storage room, he noticed large bags of flour and rice stacked to his left. He grabbed the top sack and pulled it to the floor; then he reached for the next bag and another, his efforts sent a fine mist of flour into the air. He worked feverishly, piling up several sacks in front of the door before he turned and ran toward the back. He heard men shouting and pounding on the door as he fled from the building to the parking lot.

He couldn't locate Lauren and searched until he saw her waving frantically from between two cars. He ran toward her, looking back over his shoulder every few seconds. No sign of them, but he knew the barricaded door would not hold long.

He ran between the cars and stopped. "Are you all right?"

"Yes, but what are we going to do?"

"Get the hell out of here." Scott glanced toward the restaurant. "Where's your car?"

"It's in front."

"Mine too." He scanned the area. "We can't go that way. There may be more of them." He grabbed her arm and motioned toward the mall. "Come on."

They ran through the rain toward the shopping center. Scott knew there had to be a security staff, but what he really wanted was a policeman. If there were none in the shopping center, the shooting would certainly have them swarming over the area in a few minutes. Halfway to the mall he glanced over his shoulder. Two men had burst out the back of the restaurant and were running directly toward them. He turned and yelled, "Faster. They saw us."

They increased their speed, splashing through puddles of water as they ran. When they were about seventy yards from the doors, Scott looked back and saw the pursuers gaining, but he thought they could reach the mall before the gunmen got close enough to shoot accurately. He glanced at Lauren and saw she was holding up well. She was frightened, but there was no sign of fatigue.

They dodged around two women and rushed up to the mall entrance. Scott flung open the door and shoved Lauren inside. He looked around but there was no sign of a policeman or a security guard. They had to keep moving.

He guided Lauren to one side and ran along the corridor to a large department store. "In here." Just before entering the store, he turned and saw the gunmen come through the double doors. He did not know if they had been spotted, but he knew they had to keep going. He pointed toward the rear of the store and followed Lauren as she maneuvered through the aisles. When they reached the back, Scott motioned for Lauren to stop behind a large display. Wet, scared, and breathing heavily, they peered back through the store.

Lauren pointed to their right. "Over there."

Scott swung his head and saw the larger of the two men working his way toward their location. "Damn. They saw us come in." He signaled for Lauren to crouch while he searched to their rear for an exit. There was a single door about twenty feet away. He pointed and whispered, "Crawl over there."

He followed her across the floor, all the while praying that the exit led to a storeroom and not an enclosed office. When they were halfway there, he realized the door might be locked—probably was locked, but they had no other option.

Lauren reached the door and turned toward Scott.

He caught up with her and looked back. No sign of the gunman. "We're going through the door but stay on your hands and knees." He reached for the doorknob and mumbled under his breath. "Be unlocked, dammit. Be unlocked." Scott sighed when the knob twisted in his hand. He opened the door just enough for Lauren to slide through, then he followed her.

She stood up in a large storeroom. "They couldn't have seen us."

"Maybe not, but they might have seen the door open and close without anybody going through." Scott glanced around. "Look for an exit sign or a rear door."

They were in a large storeroom cluttered with stacks of boxes and shelves full of merchandise. There had to be a loading door at one end, but which? He decided to check to their right first and led the way between two rows of crates. They entered a large open area that eventually led to a row of cardboard boxes stacked near the back of the building. Shelving ran along the rear wall but no door. A dead end.

"Damn!" Scott looked in the direction they had come from. "Quick, back that way."

They started back down the aisle when they heard the storeroom door slam. He grabbed Lauren's arm and turned her toward the back, whispering as he moved. "We've got to hide."

They hurried to the rear wall and went behind a stack of cardboard boxes. Scott moved toward the end and motioned for Lauren to crouch next to him in the corner. He did not like their position, because they would be found if one of the men checked behind the boxes, but he also knew it was their only chance. With Lauren huddled next to him, he crouched down and peered between two cartons. He saw no one. He put his arm around her and felt her shiver. Except for their breathing, they remained quiet.

They waited.

A minute went by, then two.

Nothing.

Then they heard the sound of boxes being shuffled. Scott looked through the crack and saw the larger of the two gunmen come out from a row of crates and stop. The man held a pistol as he looked about the room. His gaze shifted to the cardboard boxes in the corner, then he began walking slowly across the open area—straight toward them.

Scott felt a cold, gripping fear tear at his mind. There were still a few beads of rainwater on their faces, but the predominant moisture was sweat. He didn't need to look at Lauren to see her terror—he felt it. Scott patted her shoulder in a feeble attempt to reassure her, but he knew their lives could end in a matter of seconds.

He turned and looked along the rear wall, searching for something to use as a weapon. The shelves were full of several kinds of sports equipment, but he couldn't find anything to neutralize a six-foot six-inch man with a gun. He reached into another box on the back shelf and pulled out the first thing he touched. It was a baseball—a goddamned baseball.

Lauren turned to him with a look of astonishment, then whispered in his ear, "What are you doing?"

"I was a pitcher in college," Scott said, his voice barely audible.

"But that was a long time ago."

"Yeah, I know."

He peered through the crack and saw the huge man looking behind several cartons about fifty feet away. After a brief search, the gunman turned away from the boxes and looked in their direction. A stream of sweat from Scott's forehead caused a faint sting in his eyes. He wiped his face and looked back toward the gunman. If the man came toward them, Scott thought his only choice was to hurl the ball and try to hit their assailant in the head. He was not going to be trapped in a corner and shot down like a wounded animal.

He tightened his grip on the ball.

The gunman started walking in their direction.

Scott waited as long as he dared, then he stood and threw the ball as hard as he could.

The man stood motionless, a look of surprise outlined on his face as the baseball sailed within an inch of his left ear and thumped into a carton behind him.

Scott dropped and moved Lauren over about three feet just as a gunshot roared across the storeroom. The bullet cut through the boxes and slammed into the wall behind them. Another shot followed, ripping through cartons two feet to their right.

Instinct overcame panic, and Scott again turned and reached into the box. His hand came out with a baseball bat. He grabbed another ball and thrust it at Lauren. "Throw this toward the other corner."

She hesitated; then, she took the ball, and hurled it at the opposite wall.

The gunman turned toward the sound of the ball hitting boxes and fired a shot.

Scott jumped up at the same instant and swung the bat as if he were facing a pitcher, snapping his wrist at the instant of release. The maneuver caused the bat to sail across the room in a revolving motion like a large boomerang.

Scott focused on the bat. In that single instant, nothing mattered more than the flight of a single piece of tapered wood.

CHAPTER 10

Ray Lisowski never knew what hit him. Actually, it was a thirty-two ounce Louisville Slugger, and the sweet spot caught him just above the left eye. The gunman crumpled to the floor and did not move.

Scott moved away from the boxes. "Let's go." He led the way and ran between the rows of crates. He turned the corner and collided with Billy Barker. The impact knocked the smaller man into the air. Billy landed on his back and slid along the smooth concrete. His pistol jarred loose when he hit the floor.

Scott's first thought was to try for the gun, but when Billy rolled over and crawled after it, he knew he could not reach the weapon first. He pointed toward the other end of the storeroom and yelled at Lauren. "Run!"

He grabbed a large box and turned toward Billy. The gunman's hand grasped the pistol and he started to swing his arm around. Scott threw the box, then turned and started running. He heard a loud groan followed by the roar of a single pistol shot. Scott thought he must have hit the man squarely, but he doubted if the box was heavy enough to stop him for long. He also worried that the other man might have regained consciousness, though the bat appeared to have made a direct hit.

He came around a stack of boxes, saw that Lauren had managed to raise the loading door, and was standing on the ramp looking toward him. "Down the ramp," he yelled. "I'll be right behind you." He went outside, reached up, slammed the door shut, and then ran into a driving rain. He made up the thirty feet that separated him from Lauren, took her hand, and dashed around trash bins and past loading docks, glancing over his shoulder as he went. They came to several parked trucks and ducked behind the first one. Breathing rapidly, Scott turned and peered around the edge of the vehicle. Their position was less than a hundred yards from the loading ramp, but it was difficult to see because of the heavy rain. He brushed wet hair from his face and squinted, searching for movement.

Lauren tugged on his arm. "Do you see them?"

"No, but we can't stop."

Just as he started to turn, he saw a shaft of light streak into the alleyway from the department store loading dock. "Shit. It's the door." Scott peered through the rain-darkened alleyway and saw a blurred figure run down the ramp. The man extended his arm as if holding a gun. A larger man staggered down the ramp and fell near the bottom. The smaller gunman turned and helped the fallen man.

"It's them," Scott said. He watched the larger man get to his feet only to fall again. The man with the gun yelled something and then started in the direction of the trucks.

Scott turned to Lauren. "We have to move." They went around another truck and started to run when Lauren stepped in a pothole filled with water. Her shoe came off and she fell heavily.

Scott took her hand and helped her up. "You okay?"

She took a step and started to fall again but he caught her.

She grimaced and grabbed her leg. "I hurt my knee. I—I don't think I can run."

Panic surged through Scott as he helped Lauren. The gunman would reach them in less than a minute. A vision of Lauren and himself lying dead in a pool of water between two trucks flashed through his mind. There seemed to be no way out.

Scott searched frantically between the trucks and saw a side-door on one of them. There was only about two feet between the vehicles, but he managed to get Lauren to the door. He reached up and pulled down on the latch.

Lauren's grip tightened on his arm. "What are you doing? They'll find us in the truck."

"Your knee. We have no choice." Scott peered inside but could see only a few feet. It looked empty. "Dammit." They would be easy to find in a barren truck, but they had to take the chance. He climbed in and reached for Lauren's hand. She threw her handbag in and he pulled her up.

They heard shouts.

Scott whispered, "Hold the door open a little so I can see." He went toward the front of the truck and stumbled over a chair. He got up and ran back to Lauren. He pulled the door shut but was careful to leave it unlatched to avoid being trapped.

More shouts came from outside. They could not be more than twenty yards away.

Lauren tugged on his arm. "This looks really bad."

"There's some furniture in here. Come on."

They used their hands and groped their way toward the front of the truck. Scott passed the chair and waved his hands about until he felt plastic covering used to protect a piece of furniture. He reached down and touched the back of a large sofa.

He whispered, "What's on that side?"

"Another chair. That's all I can find."

"Over here," he said. "Quick."

Lauren reached for Scott but nearly fell because of her knee.

"I want you to—" Scott stopped short.

Shouts sounded from outside. "Let's search these trucks. Start with that one."

Scott grabbed the edge of the couch and whispered, "Let's get around to the other side. We're going to tip it over and crawl underneath." He reached forward but when his hand hit the panel, he realized the couch was too close to the front wall. He grabbed the armrest and pulled, then moved next to Lauren and did the same to the other end.

A door slammed on the next truck.

"Hurry," Scott whispered. "Pull on your end when you feel me tipping the couch but don't let it bang on the floor."

They pulled on the sofa until the weight shifted toward them. Scott held onto the back and eased it down. The bottom of the couch was now facing the back doors, and there was a narrow space underneath against the front wall.

Scott whispered, "Crawl underneath the sofa."

They heard the metallic sound of the door latch.

A man's voice sounded from a few feet away. "Ray, get up there and check it out."

"I'm still too woozy."

Billy checked his gun. "Move over, I'll do it."

Lauren had gotten as close to the cushions as possible. Scott lay on his side, his chest pressed against her, his back against the front wall of the truck. They were wet, tired, scared, and crammed together with little room to move. Scott heard someone climbing into the truck and brought his index finger up to Lauren's lips. He touched her gently, then he held his breath. She understood his signal and held still. They controlled their breathing as best they could.

A small amount of light filtered through the large back door, but the combination of approaching darkness and heavy rain made visibility difficult.

They heard footsteps coming toward the front of the truck.

A chair tumbled over and hit the edge of the sofa. The movement startled Lauren and her body jerked. Scott put his arms around her and held tight. They remained still, hidden in their tiny covert, and clung to each other in desperation. If the man turned over the couch Scott knew the truck would erupt in gunfire and their last seconds on earth would be filled with terror.

He was wrapped around Lauren, and their breathing became as one. Another chair was tossed across the truck, something crashed to the floor.

When the couch moved slightly, Lauren tensed again.

Scott tightened his arms around her.

A voice sounded from outside the truck, "Find anything?"

"Naw. Just a bunch of damned furniture. Let's check underneath the trucks, then I'll go to the other end of the alley. They've got to be close by."

The door slammed and the truck interior turned pitch-black.

Lauren let out a heavy sigh.

"We're not out of this yet," Scott whispered. "We've got to stay put for a while."

"Why?"

"If they don't find anything at the other end, they'll probably come back this way. One of them might even stay here. That big guy is still shaky from getting hit with the bat." They remained quiet and listened. Every few minutes they heard a sound outside the truck. Scott whispered in Lauren's ear, "Sounds like there's still someone out there. We'll just sit tight and wait until it's safe. The police should be all over this mall before long. That should scare them off."

"God, I hope so."

They turned quiet, and their breathing gradually returned to a normal rhythm. Though they were still in danger, Scott became acutely of Lauren's body pressed against his. He wondered how he could think of such a thing at a time like this. He tried to put his mind back on the problem at hand, but an exotic mixture of aromas from Lauren took hold of him. He could smell her skin, her wet hair, and what was left of her perfume. The power of her femininity was immediate, sensuous, and overwhelming. He was wrapped around her so tightly that he felt every curve of her body. He held on, listened to her breathing, and wondered whether they would still be together tomorrow, or if they would even be alive.

After several minutes, the occasional noises from outside stopped. Scott used his arms to push the couch out slightly, then he shoved the other end with his feet, giving them enough room to sit with their backs against the wall. When they were more comfortable, he spoke softly, "It's time you told me what's going on. Why are these men trying to kill you?"

Lauren hesitated, then she recounted the day's events and told how she had overheard Hayden Benson before fleeing the building. She gave details of seeing the men leave her apartment and about finding her roommate. Her voice faltered and she turned silent.

Scott sensed her pain and comforted her. When she continued, he listened intently and became more concerned with each new piece of information. "My God, Lauren. This is worse than I thought."

"What do you mean?"

"Did anyone see you enter or leave your apartment?"

"No, I. . . . Wait, yes. I bumped into the new neighbor while I was running to my car."

"Don't you see?" Scott said, "They're going to think you killed her. They'll probably figure you and her were mixed up in this crop report scheme and for some reason you killed her."

"Why would they think I did that?"

"I don't know. Maybe she was going to talk. All I know is that they're going to think you killed her. They even have a witness who saw you leave right after she was shot. It makes a lot of sense. I don't see any other conclusion they could make."

"Scott, I swear I didn't have anything to do with it. You've got to believe me."

He was quiet for several seconds, and then said, "I do, but I don't think anyone else will. You're in a hell of a spot."

"What should I do?"

"I don't know. I was going to flag down the cops when they search the area, but they'll arrest you for sure." Scott became increasingly worried about something else; this was not the kind of thing he wanted to get involved in. He needed to get back to the trading floor and his faltering career. Then it hit him—he already *was* deeply involved. With alarm, he suddenly realized that the odds of this turning into a life-altering event had risen steadily. "Christ, I just thought of something. They might suspect me too."

"How could they?"

"Think about it. I'm a futures trader, I was in the Ag Building when the events unfolded, and I was seen with you in the restaurant. The maître'd could identify me."

"I'm sorry," Lauren said, her voice expressing genuine sincerity. "I didn't know about any of this. I just happened to be in the wrong place at the wrong time . . . and now I've got you involved."

Scott believed her, but he felt more uncomfortable about the whole affair. He thought about his involvement and realized no one knew his identity. He might be able to slip away, or maybe he should go straight to the authorities and try to clear himself. But what if they did not believe him and he wound up in jail? He could not take that chance.

There seemed to be only one option. "They don't know who I am; so I'll try to get you out of town. Since they'll be watching the local airport, we'll have to drive to another city. Then, you can go your way and I'll go mine." He touched her shoulder. " I'm sorry if that sounds harsh, but I have no other choice."

Lauren did not answer for a moment. Then she said, "Okay, but I don't know where to go." Her words came slow, her tone full of sadness.

"I can tell you one thing. Stay away from your family. I'm sure they'll be watching them."

A car slid to a stop in the alleyway and a door slammed. A police radio squawked in the background. They heard voices outside the truck.

"Get back down."

Lauren rolled over and Scott pulled the couch back against the wall. They were in tight quarters again, and he put his arms around her. His hand inadvertently came to rest under her breast but when he started to move his arm, she held him tight—a grip of desperation.

The door swung open. They held their breath.

Someone climbed into the truck; a flashlight beam scanned the wall behind them.

CHAPTER 11

Scott struggled with his inner turmoil. He wanted to surrender to the police, but he wondered if they would believe his involvement was that of an innocent bystander. Interwoven among his emotions was a strong feeling of empathy for Lauren, empathy that clashed with his urgent need to save his career. If they could get out of town, he could think things through under less pressure. He could always consult with his attorney and decide what to do later. He kept his arms around her and waited.

A voice called from outside. "What've you got?"

"It's clean. Just a couple of chairs and a sofa, but some driver's going to have to explain a broken lamp to his boss."

"Hell, they'll just take it out of his check." Laughter faded with the slamming of the back door.

After the police car left, Scott pushed the couch out, and they sat in the dark against the truck wall in silence. He felt Lauren's body shake and put his arm around her. "You've had a horrible day."

Lauren sighed. "I just can't believe this whole thing. Why did I have to get involved in this? And poor Marilyn. She never hurt anyone." Lauren put her head against his shoulder and became quiet.

While Scott listened, he became convinced she had nothing to do with stealing the crop data or the murder. He had tuned in to the sincerity in her voice, and he sensed that her sadness over her friend's death was real. With his decision about her innocence made, his next problem was to get them to safety—but how?

"Lauren, I'll try to help you get away, but, after that, you're on your own. I can't get more involved than I already am." He felt a stab of guilt, but he needed to get back to his own world—to his own problems.

"I understand." She raised her head and spoke softly, "I can't thank you enough for what you've already done. I'll never forget it."

"You're getting ahead of yourself. The police are scouring this whole area, and don't forget about those killers."

"I know, but I was talking about your help so far. You could have left several times, but you stayed with me." After a brief silence, Lauren asked, "Any ideas about what we do next?"

"I think we should wait here until after midnight, then try to get my car and go to my hotel. It might get a little tight over the next day or two, but we'll figure out something." He wondered if his voice had concealed his own doubts.

"I'll do whatever is necessary."

Scott leaned forward. "I'm going to shove the couch out a little, but we're going to stay right here. I want you to rest your knee until it's safe to leave."

———

Lauren sat in the black silence and soon found herself thinking about Scott. His moments of gentleness reminded her of Paul, but he also had an inner core of strength—his decisions under pressure had impressed her. He had risked his life for her, and she thought few men would have done the same under the circumstances. She shuddered as her mind played out the nightmare she would have endured if he had not been there. She knew she would not have survived the attack.

———

After a long silence, Scott's body stiffened. "Damn!"

"What is it?"

"I just thought of something. If we leave my car parked there too late, the police or the gunmen will spot it. They're bound to check any cars left around the restaurant after closing time. I've got to get it before then." He looked at the luminescent dial on his watch. "There's not much time."

"They could get the plate numbers."

"Exactly. The police could get my name from the rental company." Scott paused, his mind processing, and then said, "I've got to get the car before the shoppers leave the mall." He turned in the darkness and placed his hand on her shoulder. "You'll have to stay here. There's no way we could get to the car together, especially with your injury." He gently touched her leg. "How's your knee?"

"It's sore and it's bleeding some but that's not important now." Her voice notched down and turned apprehensive. "You are coming back . . . aren't you?"

The thought flashed through his mind. If he reached his car, he could drive into the night and no one would know, but he quickly discarded the idea. The thought of abandoning Lauren in the back of a dark truck seemed unconscionable.

"I'll be back," Scott said. "Unless I get caught."

He thought about his best strategy and decided to leave half an hour before the mall closed. Three cars passed while they waited but none stopped. They heard no other sounds except for their own breathing and the occasional patter of rain on the van's metal roof.

After a time, Scott checked his watch and turned toward Lauren. Although he could not see her outline, he could easily visualize her face. "I'm going to leave now, but I want you to stay here no matter what. I'm certain the police are still checking the area so it may take a while. You've got no choice but to wait for me, no matter how long it takes."

"I know. But what if you don't come back?"

"I don't know, Lauren. I just don't know." He realized his answer had been inadequate and felt he should try to reassure her. "We're going to get you out of town. I don't know how, but we will."

Scott went to the side door, looked out, and saw that the rain had turned to a drizzle. He lowered himself to the pavement, squatted, and looked beneath the other truck. All clear. He crept to the end of the vehicle and looked in both directions. At the far end of the alleyway, to his left, he saw flashing lights from at least one patrol car, but it was not moving. He saw nothing to his right. Scott went around the trucks, made his way to the rear of the building, and then ran parallel to the wall. He skirted several trash bins and felt relieved he had not seen anyone. If he continued in this direction, he thought he would eventually come out on the far side of the mall next to the restaurant. He hoped there were still enough automobiles in the parking lot to conceal his movements.

As he approached the end of the buildings, car lights flashed into the alley. He dove behind a stack of flattened cardboard boxes and peered over the top, watching as the car eased into the alleyway and cruised past him. It was not the police. There appeared to be two men in the car, and he could see the red glow of a cigarette as the driver turned in his direction.

Scott became concerned for Lauren as they drove past his position, heading straight toward the trucks. After about twenty yards they stopped suddenly, turned, and came back the way they had come. They had obviously seen the flashing lights at the far end of the alleyway.

The car moved out of sight.

Scott waited a few minutes, then he got up and crept along the wall. He reached the corner and saw part of the large parking lot but no restaurant. He could not see the main lot from his position, but he believed he was going in the right direction. His problem now was the open space.

It began to sprinkle.

He started across the lot but did not turn toward the main area as planned, choosing instead to continue toward the street and come in from the front. Anyone searching for them would be looking toward the mall, and they would be looking for two people. If he could make it to the street, he felt his chances would improve.

Scott moved across the lot at a walk to avoid looking suspicious. He headed up the first row and glanced to his right, but there was no sign of the car he had seen in the alley. After he had gone far enough to get a better view of the mall, he looked back and saw flashing lights from several police vehicles scattered about the area.

When he reached the end of the row, he grew optimistic and quickened his pace. He did not want to leave the protection offered by the lot, which was now thinning out, and decided not to go all the way to the street. After another minute, he saw the sign: Henry's. A hundred yards from the restaurant, he veered to his right and headed directly toward the building. He saw two police cars in front of Henry's and one in back.

The sprinkle stopped as Scott snaked between the cars. He approached his rental and suddenly remembered his appearance—he was a mess. A bullet had ripped the shoulder pad on his coat and his tie was torn. Scott took off his coat, brushed his slacks, tucked his shirt in, removed the tie, and shoved it into his coat pocket. He threw the coat over his arm and headed for the car.

Fifteen feet from his car, he heard a voice. "Sir. Hold up a minute."

He looked toward the restaurant and saw a police officer walking toward him. His mind froze. Shit, what now? Scott started to run but realized that was the worst thing to do. He walked the few steps to the rear of his car, stopped, brushed a hand through his wet hair, took a deep breath and waited.

The policeman stopped a few feet away. "Sir, I'd like to ask you a few questions."

"Sure, officer. What's the problem?"

"Could I see your ID, please?" He put his flashlight on Scott. "What happened to you? You look like you've been in a fight."

Scott searched for an answer. "Well, actually, I've been wallowing around in three inches of water. I came across a young lady whose car had broken down; so I changed her tire. It was a hell of a job."

"Where was that?"

"Just up the street." Scott motioned with his head as he spoke. "About two blocks. She had pulled in between two buildings but couldn't manage the tire herself." Scott watched the policeman's reaction.

Nothing.

"By the way, officer, she was acting strange. She seemed somewhat scared and kept looking around. What's going on here, anyway?"

"What did she look like?"

"She was about thirty, medium length brown hair."

The officer looked up from his pad. "What was she wearing?"

"To tell you the truth her clothes were a mess. She had on a dark skirt, maybe black or navy blue, and a white blouse."

"Is she still there?"

"She was a couple of minutes ago."

The officer turned and looked back at Scott. "What's your name?"

"Ah—Carpenter. Jim Carpenter."

"Thanks, Mr. Carpenter." The police officer ran toward the restaurant.

Scott got into his car and started the engine. It stalled. He cursed and turned the key again. When the engine started, he pulled out of the slot and went down the row toward the mall. He looked back and saw two police cars racing down the street in the direction he had given the officer. His ploy worked, but he did not have much time. He drove to the end of the building, cut the lights, turned into the alleyway, and pulled as close to the wall as possible. Light rain began to fall. He switched on his wipers, thankful for the poor visibility.

Scott looked ahead and saw the faint outline of the first truck. After a few seconds, he pulled to a stop, jumped out, and ran to the truck. He peered around the vehicle and felt a surge of optimism. No police lights, no one in sight. He ran between the two trucks and pulled on the side door. "Lauren! Let's get out of here."

She appeared at the door, and he started to help her but she turned back. She spoke from the darkness, "I forgot my purse."

He glanced around nervously while she retrieved the bag, then he helped her down and led her around the truck as fast as her sore knee would allow. "I want you to get in the trunk."

She stopped. "The trunk?"

"A policeman stopped me when I got to the car. I got rid of him, but they're all over the place."

She hesitated.

"Don't worry; I'll let you out after a few minutes." He turned the key in the lock, lifted the trunk lid, and helped her climb into the small space. Scott could not see her face, but he sensed her trepidation. This was obviously the most tragic and harrowing day of her life.

Before bringing the lid down he said, "I won't leave you in here too long. I promise."

"I'll be all right."

Scott closed the lid and ran to the last truck. He looked up the alley to where the police car had been earlier. Seeing that the cruiser had left, he ran back to his car and got in. He did not want to go back through the parking lot by the restaurant and decided to take a chance the police at the end of the alley had been called away.

He kept the lights out, drove around the truck, and headed up the alley. He reached the end and searched from side to side, looking for the police, but he also worried about the killers, which he suspected were still in the area. He tried to remember what kind of car they had used but his mind drew a blank. He knew only that it was dark in color.

Scott left the headlights out and started across the back of the parking lot. As he approached the street, he glanced in the rearview mirror and saw lights flashing from the direction of the restaurant, but there was no one pursuing him. He reached the street and turned right. He had gone a block when a police car came around a corner in front of him, siren on, lights flashing. "Dammit. The headlights. I forgot the lights." He flipped the switch and tried to act like a forgetful driver. The police car raced past. He wiped his forehead and watched the rearview mirror.

———

When Scott had closed the trunk lid, Lauren entered a world of darkness. The loss of her visual senses propelled her mind into overdrive. It seemed as if her day of horror had now turned toward the bizarre. How else could she explain the thoughts and feelings rushing through her mind? And now she found herself confined in a small, dark space designed for luggage. But that was not all. She was cold, weary, sore, confused, and scared. She felt a crushing sense of helplessness.

Suddenly, above the hum of the tires, she heard a siren. A current of fear surged through her mind. She could not comprehend the thought of going to jail.

CHAPTER 12

Scott felt a wave of relief as he watched the patrol car continue toward the restaurant, and he turned his attention to the route ahead. With so many police units in the area, he decided against using the Fourteenth Street Bridge and drove north toward the Key Bridge. After two miles, he felt the pressure ease but he worried about Lauren. The temperature had dipped and she was soaking wet. He turned onto Fort Meyer Drive, found a parking lot, pulled into a dark area, parked next to a van, got out, checked the area, then he went to the back of the car and opened the trunk.

Lauren was curled up on her side, shivering. "Where are we?"

"Let's get you out of there and then I'll explain everything." He bent to help her and saw the rose. It did not look the same, but she still had it. She had shoved the wrapped flower into her shoulder bag and had managed to keep it throughout the ordeal.

"You still have the flower."

"No one's given me a rose for a long time, and I don't intend to lose it."

Surprised at her determination, he helped her out of the trunk and opened the car door. "I want you to get down on the floorboard. It's not comfortable but it'll be a lot better than where you were." He helped her in and went around to the driver's side. He walked past another car and saw a small blanket on the back seat.

80

After trying both doors on his side, he ran around the car and grabbed the handle on the rear door—it opened. Scott grabbed the blanket, went to his car, and opened the rear door. "You can hide under this, and it'll keep you warm."

"Thank you. I'm freezing."

He shut the door and considered his next move. Lauren was soaking wet, her hair was stringy, her clothes were torn, and the police were searching for her. He obviously could not take her inside the hotel. One mistake would send them to jail.

He pulled out of the lot and started up the street. "I'm coming to the Key Bridge. How do I get to the Jordan Colonial Hotel?"

"Take the first off ramp. That'll put you on the Whitehurst Freeway. I'll tell you how to get to K Street. It's easy from there."

"All right." Scott hesitated and then said, "I'm afraid I've got some bad news for you. I thought we could get you into the hotel so you could clean up, but it's too risky."

"My, God. What next?"

Scott said, "We're going to get tired and feel like giving up, but we just can't do that." He glanced at the rearview mirror. "I've been thinking about the hotel. If I leave my clothes there, it would look suspicious so I'm going to have to get my things and check out. You'll have to stay in the car. That means under the blanket on the floor."

"I was afraid you'd say that."

"There's no other way."

"I know, but will you do me one favor?"

"Sure."

"Will you hurry? And maybe bring me something to eat?"

"I'll just change clothes, pack, and check out. It won't take long; I Promise. When I finish, we'll stop at a fast-food place and load up. Then we'll get the hell out of Dodge."

"Where to?"

"I don't know. South, maybe. How far is Richmond?"

"I think it's about a hundred miles."

"Richmond it is."

She gave directions to the hotel.

Scott pulled in and parked in a dark spot next to a building. "I'm going to leave the keys. I shouldn't be more than thirty minutes, but if I'm not back in one hour you have to figure something happened. You'll have to take off on your own."

"You will be back . . . won't you?"

"Sure." He knew the optimism in his voice did not match his inner feelings, but he did not want to make her wait any more unbearable. Scott brushed his clothes and walked toward the hotel. He entered his room and quickly changed, packed, and then went downstairs to the front desk.

A clerk walked over. "Yes, sir. How may I help you?"

"I'd like to check out."

"Of course, sir, but you do understand we'll have to charge you for the night."

"It doesn't matter. I'm not feeling well, and I have to leave." Scott paid his bill, went outside, walked to the car, and tapped on the window.

Lauren peeked out from under the blanket and unlocked the door. "Any problems?"

"Everything's okay. You'll have to tell me how to get to Richmond, but I want you to stay down until we get out of the area."

"We'll go to the Beltway and get on Interstate 95. It's easy, and there's a fast-food place on the way. I don't usually eat that kind of food, but right now, it sounds great." Lauren gave directions as he drove.

After several miles, Scott turned off the road and parked behind the restaurant. He went inside, ordered food, and returned to the car. Lauren sat up and took the bag he handed her. They ate in silence. For those few minutes, pacifying an empty stomach temporarily blotted out the urgency of the moment.

He finished eating and thought about their immediate future. They had many obstacles to overcome, and he knew they would be under constant pressure. He also felt a nagging urgency to return Chicago. After considering their situation further, he turned to Lauren. "I'll try to get you on an airplane, if that's what you want, but I think we need to talk about going to the police."

"I can't think about that now. Can we discuss it in the morn—" Lauren stopped short. "I forgot. I've got to call Angela."

"Who's Angela?"

"A friend from work. She's a supervisor on the security staff, and she wants to help."

"How can you be sure?"

"I phoned her just before I went to my apartment, but she was called away, and we couldn't talk. I was supposed to call her at home around six-thirty."

"Can she be trusted? I mean, she does work for security."

"She believed me when I told her I had nothing to do with releasing the crop data, and I believe in her."

"But that was before you found your roommate. She might not be so trusting when it comes to murder." An uneasy silence hung inside the car, mixing oddly with the lingering odor of a cheeseburger and fries.

Lauren gazed at her lap.

Scott thought she might have misinterpreted his words. "I didn't mean that like it sounded. I don't think you could kill anyone."

"But I did kill her. Don't you see? If it hadn't been for me, she'd still be alive. I might as well have pulled the trigger myself." She buried her head in her hands.

Scott reached back and put his hand on her arm. "Listen to me. You're going to feel guilty, and it's going to hurt. It's going to hurt like hell, but it's not your fault. You didn't pull the trigger. You just got caught up in something beyond your control."

She raised her head and wiped her eyes. "I know, but I still feel guilty."

"You couldn't help what happened, Lauren." He reached up and pulled several strands of tear soaked hair from her eyes. "It'll pass in time."

She looked at him and nodded weakly.

"You'd better phone Angela. She may be able to bring us up to date on what's happened." Scott turned in the seat and looked across the parking lot. "I'll pull over to that phone booth so you can call her. Do you feel up to it?"

"I'll need a minute or two."

Scott waited a moment, and then started the engine. He stopped next to the telephone booth, reached into his pocket, and took out some change. "This should be enough."

She took the coins and got out.

He rolled down the window and called to her, "Find out everything you can but don't talk too long."

———

Lauren entered the booth and put the change on the metal ledge under the phone. Her hands shook as she picked up the receiver and dialed.

The phone rang twice.

"Angela. It's Lauren."

"Lauren! Where are you? Are you all right?"

"Oh, Angela. It's been like a bad dream."

"Listen, honey. Your nightmare hasn't even started. They're going to arrest you for Marilyn's murder, and they're going to have one hell of a case. Why did you leave the apartment? Why didn't you call the police?"

"I saw the men who killed her. I was scared."

"I've got to level with you, Lauren. It looks really bad. They have a witness who saw you leave the apartment right after he heard a loud noise. After the police arrived, he realized the sound must have been a gun shot." Angela paused, then added, "And this thing with the crop report. Hayden Benson gave a complete statement. He claims he heard you illegally giving out data, and they're saying it all fits. They think you and Marilyn might have been in this together, and had an argument, or that she found out, and you killed her."

"But I didn't. I swear it." Lauren looked down and put a hand to her forehead. "This just keeps getting worse."

"You're in a terrible spot," Angela said. "If this went to court on the evidence they've got, I don't think you'd have a chance."

"Why is this happening to me?"

"I don't know, honey. I just don't know."

Lauren sighed, then lifted her head and looked toward the car. "Did you hear anything about the restaurant and the mall? Do they have any idea who was with me?"

"I don't have many details. They seem to think there are several people mixed up in this and there was a falling-out, but I don't think they have the slightest idea about anyone's identity except yours. They have a rough description of the man from the people at the restaurant but it could fit thousands of men."

Lauren thanked Angela, then hung up and turned toward the car. Fear and doubt plagued her every thought.

CHAPTER 13

Lauren got in the car and gave Scott details of her conversation with Angela.

Scott considered the information and said, "There's only one thing in our favor, and we've got to use it."

"What's that?"

"They evidently don't have any idea who I am or what kind of car we're in. That gives us a little edge, but I think we should keep to the back roads for a while. It will take longer but our chances of getting through are better. Do you know the country south of here?"

"Only for about twenty miles. After that, you know as much as I do."

"Okay. Direct me as far as you can but stay in the corner and keep your head down." After fifteen minutes, Scott stopped at a station and bought a map. He plotted a course and started the engine.

"I've been thinking," Lauren said. "I need to change my appearance."

"I thought about that too. We'll stop at a motel near Richmond and take care of that. Any ideas?"

"My hair is the main thing. I've got to change my hair."

"All right. I'll help you with that and put you on a plane; then you'll be on your own." He worried that his words sounded too harsh, but what else could he do?

Lauren turned her head toward the side window. "I know."

Silence followed. Their brief relationship was terminal. Their paths had crossed at the wrong time in the worst possible place, but Scott wondered what might have happened under different circumstances.

After crossing the Beltway, he angled toward Highway 1, which he meant to follow for at least fifty miles. It was after one o'clock when they reached the outskirts of Fredericksburg, and Scott became worried because there were no small motels open at this time of night. If they continued to Richmond they might have the same problem, and he did not want to be stuck there at two or three in the morning.

He drove through Fredericksburg, checking the motels, but they were either fully occupied or closed for the night. He was about to give up when he saw a man leaving the office of a small motel. He made a U-turn, entered the driveway, and parked away from the light. He cut the engine and turned to Lauren. "Stay down until I get back."

He reached the office just as a nattily dressed man chewing on a dead cigar was preparing to lock the door. "Looks like I caught you just in time. Do you have a room available?"

"You lucked out, mister. Me and the boys were playing poker. Otherwise, I'd be closed up tight." The man walked around the counter and looked at a key rack. "I got four rooms. How many people?"

"Two. Just my wife and I."

The man turned with a knowing look. "No problem, mister. I suppose you want a big bed?"

"Actually, I'd like two beds."

The man's forehead wrinkled. "Hmm. This late at night I had you figured for one." He grabbed a key and laid it on the counter. "Room six. Two single beds." He pointed to his left. "Just go down this side. You can't miss it."

Scott started to sign his name on the card, but caught himself and wrote in the alias he had used earlier—Jim Carpenter. He also used a phony license plate number. If the man checked, he would just say it was the number on his own car, and he wrote it down out of habit.

The man barely looked at the information on the card. Scott paid in cash, went back to the car, drove to their room, and parked in front. He cut the engine. "I got one room, but it has two beds. I was just happy to find a place open." He hesitated. "I probably should have checked with you, although we should stay together."

Silence.

"Is that all right? Do you want me to try to get another room?"

"No. I don't want to be alone. As long as it has two beds, we can manage."

"By the way, we're Mr. and Mrs. Jim Carpenter."

She didn't answer.

The room was depressing. It was old, dark, and had a faint odor of mold. One small picture hung on otherwise drab walls, and some of the furniture should have been thrown out years ago. Nevertheless, they were temporarily safe and nothing else mattered. The ordeal of the past twelve hours had taken a toll, and neither said much after entering the room. Gloom and exhaustion are not easily overcome by a few tired words. Lauren used the bathroom while Scott got into bed. When she had finished, she turned the light out and went to bed. They said a weary good night but nothing more.

———

After a fitful night of broken sleep, Scott awoke to street sounds. Seeing daylight coming through a crack in the drapes, he reached for his watch. Almost eight o'clock. He turned toward Lauren and saw her sitting in bed with the sheets pulled up, clutching her knees, her face lined with concern.

"Did you sleep okay?" he asked, rubbing his right eye with the palm of his hand.

"Not really. Three or four hours, but that's all."

"Yeah, I had the same kind of night."

"I've been thinking," she said. "I can't try to get on an airplane without changing my hair. And I need different clothes."

"I know. Make a list while I go get some food. As soon as the stores open I'll buy whatever you need."

"I'll need quite a few things."

"I'll take care of it."

Lauren nodded, then turned her head so he could get out of bed and dress.

He went to the window and looked out but saw nothing unusual. He opened the door and spoke over his shoulder, "I won't be long." Scott walked to the front of the motel and saw a doughnut shop on the other side of the street. Not exactly a good breakfast, he thought, but it was food, and it was convenient.

A few minutes later, he entered their room carrying two white bags. "Coffee and doughnuts," he said. "It's not much but it'll keep us going."

Lauren was sitting up in bed, writing on a small pad. "That'll be fine," she said, looking up at the bags. "You know, it's funny in a way."

"What?"

"Well, when we first met, you invited me out to a nice dinner, but since I've known you all I've had to eat is junk food."

Scott smiled. "I'm glad to see you still have a sense of humor."

"That's probably the only funny thing you're going to hear from me today." She extended her arm and handed him the pad. "You're going to have to go to two or three places to get everything."

"I don't mind." Scott read the list. He came to the items for her hair and looked up. "If I just hand this to someone I guess they'll know what I want?"

"Yes, it won't be a problem. Just don't forget the scissors."

They drank coffee and ate doughnuts while going over sizes of the various items. Lauren's list included sneakers, jeans, socks, bra, underwear, and a blouse. Scott told her to add a sweater in case it turned cool.

He got up to leave at a quarter of ten. He opened the door and looked back. "I guess I don't need to tell you to stay in the room."

She nodded.

Scott drove to a nearby drugstore, went to the cosmetic counter and handed the list to a hard looking woman wearing excessive makeup.

She ran a finger down the list of items and looked up. "If you ask me, honey, you really don't need a makeover."

He didn't answer.

The woman completed the list, and he left for the department store. Scott had been gone an hour and a half when he walked out of the last store and headed toward his car. He passed a news vending machine and glanced at the front page of the paper. Startled, he dropped one of the bags. A front-page picture of Lauren glared out at him. She was headline news.

Their dilemma soared to a new level of urgency. Every police officer in Virginia would be looking for her. Scott bought a paper and hurried to his car with a single priority—he had to get her out of the state, and he had to do it now. Ten minutes later, he pulled into the motel lot. He stopped two parking slots from their room and saw a maid standing next to a cart. She had just opened the door to their room. Scott yelled at her but it was too late. He exited the car and ran toward the room.

The maid came back out just as he reached the door. She was obviously talking to Lauren. "I'm sorry, miss. I knocked twice and didn't think anyone was in." She greeted Scott. "Good morning, sir."

He nodded. Sensing that everything was all right, he went to the passenger side of the car and started removing the purchased items. He took several bags to the room and then went back for the last one.

The maid stopped her cart a few feet away, walked toward his car and bent down. "Sir, you dropped your newspaper." She picked up the paper and glanced at the front page. Her head shot up, and she looked toward the room, then she suddenly thrust the paper at him and rushed away.

Scott ran into the room and found Lauren standing in the doorway to the bathroom wrapped in a towel. "Did she see you?"

"Yes, I was in the bathroom and—"

"Get dressed. We've got to get out of here fast!"

"What's wrong?"

Scott held up the front page of the newspaper.

CHAPTER 14

The morning after the crop production report, Victor Merrick walked across his office and stopped in front of the heavy wooden door that led to his special sanctuary. He ran his fingers over a brass replica of a locomotive engine centered on the door, then he inserted a key and entered a large room his employees secretly referred to as Merrick's asylum. The name had evolved because of his habit of retiring to the room for hours with standing orders to hold all phone calls. The only telephone in the room connected to his private line.

He walked to a desk on an elevated dais overlooking the room. In front of the desk was a large, sophisticated collection of O-gauge trains arranged atop a platform containing an elaborate combination of mountains, forests, waterways, cities, towns, and farming communities. The entire layout measured eighteen by twenty-eight, taking up approximately five-hundred square feet.

His participation in the project had given him a strong sense of pride. Carpenters had constructed the framework, but Merrick completed much of the assembly. He was particularly pleased with the circuitry. Handling complex model trains required a working knowledge of electricity, which Merrick had learned over the years, and his experience allowed him to oversee much of the wiring. When the workers had finished, he secretly installed a special circuit. He had never used the pernicious device, but it was there—silently awaiting his command.

The elaborate scale model fulfilled a promise he had made to himself when, as a young boy, he had hidden from his father in the rail yards. Shortly after his takeover of Burgess, he moved an accounting unit into smaller quarters downstairs and then placed the trains in the vacated space. He did not care what the employees thought about being displaced. His attitude toward them was quite simple—fuck 'em.

The wall opposite his desk contained a commodity price board that could be seen from anywhere in the room. He had purposely installed an older style quote system that produced an audible click with each price change. Small green lights flicked on when a particular commodity made a new high for the day, red lights indicated a new low. He loved the flashing lights and clicking sounds when the market was going in his favor, a mercurial symphony that produced a high unlike any other.

Merrick had purposely entered the room a few minutes before grain trading began. With swelling anticipation, he could almost feel the excitement of viewing numbers that would symbolize his financial gains on his own quote board. When the market opened, Merrick stood and shouted as an array of red lights spread across the board. The bearish crop report took an immediate toll on soybeans, sending the nearby months down the daily limit. Other grains fell in sympathy. His short position had created a substantial paper profit in a matter of seconds.

As soon as he believed the market would continue under pressure, he flipped a switch that started a long freight train. When a series of open cars reached a scale model grain elevator, he stopped the train and pushed a lever. After the elevator mechanism had filled each car with soybeans, he again set the train in motion. He was in another dimension, his mind floating as if it had been freed from the constraints of his body.

Time, like a fading narcotic, gradually eased his euphoria, but Merrick was so pleased with himself he thought he deserved a pleasure trip. His destination would be Colorado where he had used company funds to purchase a summer home in Aspen. A vacation was overdue, and he felt pleased with the notion. Of course, he would have to wait until he had eliminated Lauren Chandler. Kill the woman; have some fun.

He stared at the price board for a considerable time before finally checking his watch. He had not heard from Billy Barker since the previous afternoon. He expected his men to find Chandler, but he also knew his future was at risk as long as she was still alive— her knowledge was a constant threat. Merrick realized that his zeal over the soybean market had blocked his objectivity. His mood changed quickly; the woman had to be eliminated.

He strode about the room, mumbling to himself, which only intensified his concern. He thought about Billy and spoke aloud, "If he doesn't call soon, I'm gonna ring that little fucker's neck."

He also worried that Hayden Benson might become more of a problem. Benson was an intelligent man who had not reached his present position by collapsing under pressure, but blood and death made this a different state of affairs. Merrick decided to fly to Washington and speak directly with Benson to make sure he would hold up. He meant to coach him, but he would also do something else—he intended to scare the hell out of Hayden Benson.

Merrick was standing by the window when the phone rang. He rushed to his desk and picked up the receiver. "Yeah."

"Ah, Victor, it's me."

"Dammit, Billy, what's going on down there?"

"We've been looking for her all night."

"Well?"

"We almost had her at that restaurant, but some guy helped her get away."

"Why didn't you call me sooner?"

"Hell, we've been looking everywhere for her. We chased her through a shopping center but lost her. Her car was still at the restaurant; so we checked the airports, trains, and bus lines but there are only two of us. She just disappeared."

"Hammitt and Navarro will be there today," Merrick said, "but it's probably too late."

"Another thing," Billy said. "Lisowski got cold-cocked by a baseball bat. He was pretty fuckin' dizzy so I had to take him to the hospital this morning. They said it's a concussion."

"Let me get this straight." Merrick's voice turned sarcastic. "You mean to tell me a woman knocked out a two hundred fifty pound man and got away?"

"No. It was the guy."

"What guy?"

"The one with her in the restaurant. I got no idea who he is."

"All right, Billy, listen up. I'm flying into National this afternoon. I want to see you at Shannon's apartment at six o'clock. I'll call Benson and tell him to be there too. When Hammitt and Navarro arrive, have them stay in your apartment. I'll have something figured out by the time I get there. You got that?"

"Yeah, I'll be there."

"And be on time." Merrick hung up, then dialed Benson's office number but was told the Deputy Secretary had gone home ill. Merrick thought the pressure must have gotten to him—a bad sign. He dialed Benson's home.

A woman answered.

"Hayden, please."

"I'm sorry, he's not feeling well."

"This is urgent. Tell him there's a gentleman on the phone regarding a margin call."

"A margin call? Yes, just a minute."

If those words did not bring him to the phone, nothing would.

A minute passed, then a shaky voice said, "Merrick?"

"Who else?"

"You shouldn't call me here."

"Listen, Hayden, I don't have time to discuss trivial bullshit. I'm going to be in town this evening, and I want you at Shannon's apartment at six o'clock. Make sure you bring the Chandler woman's address book."

"But—"

"No questions. Just be there." Merrick hung up, buzzed his secretary—his third in the last year—and told her to book the earliest flight to National. Going to Washington meant he would have to leave before the grain markets closed, but he expected soybeans to remain locked down the limit. He checked the quote board. As expected, all months still showed only one price for the day. There was obviously a large pool of sellers desperate to get out. He would call the trading floor tomorrow, and if beans opened down the limit again he would take partial profits. This was just what he needed—a quick profit.

———

Merrick's plane touched down at Washington National Airport a few minutes after five. He took a cab to Shannon's apartment, arriving at six-twenty. He walked into the living room and saw Hayden Benson in a chair, a drink in his hand, his head down.

Billy Barker was sprawled on a couch sucking on a beer, reading the *Racing Form*.

Shannon came out of her bedroom.

Merrick shot a harsh stare at Billy. "How in the hell did you let a woman get away?"

"Jeez, Victor. You had to be there."

"Be there my ass."

"We'll find her."

"You're damn right you'll find her. Are Hammitt and Navarro here yet?"

"Yeah, they're over at our place."

Merrick turned to Benson. "What the hell's wrong with you?"

Benson raised his head. "My God, Victor. You've killed an innocent woman."

"Yeah. Well, that's unfortunate, but those things happen." Merrick stared at Benson with brutal intensity. "I'll tell you something else. There's going to be more blood spilled if anybody folds on me. This is too damn important to screw up."

Benson looked down.

Merrick decided to push harder. "You'd also better think about your family. Don't you have a daughter in Boston?"

Benson's head came up. "Y—you can't involve my family in this."

Merrick went over and sat down. "Listen, Hayden, you don't understand how I work. I take care of my people. I pay top dollar, and I'm going to make sure everyone makes a chunk of money from this." He paused a few seconds to give his next words more impact. "But, I won't let anyone screw things up. If you do, your family's going to pay. It's that simple."

A look of agony spread across Benson's face.

Merrick rose, walked to the bar and poured a drink. "But it doesn't have to be that way. Just do as you're told and everything will work out." He glanced toward the hall and saw Shannon leaning against the door. He raised his eyebrows and nodded toward Benson.

She took the cue, went over, and sat next to the distraught man. She put her arms around him and whispered something in his ear. After a moment, she got up and made him another drink.

Benson took a sip and seemed calmer.

Merrick winked at Shannon. "Get him out of here. I want to talk to Billy."

Shannon took Benson into her bedroom and started to close the door.

"Wait a minute," Merrick demanded. "Did you bring the address book?"

"Yes, I've got it." Benson reached into his pocket and withdrew a small book.

Merrick walked over and yanked it out of his hand. "Good. Now shut the door." He turned to Billy. "Have you got any leads?"

"Nothing."

Merrick moved across the room. "You've got to find this woman. When you do, I want it done so there's absolutely no trace of her—none." He stared intensely. "You got that?"

"Sure."

"Okay. Go through this address book and list the names of everyone in the immediate area. People like her are going to seek out friends or relatives; so check everybody on the list. If you don't find her soon, we'll have to figure she's already skipped town." Merrick paused. "I know some people who are experts at finding people on the run."

"What about Benson?"

"Don't worry about him. He's scared to shitless." Merrick took a sip of his drink. "And Billy."

"Yeah."

"Find her, and I'll make it worth your while. Hell, you can buy another horse."

Billy's face brightened, his mind obviously fixating on the last three words.

Merrick finished his drink. The more he thought about bringing in outside help, the more he liked the idea. If his people did not find the woman soon, he would use some of his new profits and get the best hit man money could buy. His mind ran ahead, listing possible assassins. A name came to him, and he knew he had the right man for the job: Cade. On contract after contract, Cade had proved worthy of his name—he never failed. The feared assassin was one of the most expensive in the world, but he was also the best. Whatever the cost, Merrick wanted Lauren Chandler dead.

CHAPTER 15

Scott saw the shock on Lauren's face as she stared at the front page of the newspaper, but urgency displaced compassion. "Get dressed. Hurry!"

She stood motionless, transfixed by her photo.

"The maid saw the picture. We've got to get out of here."

Lauren's expression changed from concern to fear as she threw down the paper and grabbed the bag of clothes. Scott headed toward the door. "I'll be right back." He went outside and searched the ground until he found a puddle from the previous day's rain. He gathered a handful of mud, ran to the rear of the car and smeared it over the license plate. He covered the numbers and rushed back to the room.

Lauren had put on jeans and was buttoning her top when he came in. Scott reached in the bag, pulled out the sneakers, and threw them on the bed. "I'll take the rest of this stuff to the car." He ran toward the door and yelled over his shoulder. "Let's go."

He put the things in the car and rushed back to gather the last of their belongings.

Lauren came out of the bathroom. "I'm ready."

"Good. Let's move."

They ran to the car.

Scott started the engine and looked toward the office. No one in sight. He backed up and saw an alley that led to a road at the rear of the motel. He gunned the engine, drove down the lane, and turned onto the street. They had gone only a block when he heard a siren. It sounded like it came from the street in front of the motel. "They damn sure got here fast." He shoved down on the gas pedal while Lauren looked through the back window. "See anything?"

"Nothing."

An old gangster movie flashed through Scott's mind as they raced down the street. One scene had stuck with him over the years. A detective had caught a fleeing criminal he had lost track of during a pursuit. The captured man asked the cop how he had found him. The detective said people trying to escape always turned right. Scott did not know if that happened only in the movies, but he decided to turn left at the next street.

He tugged on the wheel.

Lauren screamed, "Look out!"

A car coming from the crossroad slid in front of them. Scott swerved hard to avoid a collision, throwing Lauren against the passenger door. He regained control and yelled, "Lock your door."

She pushed the knob. "God, that was close."

He didn't answer.

Lauren saw the mud on Scott's hands. "What happened to your hands?"

He glanced in the rearview mirror. "I smeared mud over the license plate. I didn't want someone at the motel to get the number." He drove several blocks and made another left turn. He followed a narrow road for several minutes and then turned right. He moved his head toward the windshield and glanced at the sky. The sun's angle meant they were going east. He turned toward Lauren. "Keep looking and let me know if you see anything."

They entered a rural area and Scott slowed considerably. There had been no sign of anyone pursuing them, and he did not want to draw undue attention. After a few miles, they were in the country. Houses and small farms dotted the countryside. Occasional dirt roads intersecting the highway were marked by colonies of mailboxes lined in rows like selfless, frozen sentinels anchored to the earth.

After crossing a stream, Scott pulled to the side of the road and stopped. "Sit tight. I need to wipe off the license and clean my hands. I don't want to get stopped by a policeman because he can't read our plates."

"Don't you think we're safe now?"

"No. Every cop in Virginia is looking for you." He thought about what he had said as he got out of the car. They would not just be searching the D.C. area now. He was right, he knew it, and he was worried. He cleaned off the plate, looked toward the bridge, then got in the car. "Hand me the map."

Lauren stared at the highway as she spoke. "That means Richmond won't be safe either."

"I'm afraid not." Scott studied the roads for several minutes before starting the engine. "Our best bet is to take the back roads and try to get to Raleigh. I think you could catch a plane there, especially after changing your appearance." He adjusted the rear-view mirror. "But right now we need to get out of Virginia."

Lauren turned her face toward the side window.

"You okay?" Scott asked.

She shook her head. "I can't believe how I got into this horrible mess. And Marilyn. . . . It's hard to believe she's gone."

Scott touched her arm. "I know, but we've got a decent chance of getting to Raleigh; then you can get away from all this."

"Yes, but for how long?" She kept her face to the window in an obvious attempt to hide her distress.

After three hours of crisscrossing back roads, Scott stopped at a small country store where they got gas and used the rest rooms. He came out of the store with one arm held behind his back and managed a slight smile. "There was a really nice old man in there. He said the state line is only about five miles away." He then brought his arm around and handed Lauren a single red rose. "Your other one got crushed along the way; so I bought you a new one. It's not a long stem but it's nice."

She took the rose with a graceful movement of her hand. Her lips parted to speak but no words came. She turned and faced the front window. After a moment, she spoke softly. "Thank you." Nothing more—just those simple but remarkable words.

After Scott pulled onto the road, she asked, "Can we stop for a while?"

"As soon as we cross the state line we'll look for somewhere to eat and rest."

They had gone about two miles when he saw a patrol car on the other side of the road coming straight toward them. When the car came within a few hundred feet, Scott put both hands on the wheel. "After he goes by I want you to keep your eye on him. If he turns around, holler and hang on. I'm going to kick this sucker in the ass."

As soon as the patrol car passed, Scott increased the speed slightly and looked in the mirror, then back at the road. "What's he doing?"

"He's still going straight."

"It shouldn't be more than a couple of miles now. Keep watching."

Lauren looked intently out the back window. After a moment, she grabbed Scott's arm. "I can't see him anymore. He went around a bend in the road."

A minute passed, then two. No sign of the police car.

He looked ahead and saw a large sign a hundred yards away: Entering North Carolina.

When they crossed the state line, Lauren sighed. "I guess our chances are better now."

"I think so. I don't know how jurisdiction over state lines works, but there should be a hell of a lot fewer people looking for us down here."

They drove for nearly fifteen minutes without speaking, enjoying the transitory relief, but Scott knew uncertainty and danger lay ahead. He finally broke the silence. "Raleigh is only about forty or fifty miles from here. Let's look for a spot where we can pull off the road and eat."

The countryside underwent a subtle change, and they came upon a long row of elm trees teeming with starlings. As they drove by, a large flock of the birds flew out of the trees and arced over the highway, curving and swooping as if a single entity. They dove as a unit, leveled off, and lighted in a field on the other side of the road.

A short time later, they passed a side road that displayed a small sign:

Montgomery Park - 2 miles.

Scott pulled to the side of the road, made a U-turn, went back to the sign and made a right turn. They drove through a small community and followed the markers. Montgomery Park was a narrow parcel of grass and trees that bordered a quiet stream. Few people about made the location ideal. He pulled off the payment and followed a dirt road to the edge of the water.

Lauren got out of the car. "It looks so peaceful. Right now that's exactly what I need."

Scott picked up the grocery bag and walked to a spot under a tree. "This looks good. Are you hungry, or did all this spoil your appetite?"

"I can eat, but for the next few minutes, all I want to do is lie flat on my back and shut my eyes. God, what a nightmare."

"I think we're safe here," Scott said, looking over the grounds. "Actually, it's kind of nice. We can eat and relax a little, but then we need to talk about getting you on an airplane." He laid out Havarti, crackers, and fruit. He saw an empty soda bottle a few yards away, which he retrieved. He took it to the edge of the stream, filled it with water, went back to the car, and put the rose in the bottle.

Lauren smiled when he set it on the grass.

Scott sat down and occasionally glanced toward the road, but mostly, he watched Lauren. She had certain qualities that gave her a natural charisma. He thought it was caused by a synergistic match of her various characteristics—a combination of the way she moved, talked, and smelled. He noticed those things about women.

Lauren opened her eyes and saw him looking at her. "What are you thinking?" she asked.

"Another time, another place . . . the possibilities."

She sat up and nodded but did not reply.

Scott motioned toward the food. "We'd better eat." He handed her a soft drink. "It's not cabernet but right now it should taste pretty good."

They ate in silence.

When they were nearly finished, Scott noticed a toddler running across the grass, his mother close behind. Because the stream was nearby, he got up and caught the boy. He exchanged pleasantries with the woman, and then returned. "Cute kid. The mother said she was going to have to tie a rope around him."

Lauren's laughter caught Scott off guard, as this was her first appearance of cheerfulness since their ordeal began. He had always felt that a sense of joy flowing through one's soul had a profound cleansing effect. So much so, that he often wondered about the healing properties of bulk lots of laughter.

A combination of the melodic flow of the quiet stream, the welcome food, and the lighthearted moment seemed to lift the sense of doom that haunted her. He knew the fleeting glimpse of tranquility could not possibly last, yet he wanted to hold on, to grasp the feeling of peace and somehow place it in a bottle.

They stared at each other for a moment; then she turned away. Scott asked, "What's wrong?"

"Nothing. I just don't want to get too close."

Scott's mind searched for the right words, but, unable to find them, he remained silent. A few minutes later, he got up. "I'm going to stretch my legs. Do you want to come along?"

"Sure."

He extended his hand. He helped her up and felt a sensual thrill at the touch of her warm skin. After a few steps, she eased her hand from his. They walked along the edge of the stream and talked some, but mostly enjoyed the peace of the moment. They stopped near a tree and Scott threw small pebbles into the water. While he watched the splashes made by the small rocks, Lauren watched him. She thought about how different he was from Paul. He had an intriguing way of being gentle one moment and strong the next. She thought of the rose, smiled, and began to wish that she had held onto his hand.

When the last pebble hit the water, Scott turned to her. "We'll have to leave soon."

"I know."

They talked a little longer before walking back to the car. Lauren put the leftover food in the back seat, then got in and looked at Scott. "We've got to change my hair as soon as possible."

"I think it'd be best if we found a small motel out in the country somewhere instead of going into town."

"Don't you think we should try to leave tonight?"

"No. We'll let things cool off overnight." Scott pondered their problem. "There's more to consider. I don't want to exchange my airline ticket in Raleigh. I'll buy a new one-way ticket to Chicago from there. Do you have any money?"

"Only what I took to work on Monday. Maybe forty dollars."

"Okay. I'll go to a bank in the morning and draw some money. We should use cash for everything. I'll cover your ticket and give you some money, but you'll have to let me know your destination by tomorrow." Scott started the car. "Do you have any idea where you'll go?"

"The only place I can go is back home."

Scott ran his fingers through his hair. "I don't think it's a good idea to go to *any* of your relatives. That Ag official could get your records, and they could easily trace you. You might even put your family at risk."

Lauren turned away. "I'll never be safe. This will just go on and on."

"Where else could you go?"

No answer.

"Lauren?"

DALE BRANDON

She continued to look out the passenger window but finally said, "There's no place else. If I went to a friend's house, I'd put them in jeopardy too. I just can't do that."

They drove back to the highway and headed south until they found a suitable roadside motel twenty miles outside Raleigh. After settling in, Lauren went to a phone booth to call her parents. Scott noticed the red around her eyes when she came back to the room. She didn't want to talk about the conversation, saying only that they believed her, supported her, and were frantic with worry.

Lauren then performed the necessary task of cutting and bleaching her hair. It took over an hour but when she finally emerged from the bathroom she had definitely acquired a new look. She stepped just inside the adjoining door and asked, "Well, what do you think?"

"You're cute like that, but I think I liked the other way better." She blushed.

———

They drove to Raleigh the next morning. Scott stopped at a bank, then headed for the airport. During the drive, they decided it would be safest to split up after he purchased the tickets. When they arrived, Lauren had still not selected a destination. She had been unusually quiet and said nothing after Scott returned the car to the rental company.

He stepped inside the terminal and turned to her. "Have you decided?"

She said nothing for a moment, and then blurted out, "Los Angeles. Buy me a ticket to Los Angeles."

"Do you know someone there?"

"No, I just want to get as far away as possible, and I think a large city is best."

Scott found a secluded spot and told her to wait. They agreed that he would buy her ticket, walk by, hand it to her and keep going.

He put down his bags to say goodbye.

Her eyes glistened with moisture.

He put his arm around her. "I'm going to give you my home number. If there's anything . . ."

Lauren did not let him finish. She kissed him on the cheek, then turned and went to a chair in the far corner and sat down. She stared out the window and did not look back.

Scott felt a powerful mixture of guilt, concern, and a sense of loss as he walked to the ticket counter. He stood in line and thought about how Lauren had looked the first time he saw her in the cafeteria, and how important she had become to him in such a short time—even under such trying circumstances.

It took thirty minutes to purchase tickets and check the bags. The longer he waited, the more he worried she might be spotted. He left the counter and had started back when he saw two police officers rush by, moving in Lauren's direction. He hurried up the corridor but lost the two men in the crowd. Scott turned the corner, hoping they had not recognized her. His gaze swept over the area, and he felt a wave of relief when he caught a glimpse of the policemen leaving the building. He looked toward the corner and felt a little tug at his heart when he saw her.

He crossed the open area, handed her the ticket folder, hesitated a moment, and then kept walking as planned.

Without raising her head, she mumbled something that sounded like thank you.

Scott walked about thirty feet, then stopped near a corner and looked back.

———

Lauren sat for a moment, gently tapping the end of the folder against her knee. She wondered what kind of future awaited her at the destination printed on the ticket—or if she even had a future. She stared straight ahead, unable to shake the vague depression that had swept through her when Scott handed her the ticket and walked away. She suddenly felt very tired—the ordeal had taken a toll. She had been cast, against her will, on a journey of terror, a journey that consumed her energy like a cancer—a slow, insidious destruction. Yet, from some arcane level deeper than thought, a voice told her to hold on, to somehow maintain her resolve no matter what the odds. She wondered if she could.

She sighed wearily, then shifted her attention to the folder in her hand. She opened it, glanced at the ticket, put it away, and looked straight ahead. Seconds passed, then she quickly opened the folder and squinted at the ticket. Her eyes focused on one word: CHICAGO.

Lauren turned her head, searching for Scott. She saw him standing, watching.

Tears streamed down her cheeks.

CHAPTER 16

With Chicago's O'Hare Field only fifteen minutes away, Scott turned apprehensive. The relief he had felt when the plane lifted off the runway proved fragile. He and Lauren were safe in the air, but the closer they got to Chicago the more he worried. He could only hope the killers were still unaware of his identity. Everything depended on it. He thought about the complexities of their problem. Lauren's life was in danger, and she was wanted by the police. Scott knew time would become their enemy; each day would bring them closer to some unknown fate—an ultimate resolution.

When the airplane left Raleigh, Scott knew his involvement had escalated dramatically. If the authorities arrested Lauren, they would detain him also, but he felt he had no choice. He believed her story, and he would have felt guilty forever if he had let her go to Los Angeles and something happened to her. His mind replayed an image of Lauren's face when she had first realized that Chicago was the destination on her ticket. He knew it was one of those special moments between two people that occur too seldom in life. Scott let the memory of her reaction sink into his mind, deeply, profoundly. He meant for it to stay there forever.

Lauren occupied a seat four rows behind him. Just before the plane touched down, he turned and looked at her. She smiled briefly, but it was not the smile he had found so appealing. She was obviously worried about what might await them on the ground. Scott had previously arranged for her to follow him to the baggage area and to stay within sight. After disembarking, he struggled with a strange, awkward feeling as he moved through the crowd, one moment checking Lauren's progress, the next casting speculative glances at anyone who moved in her direction. So this was how it was going to be.

A delay in the distribution of the luggage added to the increasing tension, but after Scott retrieved his bags and headed for the parking area, he felt a touch of optimism. He looked back several times but saw nothing suspicious. Lauren stayed about four yards to one side. The only people near her were an elderly couple pulling a luggage cart and two flight attendants. Scott slowed and scanned the area as he approached his car. He threw his bags in the trunk and started to open the door but suddenly stopped and peered through the rear window.

"What are you doing?" Lauren asked.

He went around to her side and stuck his key in the lock. "I guess I've seen too many movies. I was just checking for someone on the floorboard in the back seat. Silly, huh?"

"I don't think so. I try to live by the rule of never assuming. It seems especially important now."

"I was a little worried when we got off the plane," Scott said, "but I feel better now. Actually, I don't see how anyone could know my identity or where we are. I think we're in pretty good shape."

"For now."

"Yeah, for now." He glanced around and then opened the car door, pondering his words as he slid onto the seat. Wondering what might happen over the next few minutes, or the next few days created an ominous mood. It seemed impossible to stop the roller coaster of emotions that continually flooded his mind.

Thinking it would be best to stay inside for the next few days, they stopped at a small market and purchased food. Scott's apartment was on the twelfth floor. They managed to load the elevator and carry the groceries and luggage in one trip. He put down his bags and reached for the door. "I'd better go in first." He stepped inside, looked around, and found everything exactly as it had been when he left on Sunday. He checked the other rooms and called to Lauren, "It's okay. Please come in."

———

Lauren stepped into a remarkably well kept apartment. An Oriental rug covered the entryway floor, a hall tree stood on one side, a framed mirror hung on the opposite wall. She moved into the living room, and her gaze fell on a large, colorful serigraph on the wall behind a sofa. "That's beautiful. Thomas McKnight?"

"Yes. Do you like his work?"

"I've only seen a few, but I've liked them all."

She looked about the large room and found it warm, comfortable, interesting. On the wall opposite the sofa were a series of shelves containing a collection of pottery and other artifacts. She went over to examine the pieces and found them remarkable. This man, she thought, obviously had good taste. On another wall was an oil by Itzchak Tarkay depicting two women in an outdoor cafe. The blues, yellows, and reds from their clothing seemed to explode outward from the canvas. "I love that painting." After a moment, she turned toward Scott. "I'm very impressed with your place."

"Thanks, I'm happy with it." He started toward the kitchen. "Come on, I'll show you around."

Lauren continued looking over the surprising array of unusual objects as she made her way into the oversized kitchen, which was immaculate. It would have been hard for many to believe these quarters belonged to a bachelor.

An island stood in the center of the kitchen. Directly above it were racks containing gleaming, stainless steel cooking utensils. A large, temperature controlled wine storage unit stood near one corner. A glass door allowed a view of row after row of wine bottles stored on their sides, cork end out. Small tags, with notes written on them, hung from the necks of several bottles.

Lauren put the perishable items in the refrigerator and followed Scott back to the living room. She stopped next to an old, wooden rocking chair that had obviously been handcrafted. She slid her fingers along the top and turned to Scott.

"It belonged to my mother," he said.

"They don't make them like this anymore."

He nodded. After a moment, he glanced toward the hallway. "We haven't talked about our arrangement, or how long you'll be able to stay. I don't think we should worry about it tonight, but we'll have to do a little brainstorming tomorrow. What we really need to do is figure a way to get you out of this mess, but I'll be damned if I've got the slightest idea of what we can do." He ran a hand through his hair. "Anyway, you can have my bedroom tonight. I'll sleep on the couch."

"Isn't this a two-bedroom apartment?"

"Yes, but I converted one to an office."

Lauren gazed down the hall. "Maybe we could alter the office slightly so I could sleep there. It shouldn't be that difficult."

Scott had a strange look on his face. "Well . . . ah, not really. But it's okay. The couch makes into a bed, and I don't mind sleeping there. It's no problem. But I do need to straighten my bedroom a little."

Scott went into the kitchen.

Lauren started toward the hall and said, "Is it okay if I take a look at your office?"

No answer.

She stopped in front of the door and called again.

"I can barely hear you," Scott said. "I'll be there in a second." He came into the hall just as Lauren's hand turned the doorknob to his office door. "No! Don't go in—"

Too late.

Having already stepped inside, Lauren was stunned by the extraordinary sight before her. "Oh, my." Scott's office was the complete opposite of the rest of his apartment; it was in shambles. The walls were plastered with futures charts, maps, inspirational quotations, photos, and a large poster that displayed the wine appellation regions of Northern California. The floor was nearly invisible. Large stacks of magazines, newspapers, file folders, and books were scattered everywhere. A path led to two desks, one of which offered a glimpse of wood, but the other was covered with stacks of papers and futures charts. A computer took up most of the space on the other desk. A large, black and white photo hung on the wall directly above the computer. The subjects, two young men wearing hats and dungarees stood, arm in arm, sporting wide grins. Each held a fly rod.

Post-it notes were everywhere. They surrounded the computer console, were stuck on both desks, and on the walls. A replica of Rodin's *The Thinker* rested on a small table, a Post-it note looming prominently on statue's head. An old baseball glove and a football with faded white stripes on both ends rested of the table.

A dartboard hung on the wall, which had been covered with a picture of a prominent East coast politician. A dart was stuck in his forehead, another in his chin. Shelves, on the opposite wall, held a small stereo, CD player, and two speakers. Lauren spotted a diversity of names: Smokey Robinson, Patrick O'Hearn, and two Mozart violin concertos.

Feeling self-conscious, she stepped out of the room. "I'm sorry, I shouldn't have opened the door. I just thought it would be an ordinary office that we might be able to convert into a temporary bedroom."

Scott rubbed his forehead. "Well, ah . . . my friends have a few names for my office, but ordinary isn't one of them."

A few awkward seconds passed. "I really feel bad about barging in that way."

"It's okay," Scott said. "I guess I really should clean that place up one of these days." He offered a weak, almost boyish grin.

"It might take more than a day."

They laughed. Lauren looked through the doorway and pointed at the wall above the computer. "Who's in the picture with you?"

"Oh, that's one of my best friends. His name is Michael Tucker but everybody calls him Tuck."

"Obviously, it wasn't taken around here."

"No, we shot that at his place in Colorado."

Lauren nodded, then stepped closer. "Can I ask you a question about your office?"

"Sure. Fire away."

"How come the rest of your place is immaculate, and your office is—"

"A dump?"

"That's a good word."

Scott rolled his eyes. "Let's just say that trading futures is extremely intense. I'm in another world when I'm following markets and studying charts. I really can't describe how intense it is. Because of that I ignore everything else and things just kind of get out of hand."

"That makes sense."

He seemed surprised by her answer. "You're just being kind."

"Not at all. If this helps your trading performance who's to say it's wrong."

Scott looked into her eyes. "I liked you from the first minute I saw you, but I like you even more now."

Hesitant to respond, she turned away. After a moment, she said, "I'm hungry. Can we eat?"

"Sure. How about sharing the cooking chores?"

Lauren started toward the kitchen. "You're on."

"Do you drink wine?"

"Mostly white but I also like Pinot." She glanced at the wine storage unit as she entered the kitchen. "Looks like you might have a bottle or two around here somewhere."

"Could be." He went to the storage unit and withdrew a bottle of ZD Chardonnay. "This is what you call a big chardonnay. It seems appropriate tonight." He used a cork-puller, wiped off the top of the bottle and poured a few ounces into two oversized glasses.

Lauren took a sip. "Whew, big is the right word, but it's very good."

They sipped wine and talked while preparing dinner. Scott's apartment gave them a temporary feeling of safety, and their mood lightened considerably as they worked, but underneath there was latent apprehension—a mutual fear.

CHAPTER 17

Scott awoke at four-thirty and found it impossible to go back to sleep. As he considered their problem, his mind kept focusing on one thing—time would work against them. It seemed likely the killers or the police would eventually find them. He was now deeply involved, and there seemed to be no way out. He attempted to approach the problem in his normal fashion—analytically. But after thoroughly examining every possibility, he saw no apparent solution. He was out of his element, and he knew it.

His desire to return to the trading floor complicated his dilemma. Though their life-threatening flight had temporarily delegated market concerns to some secondary level in his mind, he felt a growing need to get back to the floor. He had to recoup his losses. Now, it was too late. For the first time, he felt a touch of anger about his involvement. He mulled the complex variables until frustration clouded his mind. He put on his robe, went into the kitchen, took coffee beans from a bag in the freezer, and ground enough for a full pot. While the coffee brewed, Scott stood against the island and tried to think safe thoughts, but the effort quickly failed. The part of his mind trying to erect a barrier against negative feelings was overcome by the sheer enormity of the problem.

As he began to pour his second cup, Lauren walked into the kitchen wearing a white robe several sizes too big.

"Good morning. The coffee smells good. Any left?"

"One hundred percent Kona. Great stuff. I'll pour you some." He studied her as she walked to the cupboard. Even with uncombed hair and no makeup, she looked stunning. Though he knew women usually fussed about their appearance first thing in the morning, he had always liked the way a woman looked and smelled after waking, preferably while still in bed. He thought it gave them an earthy, sexy appearance. His brief spell of anger melted away.

She took the cup and looked into his eyes. "I'd like to fix you a nice breakfast this morning."

"You don't have to."

"I want to, and I'm going to. It's non-negotiable."

Scott smiled. "How long have you lived here?"

She laughed.

"Okay, but we need to talk after we eat."

Her expression saddened. "I know."

They ate a leisurely breakfast of scrambled eggs, hash browns, toast, and coffee. They finished and were quiet for several minutes as neither wanted to discuss the difficult but unavoidable dilemma.

Scott put down his cup. "Did you get much sleep?"

"A little but not enough."

"Me too." He met her gaze. "I've given this a lot of thought. If we do nothing, it is just a matter of time until they find us."

"I know. Any ideas?"

"The crop report and that Ag official are the keys. Did you hear anything during his phone conversation that would give us a clue about how he got information out of the lockup facility?"

"No. He just gave a number to someone and said he was positive about the report. I couldn't hear everything."

"How in the world could he get the information?"

"I don't know," Lauren replied. "It doesn't make sense. The security system is very elaborate, and it's supposed to be impossible for anyone to get numbers out." She took a sip of coffee. "But somehow he *did* get the data. We know he couldn't go in or out of the reporting rooms. Someone had to get the information to him, but I can't imagine how."

"Okay, let's assume there's someone inside the lockup, there's Hayden Benson, and somebody was on the other end of that phone. We know at least three people are involved." Scott mulled the problem. "How about Benson. What kind of man is he?"

"That's what surprises me. I've worked for him a few times, and it just doesn't make sense. He really didn't seem to be the type of person to do something like this."

"But he made the call and someone had to place the orders to benefit from the information." Scott leaned back. "I have some good contacts and I might be able to get a report listing every short position put on before the close. It would take a lot of work to go through all the trades but it might give us a clue."

"I'll help."

"It may not tell us anything."

"It sounds like that's all we've got."

He nodded. "We'll start there, but I also want you to tell me everything you know about Hayden Benson. Think about it, and we'll talk again later." He got up from the table. "There's one more thing we need to do. I'll be right back." Scott returned with a tightly wrapped old towel. He pulled back the edges of the cloth, exposing a pistol. "Since I'll have to leave occasionally, I think you'd better learn how to use this."

Lauren said nothing but her expression made her thoughts transparent—she obviously wanted nothing to do with the gun.

"I understand how you feel," Scott said, "but let me ask you one question. If I was gone, and someone busted in here to kill you . . . and you had the gun, what would you do?"

"Since you put it that way, I guess I'd shoot the bastard."

"That's the way you've got to think. Remember, it's you or them."

Lauren nodded and looked at the weapon. "Where'd you get it?"

Scott checked to make sure the gun was unloaded. "When I was young, I saw a couple of James Bond movies. He used a Walther. I always wanted one, so I bought this PPKS. When I lived in California, I used to shoot occasionally and got pretty good, but I haven't touched it in years." He turned the gun in his hands and ran his fingers along the barrel. "Actually, it's a good size for you." For the next forty-five minutes, Scott taught a reluctant student the intricacies of the pistol. They agreed to test her proficiency every few days.

Scott began cleaning the weapon. While wiping the barrel he realized they should have two pistols. The Walther was ideal for Lauren, but he wanted something heavier. He remembered how helpless he had felt in the storeroom of the department store and vowed it would not happen again. It was impossible to know if the killers would learn his identity, but he was determined to fight back if they did. The need for another weapon turned his thoughts to his friend, Michael Tucker. Tuck, an ex-cop, operated a backpacking service in the Rockies. They had gone to school together and had remained close over the years. Their friendship was strong, their trust in each other unquestioned.

Tuck had suffered through years of discontent as a police officer in San Francisco. Fortunately, he'd had the insight to notice changes in his own personality, and when his perception of the world darkened, he knew it was time to make a change. It had been several years since he had resigned and moved to Colorado. Scott knew Tuck had several guns and that he would send a weapon if requested. Because he could also benefit from his friend's experience and advice, he decided to call Tuck the next day.

Scott finished with the pistol, went to the front door, opened it, and checked the hallway. He took Lauren to the stairwell and discussed various options she might use if someone attacked her in the building, emphasizing the importance of memorizing every exit.

They returned to the apartment, and Scott picked up the gun. "Follow me." He walked down the hall and entered his office. "If anyone tries to break in while I'm gone, here's what I want you to do." He went to the far wall and crouched in the corner behind a file cabinet. He bent his knees, propped his back against the wall, and used both hands to point the gun toward the doorway. "All right, change places."

Lauren crouched behind the cabinet and raised the weapon.

Scott bent next to her. "If you know you're in danger, run in here and get in the same position you're in now. If they come in after you, you've got to shoot."

She stared across the room, her brow furrowed.

"Lauren, there's no other way. These people want to kill you."

She hesitated. "I know, and I'll do whatever I have to do, but it's all so foreign."

The talk of guns had changed the mood, and again, Scott realized just how threatening their situation was.

———

Later that day, Lauren told him everything she knew about Hayden Benson. Scott thought about the man and agreed with her—something was wrong. He did not seem like the kind of person who would be involved in something illegal, but greed has enormous power. A man's professional standing was no guarantee against illicit activities. History had proven that countless times.

Scott sat on the couch with a yellow pad on his lap, thinking, analyzing, and making notes as he considered their options. He looked up from the pad. "What about your friend? The security person."

"Angela?"

"Yes. Do you think she would help us?"

"I think so, but I'm not sure what she can do."

"What's her position?"

"She's a supervisor."

"We'll call her in a day or two, but we shouldn't do it from the apartment. I don't want you to use my phone for any reason, especially to call your parents."

"I do need to call them."

"We'll have to get you some kind of disguise. Then we'll use a pay phone at night, but we can't do it regularly."

"That's fine." She paused. "Scott, there's one other thing. I'm going to need more clothes."

He handed her the pad. "Just list what you need, and we'll put it on your bill."

"I guess my bill is getting pretty big." Her eyes focused on him. "I owe you a lot."

"You don't have to say anything."

"Yes I do." She made a list of clothes and toiletries.

Scott remembered that he needed to go to the bank. He loaded the gun and gave it to Lauren; then, he went to the door and checked the hall. He turned and said, "I'll be back in about forty-five minutes. Stay alert and pay particular attention to any noises coming from the hall, and keep the gun close."

Scott had a palpable sense of danger as he walked to the bank, which caused him to repeatedly look over his shoulder, searching the sidewalk for the gunmen from the restaurant. He reminded himself that no one knew his identity, or at least he did not think they did, but he could not shake the feeling that everyone on the street was a potential assassin.

He left the bank and entered the lobby of a nearby hotel and went directly to a row of phone booths, pulled out his wallet, withdrew a business card, and glanced at the name: Tucker Pack Trips. As he dialed the number, a vision of two young boys, shirts off, sweating, laughing, and playing basketball flashed through his mind. A smile played across his lips as he thought about his life-long friend.

He became impatience on the seventh ring and started to hang up when a voice answered, "Tucker."

"Tuck, it's Scott."

"I'll be damned. It's good to hear your voice. Where are you?"

"I'm in Chicago, but I'm afraid this isn't exactly a social call. I'm in serious trouble and need some help."

"I'll drop whatever I'm doing for you anytime. You know that. Hell, you'd do the same for me."

"I know, Tuck, but this involves the police."

"And a woman?"

"Yeah, and a woman. How'd you know?"

"Hell, any trouble worth its salt always involves a woman. All right, what's the deal?"

Scott detailed the events of the last few days.

"Jesus, Scott. It sounds like you're running with the big boys. How can I help?"

"Two things. First, I need a pistol. Can you send me one right away?"

"No problem. What else?"

"We don't think anyone knows my identity, but I'd feel better if I had some idea of just how much the police actually do know. Can you make a few discreet calls?"

"Yeah, I've still got a few chits out. I'll try to get back to you by tomorrow on that, and I'll send the gun out right away."

"Thanks, Tuck. I knew I could count on you."

"One last thing," Tuck said. "It sounds like professionals; so you'd better watch your back. And I mean all the time."

"I know, but what worries me is that I don't have any experience at this sort of thing."

"Just keep your eyes open and if things get tight, all you have to do is come out to Colorado. I'll put you up for as long as you like." Scott thanked his friend and placed the handset in the cradle, his mind locking on Tuck's warnings. Needing a change of mood, he walked to a nearby market and bought two filets. Although they had purchased food the previous day, he thought a special dinner might raise Lauren's spirits. The talk of guns and escape routes had obviously upset her.

When he reached his apartment, he realized they should probably establish some kind of code before he unlocked the door and barged in. A certain type of knock, just like in the movies. At first, he thought the idea was a bit silly, but it actually made sense.

That evening, they shared kitchen duties while preparing dinner. Lauren had on jeans and one of his white dress shirts with the sleeves rolled up just below her elbows. They were often in close quarters as they moved about. Before the smell of food permeated the air, Scott caught her subtle aroma. Her scent was not covered by perfume—it was pure and natural, and he was drawn to it.

He turned to walk to the refrigerator at the same time she stepped away from the sink. They stopped about a foot apart, and stood facing each other for a moment but neither spoke. Lauren lifted her right hand as if to brush her hair back, and then suddenly dropped her arm as though she'd remembered her new hairstyle. The sound of ice dropping from the refrigerator's icemaker broke the tense silence. She smiled nervously and stepped to the side to let him pass.

Scott wanted to touch her, but the timing was not right. She had told him about the loss of her fiancé, and he respected her feelings. They had also discussed the terrible guilt she felt about her roommate's death. The dual tragedies bred emotional scars that were buried deep and needed time to heal. She was in a difficult situation, and he was not going to take advantage of her. He would give Lauren the time she needed, but it would not be easy. He felt more drawn to her with each encounter.

They lingered at the table after dinner.

During a lull in the conversation, Scott got up and walked toward the kitchen. "How about a small dish of ice cream?"

"Sounds great."

Scott went into the kitchen, retrieved a container of vanilla from the freezer, popped the lid and, in mid-scoop, he found himself wondering about her background. He finished his task, walked back to the dining room and placed the bowls on the table. He sat down, took a bite, and said, "Since we're sort of living together, I'd like to know more about you."

Lauren choked on her ice cream. "Scott, I don't think this is what's meant by living together."

"You know what I mean."

"Yes, I do." She tilted her head. "What would you like to know?"

"Where are you from? What did you dream of when you were a little girl? How did you get with the Agriculture Department? Things like that."

"You don't want to know much, do you?"

He laughed.

"All right," she said, "but you've got to do the same."

"Fair enough."

Lauren finished the ice cream and leaned back in her chair. "I was born and raised in a little town in Idaho you've probably never heard of: Pilot Hill. It's up in the mountains. The house I grew up in is nestled in pine trees. It's really nice."

"You're right; I've never heard of it, but it sounds great. What about your family?"

"My dad ran a pharmacy for over thirty years, but he sold the business ten months ago and retired. It's still the only drugstore in town. My mother used to help him, but she developed severe arthritis about seven years ago and has pretty much stayed home since then."

"Any brothers or sisters?"

Lauren bit her lip and looked down. "I had a sister, but she died when she was eight. Leukemia."

"I'm sorry." Scott became acutely aware of the pain Lauren had endured from the loss of loved ones. They were silent for a moment; then, he purposely changed the subject and asked about her career.

"I wanted to be an artist," she replied, "but the odds are really against you. I didn't have enough time or money to try to make it big. I've always been good with numbers; so, I guess you could say the practical side won out. I majored in statistics with a minor in art." She smiled. "I guess I didn't want to give up my creative side entirely."

"How'd you wind up working for the Department of Agriculture?"

"My dad was the big influence there. He's big on the concept of personal stability, and he felt that if I worked for the government, I would always have a job. It made sense; so, I took a series of tests and got a position with the Agriculture Department. I transferred to Washington after my fiancé died."

"You don't have to talk about that," Scott said. "I know it still hurts."

"It does but I've got to put it behind me. I guess it was the way it happened that made the whole thing so difficult." She looked down. "An automobile accident two days before our wedding." Lauren got up and walked into the living room.

Scott followed. "I'm sorry," he said softly.

"Thank you." She sat on the sofa, staring across the room at nothing in particular. "Now it's your turn."

"Born in San Francisco thirty-six years ago. I majored in economics in college. It was tough, because I had to work six hours a day. After graduation, I became a stockbroker. I didn't like the job as much as I expected, but I was fascinated with trading. Since that first day, a desire has burned inside me to beat the markets." He paused a moment. His father's ghost seemed to lurk nearby whenever he thought about his intense need to succeed on the trading floor.

"And?"

"Oh, sorry." Scott's mind shifted back to the conversation. "After accumulating a small trading fund, I came to Chicago. I had a job at the Board of Trade for two years before I was able to lease a seat on the exchange. Since then I've been a professional trader."

After a moment of silence, Lauren said, "Do you have a girlfriend?"

"I did. She left for L.A. about six months ago." Scott rolled his eyes toward the ceiling. "She thinks she can make it in the movie business. I explained the odds, but she wanted to chase a dream." He remembered what Jason had said about his tendency toward short-term relationships. "Actually, we'd only gone together for a short time."

"How about before that?"

Scott was surprised at her straightforwardness but found it refreshing. He leaned back. "I'm a pretty honest guy; so, I should tell you that my relationships haven't lasted too long in recent years. Sometimes I get too wrapped up in the market." He broke off eye contact. "Maybe I shouldn't tell you that."

"On the contrary. A person should never apologize for being honest."

They talked a little longer before watching a movie.

They said good night after the video. Lauren had started toward the bedroom when Scott stopped her. "I'm going to be gone for a while tomorrow. Remember that report I mentioned, the one showing trades for a particular day?"

"Yes."

"Jason McDonald is one of my best friends. He used to date a woman who works in the department that runs those reports. They still have a friendly relationship; so, he might get her to help. If we can find out who Benson was calling, it would be a great start."

Lauren nodded. "Could you pick up some of the things on my list while you're out?"

"Sure."

"There's one more thing: since I'll be stuck in here for a while, I wonder if it would be too much to ask you to buy a few art supplies? I'll have plenty of spare time, and I'd like to do a few sketches. It won't cost much, and I'll pay you back when I can."

Scott answered without hesitation. "Since we're living together, you can have anything you want."

Their laugh was cut short by a bumping noise at the front door.

Scott grabbed the gun and motioned for Lauren to move down the hallway toward his office. He crouched behind the sofa and focused on the doorknob. He heard a man cursing and fumbling with a set of keys.

Relief swept through Scott as he stood and called to Lauren. "It's okay. It's just my neighbor. He comes home drunk once or twice a week, and he usually has a heck of a time getting his door open. Every once in a while he tries to open mine."

She stood at the entrance to the hall.

They looked at each other without speaking, but Scott sensed her thoughts. The next time they heard noises it could easily be those made by gunmen crashing through the front door to kill them.

CHAPTER 18

Hayden Benson had spent a restless night anguishing over recent events. At a quarter to five he conceded his struggle to sleeplessness, crawled out of bed, went to the kitchen, made a pot of strong coffee, then took his cup to the terrace. Benson had been persistently troubled by his role in obtaining crop report information, but this morning he felt his concerns ratchet up to a new level. The Secretary of Agriculture had called an emergency staff meeting for ten o'clock, and Benson knew it would not be business as usual. The Secretary would undoubtedly call for an investigation, and Benson expected to play a role in the inquiry.

He thought about the brilliance of the scheme. He did not believe an investigation would uncover anything, but the whole affair had caused considerable stress. The death of the woman continued to be his greatest source of pain. Benson thought of Marilyn Shepard as he brought the cup to his lips. He looked through the steam rising from the hot liquid and saw a vision of the woman's face. He had known Marilyn for several years and knew her memory would be locked in some dark part of his mind, haunting him forever. His hand trembled as he tried to put down the cup, sending coffee splashing over the edges of the container.

He rose and paced about the brick lined terrace, reminding himself that he had not pulled the trigger, and nothing could change what had already happened. He knew he needed to put the past behind him and concentrate on the future, but he wondered if he could. He finally resorted to the one thing that would move his mind to another zone. He thought about Shannon Peterson. He knew he had been set up, but it no longer mattered because he had fallen heavily for the young woman, and he desperately wanted to maintain the relationship. The special interludes with Shannon filled a void in his life. He had a successful career, but his marriage had changed over the years. He still loved his wife, but she had long ago shifted her interest in sexual intimacy to bridge clubs, garden functions, and the like.

Benson believed a positive bond with Shannon had developed over time, and he felt his quality of life depended on his time with her. She treated him with respect and seemed to enjoy his company. Her feelings were either legitimate or she was a superb actress. He knew she did not actually love him, but there seemed to be a certain warmth in her behavior. Then, he thought of her beauty, his mind retracing every curve of the incredible body he had grown to love, and he thought of their many hours of passion. Shannon's carnal abilities were substantial, and her sexual appetite was nearly insatiable. Prurient thoughts of Shannon lifted him out of his depressed mood, and he fell into his morning routine. He took toast with his coffee, shaved, showered, and then drove to his office.

After attending to miscellaneous details, he left for the designated conference room at nine forty-five, reminding himself, as he walked, of the genius of Merrick's plan. It seemed inconceivable that anyone could uncover the scheme. The only flaw was the possibility of a participant talking, but everyone had too much to lose to contemplate such an action. Merrick had continually spoken about the invincibility of the plan, and Benson believed him. A wave of confidence swept over him as he opened the conference room door.

Several department heads, security officers, and members of the National Agricultural Statistics Service were already present. Benson became the ranking individual when he entered the room, and he moved around the table, shaking hands, chatting with everyone, purposely trying to act in his usual manner.

A few minutes past ten, Cormick Langley, the Secretary of Agriculture, entered the room. It turned quiet as the balding, heavyset man walked to the end of the table and seated himself. He opened his portfolio, looked over his reading glasses, paused seemingly to build tension; then, he spoke in a slow, powerful voice, "What in the hell is going on around here?"

No one spoke.

The Secretary continued, "I go off on a business trip, and some reporter asks me about the leak in our reporting system. Hell, he knew about it before I did. People are either madder than hell, or they're laughing at us. Both are completely unacceptable."

One of the members of NASS started to answer, but Langley waved him off. The Secretary looked around the table. "Our reports impact the whole goddamn world. Everyone who has an interest in production and prices relies on our reports. Hell, you all know that, but what you may not realize is that the credibility of our entire department is at stake." Langley leaned back in his chair. "I'm going to ask a few questions, and we're going to get to the bottom of this."

Various individuals shifted uncomfortably in their chairs. A few scribbled notes as if they had suddenly thought of something important. Everyone knew Langley did not lose his temper often, but when he did, he became an aggressive and powerful force.

Benson, seated at the other end of the table, was careful to maintain aura of equanimity. He and Langley got along well, and Benson thought he would be given substantial leeway in overseeing the Secretary's wishes.

Langley looked directly at the man to his left. "Marshall, how in the hell did somebody get that information out of lockup?"

"Well, ah . . . I just don't see how any—"

Langley interrupted. "You don't have a clue. Right?"

Marshall shook his head.

Benson saw an opportunity. "Cormick, why don't we review the security procedures to bring everyone up-to-date on how the lockup is handled?"

Langley nodded. "Good idea. Fortnoy, that's your department."

Fortnoy, a thin, meticulous man with receding black hair cleared his throat. "Where do you want me to start?"

"Tell us about the mechanical features on the fifth floor, then the electronics."

Fortnoy cleared his throat again. "As most of you know, we've installed two sets of heavy metal doors at each end of the lockup area. There is a four-foot space between each pair of doors that allows a person to enter the lockup through the first set of doors, close the door, then open the second set and enter the lockup corridor. The doors are arranged so that the left side opens on the first set and the right side opens on the other. An armed guard is stationed outside the first door."

Benson interjected. "That arrangement prevents hand signals."

"Exactly."

"How about the elevators?" Langley asked.

Fortnoy said, "Special switches have been installed to prevent them from stopping on the fifth floor during lockup."

Langley nodded. "The phones?"

A woman across the table spoke up, "I'll take that one. All telephone lines in the lockup area run through a "barge" system that enables the proper personnel to eliminate all telephone communications during lockup. We believe it's foolproof."

Langley rubbed his chin. "I didn't think the phones would be a problem, but what bothers me is the computer system. We're always hearing about hackers and such. How about our system?"

Ruth Walthrop answered again. "The local area network would be an obvious concern, but we've come up with a well-devised system. A device located in the same locked closet as the telephone barge system switches off the LAN in the lockup section. That way the LAN is still available to the entire USDA system but not to those in the lockup unit."

Fortnoy added, "We designed that system very carefully, but we'll check it again."

Langley nodded his agreement.

Benson looked toward Marshall. "Have the special shades over the windows been checked recently. I mean, could some new type of electronics penetrate the wire cores in the blinds?"

Marshall turned to the man next to him. "Allen, what about that?"

"I don't think it's possible," the man replied as he scribbled a note, "but we'll look into it again."

The Secretary was quiet for a moment, then asked, "What if someone gets sick?"

"We've got a procedure to take people out," Marshall said, "but nobody was sick on report day. That's the first thing I checked."

The meeting churned on for nearly two hours, and Benson felt more optimistic with each passing minute. The members of the meeting covered every conceivable possibility, but they were not even close. Again, he had to admit that Merrick's plan appeared flawless.

When the discussion became trivial, Langley raised his hands to quiet everyone. "All right, here's what I want done. After I leave, I want all of you to stay and form a committee to investigate everything we discussed today. Go through our entire security system and put together a report. If you find anything that needs to be changed, highlight it in your summary."

"When do you want it?" Marshall asked.

"I'm bound to catch flak about this in the cabinet meeting; so I want it in one week. Give this priority." Langley rose and glanced at Benson. "Send the report to Hayden. He'll review it with me." He looked around the table. "One more thing, I don't want you to miss a goddamn thing. Nothing. Is that clear?" Everyone nodded, and the Secretary left the room.

Benson felt victorious. Things had gone better than expected. He chaired the rest of the meeting before resuming his normal schedule.

He left his office at four o'clock and drove to Shannon Peterson's apartment. His sexual tension notched up when Shannon opened the door wearing only a bra, thong panties, and thigh high stockings.

Shannon poured two glasses of champagne and then sat next to him. They engaged in light necking until they finished their second glass. She whispered in his ear. "Are you ready?"

Benson practically leapt off the couch and headed for the bedroom.

She followed at a slower pace. "My, aren't we anxious today." Once inside she took control. She kissed him repeatedly as she removed his clothes. After several minutes, Shannon let her lips slowly trail down his body, but she teasingly skipped his groin.

She moved directly to his ankles, then she gradually inched higher again. Her wet kisses heightened the pleasure of the nerve endings on his skin.

Hayden Benson, swirling in a world of carnal lust, did not hear the front door open.

CHAPTER 19

In the last three days, Billy Barker had spent more time in public libraries than he had in the previous twenty years, and he was not happy about it. He closed a telephone book and looked disgustedly about the large room. The atmosphere reeked of bad karma. The people did not bother him—it was the quiet. When this many people gathered in one room, there ought to be a little activity. The crowds Billy usually associated with were those on city streets, at racetracks, and in bars. He rubbed the back of his hand across his forehead in the manner one uses to wipe sweat from their face after performing manual labor. As far as Billy was concerned, this *was* manual labor.

He glanced toward an elderly woman sitting quietly in a large chair, reading. He had noticed her earlier and could not understand how a person could sit still that long with a book. The racing form, maybe, but a book? He wondered how anyone could be still that long under any condition. There was no doubt about it—the library was a spooky place.

He stood, grudgingly, then placed the phone directory on the shelf and selected another. He would have left the book on the table, but it had become overloaded with other volumes he had not put away. He couldn't care less. Twenty minutes later, he closed the last directory in disgust. He had covered nearly every phone book used in the surrounding two hundred miles, and he still had no idea who Scott Q was. A team of three men had already checked potential suspects living in the immediate vicinity, and they were now working names in the more distant towns. The list of possibilities continued to shrink.

Immediately after the Chandler woman had escaped, Billy and his men spent two days checking the airports, train stations, and other obvious locations, but they found no trace of her. Their next task was to find the mysterious Scott Q. Thus, Billy found himself in the library.

He left the building and sought out a crowd more to his liking. A few minutes later, he walked into the Cloverleaf Bar. He felt comfortable here, but he was worried. Merrick was flying into town, and Billy knew he was in for an ass chewing. He ordered a boilermaker. Billy looked solemnly into the bar mirror and saw his thin, taut face staring back at him. He picked up the shot glass and downed the contents in one movement. He let the liquid spread its warmth through his stomach for a moment, then he started on the beer. He finished the bottle, left the bar, got in his car, and headed for the apartment. With Merrick on the rampage, Billy knew better than to be late.

———

Victor Merrick was pissed. His men had let Lauren Chandler escape from the restaurant, and they had not been able to find any trace of her. The chances of locating her in the Washington area now seemed nil. After his plane had landed, he picked up a rental car and drove straight to the apartment complex. He turned off the engine just as Billy pulled into the next parking slot. Billy got out of his car and wiped sweat from his forehead. "Hey, Victor."

Merrick started toward the building without answering. As soon as they got inside, he focused a brutal stare on Billy. "You really fucked up."

"Jesus, we've done everything possible to find her."

"That's not the point. You shouldn't have let her get away in the first place. Think about it. Lisowski corners an unarmed man and woman and gets knocked out with a baseball bat. Then the guy runs right over you, and they get away. A bunch of old ladies could have done a better job."

"It was one of those things where you had to be there to understand."

"Bullshit!" Merrick went to the bar, poured a drink, took a sip, and turned toward Billy. "Tell me everything you've tried."

"For the first forty-eight hours we checked the airports, bus depots, and the train station. We also watched a couple of the people in her address book, but there were only a few local names." Billy went to the refrigerator and got a beer. His fingers fumbled about as he tried to pop the tab.

Merrick mulled the information. "What about the man?"

"All we know is that his first name is Scott and his last initial is Q. I went through every damn phone book in the area and made a list of the possibilities. Lisowski, Hammitt, and Navarro are working them around the clock, but it's like looking for a needle in a haystack."

Merrick ran a finger through the condensation on the side of his glass. "We've got a perfect set up here, one that can make everyone rich, but the Chandler woman can ruin everything. We've got to locate her and the man she's with." Merrick thought a moment. "It's obvious we need more people. I know you've got a few men in Chicago we use from time to time, and I want you to bring them in right away."

Billy nodded.

"I'm going to get a copy of her personnel file from Benson; then we can check her parents and next of kin." It was time to make a decisive move. "I'm going to bring in a hit man called Cade. He's one deadly sonofabitch." Merrick looked at Billy." I'm sure you've heard of him."

"Christ, everybody's heard of him."

"Yeah, I guess they have." Merrick paused, his thoughts turning optimistic. "He's a genius at finding people, but he's expensive as hell. We need the best so I figure the potential of our setup makes it worth the price."

"When's he coming?" Billy asked.

"That's the problem. Some say Cade retired and moved to Florida, but I know someone who says he can make contact. I should hear something in a day or so."

"I'd hate to be in that woman's shoes," Billy said.

Merrick nodded, realizing he had made the right decision. He walked to the window and looked out. "Isn't this one of Shannon's days with Benson?"

"Yeah, but I don't know if he's there yet."

Merrick moved toward the door. "Let's go find out."

The two men walked past the parking lot and noticed Shannon's car in its usual place. They expected her to be home, but she did not answer the doorbell. Merrick said, "Did you get a duplicate key from her like I asked?"

"Yeah." Billy reached into his pocket. "Her bell rings in the kitchen, and it's not very loud. She said if she's in the bathroom or the bedroom with the door shut, she doesn't always hear it, and for me to knock real loud."

Merrick took the key. "Let's just go in and see what they're up to."

Billy grinned. "She'd be a hell of a piece of ass, huh, boss?"

"Yeah, Billy—she would."

Merrick twisted the knob and opened the door. They were cautious at first but relaxed after seeing the champagne bottle and two glasses. He led the way down the hall, stopped in front of the bedroom door, leaned forward, and heard Benson moan. He whispered to Billy. "This I've gotta see." He opened the door.

Shannon rocked back and forth atop Benson, cowgirl style. Merrick knew she had a great figure, but he had not seen her completely undressed, and he was more than impressed.

Benson's, head shot up. "Who's there?"

Merrick laughed. "Oh, I'm sorry, Hayden. It looks like you're a little busy."

Benson yelled, "Merrick? Dear God."

"Relax, Hayden. We'll go back into the other room and have some of your champagne. Go ahead and finish what you're doing." Merrick walked into the hall.

Billy followed, laughing hysterically. "God, I'd like to stay and watch the whole show."

"There isn't going to be any show," Merrick said. "Benson is so fucking embarrassed he won't be able to get his dick up for two weeks."

The two men erupted in laughter.

Ten minutes later, Benson walked sheepishly into the front room and headed for the front door.

"Not so fast," Merrick said. "I need to talk to you."

Benson walked to a chair and slumped down. "Haven't you had enough fun?"

Merrick ignored him. "I want you to get me Lauren Chandler's personnel file."

"I can't just go in and request that kind of information. People would be suspicious."

Merrick spoke in a harsh tone. "I'm not asking you to do this; I'm telling you. I want the damn file by tomorrow."

Benson remained silent for a moment; then his expression changed. "I just thought of something. I was put in charge of the investigation committee, and I can legitimately ask for anything related to the case."

"What investigation?"

"The Secretary called a meeting and wants a full review of our security procedures for the lockup."

"What do they know?"

"They don't have a clue," Benson said. "I don't think there's any chance of them finding anything. Actually, there's nothing to find."

"Of course there isn't, but I still want you to keep me informed."

Benson inched toward the door. Can I go now?"

"Yeah, get the hell out of here." As soon as Benson left, Merrick turned to Billy. "I'm going back to Chicago tomorrow. When you get that file, call me and let me know about her relatives. The first thing we'll do is send somebody to watch her parent's house."

Billy nodded. "I'll call you the second I get it."

Merrick thought for a moment and realized he had covered everything; then his mind shifted to what he had seen in the bedroom, specifically Shannon Peterson. The sight of her naked body had created a powerful urge. He got up and walked toward her bedroom.

He knocked once and entered the room. She was lying across the bed reading a fashion magazine. "Shannon, I've got an offer for you."

"Sure, what's on your mind?"

"I'm going to stay the night. I'll give you a special bonus to cover things."

She turned on her side, presenting a suggestive pose. "What are you doing way over there?"

Merrick held up his index finger. "I'll be right back. He walked into the kitchen and got a fresh bottle of champagne. He spoke over his shoulder as he headed for the bedroom. "Billy, get lost."

CHAPTER 20

Deep in the night, a startlingly vivid dream caused Scott to bolt upright in bed. He sat in the darkened room, rubbing his right eye with the palm of his hand, his mind sorting and replaying fragments of the strange dream. It began with him standing in the corner of his family's living room with his arm around his mother's shoulder. The day after his father's suicide, repossession agents swooped in with a squad of men to remove the household possessions.

His mother wept as the workers stripped the contents of the house. After taking the furniture, the grotesque-looking men laughed and turned on the house itself. The walls came down, but the roof remained suspended overhead as if held up by invisible cables. As Scott and his mother fled outside, another crew swept in and dismantled the roof. When it appeared the madness had finally ended, two bulldozers tore across the ground, scraping it clean. The same men who had tried to kill Lauren in the restaurant operated the huge earthmovers. Within seconds, they disappeared. Scott and his mother stood helplessly in the corner of the lot, surveying the destruction. Earth, smooth as glass, was all that remained. It was as if his childhood had vanished before his eyes.

Scott swung his legs over the edge of the bed and thought of his mother who had died three years earlier, remembering how hurt she had been when they actually did lose their furniture. It had been hard for her those first years after his father killed himself, but Scott had been able to provide substantial financial help after he began working. Still, his father should not have left her so alone, so unprepared.

He went to his office and reflected on how real the dream had seemed. He sat quietly for several minutes, and then switched on his quote machine. As the numbers flickered on the screen, he felt the familiar urge to go back to the trading floor. Circumstances made that impossible, but he could stay in touch with the markets and hope that he could return to the floor in a few days. He checked the S & P 500 Index, gold, and the grain market. The decline in soybeans had temporarily stabilized, but market action was not good and the bears were still in control. He pulled out his charts to review various trends, but realized that he had not been able to keep them up-to-date.

Scott turned back to the keyboard and punched several keys. His quote vendor offered software options that plotted charts in real time. He scanned the various futures instruments, noting recent changes, especially the robust rally in the Dow and the S & P. He brought himself current with price movements, but he also waited for Tuck's phone call. Scott was anxious to find out what his friend had learned from his police sources. He knew the information would probably be the catalyst for determining his actions over the next few days. He finished his update and looked at the clock: ten-fifteen, and Tuck had still not called. It was early, but Scott's impatience surfaced quicker than usual.

His thoughts shifted to Lauren, and he realized he had not heard any noise from his bedroom. He had assumed she was still sleeping because she was emotionally fatigued and needed several days of rest. Yet, it seemed too quiet. Concerned, he tapped softly on the door. No answer. He eased the door open and saw Lauren sprawled across the bed in a deep sleep, her breathing slow and rhythmic. Scott thought it must have been the first good sleep she'd had since the tragedy.

Her blonde hair was disheveled and her right leg was out of the covers exposing her upper thigh. One side of Lauren's face was visible, and her overall appearance stunned Scott. It was not just her beauty—it was her look of complete innocence. He could not take his eyes off her. He did not think he was taking advantage of Lauren; he was simply admiring her appearance. Still, a feeling of a guilt crept into his mind. He started to close the door but looked back briefly and again stared at legs that were well proportioned, smooth, long, and incredibly sensual.

Scott experienced a stronger wave of guilt, causing him to close the door and back away toward his office. Lauren was growing on him, minute by minute, notch by notch. He felt himself giving in to feelings unlike those he had experienced with other women. This was different; this woman was special.

Just as he turned the corner to his office, he heard the phone ring and hurried to his desk, picked up the receiver.

"It's Tuck. Everything all right?"

"We're okay. What'd you find out?"

"Good news, at least on one front. I had a friend in San Francisco call his counterpart in Alexandria. The police don't have a clue who you are."

Scott sank into his chair with a sense of relief. "Thanks, Tuck. I owe you."

"Nonsense. We've always helped each other."

"I know."

"I hope you realize that the police aren't your biggest problem."

"What do you mean?"

"Well, if you were still in the D. C. area, they'd be a real concern, but right now I'd say your biggest threat is from those gunmen. I don't know how good they are, but it's a safe bet they won't stop looking. You have to be on guard every second. The worst thing you can do is to think you're in the clear."

"I know, Tuck, but at least the police aren't going to pound on my door at any minute. How about the gun?"

"You'll get a package tomorrow."

"Good. I appreciate your help."

"Watch your back, pal."

Scott hung up and thought about the conversation. Tuck was right about the danger, but what could be done about it? He pondered the problem for several minutes and decided he simply could not sit around waiting for the killers to break through the door or shoot them down on the street. He *had* to do something.

He stared at a yellow note pad for several minutes, then wrote down two words: Hayden Benson. Since Benson was the only person Scott knew to be involved, he had to start there. He checked the clock, picked up the phone, and called Jason McDonald's office number. He did not expect to reach him because the grain market had opened, and Jason was probably in the pit. After several rings, the answering machine switched on. He waited for the beep. "Jason, this is Scott. It's urgent I talk to you as soon as possible. I'll call every thirty or forty minutes till I get you. If you come back to your office, stay there until I reach you." He hung up, walked down the hall, and stopped in front of his bedroom door. This time he knocked louder and waited.

No answer.

He knocked again.

"Scott?"

"Yes. May I come in?"

"Just a second." There was a short pause. "All right, but I look a mess."

Scott knew otherwise. He opened the door and looked in. "Actually, Lauren, you look wonderful, but I've always had a thing for women in the morning."

She flushed slightly but smiled. "You've got to stop telling me things like that."

"I promise I won't say anything more for several hours."

She smiled.

"I'll be going out for a while."

She nodded.

"I didn't want to wake you but, I think you should be up while I'm gone, and I want you to keep the gun with you until I get back."

She frowned when he mentioned the gun.

"Cheer up," Scott said. "It won't take long, and I'll bring you the things on your list." He started to leave, then turned back. "I almost forgot. Tuck called. The police don't have any idea who I am."

Lauren's face brightened. "That's wonderful news."

"Yes it is, but he also gave me a warning. He reminded me that our biggest problem is the killers. We can't let our guard down."

"I know, but if the police don't know who you are those men probably don't either."

"Let's hope not, but I want you to stay alert every second while I'm gone. When I get back, we'll go over some ideas I came up with. Tonight we'll go out so you can call your folks. I also want to talk to your friend, Angela."

"I really do need to call my parents."

"One more thing. I need Hayden Benson's office address in Washington."

Lauren's expression turned curious. "What for?"

"I don't have time to explain now. I'll tell you when I get back."

After she gave him the information, Scott cautioned her again, said goodbye, and left the apartment. He looked around carefully before exiting the elevator, then he walked across the parking area to his car. He drove about ten blocks, pulled into a service station, and parked by the phone booth. He pulled a dog-eared business card from his wallet and dialed the number printed below the name. Dave Lamberson was an old college roommate he had kept in touch with over the years. A secretary answered. Scott gave his name and asked for Dave.

After a moment, he heard an excited voice. "Hey, Scott. How are you?"

"This is very important, and I only have a couple of minutes. I can't explain but I'm in a bad spot, and I need your help."

"Sure. Fire away."

"It may sound a little strange but I'll explain everything later."

"Jesus, Scott. I hope you're okay."

"I need this done right away. Got a pencil?"

"Yeah."

"I want you to go to the Western Union office and send the following telegram. Be sure to pay in cash."

"No problem."

"Okay, take this down." Scott gave Dave the name and address of Hayden Benson, then dictated the message:

Mr. Benson:

I am aware of the release of sensitive crop data on report day, STOP.

I will contact you at a later date to discuss, STOP.

Keep this telegram confidential, STOP

"Use the name Jim Carpenter. Can you handle that?"

"I guess so, but this sounds heavy-duty. If there's anything else I can do just let me know. In the meantime, you take care of yourself."

Scott thanked him, hung up, got in the car, pulled into traffic, and thought about his strategy. By sending a message in this manner, he was sure no one would see it but Hayden Benson, and if someone attempted to trace the telegram, it would have originated in Texas under a phony name. He suspected a telegram would increase the shock value of the actual message. He would let Benson worry a day or two, then call him. Because of what Lauren had said, Benson's part in the scheme did not seem to fit, but no matter what the Deputy Secretary's involvement, the telegram was targeted to cause considerable alarm. *Make him sweat.* His next priority was to obtain copies of trading reports, and then have Lauren call Angela. Hopefully, his efforts would provide important clues.

Scott drove to a shopping area that had an art supply store. He walked to a nearby department store and handed the clerk a list, instructing her to pick clothes suitable for a thirty-year-old blonde, and that he would come back shortly to approve the selection. On his way to the art supply store, he negotiated the streets constantly checking his surroundings. He stopped at a phone booth and tried Jason's number. No answer.

He approached the supply shop and noticed a man wearing jeans and a dark shirt leaning against the building, apparently reading a newspaper. The man glanced over the top of his paper. Scott stopped and moved next to a window, acting as if he was interested in the items on display, but he had positioned himself so he could easily observe the sidewalk.

After several minutes the man pushed himself away from the building, tossed the newspaper into a trash can, and got into a car that had pulled up to the curb. He leaned toward the driver and kissed her on the cheek. Scott expelled a large breath and shook his head. This was how it was going to be—every minute, every hour, every day.

He entered the art store and gave his list to a clerk, paid for the items, put them in the trunk of his car, and then went back to the department store. The saleswoman had nearly finished. He was startled by the number of bags that awaited him. He probably should not have given her free reign, but he didn't have time to select the items himself. Besides, this was not the time to be frugal. Anything that might lift Lauren's spirits seemed worth the price.

While waiting for the clerk to complete his order, Scott again tried Jason's number. He answered. Scott relayed the urgency of his situation but did not give details. They agreed to meet at the rear of a large public parking area in thirty minutes. He paid for the clothes, left the shop, and staggered back to the car looking like a last minute Christmas shopper. Just as he started to pull away from the curb, he noticed a florist shop three doors down. He glanced at his watch—there was just enough time.

He entered the shop and purchased a long stem red rose, and wired a bouquet of flowers to a cemetery located near San Francisco. After his mother had died, he had arranged with the caretaker to place flowers on her grave whenever he sent them. Scott got back in the car and pulled onto the street. He thought about his father's gravesite for the first time in many years. He had not sent flowers or visited the grave since the funeral. His resentment toward his father's suicide had cut deep. He felt a touch of sadness that seemed to flow from the protected depths of his mind. He turned on the car radio, attempting to shake the feeling.

He arrived at the meeting site ten minutes later, pulled into the lot, and watched everyone as if they were potential assassins.

This was a new part of his life he did not like. He felt a sense of freedom lost. Scott drove to the back of the lot. Jason had not yet arrived.

Five minutes later, Jason pulled up next to him and got out. "My God, Scott, you sounded pretty damn serious. What's wrong?"

Scott walked over and leaned against the car. "I know I probably don't need to say this, but I want you to promise that everything I tell you is confidential."

"You're right. You don't have to say it but the fact that you did makes me even more worried. What's going on?"

"It's heavy duty." He then relayed the details to an obviously alarmed Jason McDonald.

Jason shook his head. "Unbelievable."

"I know, but it's true. Every word."

"I'll help if I can, but I'm really worried about this."

"Christ," Scott said. "Tell me about it." He pushed himself away from the car and faced his friend. "I do need your help, but I want you to remember that if you can't do it, it's okay. Really. It won't affect our friendship."

"Hell, I know that. What do you need?"

"You're still on good terms with Jenny, aren't you?"

"Sure, but—"

"I need some reports from her computer. If she can do it without much risk it might really help."

Jason frowned and tugged on his right ear lobe. "I'll ask but I have no idea what she'll say."

"Could you see her today?"

"I'll go right over."

He shook Jason's hand, watched his friend drive away, and got in his car wondering if this might lead to the break they desperately needed.

CHAPTER 21

Scott had already made two trips between the car and the apartment. He opened the door before his last trip and looked over his shoulder at Lauren. Her face glowed as she rummaged through the packages. The news that the police did not know Scott's identity, combined with obtaining new clothes had lifted her spirits considerably. He went to his car and retrieved the last packages and the rose. He entered the apartment and put down the bags but kept the flower out of sight as he spoke, "I have something else for you." Lauren was still on the floor when he brought his hand around and gave her the rose.

"Oh, Scott. You're about the sweetest man I've ever known." She admired the flower, smelled it, then looked at him. "I don't know how to thank you, but I'll remember everything you've done for the rest of my life—and that includes giving me the roses."

Scott said, "There's an old Chinese proverb I've always believed in. It goes something like this: flowers always leave a fragrance in the hand that bestows them."

Lauren smiled. She started to speak, but it seemed as if some new thought changed her mind. She got up and went into the kitchen, returning shortly with a white bud vase containing the rose. She placed it on a table, and then she sat looking at the flower. A warm, comfortable silence filled the room, the essence of which

Scott wished he could capture in a bottle to save for some future moment when one's soul begged for such a comforting tonic.

After several minutes, Scott went into his office. He spent considerable time reviewing the markets but found nothing worthy of a trade. He turned his attention to his magazine article but after half an hour, he realized his attitude about the project had changed. He still wanted to complete the article, but too much had happened. He decided to call the magazine and request an extension of the deadline.

He leaned back and thought about the immediate problem. He needed to go to Washington. He would meet with Angela Williams if she agreed to help, but his real objective was to find out more about the Deputy Secretary of Agriculture. Scott thought he might spend a day or two following Benson, maybe even approach him if he could do it safely.

———

They shared various household duties that afternoon, and then discussed the necessity of obtaining a wig for Lauren. Because they would occasionally go out to make phone calls, they agreed to make the wig purchase a priority. Lauren checked the phone book and found a suitable boutique about two miles away. The ad said the shop closed at six o'clock. When they were ready to leave Scott stuck the pistol under his belt and put on a sport coat. He became anxious as they approached the elevator. This was the first time Lauren had left the apartment, and the trip to the boutique proved nerve wracking. They talked some but mostly watched nearby vehicles. It seemed as if each car was full of potential assassins.

After arriving at the store, Lauren tried on several different wigs that neither of them liked. Then she came out with a long, flowing, auburn wig. She looked different, and she looked beautiful. Scott pulled out his wallet, purchased the wig, and told her to leave it on. Except for her clothes, Lauren left the shop with a very different look.

Scott selected a phone booth in a hotel lobby for the calls to Angela and Lauren's parents. They had previously discussed the need to keep the conversations short and to say nothing about her location. He stood nearby, acutely aware of the weight from his gun, watching everyone entering the lobby.

Lauren finished her first call, paused a moment, obviously struggling with her emotions, then she dialed Angela. She ended the conversation, stepped out of the booth, and said, "She's worried, but she'll try to help."

"Great."

"She also said it's hard to comprehend that Hayden Benson is mixed up in something like this, but she made it clear that she believes I'm telling the truth."

"Did she agree to meet me on Thursday?"

"The Lincoln Memorial. She'll be at the top of the steps at three o'clock."

"How will we recognize each other?"

Lauren spoke without hesitation. "I told her to look for the handsomest man there."

Scott felt a surge of emotion. This was the first time she had said anything with a romantic implication. He changed lanes and glanced at her. "Well, I've got this thing for a cute blonde I'm living with, but I just might kick her out and have you move in."

She laughed.

They stopped at a market and bought groceries. Lauren looked different, but Scott still felt nervous. Living in constant fear seemed inevitable. He felt exposed while on the streets, but the pressure eased when they stepped into the apartment. After he placed the grocery bag on the counter, the phone rang. He picked up the kitchen extension.

"It's Jason. I've been trying to reach you and got worried."

"We had to run a few errands but we're fine. Did you talk to Jenny?"

"Yeah. It took forty-five minutes and I had to promise her an outrageously expensive dinner, but she agreed to help."

"Jenny always was a good negotiator."

"Tell me about it. Remember, I dated her for three years." Jason's tone changed. "Are you going to be there the rest of the evening?"

"Yes."

"I'm on my way over. I'll explain everything when I get there."

Jason arrived twenty minutes after they had put away the groceries. Scott introduced Lauren and asked about the reports.

"You've got a modem and a printer, right?"

"Sure."

Jason said, "Can two people fit in your office at one time?"

Scott saw Lauren grinning and rolled his eyes.

The two men went down the hall to Scott's office.

"All right," Jason said. "Here's the deal. Jenny gave me a phone number to access the system, but the password is only good for twenty-four hours."

"How will I find the right system for the reports I need?"

"That's why I'm here. Jenny gave me a list of the proper keystrokes. Between the two of us, we should be able to figure it out."

Ninety minutes later, they had produced a stack of reports showing all trades placed during the last thirty minutes on the day the USDA crop report was released.

"That's the easy part," Scott said.

Jason grabbed a stack of printouts. "I'll stay and help you go through these."

Lauren entered the room with a large tray containing three dinner plates. She had changed into jeans and a denim shirt. "If one more can squeeze in here, we can eat and then I'll help."

At two thirty, they had a final printout that listed only those new short positions placed right before the market closed. Somewhere among those names and account numbers, Scott hoped to find a few large trades that would lead to the identity of the person controlling the scheme. He went through the list, then leaned back in his chair and threw his pencil on the desk. "Shit—"

"What's wrong?" Jason asked.

"I should have known whoever came up with something this good wouldn't use one account number. There isn't a single large order on this list, but there were a lot of medium-sized orders entered right at the close."

Jason leaned over. "What are the names?"

"That's the other problem. Most of these accounts look phony. The rest are legitimate hedgers."

"What do you mean by phony?"

Scott pointed to the list. "They look like corporate shells. I've never heard of any of them."

"How about the others?" Jason asked.

"Let me separate them and print out a new list." He punched several keys and activated the printer.

"These are the hedgers. Let's take a look."

They scanned the first page:

Arwood Inc
Burgess Grain
Consolidated Ohio Grain

Barry T. Hanson
Harper Exports
E. II. Newbury
Victor Merrick
Natco Northern Ltd
Turner Grain Exporters
Oliverio & Sons
Paul R. Oppenheimer
R & R Grain
Staten Grain
Peter M. Stonebridge

"There's another page," Scott said, "but it's just more of the same. Every one of these accounts had a legitimate reason to be in the market. It's those names on the other report that are suspect."

"How do you trace a corporate shell?" Lauren asked.

"Damned if I know. There's probably a whole series of bogus names behind each one, and I'll bet they all lead to a dead end."

The results of their efforts combined with the late hour had changed everyone's mood. "That's enough for tonight," Scott said. He got up and stretched. "I'll sleep on this and take another look later. Let's hope the devil's in the details."

Lauren excused herself and went to bed.

The two men talked for several minutes, and Scott arranged for Lauren to stay with Jason while he was in Washington.

———

After a restless night, Scott spent the next day sifting through the trading reports but found nothing new. He realized it was possible that one of the legitimate hedgers listed could be involved, but it did not seem likely. He thought the list with the apparently fabricated names and accounts were set up by whoever had access to the USDA information. They were probably hooked into Swiss numbered accounts. The individual who used the illegal data had evidently thought of everything.

Scott worried that someone that clever would be equally as resourceful in his search for Lauren.

CHAPTER 22

Scott took Lauren to Jason's apartment Thursday morning before driving to the airport. Thinking it best to avoid both Dulles and National, he had booked a flight into Baltimore-Washington International. His plane landed at BWI at twelve-forty. He rented a car and headed south on Highway 295. He had planned his trip to allow for potential travel delays, but the flight landed on schedule, and he arrived early at the Lincoln Memorial.

At two-fifty, a well-dressed black woman, matching the description Lauren had provided, came across the walkway and started up the stairs. Scott waited until she reached the top, then he stepped from behind a column. "Angela?"

"I know you're Scott," she said. "Lauren told me that you'd be the handsomest man here."

Scott smiled as he looked around. "Angela, there are only two other men up here, and they're both over seventy."

She laughed and shook his hand.

They walked to a secluded area that offered a panoramic view of the grounds. Angela spoke first. "That girl's got herself in a hell of a mess."

"It's been a terrifying experience for her." Scott turned from the view and looked directly into Angela's eyes. "She said you believed her story. It's important that I hear it from you."

Her answer was immediate. "I believe her. I haven't known her long, but I know she would never get involved in this sort of thing. It's just not in her."

"Thanks, Angela. We're going to need help from people like you."

"I have a loyalty to the USDA, and I certainly don't want this sort of thing going on, but I've got to be careful. There's really only so much I can do." She looked toward the reflecting pool. "Just what did you have in mind?"

"Two things. The first is easy."

Angela rolled her eyes. "That sounds like a good news, bad news situation."

"Close."

"All right. You tell me what you want. I'll tell you if I can do it."

Scott watched a jet crossing the sky to his right. "I want you to take me to the executive parking area at the Agriculture Department and point out Hayden Benson when he leaves the building."

"No problem," she said, turning to look him in the eye. "Number two?"

"With your help, I want to track Benson's activities on the day the next report is released."

"That could be easy or really messy. It all depends on what he does." She paused, considering his request. "I'd have to be careful, and I couldn't do it by myself."

"I'd like to be there," Scott said. "Can you get me some sort of pass that'll give me access to most floors?"

"That's tricky, but I think I can handle it. Actually, I know the perfect person to help us. My uncle is on my staff. He's worked the night shift for years, but I could change his schedule temporarily. That would give us three."

"That should be enough."

"The real problem is that we have no idea if Benson even leaves his office. Maybe someone delivers the information to him."

"I don't think so," Scott replied. "Lauren said he used the phone in a small library on the fourth floor. If he did that for the last report, it means he had to go somewhere to get the data."

Angela nodded. "Makes sense."

"You'll help?"

"Yes, but if something happens, and it looks like I might get caught, I'll have to back out. I couldn't bear causing my uncle to lose his job."

Scott nodded. "I understand. . . .There is one more thing."

Angela rolled her eyes again, and said, "I thought you said two things."

"I forgot one but it's easy. Can you get me Hayden Benson's home phone number?"

"No problem."

"I really appreciate your help. Lauren's special, and she needs friends like you."

Angela looked curiously at Scott. "I know you haven't known her for long, but I want to ask you something."

"Sure."

"Are you in love with her?"

Scott felt a jolt from the unexpected question. It seemed improbable he would have fallen in love so quickly, but he heard himself uttering one simple word. "Yes."

"I knew it. I had this feeling about you and her."

"I'm afraid it's pretty one-sided at this point. She's still hurting from the death of her fiancé and doesn't want to get involved in a relationship. She also feels terribly guilty about Marilyn. This whole mess isn't exactly a tonic for romance."

"I know," Angela said. "I've been trying to get her to start dating again, but she won't even discuss it. She always says she needs more time."

They talked a little longer, then Scott followed Angela to the USDA complex. They sat in his car and watched the parking area. Scott took an immediate liking to Angela. She was honest, forthright, obviously loyal, and it was easy to see why Lauren had formed a strong bond with the woman.

After thirty-five minutes, Angela pointed toward a distinguished-looking man walking across the grounds. "That's him."

"Lauren was right," Scott said. "He doesn't look like the type who would be involved in something like this." He thanked Angela as she got out of the car.

She started toward the sidewalk but turned back. "I just thought of something. What if they skip the next report?"

"That's a chance we'll have to take."

He followed Benson's Lincoln Town Car out of the parking area and onto the street. Scott had no experience at this sort of thing, but he decided to stay as far back as possible, yet close enough to make it through any stoplights before they changed. Angela had told him that Benson lived in McLean and gave Scott his probable route. He soon found himself on the anticipated course and believed the Deputy Secretary had no idea he was being followed, but he was disappointed that Benson seemed to be going home. It was a long shot, but Scott hoped to discover something that would provide some kind of clue about the identity of others who were involved.

After several miles, Benson turned off his expected route and drove through a residential area. Scott straightened in his seat and became more alert as he tried to maintain contact without arousing suspicion. A few blocks later, the Lincoln turned into the parking area of an apartment complex. Scott sped up slightly. If Benson was meeting someone, he did not want to lose sight of him before he disappeared into the maze of buildings.

Benson parked next to a row of apartments on the right and started up the walkway. Scott stopped at the far edge of the parking lot, got out, and hurried toward an area of trees and shrubs that covered the grounds on the near side of the complex. The greenery provided a buffer between a wall that bordered the street and the apartments. He stopped next to a large bush.

He caught a glimpse of Benson about halfway down the walkway. Scott moved through the trees to an area of thick shrubs and looked up in time to see Benson going up the stairs to the second floor. Scott backed up toward the wall to get a better view of the upper floor. Benson stopped at an apartment and rang the bell. Scott's pulse quickened. Maybe, just maybe, Benson was meeting with an important member of the group. The door opened, but he was unable to see who answered. He waited ten minutes but nothing happened. He guessed the visit would be lengthy and decided to wait in his car.

After an hour and a half, Scott knew he would not make a good policeman. He had lost patience and was bored. He glanced at the sky, noting that the sun would go down in about an hour, and knew he would not feel as comfortable if he had to wait in a darkened parking lot. He got out to stretch, looked toward the building and realized he had not written down the apartment number, something he should do before it got dark. He walked toward the trees, reached the first row of shrubs, and stopped to look for Benson, but there was no sign of anyone.

When he was sure no one was watching, he walked between the trees and made his way to a position where he could see the door. He jotted the number on a small pad and headed back toward the parking lot. He stopped behind the last tree and checked the lot, which was half-full of cars. He saw a woman carrying a shopping bag, nothing else. When it appeared safe, he headed toward his rental. After going about ten yards a car door opened three rows away.

A man got out and looked in his direction, then turned back toward his car as if he were talking to someone. Because he did not recognize the man, Scott decided to act natural and continue to his car. A few seconds later, two more men got out of the same vehicle. Scott stopped suddenly. He recognized the last two men: one was short, the other very big. They were the gunmen who had chased him and Lauren from the restaurant.

He froze momentarily, then started to duck but it was too late. The man he had hit with the baseball bat pointed at him and yelled something. Scott glanced toward his car but knew he would never make it in time.

He looked back at the three men.

They were running toward him.

Shit.

CHAPTER 23

Lauren's concern for Scott grew with the passage of time, and she soon found herself unable to concentrate on anything else. Jason's apartment contained an abundance of reading material, but each time she picked up a book, she quickly lost interest, tossed it aside, and again found herself pacing the room. This was the longest she had been separated from Scott, and she was surprised by her feelings—she missed him terribly. Surely, she could not miss him this much. It was obviously just concern for his safety. After all, he had helped her and had put himself in extreme danger in the process. She should be concerned.

Lauren went back to the couch and picked up a magazine, but after skimming a few pages, she put it down, pulled her legs up, hugged her knees, and stared across the room. She thought of Scott and a warm, longing sensation washed over her. Confused by her feelings, she got up, went to the kitchen, and began to prepare a snack. She was nearly finished before she realized she was not hungry. Lauren brought a hand to her cheek and leaned against the counter. She had repeatedly told herself not to get involved again—at least not yet. Another loss would be unbearable. Yet, she found herself thinking seriously about another man who might be in danger at this very moment. This was completely opposite of what she had wanted.

She found herself caught up in a strange inner struggle. Part of her mind was trying to keep thoughts about Scott out while another part was letting them in. She stared across the room and pictured him in her mind. His unique way of showing gentleness while maintaining inner strength intrigued her. She made a mental picture of his lithe body and the way he moved, and she held onto it for a long moment.

As the day progressed, she became increasingly concerned about Scott's safety. She wondered how many times she had looked at the clock. Jason had called twice to check on her and said he would come home early and stay with her. A little after three, she heard his coded knock on the front door, the same one she and Scott used.

Jason entered the apartment, threw a newspaper on the entry table, and walked into the living room. "Everything all right?"

"It's been quiet but thanks for checking on me today. I really appreciate it."

"My pleasure." He looked directly at her. "Did Scott call?"

"No, but it's still early. He said it would probably be at least seven before he could phone."

They talked casually for a while, exchanging pleasantries. As they grew more comfortable, they discussed their backgrounds. Lauren discovered that Jason already knew much about her, including the loss of her fiancé, and that Scott had talked about her on several occasions.

When the conversation languished, Jason left the apartment to buy something for dinner. When he returned, they decided to eat early and then wait for Scott's call. After the meal, they went into the living room and read for a short time. Lauren was quickly bored. Her mind simply would not let go of thoughts about Scott.

Jason had looked at her several times as if he knew what she was thinking. He finally moved across the room, sat in a chair near her and spoke in a soft voice. "There's something I'd like to talk to you about, but I've got to warn you that it might be painful for you. Some might even say I was patronizing you, but that's not my intent."

Lauren felt surprised by his declaration.

Jason shifted in his chair. "When you get to know me better, you'll find out that I sometimes speak my mind when I shouldn't."

"I know you well enough to know that you wouldn't hurt someone on purpose. You've got my full attention."

Jason leaned back and glanced at the ceiling as if he were collecting his thoughts, then he looked directly at Lauren. "I'm going to tell you a story. Emma, a friend of my mother's, died about five years ago. She was sixty-four. I was in the room with my mom when Emma passed away. She didn't have any family so we were all she had. Her husband died when she was thirty-six, and she never recovered from the loss. She never remarried and gradually became more reclusive. She led a very unhappy and sheltered life right up to the day she died. You see, during all those years she could never let go of the past. It was not until she lay on her deathbed that she realized what she had done. Then, of course, it was too late."

Shaken by her emotional response to the allegorical nature of Emma's story, Lauren excused herself and went to the privacy of a bedroom. Jason's methods were startling forward, but his story had touched her heart and she felt a profound connection. What surprised her most was that she had told herself the very same thing on many occasions, but she had not acted on her thoughts. Perhaps she had been too close to her own sorrow.

Time seemed to collapse, and in that brief instant, she understood. She had to move on with her life and look to the living, to the future. A few minutes later, she walked back into the living room, clutching a tissue and said, "Thank you."

They sat in silence, in an atmosphere of mutual understanding. As Lauren grew more comfortable, she spoke softly. "I want to know more about Scott."

Jason laid his newspaper aside and smiled. "What would you like to know?"

"Well, for starters, how did you meet?"

Jason laughed. "The first time I saw Scott we almost got in a fight."

"A fight? You two don't seem like the type."

"We're not, but you've got to understand where all of this took place. It was in the Dow Jones pit at the Chicago Board of Trade. It was my third day on the floor, and I made a rookie mistake and wouldn't admit it, although I'm sure I would have later. It turned out that the person on the other side of the trade was Scott." Jason gave details of that first meeting and how they had finally solved the problem, shook hands, then went out for a drink. "I'll never forget one thing about that day," he added. "As soon as I said it was my fault and I was sorry, he stuck out his hand and said it never happened. Our friendship was sealed at that moment."

Lauren smiled. "He's easy to like."

Jason tilted his head and looked at her. "Just how much *do* you like him?"

Lauren hesitated. "I'm not sure, but I'm worried sick about him." After another pause she said, "I'd like to know more about his work. Specifically, why does he trade futures? I mean, is it just the money?"

"Hopefully you're making good money," Jason said, "but there's more to it than that. I'd say it's a combination of excitement, independence, and the chance to make a big score."

"I certainly understand the reason for futures markets, but I don't know much about speculative positions. How does it work? Why do I hear so many wild stories?"

"One word—leverage. Let me give you an example. Each contract of soybeans is five thousand bushels. If beans are selling for eight dollars a bushel, that means one contract is worth forty thousand dollars. But a trader only has to put up a fraction of that amount."

"How much?"

"It depends whether you're a speculator or a hedger, but we'll say about two thousand dollars. As you can see, you can control a large amount of a particular commodity with a small amount of capital. You can do nearly the same thing with the Dow and S & P indexes. If the market moves in your favor by a few percentage points, you'd double your investment."

"That's incredible."

Jason laughed. "It is if you're on the right side of the market, but don't forget one thing—it moves the other way just as fast." Jason paused, then said, "It's the only place I know where you can find despair and euphoria sharing the same breathing space. There's no other place like it."

Lauren nodded slowly. "I'm beginning to see why you and Scott are so involved."

"It's exciting, it's scary, and it's harder than hell. A lot of traders lose money, but the rest make extraordinary profits." Jason paused and looked at Lauren as if he wanted to say something, but he seemed to change his mind.

Lauren leaned forward. "What is it?"

"You said something about Scott being so involved in the markets. Actually, I think he's too involved."

"I don't understand."

"It's hard to explain, but I think it might have something to do with the way his farther died. He lost everything in the stock market and committed suicide."

"Oh. . . . I didn't know." Lauren frowned as she reflected on Jason's surprising statement. "But how do you tie that in with Scott's behavior in the market?"

"I'm just going on bits and pieces from things he's said over several years. It's just speculation, really. But whatever it is, he seems overly obsessed at times. That's probably why he has occasional bouts with insomnia." Jason acted as though he were suddenly sorry for what he had said. He looked back at Lauren. "Please don't get me wrong. He's a wonderful person, and I could be way off on this."

"I understand." Her interest piqued, Lauren asked several questions over the next thirty minutes but when seven o'clock passed without Scott calling conversation grew sparse. Lauren checked the clock every few minutes. The hours wore on, and she became increasingly worried that something had gone wrong—very wrong.

CHAPTER 24

Propelled by a burst of adrenaline, Scott sprinted toward the trees. Fear and flight narrowed his vision, sending only snippets of blurred objects to his brain. He jumped the curb and passed the first bushes without looking back, concentrating on a single objective—speed. He had expected gunfire from the three men chasing him, and he felt relieved when he heard none. He maintained his pace through the shrubbery, veered toward the wall bordering the complex and came upon a level surface of loose gravel that extended along the edge of the wall. He picked up speed and headed toward the rear of the building, his shoes making crunching sounds and spitting out bits of rock with each footfall.

He ran about twenty yards, glanced over his shoulder, and saw that two men had crossed to the wall and were in full pursuit. Why just two? They must have sent one man up the other side of the apartments to prevent him from doubling back between buildings.

Still no shots. *Why?*

He turned his head again and saw they were within range. Maybe they lived in the apartment Benson had entered and were afraid that shots would bring the police. He had gone a few more yards when he suddenly understood why they had not shot at him. He was their only link to finding Lauren.

Scott looked ahead and saw that the wall turned to the left about thirty yards away. Where did the wall go? If it surrounded the entire complex, he would be trapped inside and might be funneled toward the third gunman. He began to pull away from his pursuers, but when he reached the end and made the turn, his hopes sank. The wall extended all along the rear of the complex. He wondered if he could go all the way around and outrun them. Maybe, but where was the third man? Another thought jolted him. Even if he successfully got to his car, they would probably see the plate number and might be able to trace him. He had to try something else.

He scanned the trees ahead, selecting the third one. Scott eased his speed and made a lunge at the tree. He threw his hands overhead and grabbed a large overhanging limb. Shouts sounded as he shimmied up the tree to a limb that extended over the wall. He moved out on the branch until the top of the barrier was directly below him. He looked down and discovered that the wall was farther away than he expected.

He hesitated.

The shouts grew closer.

He jumped from the tree. His chest struck the top of the wall, knocking the wind out of him. It was the same feeling he had gotten in high school when he fell on a football after a two hundred sixty-pound nose guard tackled him. He inhaled deeply, filling his lungs with air, and scrambled over the edge. He meant to hold on and drop but the impact momentarily sapped his strength, causing him to lose his grip and plunge headlong to the ground. The fall was painful, but he was fortunate to have landed on grass instead of the nearby concrete.

He rose to his knees and shook his head.

Voices sounded from the other side of the wall. To reach him, they had to climb the tree or go around. He had to make good use of the time.

He tried to get up but fell back. He finally stood and put his hand against the barrier for support, then he looked at the branches of the tree. No movement and the shouting had stopped. His pursuers were probably running back toward the parking lot to get their car and drive around the wall. Scott went to the corner and looked for his best escape route. The street went straight for several hundred yards, then curved to the right and disappeared around a low, tree-covered knoll. Homes and apartments lined the left side of the road, but there was an extension of the tree-covered hill directly across the street. Concealment was plentiful on the slope—it was an easy choice. *Run.*

He started across the street but fell again. A sharp sting shot through his right leg when he stood, but something inside screamed at him to ignore the pain and run. He crossed the road and glanced to his right before attempting the incline.

Tires squealed as a car slid sideways onto the street from the parking area. The gunmen saw him. "Fuck!"

He was halfway up the slope when he heard the car screech to a stop. He looked back. Doors flew open and three men started running toward different sections of the hill. With adrenaline surging through his veins, Scott felt his strength coming back. He put forth an extra effort and powered up the slope. When he reached the crest he had planned to turn either left or right, but he now decided to go over the top and continue straight ahead.

He churned on, his mind forcing the pain signals from his legs and chest to some hidden reservoir. Survival instinct had taken over, pushing him onward with a single goal—outrun the bastards. With each stride, he felt thankful for his athletic abilities and his years of jogging.

Thirty yards after cresting the hill, he looked back but saw nothing. They were obviously still climbing, but what should he do when they came over the top? He had to run and keep running. His breathing had been rapid while going up the hill, but it had settled into a more sustainable rhythm. Scott was gaining confidence until he came through the trees and found himself at the edge of a large, open area of grass surrounded by a high chain-link fence. Through the space he could see an old, Victorian style house.

Instinct told him not to climb the fence because he would be exposed too long, and though he believed the killers wanted him alive, he could not be sure. They might cut him down in the open. He turned to his right and ran a short distance into the cover of nearby trees, then he moved parallel with the fence. He heard someone yell and ducked behind a tree. Because they were on this side of the hill, probably fanning out, he could no longer afford to run blindly through the trees. He shifted into stealth mode.

There were noises above and behind him now. His pursuers were thoroughly searching the trees and brush. He saw movement above him—he had to find better shelter. Perspiring heavily, he looked around. The combination of running and fear caused a heavy sweat and several trickles flowed into his eyes, blurring his vision. He used the back of his hand and wiped away the moisture.

The noise from above grew closer.

He had to move.

Scott wiped at his eyes again, then searched through the trees and saw what looked like a small limestone wall about seventy feet away. He crouched and made his way toward the formation. He moved closer and saw a narrow crevice that would offer protection, but he wondered if it would be good enough. His plan was to hide there until they went by and then try to escape back up the slope.

He reached the rock, slid into the crevice, and wiped his face. The location left him far more exposed than he had expected. His mind raced. What were the alternatives? He either stayed here or made a run for it through the trees. They would probably see him if he tried to run but it seemed to be his only chance.

He crawled out of the crevice. The noise from above grew louder. It sounded like someone was beating the shrubs with a large stick, and he was very close.

Too late to run.

Frantic, his pulse racing, Scott sought a way out. He did not want to be captured, and he did not want to die like a trapped animal. Panic stabbed at his mind as he searched nearby. A limb lay about three yards away. It was crooked and knobby but he needed a weapon—any weapon. He lay on his stomach, crawled to the branch, retrieved it, and crawled back. He stood with his back against the rocks and grasped the limb. It was about four feet long and thicker than he had first thought.

Thwack! The nearby noise grew very loud.

Scott waited, his hands tightening around the rough bark. Fear tore at him as the sound came closer, louder. He edged to his left and drew back the limb. Seconds ticked by that seemed like minutes.

Still, he waited.

A few more seconds passed, then a large man came around the edge of the rock formation. The man saw Scott out of the corner of his eye and started to swing his gun around.

Scott swung the limb, putting the full force of his body behind the blow. The sound of wood breaking and bone crushing exploded through the air.

His weapon shattered, Scott pounced on the gunman expecting a fight, but the big man was unconscious—blood spurting from his nose. It was the same man he had hit with the baseball bat.

Scott shook his head. "Jesus, if he ever gets hold of me."

A noise startled him. Someone was coming through the trees. He reached down, grabbed the man's gun and ran into the nearby growth. He sprinted for several minutes before he dared to stop. Finally, he ducked behind a tree and looked back.

Nothing.

He stood with his back against the tree for a moment, panting, sweating. The hard steel he gripped in his right hand gave him new confidence. He had a gun now—things were different. He waited. Hearing nothing, he took a few deep breaths and continued on the same course. He had noticed the wooded area, on his right, when he drove up the street behind Hayden Benson, but he could not remember how long the section was. A mile, perhaps, probably less. He realized he had only two choices: he could continue straight or turn up the hill and try to make it to the street.

Though he did not know where he might come out, it seemed prudent to stay with his present course and hope he could get out of the trees and reach safety. After another hundred yards, he crawled through a dilapidated rail fence and saw a shed behind an old house. He dashed around some high grass and dove next to a large pile of firewood stacked against the shed. He edged up against the wood and peered back through the trees. Had they seen him?

He waited.

After several minutes, he saw two distant figures coming in his direction. He looked to his left and found a narrow space between the stack of wood and the shed. It was not wide enough for his purpose, but if he could move a few logs, he thought he could squeeze into the narrow gap. He pulled out three lengths of wood, then he slid against the wall of the shed. Cobwebs clung to his face as he moved into the dark crawlspace. He wiped and spit in an attempt to clear the dusty webs. He reached out and pulled the cut pieces back over the end to enclose himself. There was a crack on the opposite side but someone would have to squat down and look in to see him. If anyone did, he meant to blow the man's head off.

Scott checked his weapon and waited.

A moment later, he heard voices coming toward him. When they were a little closer, he strained to hear what they were saying.

One of the men said, "This tall grass looks like it's been walked through but I don't see any foot prints where he would've come out."

"Billy, there's some dog tracks over here. Maybe it was just a damn dog."

"Maybe. Hell, he could have gone to that house, or he might have gone back up the hill and gotten away."

"I don't know, Billy. I think he's still around here."

There was a short silence. "The car! His fucking car is somewhere in that lot. He's got to go back for it."

"Hell, yes."

Scott gritted his teeth. It just kept getting worse.

The next voice sounded farther away. "Let's look around a little more, then we'll go over and stake out the parking lot. Sooner or later, he'll come back for his car. When he does, we'll nail his ass."

"Yeah."

Scott heard scattered bits of voices fading in the distance and, then, it turned quiet. He remained vigilant. After several minutes, he heard a swishing noise coming from his left. He brought the gun up, rested it on his knee, and peered through the gap in the wood. He could feel his heart pounding as he brought his finger against the trigger.

For a few seconds everything was quiet, then he heard the noise again. He gripped the pistol and concentrated his whole being on the narrow gap. He expected to have to pull the trigger at any second.

There was a sudden movement near the wood.

Scott's finger tightened.

A Golden Retriever appeared at the hole. The dog turned his head sideways and emitted a low whine.

Scott's gun hand dropped. "Easy, boy." His voice a mere whisper. "Don't bark, fella."

The dog pawed at the wood but made no other sound.

Memories of Golden Retrievers flashed through his mind, reminding him that the breed was more apt to lick you to death than bite you. The dog persisted at the wood. When it became obvious the animal was not going to leave, Scott quietly removed three logs.

The dog was next to him in an instant, his tail wagging so hard it alternately banged on the stack of wood and the wall of the shed. Scott was relieved the dog had not barked, but he worried that the gunmen might have seen the animal enter the pile of logs. He raised his gun, then sat in the darkened space with cob webs clinging to him, the dog licking him and breathing in his face—and he waited.

CHAPTER 25

Darkness came so rapidly Scott felt as if someone had dropped a blanket over him. He waited in the woodpile for over an hour and thought the searchers had probably left but he could not be sure. Though he was sore, tired, and cramped, he had no interest in leaving his covert. Why should he? He could not get his car, and there was no place else to go. He also worried that the killers might have gotten flashlights and more help to patrol the area. They might even be on the other side of the rail fence, waiting for some kind of movement. Perhaps they were watching the nearby house in case he had gone there. He decided to wait before trying to make it back to the road, then he would look for a phone and call a cab. That still left him with the problem of an abandoned car.

But he had at least one new friend. The dog had made no attempt to leave and was now sleeping with its head lying on Scott's left foot. Weariness caused Scott to rest his head on his knees and shut his eyes. Just for a moment, he told himself, just for a moment. Fatigue gave way to sleep.

The dog's movements woke Scott. Startled, he rose up and struck his head on one of the logs. He listened for several minutes but heard only crickets, the dog breathing, and a distant owl. Judging from his position, he knew he must have been lying with his head resting on the dog. The next thing he noticed was the cold, and he wondered how the temperature had dropped so quickly. He glanced at the luminescent dial on his watch but did not believe what he saw. He squinted and read the dial again. It was a little after midnight.

Scott suspected he had slept that long because of a combination of stress, fatigue, and his recent lack of sleep. Whatever the cause, he now had additional problems. Because of what he had overheard, the gunmen were undoubtedly patrolling the area, especially the parking lot and the streets. Any attempt to leave the woods and try to get a taxi would be extremely dangerous.

He also worried about his appearance. He was covered with dirt and cobwebs and his clothes were torn and soiled. If a police cruiser saw him, he would certainly look suspicious. For Lauren's sake, he had to avoid any contact with the police. He also worried that if they discovered his identity they would arrest him as an accessory after the fact.

He was not certain what his best option was but one thing he was sure of—his legs were killing him. They were sore, cramped, and demanded relief. He decided to crawl out to stretch but only after thoroughly inspecting his surroundings. He looked between the slats and scanned the nearby grassy area. Next, he put his attention on the trees beyond the rail fence. As his gaze swept over the area, the woods seemed to abound with dark holes and foreboding shadows. He visualized assassins waiting, lurking, ready to strike as soon he stepped from his covert.

Scott paid special attention to one dark area where he thought he saw movement. He continued to concentrate on the spot until he thought his eyes must be playing tricks on him. He moved his line of vision slightly to the left and realized there had been no movement at all. He gradually felt more secure. He waited a little longer, then picked up the gun and prepared to get up. His movement woke the dog. The animal's show of friendliness was instant. His tail banged back and forth against the logs and the shed but he did not bark.

Scott removed two pieces of wood and stuck his head out. He heard crickets but nothing else. Satisfied, he patted the dog on the head, crawled out and started to get up but his legs cramped and gave way. He rubbed his thighs for a moment, and then slowly stood. With only a quarter-moon in view, it was quite dark. Still wary, he stood against the shed for several minutes and listened, moving his head from side to side as he scanned the darkness, his gun ready. No sound, no movement, nothing.

Hoping for more options, Scott thought he should check the other side of the house before deciding what to do. He crept through the grass and made a circle around the house. There had been no sounds from the main building since he crawled under the wood, and there were no lights showing anywhere. It seemed the owners were away.

After twenty yards, he came to a dirt road that led away from the house. It was hard to see but it appeared that the narrow lane wound its way through the trees for a considerable distance. Did the track go to the street he had used earlier? He could not be sure but he suspected it did. His first thought was to follow the road, but he changed his mind because it looked like the perfect spot for an ambush, and besides, what could he do at one o'clock in the morning? He crossed the dirt lane and went about fifteen yards before he came to thick woods.

The risk of wandering through the trees seemed higher than the potential reward. He decided to go back to the woodpile and stay until just before daybreak, then make his way out. The dog nudged his leg and he knelt down to pet the appreciative animal. Even in the dark, he could see the dog's tail wagging rapidly. Scott went across the road, crept along the edge of the old house, and rounded the far corner until his hand touched a wooden swing. He saw something light in color, reached over, and found a blanket draped over the swing. It felt tattered and dampish but it would keep him warm. He grabbed it and headed for the shed.

Scott stood next to the woodpile and waited until he was sure it was safe; then, he crawled through the opening. It was not until he was inside that he noticed the dog was gone. He moved his hands around the small hole to clear the remaining cobwebs and to determine whether he could widen the space and make it more comfortable. After some trial and error, he was able to remove a few logs without weakening the structure. He lay down and wrapped himself in the blanket, with his head next to the narrow slit he had used as an entryway. This position would allow him to hear any nearby movement. The gun rested on a log within easy reach.

After a few minutes, he began to feel warm and his mind drifted away from the urgent matters at hand. His thoughts turned to Lauren. He was in love with her and it felt good to admit it. He shut his eyes for a few seconds, then suddenly opened them and whispered. "Lauren." He remembered he was supposed to have called Jason's apartment to let them know he was all right. After this long, they might fear that the police or the killers had caught him. A high-pitched whimper interrupted his thoughts. The dog's nose poked between two logs, his paws scratching at the wood in an effort to get inside.

Scott removed two slats and prepared himself for attacks from tongue and tail. It took only a few seconds to know where the animal had been; the strong smell of dog food hung in the still air. Scott groaned, rolled over, and shut his eyes. "At least somebody got dinner."

———

It was five-fifteen when the dog's movements woke Scott. He peered through the logs at each end of the woodpile. All quiet. The golden suddenly barked and pawed at the wood, signaling that he wanted out. Scott checked that side again before removing the slats to free the animal. The dog ran through the grass, stopped by a tree, and hiked his leg.

Scott grabbed the gun, crawled out, stretched, dusted himself off, and took a deep breath. Instead of breathing the strong odor of cobwebs, dust, and an overly friendly dog, his senses captured the welcome bouquet of crisp, early morning air, air that always seemed to be reborn, somehow, at first light. He enjoyed his mobility for a moment and then focused on a single priority: somehow, he had to get his car. As an afterthought, he decided a little food was also in order. He noticed the dog at his side and bent to pet the animal. "What's your name, fella?"

The dog wagged his tail enthusiastically.

Scott moved through the grass and entered the trees cautiously. Because he had sheltered all night he thought the immediate area was safe but he remained wary. After going about seventy yards, he altered his path until he could see the dirt road, which he meant to follow on a parallel course. He wanted to be far enough from the road to avoid an ambush, but still use the lane to guide him through the trees, hopefully, to a public street.

He eventually came to an old rail fence. The dog stopped abruptly and refused to go any farther. Though there were holes in the fence, the golden acted as if the weathered pieces of railing symbolized a boundary that was not to be violated.

Scott kneeled and said goodbye to the dog before sliding between two rails. Ten minutes later, as the first rays of sunlight began to filter through scattered clouds in the Eastern sky, he came over a small crest and saw a street below. Scott could see a few houses and a service station off to his left. The lights of the station blinked on as he watched.

He went to the edge of the road, scanned the area until satisfied, crossed the street, and approached the station. He brushed himself off, though he knew it would not do much good. The large doors to the service area were up, and he could see a man sipping from a steaming cup. Scott walked toward the workbench and forced a smile. "Good morning."

The man stared at Scott's clothes.

"I ran into a bit of trouble last night, and I need a little help."

No answer.

The man wasn't exactly a friendly sort, but Scott had another tactic in mind. For emergencies, he had brought three thousand dollars in hundred dollar bills and he felt pleased with his foresight. Everybody has a price.

He took a step closer. "I'm willing to pay for some help."

The man finally spoke. "What kind of help?"

"Well, I've got to get my car from the parking lot of that big apartment complex up the road, but there are a couple of men who'd like to do me a little harm. So—"

The man turned away.

Scott realized his approach had not been the epitome of finesse. He retrieved his wallet and took out some bills. "They don't know which car I'm driving. If you get it and bring it back, I'll pay you four hundred dollars."

The man turned, his expression unchanged. "That much money means it's a whole lot of trouble. Not interested."

Scott pulled out more bills. "Eight hundred. Four now and four on delivery."

Before the man could answer, a much younger man peeked out from under the hood of a car. "I'll do it, mister."

Scott looked over and saw a skinny, redheaded kid, not more than nineteen, smiling at him.

"I just got married," the kid said, throwing a greasy rag on the bench, "and I can damn sure use the money."

Scott went over to the car. "What's your name?"

"Kevin."

Scott handed the kid four hundreds, then followed him to his truck and got in. They discussed tactics and drove to the rear of the apartments. Scott told Kevin the color and exact location of his car, then helped him scale the rear wall.

The plan was for Kevin to proceed between the buildings to the parking lot as if he were leaving the apartments to go to work. If Kevin sensed any danger, Scott had warned him to keep walking. He climbed in the truck and drove down the street to a point that allowed him partial vision of the parking lot. He did not think Kevin would be in harm's way, but he wanted to be close by just in case. From this distance, he could see a man pacing at the edge of the lot. Scott knew it was one of the gunmen and his concern for Kevin escalated.

Two cars came out of the lot and drove by. Neither was his. Five minutes later, his rental car turned onto the street. Scott gunned the engine, pulled the truck onto the road, glanced in the rearview mirror, and felt relieved that his rental was the only car in sight.

He reached the station, parked, and got out just as his car pulled in behind him. Scott walked over and handed the young man the other four hundred. "Thanks, kid. You saved my butt."

"And you saved mine," Kevin said with a grin. "The rent's due."

Scott smiled as he looked back up the road. No cars in sight. He turned to Kevin. "Can I use your bathroom to change clothes and clean up? Maybe get a cup of coffee?"

"You got it, mister."

Scott pulled out two more hundreds and handed it to Kevin. "I like your attitude."

"You already paid me."

"Believe me, you earned it."

The kid took the money and smiled as though he had just won the lottery.

CHAPTER 26

Scott changed clothes, left the station, headed west until he came to the Capital Beltway, turned north until he connected with highway 270, then drove several miles until he found a motel and a restaurant. He got a room, went outside to a pay phone and dialed Jason's number.

"It's Scott. Sorry I'm a little late."

"We've been worried sick," Jason said. "Are you all right?"

"I ran into some trouble, but I'm okay."

"Why didn't you call?"

"There wasn't a phone handy."

"No phone? Where'd you stay last night?"

"Inside a wood pile with a dog."

"Seriously," Jason said.

"I am serious. I slept underneath a stack of firewood." Scott briefed Jason on his encounter with the gunmen, and then asked to speak to Lauren.

"She was up and down all night worrying about you. Hell, we both were. She just got to sleep a couple of hours ago. Do you want me to wake her?"

Scott wanted to talk with her but decided against it. She would undoubtedly want details, and he did not want to frighten her. "Let her sleep. When she wakes up, tell her I'm all right but don't give her any specifics."

"Sure, if you think that's best."

Scott gave Jason the name of the motel and his room number, and said he would call back later in the day, and that he expected to be home tomorrow.

Just before they hung up, Jason said, "Wait a minute; I almost forgot. There's a big speech and reception for the Russian trade delegation in Washington this afternoon. It'll be at one of the big hotels. The Jordan, I think."

"Who's speaking?"

"The Secretary of Agriculture. Everybody's going to be there, including the Vice President and the Deputy Secretary of Agriculture. I thought that might get your attention, but it gets better. I've got some contacts, and I think I can get you in if you want."

"Hell, yes. It would give me a chance to follow up on the telegram I sent to Benson."

"Do you think that's wise?"

"I have an idea that I think will prevent Benson from doing anything if I approach him. Right now, I need to take a shower and get something to eat. While I'm doing that, you make some phone calls and see if you can get me into the reception. Call me back when you find out. Wait, one more thing. Ask your contact if there's any chance of getting in with a pocket tape recorder."

"You'd better give me your driver's license and social security numbers in case I need them."

Scott repeated the numbers.

"One more thing," Jason said.

"What?"

"Be careful."

Scott felt renewed after a shower and a large breakfast. His spirits were up, and he was determined to confront Hayden Benson at the reception. He was aware of the inherent risks of challenging the Deputy Secretary at such an event, but he had a plan. It required a certain amount of bluffing but Scott felt he needed to take the risk.

He sat at the table in his room and wrote a message he planned to have delivered to Benson at the reception. He signed the same name he had used in the telegram, and then reread his note.

Mr. Benson:
You should have received my telegram a few days ago. I am fully aware of your illegal release of report data and your contact with certain individuals at the Oak Knoll Apartment complex. I demand that you speak with me immediately. Any attempt to have me arrested will cause harmful information to be released to your family and the press. If you agree, put this note in your left front coat pocket and walk to the rear exit. Wait there.
Jim Carpenter

Scott placed the note in an envelope, sealed it, wrote Hayden Benson's name on the front, then he called the airline and changed his return flight to Saturday morning.

The phone rang a few seconds after he hung up. It was Jason. "It took a bit of arm twisting but you're all set."

"Great. How's it going to work?"

"Go to the main entrance at three-thirty. A man named Ronald Parkinson knows what you look like and he will contact you. He'll probably ask a few questions before giving you a pass."

"Thanks. I really appreciate your help on this."

"I'm happy to help. There is one problem though. If you try to take a recorder in, it'll set off the metal detector. I doubt if you want to draw that kind of attention."

"Damn—"

"Listen, I've got to get back to the floor, but do me one favor."

"Sure."

"I went out on a limb; so don't do anything either of us will regret."

———

Scott spent the next three hours resting, but Jason's last words kept nagging at him, and he wondered if he had made the right decision. He reviewed his plan and still felt he had to take the risk. If his bluff worked, there should be no repercussions. He rolled on his side and thought about Lauren. Twenty minutes before it was time to leave, he got up and dialed Jason's apartment.

She answered.

"Hi, it's Scott."

"My God, where are you?"

"I ran into a little problem last night but I'm in a motel room and I'm safe. Is everything okay on your end?"

"Scott Quinn, don't you ever do this to me again. I was up all night worrying about you. Don't you dare leave me hanging like that."

Scott felt surprised at her intensity, but he took it as a positive omen. "Does this mean you're growing fond of me?"

No answer.

"Lauren?"

"I'm thinking . . . I'm thinking." Her tone had turned flirtatious.

Scott chuckled.

"What are you laughing at?" Lauren asked.

"Oh, I was just thinking. I've made more progress with you on a trip to Washington than I did when I was with you twenty-four hours a day."

"You're dancing right on the edge of trouble, Mr. Quinn. Do you know that?" Her words gave way to laughter.

They talked until it was time for Scott to leave. Before saying goodbye, Lauren said teasingly. "There's one more thing I'd like to tell you. I made something for you, but you'll have to wait until you get home to find out what it is."

Scott tried but he could not pry any details from her. He hung up and found himself caught up in a feeling that approached giddiness. He wanted to enjoy and extend the mood, but his thoughts changed when he pulled out of the parking lot and headed for the hotel. Anything could happen during the next few hours.

He arrived at the Jordan Colonial a little after three. He was pleased the reception was at a hotel he was familiar with, but he became increasingly nervous as he waited. A few minutes before the appointed time, he placed the pistol in the glove compartment and got out of the car. He tried to be both vigilant and inconspicuous as he walked toward the designated hall. He checked his surroundings, his insides churning by the time he reached the entrance.

He glanced at his watch: three-thirty.

A man in a dark suit approached him. "Scott?"

"Yes."

The man extended his hand. "Ronald Parkinson. Happy to meet you."

Parkinson asked Scott several questions and wanted to see his identification. Parkinson then took him to the door and assisted his entry into the hall. Scott stood behind a group of people just inside the large room. He was so intent on looking for Hayden Benson that he failed to notice that the group funneled into a line, and he soon found himself standing in front of a member of the Russian delegation. Scott extended his hand to the smiling delegate. The man greeted him in excellent English.

A moment later, he stood in front of Deputy Secretary of Agriculture, Hayden Benson. Scott had not expected this, but he would play his part. He nodded, shook hands, then quickly moved on. He proceeded through the line and came to Vice President, Donovan Kenney.

Kenney extended his hand. "We've met before, but I'm not sure where."

"Yes, we have," Scott said. "A dinner in Chicago last fall; you have a very good memory."

"Yes," the Vice President said, "but, alas, I can never remember my anniversary."

The comment brought laughter from those nearby.

After a brief conversation, Scott excused himself. He walked into the crowd, acutely aware of his increased tension. He knew he was in danger, and he was nervous, but he also felt strangely in control. It seemed as if every nerve in his body had snapped to attention, manifested by an odd, electric mixture of feelings he had never felt before.

He moved to one side of the hall to watch Benson and was impressed. The man seemed perfectly at ease, even charming, but Scott knew the Deputy Secretary's comportment was about to change. He decided to wait until Benson separated from the large group he was conversing with before asking a waiter to deliver the message. After fifteen minutes he grew impatient. Every time Benson moved, he quickly entered a discussion with other dignitaries. Scott decided he had to make his move soon. He was looking for a waiter when an attractive woman with short, black hair came up and started a conversation. Scott chatted politely but kept his eyes on Benson. The woman talked continually and even asked if he would like to attend a dinner party with her.

Christ. *The woman's making a pass at me.* He decided to change tactics and blurted out that he was married, had six kids, and was faithful.

The woman scowled, turned abruptly, and disappeared into the crowd.

Hayden Benson was talking with two men when Scott summoned a waiter. He pointed to Benson and asked the young man to deliver the envelope; then, he moved a safe distance from where he had been standing in case Benson asked the waiter to identify the sender. He watched and waited. His vision narrowed, and it seemed as if there were only two men in the entire room—Hayden Benson and himself. Dozens of people milled about but Scott did not see them. His stare remained fixed on Benson.

The waiter approached the Deputy Secretary and handed him the note.

Benson took the envelope but did not open it immediately. Instead, he continued in an animated discussion with one of his associates.

Scott's nerves were electric. He muttered to himself as he concentrated on the envelope. "Open it. . . . Open the damn thing."

Three minutes passed before Benson turned his attention to the envelope.

He opened it and began to read. Even from this distance, Scott could see the color drain from Benson's face. The Deputy Secretary looked up from the paper, searching the crowd. His posture changed, and he suddenly seemed older. He acted confused, then moved away from the crowd and read the note again. He stood for a long time, with his head down, then he put the envelope in his left front pocket and walked slowly toward the rear exit.

Scott thought Benson's reaction was further evidence that something did not fit. The Deputy Secretary's involvement was not consistent with his style and manner. He watched carefully to make sure Benson spoke to no one. After Benson had reached the designated spot, Scott took off his nametag, slipped the card out of the plastic cover, turned it over, wrote Jim Carpenter on the back, and replaced it on his lapel. He looked around as he made his way toward the exit.

"Mr. Benson, I'm Jim Carpenter."

No reply.

"Mr. Benson, let's step through here so we can have a little privacy."

Benson hesitated.

Scott spoke calmly, sincerely. "I promise I'm not going to do anything. I just want to talk for a few minutes." He motioned toward the exit, then followed the shaken man into a large hallway.

Benson walked to a corner and turned. "How did you find out about Shannon?"

The comment caught Scott off guard. What was in his note that caused Benson to make such a remark? And what did it mean? Did it have something to do with the apartment complex?

He took a chance. "I've had you followed."

Benson covered his eyes with his left hand and looked down. His movements reflected a man in agony. He spoke slowly. "I—I guess you want money."

Scott felt surprised by the man's reaction. He had expected Benson to be hostile or to deny everything. It was obvious to Scott he had the upper hand. *Seize the opportunity.* "Tell me more about Shannon."

"What can I say? It was a setup, and I fell for it like an idiot."

"A set up?"

Benson raised his head. "Your note. I—I thought you knew."

Careful not to push his bluff too far, Scott chose his words carefully. "I know enough, but what I really want to know is who's in this with you?"

"I can't tell you that. H—he'd kill me."

"*Who* would kill you?"

"Christ, man. I can't give you his name. I'll give you money, but I'm not going to say any more about this." There was sorrow in Benson's face as he shook his head. "My God, I'm being black-mailed twice for the same mistake."

That one sentence said it all, and Scott realized that Hayden Benson was, indeed, a victim. He had obviously made a terrible blunder but he was a victim nevertheless. Scott put his hand on the man's shoulder. "Mr. Benson, I don't want money. I'm a friend of Lauren Chandler. I'm just trying to help her."

Benson appeared shocked. Scott was about to continue when he noticed two men watching them. He grew nervous and spoke quickly. "I'm leaving, but I'll be in touch with you in a few days. I want to know who is behind this."

"I—I need time to think. You've got to give me some time."

"You do that," Scott said firmly, "but I want some goddamned answers when I call."

Scott turned and headed for the exit. He glanced covertly at the men who had been watching and worried that he would be followed.

CHAPTER 27

Hayden Benson feigned illness and abruptly left the reception. The telegram had shaken him, but the face-to-face confrontation with the sender was catastrophic. He left the hotel, drove to a secluded location, and parked. For a long moment, he sat motionless, staring, but not seeing, his mind swirling in a plethora of emotions. Against his will, his mental faculties seemed to lock onto all that was negative, to grasp the worst possible thoughts, and amplify them into a scenario of horror. He likened himself to a fly inside an endless world of spider webs, and he thought he would soon become caught in a similar trap, doomed forever.

Gradually, he suppressed his anguish enough to give thought to seeking a way out of his dilemma. He concluded it was probable that his family and the outside world would eventually learn about his activities. He agonized for nearly an hour, but all he could think of was to tell Victor Merrick about the man named Jim Carpenter. The more he thought about this option, the more it worried him. Even if Merrick's men found the man and killed him, Lauren would still be a threat. Benson would have to live with the possibility of her coming forth at any time, and he would have to live with the death of yet another innocent person. A new flash of anxiety swept through Benson as he considered another possibility. What if his disclosure about Jim Carpenter caused Merrick to believe he had become a liability? Merrick might decide to kill him.

His thoughts shifted to Shannon Peterson and a desperate idea took hold. A surge of hope caused him to think in a shallow manner, to not fully analyze the consequences of his plan. All he could think of was that he might have found a way out. He started the car, drove to a phone booth, and dialed Shannon's apartment.

She answered.

"It's Hayden. I have to see you. It's important."

"But, Hayden, sweetie. It's not your day."

"I don't want to come over for that, but it's urgent that I talk to you."

Shannon paused, and then said, "All right, but only for a few minutes."

He drove to Shannon's apartment and went in. "I need a drink. A double."

Shannon turned toward the bar. "Sure, hon. You just sit down and relax." She walked over with the glass, handed it to him, and sat next to him. "Now then, what's this all about?"

"Think about this before you answer." Benson took a large swallow. "I—I want you to go away with me. I have some money, and we could go somewhere nice. I'll take good care of you."

Shannon rose, walked to the refrigerator, took out a bottle of white wine, poured a glass, and looked back at Benson. "What kind of money are we talking about?"

"I can raise at least eight hundred thousand, probably more."

"Honey, you come back when you're on the sunny side of five million, and we'll talk about this. Until then, I'm not interested."

"But I've got to get away from all this." He looked down, paused, and then said in a low, breaking voice. "You must know I'm in love with you."

"That's sweet, but this is strictly business. I would only be interested if you came up with some very serious money."

Benson felt crushed. He should have known what her answer would be; yet he had made a fool of himself. He swallowed the last of his drink and set the glass on a table.

Shannon moved next to him and put her arm around him.

"Listen, there's nothing wrong with this arrangement. It's actually working out very well for everyone."

He did not answer.

"Did something happen?"

He started to tell her about the telegram and the man at the reception, but held back. He would be a fool to do that. She had just reminded him of a conclusive fact—she was Merrick's employee. He got up, went to the bar, and poured another drink. "No, nothing happened. I just thought that . . . well, maybe you'd go away with me."

"You know, Hayden, you need to learn to enjoy things as they are. Don't push it."

Benson was drinking on an empty stomach, and the alcohol acted quickly. Shannon walked over, gave him a soft peck, and followed it with a long, wet kiss. Her perfume enveloped him like a cloud. Her touch, her smell, and the alcohol mixed, his senses taking over. His distress eased. "I know we agreed I couldn't stay, but maybe you'll reconsider."

Shannon looked at her watch. "I guess I should have told you. Victor's going to be here in a few minutes."

"He's coming *here*?"

"Yes, he flew into National, and he's on his way over."

"What for?"

Shannon hesitated. "He just said he wanted to see me about something. He also said he was going to call you today because he wanted to see you on Saturday. Didn't he reach you?"

"No, I've been out all day." He rubbed his chin. A grilling by Victor Merrick was the last thing he needed right now. An idea took hold. He would leave town on family business and stay away a day or two. He simply did not want to talk to Merrick, maybe in a few days but not now. He started for the door. "I have to go, but I'll see you Tuesday." He opened the door to leave, stopped, and turned. "You won't say anything about this to Merrick, will you?"

"Relax, Sweetie. I won't say anything. Besides, if you come up with the right kind of money, we might have something to talk about."

She was shrewd, but her answer gave him a feeling of relief and a slight touch of hope. Maybe there was still a chance. Benson was halfway down the stairs when he let out an audible groan. Merrick was coming up the walkway and had seen him. Benson stopped and mumbled as he watched the dark eyes lock on him. "Son of a bitch—"

————

Victor Merrick intended his trip to Washington to be a combination of business and pleasure. Every man who had spent a night with Shannon Peterson always came back for more, and he was no exception. He had arranged to stay with Shannon and was looking forward to another long, intense, carnal experience. But the news that Lauren Chandler's friend had eluded his men, for the second time, was the primary reason for his trip. The details of the escape had sent him into a rage, and it was lucky for Billy Barker that Merrick was in Chicago when he had heard the news. Merrick had screamed obscenities over the phone, but that was not enough; he intended to have somebody's ass when he got to Washington, and the person on the wrong end of the stick was Billy Barker. However, Merrick had just received good news that significantly changed his attitude. He had finally received the phone call he had been expecting for two weeks, and his tactics for finding Lauren Chandler were about to change.

He walked up the steps and stopped next to Benson. "This is Friday. What are you doing here?"

"I had to see Shannon for a few minutes, but I was just leaving."

Merrick put his hand firmly on Benson's shoulder and nodded toward the top of the stairs. "Come up to the apartment. I need to talk to you."

Merrick went in first and spoke to Shannon. "Call Billy and tell him to get over here."

Billy arrived five minutes later, his manner showing that he obviously expected a verbal onslaught. His eyes shifted around the room, and he twitched nervously.

Merrick stared at him for a moment. "Billy, you really fucked up." Merrick paused but continued to glare. "You and I are going to have a little talk later."

Billy flinched.

Merrick started to light a cigarette but changed his mind. Smoking was one thing Shannon simply would not stand for, and since he meant to stay the night, he felt it best to submit to her wishes. Besides, he thought, keeping her happy probably meant a better blowjob.

She gave him a little victory smile.

He went to the refrigerator. "I've got some good news. Let's have some champagne." He grasped a bottle, removed the wire, twisted the cork until it popped, and then poured a glass and turned back to his attentive audience. He made them wait.

Billy finally looked up. "You know where she is?"

"No, but I will soon. Remember that assassin I mentioned? Cade is very skilled at certain types of jobs, and what we need just happens to be his specialty. I heard one story about him finding a man in two weeks that certain other people couldn't find in three years. Of course, the man's dead now. Seems he caught a bullet in the temple from three hundred yards." Merrick lifted his glass in a mock toast. "Hell of a shot."

"Is Cade here?" Billy asked.

"No, he's in Europe. I understand he goes over there a couple of times a year to collect art, but his next stop is Chicago. The important thing is that I found him. Actually, I located a woman named Zina Martell. She's his assistant and is responsible for relaying our messages back and forth. I hear he never negotiates in person." Merrick poured more champagne. "He'll be here in a week, but I want everyone to remember we're still vulnerable as long as Lauren Chandler is alive. I don't want you to let up on the search." His penetrating eyes stared at Billy. "You got that?"

"Got it."

Merrick glanced around the room. "You all know how I treat my people when things are going right. Well, I think we may be able to throw a hell of a party before long. If things go as I expect they will, I'll fly everyone to my place in Aspen for two or three weeks. I'll pay for everything." Merrick's mind shifted gears, and he turned toward Billy. "How many new men do we have now?"

"Five, but Hammitt said we'll have another by tomorrow."

"Good. Tell him I want three men sent down here right away. I want Hammitt and the others to stay in Chicago, but tell him to be ready to go anywhere on a moment's notice."

"I'll take care of it," Billy said.

Merrick turned to Benson. "There's another problem. I've had some unexpected expenses so my cash flow is a little tight right now, and I have to come up with some very serious money to pay Cade. Since he gets half his fee up front, I can't afford to lay off the next report as we'd planned."

Benson got up from his chair. "My God, this whole thing is too hot right now. We should ease up for a month or two."

"Can't do it, Hayden. You really shouldn't worry so much. If they tripled the security, they still wouldn't have a clue about how we get the information out of the lockup. There's not a chance in hell of them catching us. The goddamn thing is foolproof."

The others nodded, but Benson was obviously disturbed. He took another drink and sulked quietly.

Billy asked, "So how many men is Cade bringing?"

"You won't believe it," Merrick said. "He works with one woman. That's all."

Billy's face expressed surprise. "One woman?"

"Yeah, the one I mentioned earlier. She'll be here a few days before he arrives."

Billy shook his head in apparent disbelief.

Merrick nodded. "She does all of his negotiating, but she also comes early to check out the museums. She evidently gives him a report on everything worth seeing in each city he visits."

"Jeez," Billy said. "This guy doesn't sound so great to me. If he spends all his time looking at art how's he going to find the Chandler woman?"

Merrick sat down, leaned back and stared at the ceiling, his mind going forward in time. "Lauren Chandler will be dead within two weeks."

CHAPTER 28

Saturday morning, Scott boarded a flight to Chicago. He had arranged for Lauren and Jason to meet him at his apartment, and he was anxious to return home. He turned vigilant when the plane landed; searching for people he hoped he would never see had become habit. Scott felt vulnerable because he had disabled the gunman's pistol and thrown it into a trashcan on his way to the airport. He arrived at his apartment and used the coded knock. The door opened and two beaming faces greeted him but only one person hugged him—Lauren. She held him tightly and gave no indication of wanting to let go. He could feel her, he could smell her, and he was content.

Jason cleared his throat. "Would you two like me to leave?"

Lauren stepped back with a sheepish grin.

Scott did not like clichés, but one flashed through his mind. Had absence made Lauren's heart grow fonder? Reading a woman was always hard, an art form, actually, but he sensed a definite change in her manner, and there was something different about the way she looked at him. Something intimate.

Receiving no answer, Jason repeated his question.

"I'm sorry," Scott said. "It's been a rough couple of days. I'm not thinking straight, but please stay."

"I should be going anyway, but I want to hear the details of your trip later."

Scott and Lauren said goodbye to Jason, shut the door, and stared at each other. A moment went by without either speaking. Lauren looked toward the other room. "I want you to see what I made for you. It's not finished, but you'll get the idea."

"What is it?"

"Shut your eyes."

She guided him into the living room and he became very conscious of her soft, warm hand upon his.

She stopped after several steps. "Turn to your right, and no peeking."

She let go of his hand, and he sensed she had moved a few steps away.

"All right, you can open your eyes."

Scott's eyelids blinked open and he looked in front of him. A beautiful oil painting of the trading pit at the Chicago Board of Trade hung on the wall. Scott was dumbfounded. How could she have nearly completed something so extraordinary in the short time he was gone? Then a more important question struck him. Why had she painted it? Was it gratitude for what he had done, or was it something deeper?

"Don't you like it?"

"Oh, Lauren, I think it's wonderful." He edged closer, looking at the brush strokes. "You're very talented."

She pointed at one of the traders, "That's you."

Scott laughed. "With so many traders it's hard to tell."

"That's because the scene is too big for a close up. Nevertheless, that's you."

They talked about the painting for several minutes, then Lauren asked, "Can I ask a favor?"

"Sure."

"We don't have much here to eat, and well . . . I'm sort of getting cabin fever. If I put on my wig, a hat, and sunglasses, could we go for a walk and do the shopping while we're out?"

Scott hesitated, calculating risks.

"We don't have to be gone long."

"All right, but we're not going very far."

She smiled and rushed toward the bedroom. "I'll be ready in a jiffy."

Fifteen minutes later, they walked outside and joined other strollers enjoying a glorious afternoon, stopping occasionally to talk about various window displays. They came to a bookstore and compared favorite authors, then discussed their mutual love of pasta in front of an Italian restaurant. They came to a small floral shop featuring an outdoor display of two rows of white, water-filled buckets of cut flowers. Lauren stopped in front of the roses, stared at them for a time, then she took Scott's hand in hers. Her skin was warm and soft, her gesture full of meaning. Their hands never separated until they reached the market, and then only for short periods.

Scott was amazed by his reaction. That simple touch was a heartfelt connection that stirred feelings of such depth that he experienced sensations that were completely new. No other woman had ever affected him in such a way, not even close.

Though they hardly spoke as they walked, their actions in the market were an enjoyable combination of flirting, teasing, and laughter. After they left the store, the grocery bag pressing against Scott's gun brought him back to reality. He checked the street but saw nothing of concern. He was happy Lauren did not notice his vigilance, but he reminded himself that he must stay alert. The walk back was much the same except for Scott glancing at people on the street. They reached the apartment, and he gave Lauren his full attention. They went to the kitchen and put away the groceries. The discussion at the Italian restaurant had caused an appetite for pasta, and they decided to cook spaghetti. Lauren started the sauce.

Scott came up behind her.

She turned.

He looked into her eyes for a moment, then leaned forward and kissed her—softly, delicately. Her lips were soft, warm, accepting. She seemed to weaken under his touch, to want more. The kiss lengthened. After several kisses, she put her arms around him and nestled the side of her face against his chest. He held her, breathed in the sensual smell of her hair, then he lifted her head and kissed her again. When they finally separated, Scott went to the wine cabinet. He selected a Pinot Noir from the Russian River appellation and held up the bottle. "We need some of this for the sauce, and since it's open—"

"Yes," Lauren said with a smile.

There was a charming brightness in her face he had not seen before. Her new glow tugged at his heart as he took down two of his best oversized glasses.

Their dinner that night was a special experience, not because they did anything out of the ordinary, but because there was a new depth and richness to their relationship. It was as if someone had lifted an invisible barrier that had prevented Lauren's true feelings from surfacing. Scott realized she had changed while he was away. He doubted her anxiety of losing another loved one had completely vanished, but she seemed to be coming to terms with her fears. He thought she was an exceptional woman, and he knew he was deeply in love with her.

Over the next few days, their adoration for one another strengthened considerably. They increased the level of touching and intimacy, and Scott found it difficult to maintain a promise he had made with himself—a promise to not rush.

———

The following Thursday afternoon, Scott made his first trip to the Chicago Board of Trade since his return. He had important paperwork to attend to, but he had also noticed that a low-volume technical rally had occurred in soybeans over the last ten days. He thought the move lacked intensity and was unsustainable. He entered the trading pit and watched the market for a time, and then he established a short position in November soybeans by selling two hundred contracts. He spent an hour in the pit and was astonished to find himself somewhat bored. He placed a series of stop-loss orders to protect his position and left the floor.

To his amazement, his daily obsession with the markets had been altered, and he seemed unable to concentrate on anything but Lauren. He found this development not only surprising but also almost unbelievable. Potential danger might be responsible for his attitude, but he suspected that the real cause was Lauren. No woman had ever changed his thought processes so completely. He admitted to himself that he was profoundly in love for the first time in his life. There had been many infatuations and physical relationships but never anything like this.

He returned home and took a seat on the couch. Lauren was curled up in a chair reading a novel, but she occasionally looked toward him and smiled. He watched her and felt elated that she now shared some of his feelings.

She stood, crossed the floor, sat next to him, snuggled up, and rested her head on his shoulder. She tilted her head, and he pressed his lips to hers. The kisses quickly turned passionate.

Lauren moaned softly, and then whispered in his ear. "Let's make love."

Scott's body shouted yes but his mind told him to wait—just a little longer. He looked into her eyes. "Not yet, but soon."

She sat back with a curious expression.

"Don't get the wrong idea," he said. "I want to, but I want you to be sure."

"I'm sure."

"Well, there is this other reason."

"Do you have a rule book?"

He rubbed his forehead. "No, and you might think this is strange, but I've always believed it's better to savor anticipation for a while before doing something as wonderful as making love for the first time. It not only makes the lovemaking better, but anticipation, itself, is a remarkable experience too few people enjoy."

"It's also torture."

"Yes, but it's a wonderful kind of torture. You can make love with the same person many times over a period of days, weeks or years, but the anticipation before that first time only happens once. It's a fleeting thing never to be repeated. It takes over your mind at unexpected moments with an incredible intensity. It goes to your very core." He sensed she understood, but he wanted to make sure he had not hurt her feelings. "I'll tell you what. I'm going back to Washington Tuesday. Monday night you and I have a date. We'll go out to dinner, then come back and make love all night."

"I can't wait."

"I should warn you. I'm very big on foreplay"

"Thank God."

"There's more," Scott said. I want you to think about it every minute until then. I mean, *really* think about it." He gave her the most seductive look he could manage. "I should warn you. Your sensual thought process will go into overdrive, and you mind will start painting images at odd moments."

She nodded slowly, her mind processing. "All right, but we can touch can't we?"

Scott smiled. "Try and stop me."

———

The kissing and touching increased until Monday when they agreed to refrain until after their dinner, but that did not stop Scott from looking. Actually, it would have been hard not to notice Lauren. She had purposely dressed to stir his desire to a high level—and she was succeeding. She wore a low-cut, scoop neckline top without a bra underneath, and she was obviously wearing the tightest jeans she owned. But that wasn't all. She occasionally got as close to him as possible, without touching, and hinted of what was to come. Scott became delirious with lust and found himself suffering because of his own rules.

Lauren had purchased a new dress, and two hours before their date she disappeared. Fifteen minutes before their dinner reservation there was still no sign of her. Scott knew what she was doing, and it excited him. She was purposely taking her time, creating a mood of increasing sexual tension, and it caused him considerable discomfort. His body ached for sexual release. Testosterone at work.

She made her entrance after he called her for the third time. Scott was speechless. He had always thought her pretty, but, tonight, she was beautiful. Lauren stepped just inside the room, wearing an elegant black velvet evening gown with an off-shoulder design that dropped to a sweetheart neckline. Shirred sleeves emphasized the fitted bodice. Her auburn wig cascaded over bare shoulders.

She smiled coyly. "Do you like it?"

"I love it. You're absolutely beautiful." He walked over and started to kiss her, but she stopped him.

"Uh, uh . . . remember our arrangement. No touching until after dinner."

"What have I done?"

"You've created a monster."

Scott had picked his favorite restaurant, the Chateau de Montreuil. Though French in name, the restaurant provided a wide selection of both French and Italian cuisine, complimented by an exceptional wine list. Scott knew the owner well. Claude Brunet was a gentle-hearted man who was meticulous about details. He greeted them warmly before guiding them to one of his best tables.

Brunet made sure they were comfortable, then asked, "Can I get you anything?"

"Yes, Claude. Do you have any of that '85 BV Reserve left?"

"Mr. Quinn, I have a full case with your name marked on the side. If the president himself came in and ordered it, I'd tell him I was out."

Everyone laughed.

The bottle arrived, and Scott offered a toast to their future. The sounds in the room seemed to soften, to mellow as they sipped wine. They stared at one another and became immersed in a private world all their own. It seemed as though a curtain of privacy had been drawn around them, shielding them from the rest of the world.

They both had soup and were just starting their entrees. After only a few bites, Lauren leaned forward. "I have a few confessions to make."

Scott leaned over and put his hand over hers. "Oh? I'm listening."

Lauren looked him straight in the eye. "I've never wanted anyone so badly in my life. I've thought about you every second since we made this date." She raised her other arm and ran her index finger lightly along the back of his hand.

The words and her touch sent Scott's pulse into overdrive. "I feel exactly the same way. I told you waiting a little longer would be worth it."

"And it has," Lauren said. "But there's more. I've fallen in love with you."

Scott looked across the room and raised his arm. "Waiter, check please."

Lauren looked at him in surprise. "Scott, we've only eaten a small portion of our dinner."

He gave her the most seductive look he could muster. "Do you want to stay?"

"No," she said instantly.

Scott paid the bill and left the astounded waiter a sizable tip.

Although they had bent their rule by holding hands in the restaurant, they again refrained from touching during the drive home and the walk to the elevator. It was a strange, exquisite sort of torture. They stepped into the elevator and stood against opposite walls, expressing mutual love through their eyes. The elevator began to climb, and the outer world seemed to recede a little more with each passing floor.

An urgent lust grew within them, driven by the heightened anticipation of the last few days.

Lauren entered the apartment and went directly to the bedroom. She had previously prepared the room by pulling back the covers and placing two candles at the head of the bed, one on either side, which she now lit. She turned and watched Scott's expression as his gaze swept the room.

He smiled and then went to the opposite wall to adjust the lighting.

She unzipped her dress, timing her movements so that the garment fell to the floor just as Scott turned toward her. She wore a Victoria's Secret lace bra, panties, and matching garter belt. The undergarments were a stunning shade of deep amethyst.

He crossed the room, stopped before her, touched her cheek with the palm of his hand, then he kissed her softly. The intensity of the kissing increased. They necked feverishly as they undressed one another.

She moved onto the bed with Scott at her side. His mouth was everywhere—kissing her, caressing her eyelids, glancing over her neck, then running his tongue over her breasts. His hand inched down her body and moved slowly between her legs, teasingly at first, then with purpose.

She felt an exquisite ache spiraling up from deep inside. Caught in a whirl of sensations, Lauren caressed his body, then reached down and took him in her hand. She massaged him gently at first, and then matched her movements to his response. She felt buoyant, dizzy, her lust hot and demanding, driven by a depth of love and anticipation she had never experienced before.

At the moment of maximum need, Scott moved over her as if he had read her mind. He inched into her, barely penetrating and withdrew. With each measured stroke he gave a little more of himself until, with a sudden thrust, he gave her his full length. She gasped at the enormity of the pleasure sweeping through her. Their bodies moved and flowed together in mutual passion, reaching for the final, exquisite explosion of physical sensation. They rested for a time, then Lauren rolled on top and they made love again.

Afterward, they clung to each other, wrapped in a cocoon of love and tenderness.

CHAPTER 29

Scott and Lauren had no interest in getting up the next morning, but he had to catch a plane to Washington before noon. They made love, gently, comfortably, and then held each other as long as they could. They finally got out of bed and went into the kitchen.

They smiled at each other over breakfast and shared special looks that only lovers understand, but as Scott's departure time approached Lauren's demeanor changed, and she repeatedly expressed concern about him leaving. Several times, she made him promise not to take undue risks in Washington. Lauren held Scott's hand while they drove to Jason's apartment but she said little. They spent several minutes embracing and saying goodbye before Scott left for O'Hare Field.

Though he was preoccupied with thoughts of Lauren, Scott knew he had to change his focus. He had a position in soybeans, and it was imperative that he protect it. He entered the terminal, went to a phone, and called the trading floor. He had a small profit in his short position and wanted to retain the trade through the crop report, but he felt uncomfortable with a naked position.

Because of smaller reserves, he expected wheat to have greater relative strength than soybeans during the next several weeks. Anticipating this, he placed a buy order for an equivalent amount of wheat futures, thus creating an intercommodity spread. If the report contained a major surprise and soybeans rallied, his long position in wheat would probably offset much of his loss in soybeans. He received his confirmation and hurried through the terminal.

Wishing to avoid both Dulles and National, Scott again flew into Baltimore. He rented a car, drove to his motel, and checked in. He sat on the bed with his back against the headboard and thought about his plans for the next day. He had talked with Angela Williams several times to discuss tactics prior to the release of Wednesday's USDA Crop Report, and they had arranged a meeting to review the various details of their strategy; there was no room for error.

Angela and a male companion drove into the motel parking lot at precisely six o'clock. Scott met them outside. Angela got out and smiled broadly. "Scott, I'd like you to meet my uncle, Switch Williams."

Scott shook hands with a smiling man who appeared to be well over sixty. Switch was a lanky man who walked with a slight limp. Scott could only guess how the man got his name, but one thing seemed certain—members of the Williams family had a friendly air about them.

Switch entered the room and turned to Scott. "Aren't you going to ask me about my name? Everyone does."

"I was wondering about that."

Switch let out a high-pitched laugh but did not offer an explanation.

"He always does that," Angela said. "He'll bait you and leave you hanging. Actually, he used to switch shifts so much no one could keep track of him. He once disappeared for a whole week before anyone knew he was missing. Everyone thought he had switched to another shift."

"They owed me that week for over a year," Switch said. He laughed again. "That was before computers. Now they always know where I am."

Scott talked with Switch for a few minutes, then Angela broke in. "That's enough of that. I want to know if anything has happened between you and Lauren?" She inched closer. "Details, Mr. Quinn."

Scott grinned. "Well, I guess you could say we're an item."

Angela smiled and grabbed his hand with both of hers. "I'm happy for you. That poor girl's had a rough time, and I think you're just what she needs."

"No argument there."

Angela went to the table and laid out a floor plan of the Agriculture Department's campus. "I feel like a military officer planning for a war."

Scott leaned closer to the map. "In a certain way we are." He studied the building, giving special attention to the fourth and fifth floors and the exits. "We should be able to cover him with three people, but can I get some kind of internal communication device just in case?"

"Yes," Angela replied, "but you'll have to turn the volume down and keep it out of sight."

"No problem. How about my pass?"

"I'll have it for you in the morning, but there are certain places you can't go." Angela indicated the restricted areas on the map; then, she pointed to a red X. "That's Benson's office." She tapped the spot with her index finger as she spoke. "I'm still worried about something. What if he stays there and doesn't go out?"

"I think he will. Lauren heard him in the library on the fourth floor. If someone had delivered the information to his office, there wouldn't have been any reason for him to phone from someplace else."

"That makes sense," Angela said, "but I'm still concerned."

Switch ran his hand over a section of the map. "Is everybody going to be on the fourth floor?"

"Scott can't go to the fifth," Angela said; "so he and I will cover either end of the fourth. You stay by the elevator and follow Benson if he goes to another floor. Radio me so I can help you, but make sure you stay a good distance away from him."

"One other thing," Scott said. "Our goal is to find out *how* he gets the information. If we can't do that, the next best thing is to find out where he obtains the data or who delivers it."

Switch slammed his fist on the table. "I want to get that sonofabitch. Nobody has the right to steal this information, especially the Deputy Secretary of Agriculture."

Scott nodded. "If we all work together, maybe we'll catch him in the act."

"Anything else?" Angela asked.

Scott sighed. "Unfortunately, there is one other problem. Benson knows what I look like; so I'll have to keep a safe distance from him."

"He knows what you look like? How did that happen?"

"It's a long story, Angela. Let's just say I tried to shake his tree a little."

They reviewed details for another twenty minutes; then Angela and Switch left.

Scott spent another hour familiarizing himself with the floor plans. When he felt confident he knew every entrance, exit, and elevator, he put the plans aside with the intention of studying them again before going to bed.

He walked to a nearby restaurant for a quick meal, and then went to a phone booth to call Lauren. They discussed several things but mainly how much they missed each other. Scott was surprised when he realized they had been on the phone for nearly an hour. He couldn't think of a better way to run up a phone bill. After Lauren told him to be careful for the third time, he said goodbye, went to his room, checked the floor plans again, and turned in. Though the events of tomorrow would be intense, and possibly dangerous, he fell asleep amidst thoughts of Lauren.

———

Scott rose early the next morning amazed at how well he had slept the last few days. His occasional bouts with insomnia seemed to have vanished. Was it because of Lauren? He decided it must be. He drove to a designated location and met Angela. They reviewed their strategy and set a rendezvous time. According to plan, Switch had already stationed himself in position to watch Benson's office before the Deputy Secretary arrived. There were still three hours before the preliminary data would be compiled, but they meant to take no chances. After their meeting, they went in separate directions.

At eight-thirty, Scott went to a predetermined site and waited for Angela. Six minutes later, she came by, handed him a two-way radio, and kept walking. He then went to his designated station on the fourth floor. Angela had picked a waiting area where Scott could stay for an extended time without looking conspicuous. The plan called for him to go to a different location in ninety minutes.

He sat at the edge of the waiting area and acted as though he were reading the newspaper before an appointment. Forty-five minutes later, he got his first call on the radio. Switch reported that the subject was in the building but he had not left home base. At ten o'clock, Scott moved to his new position. Ten minutes later, he received another call from Switch. "Subject is heading north on four. Alpha to follow."

Scott rose and moved a few yards down the hall. Two minutes later, he saw a man that looked like Benson turn and go through a door.

Another radio call. This time from Angela. "Subject entered rest room. Will advise on departure."

It was Benson, but he was just going to the bathroom. Scott sat down and waited. A few minutes later, he received another call notifying him that the subject had returned to home base. Scott looked at his watch. Ten twenty-five.

When nothing had happened by eleven-thirty, Scott moved back to his first location as planned. He received another report from Angela at eleven forty-seven. "Subject leaving home base. Sierra to pick up."

Scott got up as soon as he heard his code name. He moved to a spot that afforded a view of the long hallway, yet kept him out of sight. His first glance located Benson about thirty yards away, coming straight toward him. He reported the subject's movements, stepped back a few yards, then observed Benson go through a door. Because it was nearing the time when they expected something to happen, Scott rushed to the door to record the room number. When he was fifteen feet away he stopped short—it was the men's room.

Expecting Benson to exit the room in a few minutes, Scott retreated and clicked on his radio. "Subject in bathroom near mid-point." He hit the off switch. *He must drink a lot coffee.*

A moment later, Benson came out and headed in the direction of his office. Scott reported his movements until he was out of sight. Ten minutes later, he received another report. This time he reacted with excitement. It was close to the expected time of an information transfer, and Benson had stayed in his office for only a few minutes. This might be it.

The message said the subject was headed toward Scott. He looked down the hall and spotted his target. He watched to see if anyone walked by and slipped something to Benson, but the Deputy Secretary turned and went through a door. Scott hurried to the location only to discover that Benson had gone into the same men's room. *What the hell?*

Something was wrong.

Scott walked far enough away to conceal himself, and then stopped, pondering his observations. What the hell was going on? He reported Benson's location on the radio and waited. A few seconds later, it struck him. "The bathroom! It's the goddamned bathroom."

CHAPTER 30

The more Scott thought about it, the more it made sense. The Deputy Secretary of Agriculture was not going into the bathroom to take a piss—he was going there to get the crop data. *But how?* After only two minutes, Benson left the men's room and headed toward his office. Scott immediately radioed a request to shift another person to his location.

Angela rushed down the hall. "What happened?"

"You won't believe it, but they somehow make the transfer in the bathroom."

"The bathroom?" She arched an eyebrow and tilted her head. Are you sure?"

"Ninety percent. We'll have to hope he didn't get the information this trip. I don't think he did because of his body language."

"Body language?"

"He looked frustrated." Scott gazed toward the men's room. "I can't imagine how they do it, but I'm going inside and try to find out. If you spot him, tap three times on the door."

"You sure about this?"

"I'm sure."

Scott entered the bathroom and breathed in the strong odor of disinfectant. He checked the stalls but there was no one else inside the room. He thought back about Benson's previous trips, aware that there had been no visible contact with anyone. How could they transfer the information? He analyzed the possibilities. Another person must somehow get the data to the bathroom; then Benson comes in and retrieves it, but how did they get the information out of lockup and why would they go here for the transfer? It would be much safer to use the privacy of the Deputy Secretary's office. It didn't make sense.

Because no one had been there when Benson went in, Scott wondered if his accomplice hid the information somewhere. He made a quick search of the trashcans and each stall but found nothing. His frustration growing, he nearly tore the towel dispenser apart.

Nothing.

He went to the door and called Angela. "I can't find anything. We can only hope he's going to make another trip. I'm going to wait in one of the stalls. When you see him coming down the hall tap three times, then get out of sight."

"This is really weird. I sure hope you're right about this."

"I do too, Angela. I do too."

Scott entered the stall at the far end, locked the door, pulled his pants down, and sat on the toilet seat. If someone was passing illegal information in the bathroom, they would be suspicious of everyone. He had to make it appear as though he was simply tending to personal business.

Three people came in over the next ten minutes, but not his target. Scott had previously made a note of Benson's clothes and each time someone came in, he bent down and looked at the color of the man's pants and shoes. None matched so far. After hearing three taps on the door, he bent down and saw a man enter wearing dark gray slacks and black shoes. This was it. He watched Benson enter a stall and get down on his hands and knees. Scott quickly raised his head to avoid being seen. A few seconds later, he barely heard one word.

"Damn." With that utterance, Benson left the bathroom.

Scott waited a moment, and then went to the door.

Angela rushed over. "What happened?"

"I think we're onto something."

Angela's face beamed with intensity. "This is getting interesting."

He put his hand on her shoulder. "I'm going to check it out. Remember, I need as much warning as you can give me."

"You got it."

Scott hurried back inside, entered the second stall and started to search when he realized that Benson had been in the third stall. Cursing himself, he moved to the next toilet, went in and shut the door. He looked around in a random manner, not sure what he should be looking for, but he saw nothing unusual. Since Benson had gotten down on his hands and knees, Scott did the same and he began a careful search. There was nothing on the right side of the toilet. He switched to the left and looked for a full minute before he saw it. A single tile was slightly out of line with the others. He grabbed the edge with his fingers and pulled back. The tile came out from the wall. He peered in and saw a vertical pipe with a cap on the bottom. The pipe had a notch cut out to allow access.

"My God! Brilliant—fucking brilliant."

He stuck two fingers in and moved them around. Empty. He thought back to Benson's actions in the stall. He distinctly remembered him saying, "Damn." Benson would not have said that if things had gone as planned. Had he been upset because the message had not yet arrived? Scott could think of no other answer. He stood and thought a moment, trying to decide on his next action when he heard a strange noise.

Thunk!

He bent down and looked into the pipe. Something had fallen from above, but what? He reached in and grabbed the small object, pulled it out, and opened his hand. An eraser, a simple, common, ordinary eraser. *What the hell?*

It didn't make sense, but when he turned over the eraser everything came into focus. There was a large -5 written in black ink on the other side. It was obviously a code but what did it mean? If a minus was used, Scott thought their system must also include a plus value. But how high did the numbers go? While Scott tried to figure out the code, three taps sounded at the door.

"Shit!"

His mind raced, frantically searching for a course of action. Suddenly, he locked onto a single thought—alter the number. But how? He reached into his coat pocket, withdrew a pen, and started to make the change but realized his pen was blue. He jumped up, ran to the door, and peeked out. Angela was about fifteen feet away.

He looked the other way. Benson was still about forty yards away, but they could not afford to raise his suspicions. He took a chance and called in a low voice. "Angela."

She kept walking.

"Angela."

She turned and stared at him with a puzzled expression.

He signaled to her. When she was a few feet away he said, "A black pen. I need a black pen."

She reached into a pocket and pulled out two pens. He grabbed them and glanced down the hall. Benson had closed to within twenty-five yards. Scott ran back to the stall and looked at the pens. One was blue, the other black. He pulled out a piece of paper, scribbled to get the ink flowing and check the color, then picked up the eraser.

How should he change the number? Fighting off indecision, he took the pen and made a stroke through the minus sign, changing the number from -5 to +5. He shoved the eraser back in the pipe and replaced the tile, but when he started to get up the tile fell out. He had moved too quickly and failed to check the fit. He carefully adjusted the tile and shoved it back in place.

He heard footsteps by the door.

Fuck.

He lay on his back and slid under the sidewall to the next stall, then slid under another to get two stalls away. He got up, dropped his pants, and sat on the toilet.

Thoughts ricocheted wildly through his mind.

The door on the third stall opened and closed. Scott wanted to bend down and watch but he thought it too risky. He waited, then he heard an expression of disbelief.

"My God!" It was Benson's voice.

Scott heard the stall door slam, followed by the sound of someone rushing from the bathroom. He checked his watch and made a mental note of the exact time Benson got the eraser. Ten after one. Grain futures would be open for another hour and five minutes. He waited a few seconds, then headed toward the door but stopped when he heard three taps. He peeked out and saw Angela.

She stepped in front of him. "He ran out of here like he'd been shot from a cannon. What happened?"

"You won't believe it, but first let's get away from here."

Angela radioed Switch to meet them; then they went to a remote area on the first floor and waited. A few minutes later Switch came running up the hall. The slight limp in his gait made it look as though one leg was shorter than the other, but it didn't seem to hamper his speed. At five yards, he waved one arm and yelled, "You should have seen him. Good lord, I never saw a Deputy

Secretary of Agriculture move so fast in all my life. What the hell happened?"

Scott looked into the eager face. "You know what your nick-name is? Well, that's what we did to him."

"A switch. You pulled a goddamned switch on him?"

"I think so," Scott said. "I don't know their code but there's a good chance we just put their ass in a sling."

Switch laughed. "Mr. Quinn, you're welcome around here anytime. You really know how to liven things up." Switch rubbed his chin. "How'd you do it?"

Scott explained finding the tile in the bathroom and how he changed the eraser.

They laughed for a moment, then Angela turned serious. "You do know I'll have to report this."

"I know," Scott said, thinking ahead as he spoke. "How would your department normally handle this?"

"We can't prove anyone committed a crime unless we catch them in the act, so there's nothing we can do until the next report."

"Angela," Scott said, his right hand on her shoulder. "I need you to do me a big favor. Can you hold off telling your people for a while? I'm going to try to discover who's behind this whole thing. If I don't, Lauren will always be in danger."

She thought a few seconds, obviously weighing options, and then said, "There's nothing we can do until the next crop report and that's a month from now. I really shouldn't but I could hold off until about three days before then. Will that do?"

"It'll have to," Scott said, looking down the hall, his mind working forward in time. "I've got to get back to Chicago." He thanked them as they walked to the exit.

When he said goodbye, Switch vigorously shook his hand, and Angela gave him a hug. He started outside but suddenly stepped back.

"What's wrong?" Angela asked.

"Out there, across the lot. See that short fellow standing next to the blue car? He's one of the men who shot Lauren's roommate and tried to kill her at the restaurant. I don't know what he's doing here, but—." Scott stopped in mid-sentence, then said, "Of course, it's report day. They're probably keeping an eye on Benson." Scott reached into his pocket, took out his keys, and handed them to Switch. "Is there another exit on the other side?"

"Sure."

"Good. Switch, you stay here. Angela and I will go to the other exit. If it looks clear we'll radio you, then you get my car." Scott pointed across the lot. "You see that brown panel truck next to the walkway?"

Switch turned his head. "Let's see. Yeah, I've got it."

"Okay, there's a white Buick Regal next to it. That's my rental. Drive it around the building. We'll be waiting."

Switch's eyes sparkled as he opened the door. "Done."

They walked to the other side of the building and looked through the glass, scanning the area. After a moment, Scott said, "I don't see anything suspicious. I think we're okay."

Angela radioed Switch to bring the car.

A few minutes passed, then his car came around the corner and stopped as close to the building as possible. Scott checked the area again. "I'll have to go across that open stretch, but I've got no choice." He bent over and kissed Angela on the cheek. "Thanks for your help." He opened the door. "And cross your fingers."

Scott walked briskly, glancing from side to side, but it appeared safe. He reached his car and extended his hand to Switch who beamed with pride. Within minutes, Scott was safely on the parkway. He repeatedly checked the rearview mirror but saw no evidence of a vehicle following him. He drove to the motel and checked out. He then stopped at a phone booth and called Lauren, but he had only enough time to make sure she was safe, give her his flight information, and tell her how much he loved her.

He got back in the car and headed for the airport, his mind racing ahead in time, wondering what would happen next.

CHAPTER 31

On the plane, Scott replayed his incredible experience at the Department of Agriculture. His thoughts seemed unusually volatile as his mind shuffled the implications of his actions. What if his strategy backfired and tipped them off? Maybe he should not have taken the chance. There was no way of knowing, but he found himself unable to shake his doubts. He could only hope that his hasty alteration of the code on the eraser fell within the parameters used in the scheme.

It was not until the plane was on its approach to Chicago that he thought about his spread position of long wheat and short soybeans. It seemed incomprehensible that he had not considered it sooner. He had no idea what the report meant to him, because he could only speculate about the coded eraser. The minus sign could mean to sell, but it could also indicate a smaller yield than expected. That meant the report might be bullish. There was no way of knowing what the number meant until he saw the actual report—it could go either way.

———

Lauren and Jason were waiting at Scott's apartment. He had barely gone through the door when Lauren embraced him. After separating, Scott kept his arm around her and turned to Jason. "How'd the crop report come out?"

"Record yields are predicted for soybeans. It was very bearish."

Scott threw a fist in the air. "Perfect!"

"You must be short soybeans," Jason said.

"I'm short beans and long wheat, but that's not the best part."

Jason cocked his head to one side. "What do you mean?"

"We found out how they get the information out of the lockup, and I altered the numbers without them knowing. I think whoever is behind this bought a lot of soybean contracts before the close. If I'm right, he probably had to change his underwear when he saw the report."

Scott spent the next thirty minutes giving details of the events in the Agriculture Building, and repeatedly answered questions about changing the coded eraser.

Jason shook his head and said, "That's absolutely the most incredible story I've ever heard. Do you realize how much money they could make with a set up like that?"

"A fortune," Scott said, "but do you know what I'd really like to find out?"

"Yeah, who's behind it?"

"Exactly. And I'd like to see his face when soybeans open tomorrow morning."

"So would I," Lauren said.

"Unfortunately, we don't know who he is," Scott said, "but I'll tell you one thing. I'm going to be in the soybean pit tomorrow morning. Watching beans crash will be the next best thing."

"I want to go," Lauren said. "Can I get on the floor?"

"I can get you a visitor's pass," Jason said, "but—"

"I don't like it," Scott interrupted.

"This is important to me," Lauren said. "I want to be there."

Scott saw the determination in her face. "All right, but on two conditions."

"Name them."

"You've got to disguise yourself, and we can only stay for the first hour. We have to think of your safety."

Lauren beamed. "You've got a deal."

"Hell," Jason said, "We'll go to the floor together; then we'll all go out to lunch and celebrate."

"We're assuming beans will go down," Scott said.

"Don't worry about that," Jason replied. "I analyzed the report, and I expect soybeans to open sharply lower. I'd be shocked if it's not limit down."

They talked until Jason left. After the door closed, Scott and Lauren stared at each other, but it was a different kind of look than they shared when he first came into the apartment. Scott took Lauren's hand and moved toward the hallway. When they reached the bedroom door, he stopped and kissed her. Lauren then took his hand and moved toward the bed. She turned and put her arms around his neck and kissed him. After a moment, her hands moved to his belt.

———

Scott was not surprised to see Lauren up early the next morning. She had repeatedly expressed excitement about going to the trading floor, but he also knew she was pleased to be going anywhere. She had been out for occasional rides and short walks, but, due to necessity, she had spent most of her time indoors. Scott checked the Beretta Tuck had sent him and stuck it under his belt. He knew he could not take the gun onto the exchange floor, but he could take it to his office, lock it in his desk, and retrieve it before leaving the building.

They arrived at Scott's office at eight-thirty as previously arranged. That gave them an hour before the grain markets opened.

Jason greeted them. "Did you see the crop report?"

"Yes, and I think you're right. November should open sharply lower."

Jason nodded. "We need to take Lauren down to get her visitor's pass. We don't want to miss the opening."

Scott locked the Beretta in his desk and extended his arm toward Lauren. "Are you ready?"

"Excited, actually," she said as they walked to the door.

They obtained Lauren's badge and went to the trading floor. Scott answered several questions about procedures and explained how most orders came to the floor electronically or by phone.

Lauren scanned the floor. "Then they're sent to the pit by runners."

Scott nodded. "And by hand signals."

"You mean someone could take an order by phone, then signal the pit for execution in practically the same instant?"

"Yes, but electronic trading will change everything someday."

They walked to a spot about thirty feet from the soybean pit and stopped. Conversing was still easy because the noise associated with trading had yet to begin.

Lauren looked around with obvious interest. "How are the orders executed in the pit?"

"Good question. Specific rules require trading to be conducted in an open auction style," Scott said. "Traders stand on certain steps according to the month they wish to trade and shout out prices."

"But I've heard it gets so noisy you can't always hear each other."

"That's right. You'll see that happen right after the opening bell. That's why we also use hand signals to communicate both price and quantity."

An increasing number of traders filtered into the pit.

Scott glanced at the clock. "All right, it's time to get in there." He leaned and spoke directly in Lauren's ear. "Stick right next to me. No matter what."

"Don't worry."

When the opening bell sounded, the eerie calm exploded in a frenzy of waving, jostling, and shouting. With the market going in his favor, Scott did not expect to make any trades, but he watched the action closely. The opening range, for soybeans, was down between twenty-six cents and the thirty-cent limit. The first trades, after the opening, were down the limit.

Scott checked the action, but he also watched Lauren. Clearly, she was fascinated by the scene around her. He continued to monitor both soybeans and wheat until it seemed fairly certain that beans would remain limit down for the entire session. Bids were almost non-existent and the pool of sellers continued to grow.

He spoke in Lauren's ear. "Follow me." They went to the wheat pit. Scott was gratified that wheat had dropped only six and a half cents. He checked the bid, then yelled out his offer, and, simultaneously, gave a series of hand signals. He sold his entire position in a matter of seconds. He made trade notations on a card.

They left and walked toward the soybean pit. "I lost six and a half cents in wheat, but I've got a thirty-cent profit in my short position in soybeans. Unless the market changes, I'll hold that overnight."

While they were talking, Jason joined them. "Well, I'd say your boy took it in the ass today." He glanced at Lauren. "Ah, sorry about the language."

"No problem," Lauren said. "That's exactly where I wanted him to take it."

They laughed.

"Even if he wanted to get out," Scott said, "the market wouldn't have let him. He probably has a big position, and there just aren't any bids. I'd say he's locked in and suffering this very second."

"No doubt about it," Jason replied.

"This is the best I've felt in a long time," Lauren said. "I'm ready for that lunch and maybe a glass of wine."

Scott took Lauren's hand as he spoke to Jason. "We're going up to the office, but we'll meet you at the restaurant in forty-five minutes."

———

After a pleasant lunch, Scott and Lauren walked to a nearby hotel. He wanted to call Hayden Benson, but he did not want to use the phone in his apartment. They entered the lobby and went directly to the pay phones. Before phoning Benson, he called the trading floor and verified that soybeans were still down the limit. He then dialed the Agriculture Department and found out that the Deputy Secretary was ill and would not be in today.

While retrieving Benson's home number from his wallet, he became convinced the Deputy Secretary was not sick—he was starting to crack. He had put considerable pressure on Benson, and Scott believed his efforts were having a strong impact. His mind churned with thoughts when Benson answered the phone.

"This is Jim Carpenter. If you hang up, I'll go to the press."

Silence.

"Mr. Benson, are you there?"

"Yes. . . . I'm here." His voice wavered. "What do you want?"

"You know why I called. I want the name of the person who's blackmailing you."

"I—I can't give you his name. I told you he'd kill me if I did."

Scott had anticipated his answer and quickly replied, "The way I figure it, Mr. Benson, you're in a hell of a mess either way. I told you I'd release certain information to the newspapers, and I will. Now give me the damn name."

Benson did not utter a word, but Scott could sense his pain. It was a moment when silence said everything. The man was obviously immersed in agony.

"Mr. Benson, I'm going to ask you one more time. If you don't tell me, I'm going to the press."

"Good Lord, man, you can't do that. I—I'll be ruined."

"You've got ten seconds."

"But I can't tell you. If I did, Mer—" Benson stopped short.

"Is that part of his name? What's the rest of it? Mer what?"

"Oh, God. . . . I can't talk anymore. I just can't say any more." The line went dead.

He's on the edge. Press him. Scott dialed the number again. By the fifth ring, there was no answer. He listened to the drone of the rings, one after another, but it became obvious that Benson was not going to pick up the phone. Scott hung up and slammed the palm of his hand against the wall. He thought about redialing but knew it was useless and stepped out of the booth.

Lauren rushed to his side. "What happened?"

"He told me part of the name but didn't finish. Mer something. What could that stand for?"

"Merrill?"

"Maybe," Scott said. "Let's go back to the apartment and make a list of the possibilities. Maybe we'll get lucky."

When they reached the apartment, Scott pulled out a yellow pad and began jotting down names. "All right, so far we've got Merrill, Merlin, and Meredith. There has to be more than that. Let's check the phone book."

"How about Merritt?" Lauren said.

Scott started to write down the name when he suddenly jumped up. "Holy shit!" He rushed down the hall and into his office.

Lauren was right behind him. "What? What is it?"

"I need that trading report Jason gave us. The one we worked on until three in the morning." Scott searched a stack of papers near his printer. "Here it is." Lauren stood next to him as he flipped through the pages, found the one he wanted and ran his finger down the sheet until it stopped by a name.

"Merrick—Victor Merrick."

CHAPTER 32

Cade, the internationally feared assassin, moved in a world of secrecy, and only one person had ever learned Cade's true identity. By coincidence, Joseph Mancuso discovered that Cade was actually a woman whose most recent alias was Zina Martell. Everyone assumed they had to negotiate with Zina because Cade wanted to keep his identity secret. In the beginning, the original Cade, Larry Pendergrass, had operated in exactly that manner. Zina had been his assistant.

But Pendergrass had been dead for eight years. Until Mancuso discovered the truth, no one suspected that Zina had taken the assassin's place, and that Cade and Zina Martell were the same person. The first two years had gone smoothly for Zina and Larry Pendergrass. After a torrid romance, they had been married during a holiday in Las Vegas. Trouble began six months later when Zina discovered that Pendergrass was the type of man who liked to spread his seed among many women.

She caught him twice, and each time he had promised it would never happen again. The second occurrence had put Zina under a tremendous strain, and she gradually became obsessed with his promiscuity. She vowed she would never again share her lover with another woman.

The third incident pushed Zina over the edge. When she caught Pendergrass in bed with a hard-looking blonde, she promptly emptied her pistol into their naked bodies. With the gun dangling from her hand, she stared at her blood-soaked lover and knew that her attitude toward men had changed forever. A few days later, Zina decided to assume Cade's identity. After all, he had taught her everything he knew, and she had been an exceptional student. Moreover, being female was a distinct advantage because she could get closer to her targets than men could.

Excellent hand-eye coordination combined with continual practice brought her expertise with a rifle to a world-class level. She stayed current with the latest electronic surveillance equipment, and she had developed special techniques for her needs. Zina became so good that Cade's reputation soared to new heights and her personal wealth grew rapidly. In the next few years, she put all of her time and passion into two things: she learned everything she could about killing—and fine art.

Joseph Mancuso had hired Cade and accidentally discovered her identity. Though she had worked for Mancuso on two different occasions, she detested him. True, she was an assassin, but he was nothing more than a leech that preyed on the weak. Besides, she thought, he was a man, and the only men she liked were dead artists—the great masters in particular.

Zina knew her longevity depended on keeping her identity a secret. It became a simple business decision—Mancuso had to die. The thought of having sex with him repelled her, but it was the only way she could get Mancuso alone. She purposely succumbed to his incessant advances and quickly found herself in his bed. After an unpleasant sexual marathon, Mancuso finally rolled over, closed his eyes, and drifted off to sleep while Zina softly stroked his chest. When his breathing deepened, she pulled a silencer-equipped pistol from her handbag. Fifteen minutes after the last orgasm he would ever have, Joseph Mancuso took a single bullet in his left temple.

Mancuso's death had occurred five years ago, and Cade dropped from sight three years later. With the money Zina had accumulated, she moved to a beachfront home in Florida and pursued her dream of collecting great works of art. She searched the world for paintings, making impressive additions to her collection.

She did well during the surge in art prices, but she had borrowed excessively for her larger purchases, which caused her to become overextended when the price of world art topped out. In recent years, Japanese buyers had virtually taken over the important auctions and had pushed impressionist's masterpieces to unsustainable levels. The natural laws in all markets have certain characteristics that are equivalent to those of a rubber band. When prices and euphoria reach extreme levels, the market snaps. Thus, fine art prices corrected sharply. The worsening conditions made it necessary for Zina to seek new income, and she soon found herself back in the world of marketing death. Cade had returned.

She had completed her first hit four months ago and would eliminate her next victim today. She was crouched in a wooded area, outside of London, waiting for her target. After the kill, she would fly to Washington, D.C. to meet a new client named Victor Merrick, and finalize the details of her next contract.

It was still dark, but the first hint of light showed in the eastern sky. Zina opened a narrow case and removed two pieces of a specially designed rifle. She screwed the sections together, loaded the weapon, adjusted the scope, and waited.

After three weeks of stalking Perry Clayton, she knew he stayed at his country estate from Thursday evening through Monday morning and that he rode his prized stallion every morning except

Sunday. She even knew the name of his horse: Trojan. Zina discovered that he always used one of two routes, and she had taken great care to locate a position that gave her a good firing angle for either trail, yet one that provided good cover and a safe avenue for escape.

Just as the edge of the sun broke above the horizon, she saw movement around the stable. She focused her binoculars on a single individual. It was Clayton. She did not care who he was or what he had done; it didn't matter. Zina felt her activities were business transactions, and she never experienced remorse. It would be the same today. Twenty minutes later, she raised her rifle and sighted on a turn in the trail. Clayton had disappeared behind a small knoll, but she knew he would come back into view in less than a minute.

She waited.

After a few seconds, he came around the bend.

She looked through the scope, controlled her breathing, and sighted on his heart. Five seconds later, she pulled the trigger with delicate, deadly precision.

The roar of the gun shattered the still morning air.

Perry Clayton fell heavily to the ground.

She looked through the scope for any sign of life. He was probably dead, but she methodically placed two more bullets into the limp body. In swift movements, she put away the gun, moved down a small slope, and disappeared into the woods.

Three hours later, she used one of her many aliases to board a flight bound for Washington, D.C. She had discarded her blonde wig and her natural, black hair was twisted into a roll and pinned at the back of her head. She had changed into a conservative business suit and carried a small briefcase. Her passport was a perfect imitation of the official document. When Cade was safely on the plane, the assassin's mysterious identity disappeared and the persona of Zina Martell reappeared. She felt the same after every killing she forgot about it. The man was dead, she had been paid, and she was about to leave the country.

After the plane had reached cruising altitude, she enjoyed a glass of Puligny-Montrachet and perused the latest issue of *Fine Art Magazine.*

CHAPTER 33

Victor Merrick's first reaction to the crop production report had been one of total disbelief, but after confirming the data, his volatile temper erupted. He slammed down the phone, yanked it off his desk, threw it across the room, and then strode about his office, the veins in his forehead pulsing with fury. At the height of his tantrum, he kicked a chair, sending it skidding across the floor. It was several minutes before his fury diminished, which was then replaced by another emotion—anguish. He went back to his desk, slumped into his chair, and stared at his computer. His eyes fixed on large, bold, caps at the top of the page:

RECORD YIELDS PREDICTED FOR SOYBEANS

After Hayden Benson had reported a + 5 rating, Merrick placed large buy orders for his various accounts. The new position had been his largest yet, and he had anticipated huge profits when trading opened. With the release of the report, he now expected heavy loses. How the fuck did this happen? He felt an insidious darkness creeping over his mind.

Merrick went directly home and opened a bottle of scotch. He had just finished his fifth drink when his current mistress came in. Trisha Baldwin had been with him for seven months—nearly a record.

She spoke to him but received no answer. She tried again. "Looks like you had a bad day, honey. I know just what you need." She unbuttoned her blouse and threw it on a chair.

He watched as she unfastened her skirt and let it drop to the floor. He finished his drink and continued staring while she walked toward him. His alcohol distorted vision seemed to amplify the contrast between her red hair and milky skin, and it created a powerful urge. He took her on the floor, quickly, roughly, satisfying only himself. When it was over, he went back to his scotch and drank steadily.

At eleven-thirty, Trisha tried to get him to stop drinking and go to bed, but she received the back of his hand for her efforts. The blow produced a large welt over her left eye. Very early in the morning, he passed out on the couch. A bottle of Scotch fell from his hand, causing some of the remaining contents to gurgle onto the carpet.

———

Merrick woke at eight fifty-five the next morning. His eyes hurt, his mouth was dry, his tongue tasted like a dirty sock, and his head throbbed—it was a bitch of a hangover. He lay there for a few minutes, then he got up and staggered into the kitchen, rubbing his eyes as he went. He reached for a glass and saw the clock—five after nine.

"Jesus!"

It would be impossible to get to Burgess Grain in twenty-five minutes. He walked to his office and turned on his quote machine.

The dollar was down. That should help a little. He switched to a review of the crop report, scanned the summary, and then yelled, "Shit!"

After further study, analysts proclaimed that the previous day's report was even more bearish than they had first thought. State after state had predicted increased yields. He grabbed the phone and dialed his broker. A voice answered. "Floor."

"This is Victor Merrick. Let me talk to Mort."

"He was here a minute ago. Hold on a sec—" There was a pause. "I don't see him. You want him to call you back?"

"Hell no. This is important. I'll hold until you find him."

"Sure, Mr. Merrick. I'll be right back."

Two minutes went by, then a voice said, "This is Mort."

"Merrick. What's the opening call?"

"Jeez, Victor. It looks weak as hell. I wouldn't be surprised to see a limit move on the first tick."

Merrick expected as much, but he was still shaken. He rubbed his forehead, hoping to assuage the hangover that had rendered him lightheaded and dizzy. He tried to clear his thoughts and make a decision, but anguish corrupted logic.

The voice brought him back. "Victor?"

"What do you think I should do?"

"There's only one thing to do. You've got to put in market orders and hope you can get out before it hits limit."

"I can't do that."

"Well, you could hold on and hope for a decent rally, but it might take weeks. If it keeps going down, you'll have to put up a ton of margin."

Merrick's mind went blank. He had not planned for anything like this. He thought for a moment and realized he did not have the funds to hold on. In an uneven voice, he spoke to the broker. "Sell me out."

"I'll try, but I can't promise anything."

"Shut the fuck up and do it."

He slammed down the phone and switched to a display that would show the opening prices for soybeans. For the next fourteen minutes, he sat motionless, staring at the screen, his mind commingling thoughts of anguish and revenge.

The first quotes appeared at nine thirty-one. Old crop beans opened down sharply but not quite the limit. He clung to hope until he saw new crop contracts open down the limit. Within seconds, all months rested at limit down. Merrick glared at the unchanging prices for the next half hour. He was attempting to ease his hangover and his misery with a beer when the telephone rang.

"It's Mort. I only got about 10 percent of your order filled. It looks bad. I think it's going to stay locked limit down all day."

Merrick yelled into the phone. "Thanks for nothing." He hung up and stared at the screen a moment, then said aloud, "Fuck me." He finished his beer and threw the empty can across the room. A sinister mood had swept over Merrick when he first saw the crop report. As time passed, malevolent thoughts took hold and expanded. He rose, started to leave the room, but stopped in mid-stride. Who was responsible for his losses? Obviously, someone had screwed up by reporting the wrong number. His first thought was to kill whoever was to blame, but he could not afford to lose Hayden Benson, his key to future profits.

Merrick went back to his desk and dialed Billy's apartment. He glanced at his calendar while he waited. It was Thursday, and his soybean position required that he stay in town on Friday. He had scheduled his meeting with Cade for Sunday, and he decided to fly to Washington on Saturday and find out who was to blame.

Receiving no answer, he hung up and left his office. When he reached the hall, he saw Trisha coming out of the bathroom. She had just finished taking a shower and had a towel wrapped around her. He had forgotten about striking her until he saw the welt above her eye. What the hell, he thought, that's what she gets paid for.

Merrick walked over and yanked the towel from her. He had a bad case of hangover hornies. Sex would temporarily ease the aches in his mind and body.

She turned away and said, "Stop it, Victor. I'm mad at you."

"Get in the bedroom. When we finish, I'll give you a few hundred bucks so you can go out and buy some new clothes."

"I'm not a whore. You've got to quit treating me like one."

"You're a whore, all right, and a damn good one. But if you don't like it around here, you can always leave."

She was silent for a few seconds, then she dropped to her knees and began to unfasten his belt.

A thin smile crossed his lips.

She was a whore, and they both knew it.

———

When Merrick instructed his broker to "sell at the market," his orders had been entered on an open order basis, valid until filled or canceled—whichever came first. Friday morning soybeans opened down the limit again. Merrick received a large margin call and had to dig into corporate funds to meet the cash demand. The rage that had swept through him the previous two days shifted to agony. Though his controller complained, Merrick diverted monies slated for accounts payable to meet his margin calls. The financial condition of Burgess Grain tumbled to new lows.

A few minutes before Friday's close, November soybeans came off limit down for a few seconds. Merrick's broker was able to sell a substantial number of contracts, but he still held thirty percent of his original position.

Saturday morning, he took a flight to the National Airport in Washington. Being spared from another day of collapsing prices allowed Merrick to concentrate on what had gone wrong. He was determined to find out who had screwed up. It might not happen immediately, but the guilty party would eventually pay a high price. Merrick called Billy and instructed him to gather everyone at Shannon's apartment before he arrived. He specifically demanded that Hayden Benson and Kenneth Lindsay be present. They were the only two people who had touched the eraser, and one of them had obviously made the error.

Merrick flew to Washington, drove to the apartment, walked in, and confronted Benson. He grabbed the shaken man by his lapel and jerked him out of his chair. "I should stick a gun in your mouth and pull the fucking trigger."

Fright showed in Benson's eyes. He opened his mouth to answer, but no words came. A string of spittle dribbled down his chin.

Merrick slammed him back into the chair. "What the hell happened?"

Benson straightened his shirt and dabbed at his chin. "The eraser said +5. That's what I reported."

"I don't believe you."

"I—I swear it, Victor. I'm telling you the truth." Benson suddenly jumped up and shoved a hand in his right pocket. "Here! I brought it with me." He pulled out the eraser and turned it over. "See, right here. A +5, just like I said."

"Do you think I'm an idiot? You could have bought an eraser and put any number on it."

"But it's not my writing. It's Lindsay's. See, he always crosses the top of his fives like a T."

Merrick looked at the eraser. The top of the five had been crossed like the letter T, but that did not prove Lindsay made the error. Still, it could have been Lindsay's fault.

Lindsay said, "I gave the report a -5, and that's what I wrote on the eraser. I swear to God."

Merrick glanced at the eraser, then at Lindsay. "Even if you did screw up, you'd deny it."

"I always check the number twice before I put the eraser in the pipe."

Merrick thought about what the two men had said and realized there was no way of knowing the truth, though he began to suspect Lindsay had made the error. He weighed the incident against the future profit potential and knew he had to control his anger. He wanted revenge, but he desperately needed the two men. He shifted his stare from one to the other and warned that he would cut out the heart of the next person who made a mistake. He wanted to plant the seeds of fear in their minds, and he could tell by their faces he had succeeded.

Merrick spent the night with Shannon Peterson. The woman's sexual prowess continued to amaze him, but it was her beauty that made him think about a more permanent relationship. He was still certain he would eventually amass huge profits and eliminate the need for Hayden Benson. He could then move Shannon to Chicago and screw her brains out whenever he had the urge.

———

The next morning, Merrick concentrated on his immediate problem. He had experienced a major setback. The continued availability of report information guaranteed huge profits over time, but only if Lauren Chandler was found and killed. Her knowledge was a constant threat.

His meeting with Cade's assistant was set for one o'clock. He wanted to talk directly with the assassin, but he had repeatedly been told that all negotiations went through Zina Martell. Merrick had agreed because of Cade's exceptional reputation for quick success. He needed the best.

At one o'clock, he took Billy and Ray Lisowski to the designated meeting site near the Washington Monument. He had previously given his description to Zina, and was told she would approach him when it appeared safe. After waiting for over thirty minutes, Merrick's thinning patience began to slide toward anger. He rose from the bench and began pacing about the area. He went about thirty feet and turned to walk back. A woman stood where no one had been only seconds before, and he wondered how she had gotten so close without him seeing her. She was a handsome woman with shoulder length, black hair that complimented her olive skin. He guessed her age at about thirty-five.

She spoke as he approached. "Mr. Merrick, I'm Zina Martell." Her voice had a low, melodic tone.

"I should have known Cade would work with a beautiful woman."

"Let's skip the bullshit and get down to business." Her voice was direct, controlled. "I believe you have a job for us."

Instead of being put off, Merrick appreciated the woman's attitude. The sooner he had a contract with Cade, the sooner he could eliminate Lauren Chandler. He nodded. "I believe our mutual friend told you what I need?"

"You want him to locate two people and take them out."

"I need it done right away."

"We'll get to that, but first we need to discuss the payment. Did you bring half of the fee our friend mentioned?"

Merrick nodded and pulled out two thick envelopes.

She put the money in her bag. "I'll need everything you've got on the two men."

"Actually, it's a man and a woman."

Zina started to retrieve a small notebook from her purse, but stopped suddenly. "Cade doesn't kill women."

"What? What do you mean he doesn't kill women? That's absurd."

"We've nothing to talk about." She returned the money, turned, and started to walk away.

"Wait!" Merrick struggled for a solution as he hurried to catch her. "We can still work this out."

She kept walking.

He *had* to have Cade's help. An idea struck. "Wait, hear me out."

She stopped and turned. "You've got thirty seconds."

"Tell Cade to find them and kill the man; then, let me know where the woman is. I'll have my people take care of her. Hell, I'll even pay you the full rate for both."

Zina looked at Merrick, hesitated, and then said, "Done."

"Don't you have to call Cade on this?"

"No," Zina replied. "I know his demands. He lets me negotiate as I see fit." She pulled out her notebook. "I need details."

With Billy's help, Merrick gave Zina all the information available on Lauren Chandler, including their belief that she was in hiding with an unknown man.

"We've got a good picture," Billy said. He handed her the photograph he took from Lauren's apartment.

Zina looked at the photo. "This helps, but she probably doesn't look like that anymore."

"I guess she would change her appearance," Merrick said.

"Unless she's an idiot," Zina replied.

"How?" Billy asked.

"If I were her, I'd cut my hair and bleach it, then buy a couple of wigs, sunglasses, and different makeup. What else have you got on her?"

Billy provided what little he knew.

Zina scribbled in her notebook, and then looked up. "Do you know anything about the man?"

"Part of his name but that's all."

"What is it?"

"His first name is Scott. The first initial of his last name is Q."

Zina wrote the name in her book and closed it. "This will be easier than I thought. There's a good chance I can find them within ten days."

"How are you going to do that?" Billy said in a tone of disbelief.

"Unless they're hiding in some swamp in Louisiana, I'll find them." She glanced at Merrick. "I'll need access to that Agriculture official you mentioned. I think his name was Hayden Benson."

Merrick nodded. "Sure, but I don't see how he can help."

"He may be the key to the whole thing." Zina took the envelopes from Merrick. "They're as good as dead."

CHAPTER 34

Scott did not get to sleep until a little before two o'clock, then he had slept for only four hours. Since he had seen Victor Merrick's name on the trading report, he had thought of little else. There was no way to be certain Merrick was the key figure behind the crop report scheme, but it made sense. Occasionally, he had seen Merrick on the floor of the Chicago Board of Trade and he recalled his initial impressions of the president of Burgess Grain. He remembered Merrick as loud, brash, and egotistical. Scott had disliked him immediately.

But there was one glaring inconsistency. He had heard rumors of financial problems at Burgess, and he wondered how a man with advance knowledge of crop reports could be anything but a huge financial success. Although it was possible that Merrick had just started the scheme and had not had time to profit from the information. Maybe the mastermind was not Merrick at all. There was no way to be sure, but it was the best lead he had. Scott shifted his thoughts to the market. His short position in soybeans was potentially a big winner, and it was important that he monitored trading carefully before the weekend. He needed to be on the floor.

He left his apartment and arrived at the CBOT before trading began. He read the overnight news summary and checked cash prices before discussing the opening with Jason McDonald. They agreed soybeans would probably extend the decline of yesterday and might even open down the limit. On the way to the floor, Scott was thinking about Victor Merrick and failed to hear Jason's comment about cash prices.

"Scott?"

"Oh, sorry. I need to ask you something. What do you know about Victor Merrick of Burgess Grain?"

"I don't like the son of a bitch if that's what you mean."

"We certainly agree on that," Scott said. "Do you know anything about his financial condition?"

"I know Burgess is in bad shape. There have even been rumors of them being forced into chapter eleven."

Scott mulled the new information as they walked to the pit. Although there were a few inconsistencies, he still thought it probable that Merrick was the key figure behind the stolen reports. Too many things pointed to it. He decided to spend the next few days gathering information about Merrick and his operation, then call Angela Williams and discuss their action plan for the next crop report. If they could catch Hayden Benson in the act, he might implicate Merrick.

A few minutes after Scott reached the pit, Jason yelled at him. "A private report substantiating the federal yield estimate just came over the wire. The pre-call is limit down."

"Great! It looks like we'll get some of our capital back quicker than we thought."

Soybeans opened down the limit and remained there for the first two hours. Scott held his entire position, but he decided to take partial profits on any further decline on Monday. As the trading session wore on, his thoughts shifted to Lauren. He always worried about her safety when she was alone, but he was especially concerned now because Merrick was here in Chicago. The threat was too close. Scott left the pit and went to a phone. He let it ring twice, then hung up and redialed so Lauren would know it was him. After he determined she was safe, he told her he would be home in an hour or two. He hung up but could not shake an underlying feeling of trepidation.

A late session flurry of short covering brought soybeans off the limit, but the move lasted only a few seconds. Massive sell orders flowed into the pit and drove prices down the limit. Scott believed a substantial number of traders with weak long positions were trapped, and he suspected they would use every opportunity to liquidate their position.

While he watched for any sign of a change in soybeans, he again became concerned for Lauren. He told Jason he was going home and would monitor the market from there. During the drive to his apartment, Scott decided to scale out of his entire soybean position the following week and stay with Lauren until things were resolved. Because the scheme's mastermind was headquartered in Chicago, the danger had taken on a new urgency.

He entered the apartment and noticed that Lauren did not have the pistol within easy reach. Upset, he did not return the intensity of her kiss.

She stepped back. "What's wrong?"

"Remember what I told you about the gun?"

"It's over there on the table. I can get to it quickly."

"Not fast enough. Someone could bust in here and be on top of you in seconds. I want you to carry the gun with you all the time. If you don't, I'm going to get a holster and make you wear it day and night."

"You wouldn't do that; would you?"

"I would."

She bit her bottom lip as she often did while thinking. "You're right. I promise." She put her arms around him. "I need to get away from here for awhile. Do you think we might be able to go out to dinner?"

"No, but we might be able to go away for the weekend."

Her expression brightened instantly. "Really, where?"

"I know this quiet little resort on a secluded inlet at Lake Geneva. We can get a private bungalow with a great view. It's very romantic. How does that sound?"

"When are we leaving?"

"Let me call to make sure they have a vacancy. If they do, we'll leave in a couple of hours."

Radiating excitement, Lauren ran to the phone, picked it up, and handed it to him. "I'll be ready in thirty minutes."

"One more thing," Scott said. "Late next week, I'm going to stop trading until after the next crop report. I want to spend all my time with you." This was the first time he had ever allowed any individual to be more important to him than the markets. He looked at Lauren. *God, I love this woman.*

"Wonderful," Lauren said. She then got a puzzled look on her face. "Has something happened?"

"No, it's just that Merrick is so close. Our situation is more dangerous than we ever believed."

CHAPTER 35

After Zina Martell had met with Merrick, she spent the rest of Sunday afternoon at the National Gallery of Art. That evening she ordered room service and ate dinner before studying her notes about Lauren Chandler and Scott Q.

Monday morning, Zina transformed herself into the persona of Cade. Her actions were precise, methodical, and confident. She dressed differently, thought differently, and completely absorbed a new identity. From this moment forward, she would spend every minute attempting to find her target, and she would use every conceivable method in her search. The strategy she had outlined Sunday night set a priority on Lauren Chandler's work place—the Department of Agriculture. She called Merrick and requested that he arrange a meeting with Hayden Benson.

Merrick called back and said Benson would meet her at noon.

Zina drove to the appointed location, arriving at eleven-thirty. She watched carefully for the next forty minutes, then she walked up to a nervous-looking man in a gray suit. "Benson?"

"Yes."

"I'll make this short. I need information about the Chandler woman and the man she's with."

"I don't see how I can help."

"Just answer my questions. I have most of what I need on the woman, but I'm interested in the man. Do you know anyone working in your department named Scott?"

"There are hundreds of people in several different buildings."

"Just answer the question."

"No, I don't."

"All right. I need two things from you. First, I want to see a computer printout of all employees with a last name starting with the letter Q."

"But—"

"Let me finish. Second, I want a copy of the visitor logs for all the buildings on the day you last saw Lauren Chandler. That's the day her roommate was killed."

Benson appeared shocked. "I can't go around getting those kinds of things. I—"

"Merrick said to call him if you don't cooperate. Do you want me to do that?"

Benson raised both hands and gestured with his palms toward the woman. "All right, all right. I'll get the information."

"One more thing. I want everything by tomorrow morning. You're not to tell anyone about this. No one. Do you understand?"

"I understand, but damn—"

"Be here tomorrow at nine o'clock." She turned and walked away.

———

The next day Zina followed the same procedure. She watched Benson for thirty minutes and then approached him. "What've you got?"

He handed her a large envelope. "It's all there."

"Good. Stay here while I review everything." She sat on a bench and went through the computer printout. There were only three people with last names that started with the letter Q. None matched. She looked at the visitor's records. The first was a small log for the Annex Building. She ran her fingers down the sheet, but there was no entry listing Scott as a first name. Next, she searched through a much thicker log used for the Administration Building. She scanned the names and suddenly stopped. She moved back up the page and rested her finger on a name: Scott Quinn.

She looked across the sheet to see whom he had visited, then turned toward Benson. "Do you know Leon Gains?"

"Sure."

"I want you to go into his office and check his correspondence for the two-month period prior to the date on this log. I suppose you're going to bitch about this too?"

"No. Actually, I can get into those files with no problem."

"Good. I'll meet you here at one o'clock."

Zina came back that afternoon and noticed a change in Benson's attitude. He almost smiled when she walked up to him.

He handed her a manila folder. "I think this is what you're looking for."

She opened the folder and found copies of three letters, one confirming an appointment between Gains and her target on the day of the crop report. She glanced at the top of the letterhead and saw Scott Quinn's name and a Chicago address. "You haven't told anyone about this?"

"No."

"You're not to mention this to anyone, including Victor Merrick, under any circumstances." She turned and walked away.

Zina went back to her hotel, packed, checked out, and then went directly to the airport and purchased a one-way ticket to Chicago.

———

Scott and Lauren returned from Lake Geneva Sunday night. Although they were in love before the trip, two days away from the constant fear of someone busting through their front door brought them even closer. The dozen red roses Scott had sent to their room before they arrived at the resort set the tone. They talked, hiked, picnicked, drank wine, laughed, and took baths together. They shared themselves with each other in every way— physically, emotionally, and spiritually.

During those two days, they attained that special level of trust that resulted in the ability to share every thought, no matter how personal, because they knew they would support one another without question. They had found the pathway to true friendship. There was a great deal of laughter in their relationship, but there were also quiet moments when they just sat and looked at each other, communicating with their eyes.

Lauren had wanted to stay over another day, but Scott explained that he had to maintain close management of his market positions. He promised he would stop trading by Friday; then, they would be together until the next crop report. If things went as planned, and they caught Benson in the act of stealing data, he might implicate Merrick and end the nightmare.

———

Monday morning, Scott entered the soybean pit at the CBOT. Jason brought him up-to-date on news developments, including higher-than-expected export figures. Soybeans opened down six cents a bushel, but rallied slightly before backing and filling for the remainder of the day. Scott covered twenty percent of his position on the opening. A late rally gave soybeans a one-and-a-half cent gain on the day. Tuesday brought more of the same. After opening up two cents, beans drifted lower until they hit support at midday. A flurry of short covering pushed soybeans slightly higher at the close. Scott knew the market was consolidating recent losses, but he expected the downtrend to resume before the end of the week.

His short position profit exceeded $642,000. Not bad, he thought, especially since he had put up only a fraction of that in margin. However, concern for Lauren reinforced his desire to step away from the market by the end of the week.

On his way home, Scott thought about his unusually casual attitude toward his recent success in the market. Normally, he would have been filled with excitement, and he would have replayed every price tick of the past few days. His relationship with Lauren had changed everything.

———

At that same moment, the wheels of a DC-10 sent puffs of blue smoke into the air as the plane touched down at O'Hare Airport. The flight, originating in Washington, D.C., carried a woman with black hair and olive skin traveling under a false name. Cade had arrived in Chicago.

CHAPTER 36

Zina Martell had a reservation at a small hotel under the name of Lisa Cunningham. She intended to use the alias while in Chicago, then switch to another name after she completed the contract. Before leaving Washington, she had placed a call to one of her contacts in New York, and he agreed to send the requested rifle and ammunition by overnight carrier. By prior arrangement, her supplier always test-fired the weapons to insure accuracy. The selected rifle came in two sections to facilitate shipping and concealment.

The package arrived thirty minutes after Zina checked into the hotel. She retrieved the box, entered her room, locked the door, put on a pair of surgical gloves, and examined the rifle. Satisfied, she returned the weapon to its case and secured the lock. Then, she checked her electronic equipment, reviewed her notes, and made plans for Wednesday. Scott's letterhead indicated that his office was approximately eight blocks from her hotel.

Wednesday morning, she dressed in a conservative business suit and walked throughout the Jackson Street area, near the Chicago Board of Trade, until she had memorized every street and building. The contents of Scott's letter indicated his primary interest was in grain futures. Zina phoned the exchange and learned that trading ended at one-fifteen. An hour before the market closed, she entered the exchange and walked up to a member of the security staff. "Excuse me. Do you happen to know a trader named Scott Quinn?" She kept her tone soft and polite.

"Why yes, I do."

"Oh, great. He's my cousin, and I haven't seen him since we were kids. I'm in town until tomorrow and wanted to visit him."

"You could call his office."

"Well, it's a surprise, and I don't want him to know I'm here until the last minute. Would it be possible for you to point him out to me?"

He scratched the side of his head and raised his eyebrows. "I don't know."

She stepped closer, close enough for her breast to graze his arm. "It would mean a lot to me."

"I guess I could take you up to the visitor's gallery and try to spot him from there."

She moved directly in front of the man and placed her hand on his arm. "Please."

"I suppose it can't hurt, but he may not be there."

The man guided her to the observation gallery and scanned the pits. "I'm afraid I don't see him. Wait, there his is." He moved his arm and pointed at a small group of men standing next to one of the pits. "The one in the blue trader's jacket with the blondish hair. See him?"

"No, I—"

"More to your left. There, he just raised his right arm."

"Oh, yes. Hmm . . . even after all these years, he still has that same face. Thank you very much." Zina immediately left the building. She waited outside for over two hours until she saw her target leave with a companion. She observed Scott's physique and hair coloring, noting they matched the description she had obtained from Billy Barker. The two men turned left and headed down the sidewalk. She followed them to a parking garage.

———

Zina spent Thursday morning scouting several buildings across the street from the route Scott and his friend had taken. Just before noon, she found what she was looking for—a large, older building with several vacant offices overlooking the street. Thirty minutes before the market closed, she positioned herself outside the Board of Trade to see if Quinn used the same route. Fifty minutes after the market closed, her target left the building and walked in the same direction he had gone the day before with the same companion.

Zina's lips formed a slight smile. "This is going to be easy."

She went to the library and checked the city directory. She found Scott's name and address and drove to his residence, which turned out to be a high-rise apartment. She retrieved an envelope from her briefcase and addressed it to Mr. & Mrs. Scott Quinn, but she entered the street number of an adjacent building.

Zina placed her hand over the uncanceled stamp and approached the doorman. "Excuse me. I live next door, and I received some mail for one of your residents. I guess they somehow got the wrong address. It's for Scott Quinn. I believe he lives here. If you give me his apartment number, I'll stick this in another envelope and mail it to him."

"I'll see that he gets it."

"Well, it is U.S. Mail." She held up the envelope. "I think it would be best if I just dropped it in the mailbox."

"Okay, sure. He's in 1208." The doorman leaned forward and squinted at the envelope. "That's funny. It's addressed to Mr. and Mrs. Quinn. Scott lives alone."

She thanked him and left the building. She had learned that he was not married and had no roommate. Zina felt sure she had the right Scott Q, but she needed conclusive evidence that Lauren Chandler was hiding in his apartment. She went to her car and watched the building for nearly an hour as she did not want to re-enter the apartment while the same doorman was on duty. She had hoped he would be relieved at four, but he was still there at a quarter after the hour.

She asked a passerby for directions to the nearest deli, and then walked two blocks to the restaurant. After consuming an avocado sandwich and iced tea, she went back to her car, arriving a little after five. A new doorman stood near the entrance. Zina transferred equipment from a briefcase to her oversized bag, then she waited until she saw a group of four people strolling toward the apartment entrance. She hurried across the street and fell in behind them, walked to the elevator, and selected the twelfth floor.

She stepped into the hallway, avoiding eye contact with two men coming toward her. Zina continued walking until the pair entered the elevator and the doors had closed; then, she moved swiftly, following a procedure she had rehearsed many times. She grabbed a terra-cotta pot containing a dieffenbachia, and slid it a few feet closer to Scott's door. Next, she removed a contact microphone and a small transmitter from her bag, which she had purposely left on the floor. If someone came out of an apartment, she would act as if she was retrieving a dropped handbag.

Zina had found this method of eavesdropping to be very successful. Unlike a conventional microphone, a contact mic does not respond to air vibrations. It will pick up minute vibrations caused by sound striking a sounding board such as a wall or a window. After taping the mic to the apartment wall, Zina secured the transmitter to the backside of the pot. The unit had a range of nearly one thousand feet. She felt a familiar flash of excitement while performing her task, but she remained cool and focused, her hands moving rapidly, her ears alert for any noise from the hallway.

She completed the installation and checked the connections. Satisfied the mic could not be seen without looking behind the pot, she picked up her bag and walked to the elevator. She exited the building, went to her car, opened a thick briefcase, and removed a metal box containing a small receiver and amplifier. The state-of-the-art unit exceeded the amplification factor required to transfer minute sounds to useable levels. Headphones completed the system.

Zina worried about interference from mechanical vibrations and common noises present in a structure such as an apartment building. She plugged in the headphones and turned on the unit. As expected, ambient sound was the first thing she heard. No voices. After a few minutes, she heard noises she thought might have originated from the kitchen; then, she heard a man talking. Zina turned up the volume and concentrated on the voice. Seconds later, she heard a woman's voice, but it could be anyone. She had to be sure it was Lauren Chandler.

She listened for fifteen minutes, her mind filtering the ambient sounds through sheer concentration. Then, she heard what she wanted. The man addressed the woman by name: Lauren. Zina went back upstairs and quickly retrieved her equipment, took the elevator to the first floor, and exited the building. A surprisingly strong feeling of success swept through her as she drove to her hotel. She had quickly done what half a dozen men could not accomplish over a much longer period. Her opinion of men fell to a new low.

She entered her room, checked her equipment, and completed plans for Friday. When she was satisfied, she placed the rifle, the scope, and the cartridges back in the case and secured the lock. Her oversized handbag contained a pistol, extra clips, gloves, and a small packet of tools for picking locks. She went to bed early and fell asleep almost immediately.

The next morning, she phoned the airport and booked a late afternoon flight under her new alias—Lydia Brunelli. After the contract, she planned to fly to Atlanta, rent a car at the airport and drive to Florida.

Zina checked out of her hotel a little before noon and went to her car. She put on a light brown wig and drove to a location three blocks from the building she had previously selected. At twelve forty-five, she entered the lobby with an oversized briefcase. She immediately went to a phone booth and dialed Merrick's private line.

He answered on the second ring.

She spoke quickly, "You can deliver your margin call to the lady right here in Chicago."

"She's here?"

"Yes." Zina gave a surprised Victor Merrick the address and apartment number.

"I don't believe it."

"I don't have much time," Zina replied, "so listen carefully. The gentleman's margin call will be delivered within the hour at a downtown location. I suggest you see the lady right away." She hung up, took the elevator to the fourth floor, put on gloves, and went down the hall to an empty office. She picked the lock in less than a minute. Zina stepped inside, glanced around, then moved across the empty room, her steps echoing as she walked. She went to the window and raised it slightly, grimacing at the smell of fresh pigeon droppings on the sill. She opened her case, screwed the two rifle sections together, and loaded the weapon.

She waited.

Her position was perfect, and she was not the least bit worried about the hit. It would be an easy shot. She estimated the chance of missing the target at one in a hundred. She glanced at her watch. It was ten after one. The grain market would close in five minutes. If Scott kept to his schedule of the last two days, he would come out around two o'clock. She became more vigilant and carefully watched everyone leaving the building.

Scott exited the building a little before two.

Zina's location allowed her about two minutes before he would be directly across the street. She raised the window another four inches and placed the barrel of the rifle near the opening, but she was careful to keep the gun from extending beyond the ledge.

One minute went by.

The target and his companion were involved in an animated discussion as they walked; then, they stopped and continued their conversation while facing each other. After a moment, they resumed walking. When they were almost directly across the street, Zina looked through the scope and sighted just in front of Scott.

The two men stopped again. They seemed to be involved in a serious discussion.

She moved the rifle slightly.

Her target faced the street, giving her a full view of his upper body. She sighted the cross hairs on his heart and rested her finger against the trigger.

He had not moved.

She held her breath and started to squeeze the trigger, but just as she applied pressure, a grayish blur appeared in her scope. Her head jerked up as the rifle discharged.

Three pigeons had flown across her field of vision, heading for the ledge to her right. The horrified birds flapped their wings frantically in an attempt to get away from the explosive sound.

Zina glanced at the birds. "Pigeons. Stupid fucking pigeons."

She looked toward the sidewalk.

She did not see her target.

Had her bullet struck its mark?

CHAPTER 37

Victor Merrick was dumbfounded. He had expended a great deal of effort to find Lauren Chandler only to learn she was in Chicago—right under his nose. His previous decision to send Mac Hammitt back to Chicago to recruit more help had been a wise move. He now had four men at his disposal. He decided to accompany them to Quinn's apartment, thus making a total of five. That was certainly more than enough for one woman, but he wanted to make sure she could not get away.

Merrick picked up the phone and punched in a number.

"Mac, we've got work to do." He gave the address and instructions to meet him across the street from the apartment.

"Jesus, Victor. I'll need a little more time to round everyone up."

"I'll give you until two-fifteen, but that's all." Merrick hung up, reached into a drawer and pulled out a loaded 9mm Sig Sauer, which he stuck in his jacket pocket. He put a loaded clip and shells in the other pocket. He left his office at one-thirty, drove to the address, parked across the street from the building, and waited. His problems would soon be over.

He thought back to what Zina Martell had said about the Chandler woman changing her appearance. It made sense, and he suspected she would be wearing a wig or that she might have shortened and bleached her hair. He watched everyone entering or leaving the building, but no one matched that description.

At ten after two, Mac Hammitt parked two car lengths in front of Merrick, walked up to the passenger side of Merrick's car, and got in. Three men waited in the other car.

"We're ready," he said. "Where is she, and how do you want it handled?"

"Send one man to the back of the building, and leave somebody in front. You and one other go inside. She's in 1208."

"What about the dude?"

"He's being taken care of downtown; so she should be alone." Merrick watched the apartment entrance, then he swung around and faced Hammitt. "I want her dead. Do whatever it takes and don't fuck it up."

"No sweat."

"All right, get to it."

Hammitt hesitated. "I noticed a doorman over there. What should we do about him?"

"Just walk up and stick a gun in his ribs, then take him to a closet or somewhere out of sight and bang the son of a bitch on the head. Use some of that duct tape in the back seat. Put it around his hands and feet and cover his mouth; then get on with it."

Hammitt nodded and grabbed the tape.

Merrick scanned the street while the four men walked toward the apartment building. Seeing nothing suspicious, he allowed himself the luxury of thinking ahead. With Lauren Chandler out of the way, he could use the crop data for the next two or three years and make a fortune.

———

Lauren was pleased it was Friday. Scott had promised this would be his last day on the trading floor until their problems were resolved. Hopefully, that would be after the next crop report. He had said he would stay with her every day and arrange for them to move out of Chicago temporarily. He had not told her where, but he hinted it would be secluded and romantic, and that they might leave as early as Monday. They would stay until one week before the next crop report, then leave for Washington to meet with Angela Williams to prepare a strategy to catch Hayden Benson and Victor Merrick.

She went into in the kitchen to begin preparations for dinner. Her menu included lasagna, salad, French bread, wine, and a soufflé for dessert. Lauren was standing next to the cooking island when she heard a loud crash from the direction of the front door.

She froze.

The very thing she feared most was happening—someone had broken through the front door. She dropped to the floor, crawled to the counter, and reached up for her gun. It wasn't there.

Terror quickened her pulse as she tried to retrace her movements. She knew she had placed the pistol on the island countertop when she entered the kitchen. She slid to her right and tried again, her hand searching for the weapon.

She heard voices from the living room. "Check the back bedrooms. I'll go into the kitchen."

The gun? Where's the goddamned gun?

She reached farther back on the counter. Her fingers groped desperately, then her hand touched the cold steel of the pistol. She pulled it off the counter. Lauren grasped the weapon and thought back to the instructions Scott had given her. Knowing she could not get to his office, she looked around, and then slid across the floor toward the large wine storage unit.

She heard movement.

Hurry.

Lauren crawled into the narrow space next to the wine cabinet, put her back to the wall, and raised her knees in the manner Scott had shown her.

Her heart pounded.

She grasped the gun with both hands and rested her arms on her knees. When she heard footsteps strike the kitchen floor, her hands began to shake and her skin turned clammy. She froze for a terrifying eye blink. She gritted her teeth, thought of what Scott had told her, and mouthed the words. "It's you or them." The pistol's cold steel against her skin sent horrifying messages racing up her arm to her brain.

The top of the man's head came into view. He took two steps toward the rear of the kitchen. She could see his chest.

In the same instant, the gunman saw her and started to raise his pistol.

Her mind locked on a single thought, *Shoot the son of a bitch!*

She fired three shots in rapid succession. The first went wide, but the second and third tore holes in the middle of the man's chest as his own gun exploded. A bullet smashed into the glass door of the storage case.

The man crashed heavily to the floor.

Lauren wanted to scream, but there was another man searching the bedrooms.

Run!

She jumped up, vaulted over the bleeding gunman and made a dash for the front door. She had nearly reached the hallway when she heard a voice behind.

"What the—"

She leaped over the fallen door and turned right.

The roar of a gunshot sounded behind her, then another. Bullets slammed into the wall across the hall as she began running. She was twenty feet from the elevator when the door opened; a woman with a shopping bag stepped out.

Lauren dove into the elevator. Two bullets dug into the wall above her.

The woman screamed and dropped her bag of groceries in the hallway. Oranges rolled across the carpet.

Lauren spun on the floor and fired two shots at the man, then she reached up and punched the ground floor button on the panel. She fired more shots while she waited for the door to shut.

The woman in the hallway was on her hands and knees, screaming hysterically as bullets ripped into the closing elevator door. When the elevator started moving Lauren felt a wave of relief, but it was short-lived. The man would obviously take the other elevator and follow her down, and there might be others in the lobby or outside the building.

She tried to switch control of her mind from fright to logic. What were her options? She rose and stood in the corner of the elevator next to the control panel and decided to peek out when she got to the first floor. If it looked clear, she would run out the front of the building, but if she saw anything suspicious, she would stay in the elevator and go to a different floor to hide.

The elevator stopped with a slight jolt. Her body tensed as her hand tightened around the gun. She wondered how many shots she had fired and how many bullets were left. She had no idea.

The door opened.

She looked out but saw no one—not even the doorman. The other elevator might open any second. She had to move.

Lauren stepped out and ran toward the large double doors. She hesitated at the entrance, but when she heard the other elevator stop, fear propelled her onward. She went through the doors and broke into a run toward the street. It was nearly twenty yards to the sidewalk, and she had to cross the drive and an open area beyond.

Halfway across she heard shouting, then two shots rang out. Adrenalin surged through her body, driving her forward, increasing her speed. She was nearing the street when she heard more shouts and gunshots. Several bullets whizzed by her and slammed into a parked car.

The gunfire sent a burst of energy through her limbs, and she reached full speed, angling to the left, her breathing coming in sharp gasps. She reached the sidewalk, looked over her shoulder, and saw two men in pursuit with their weapons raised.

Two gunshots exploded behind her.

CHAPTER 38

When Cade's bullet tore into the hood of the car next to Scott, he dived headlong for the pavement and yelled at Jason. "Down! Get down."

Scott's first priority had been to determine where the shot had come from. Since the bullet went through the top of the hood, it must have come from above street level. If the sniper were firing from a building across the street, the car offered temporary safety.

He turned to see whether Jason was all right, then he looked up and down the sidewalk to see if anyone were coming toward them in a hostile manner. Everyone in his line of vision was lying on the pavement or crouching in doorways. A woman behind him screamed. Satisfied he was not in immediate danger of attack from gunmen on foot, Scott gripped his Beretta and crawled to the front of the car. Because of where the bullet had struck, the sniper was probably in one of two buildings directly across the street.

He chambered a shell and peeked over the hood. There was no sign of anyone in the first building. He ducked and moved forward two feet, then inched his head around the bumper and looked at the second building. His eyes focused on an open window on the fourth floor. All of the other windows were shut. He squinted and thought he saw a rifle barrel.

A split second after he dropped back to the pavement, a bullet ricocheted off the sidewalk, shattering a window behind him.

"Jesus, that guy can shoot. That would have taken my head off."

"Watch out," Jason yelled.

A sudden, shockwave of fear swept through Scott. If they knew where he worked, they probably knew where he lived. "Lauren! I've got to get to Lauren." He glanced at Jason and yelled, "Stay down—"

Scott rose to a squatting position, raised his arm over the hood and fired three shots at the open window. Then, he moved forward, sprang to his feet, and went into a full sprint down the sidewalk. Shots rang out from behind, but his speed made him a difficult target. After several yards, he turned and bounded across the street to take away the sniper's angle. He reached the other side and continued his sprint toward the parking garage.

His only thoughts were of Lauren. It had taken him all of his life to find her—he couldn't let them take her from him now. A vision of her lying dead on his apartment floor flashed through his mind. The horrifying thought quickened his pace. He crossed the street, thankful that the shooting had stopped. A block away from the garage, Scott thought about stopping to call the police but discarded the idea. He knew if Lauren were safe, they would arrest her; if she were in danger, he could get there as fast as the police could—probably sooner.

He ran into the garage, got into his car, and sped onto the street. His apartment was not far, and by driving at high speed, he would be there in a few minutes. Scott laid his gun on the seat and shoved down on the gas pedal. He darted in and out of traffic for five blocks, then made a left turn. After four blocks, he turned right against a red light, nearly hitting another car. He drove recklessly but nothing else mattered now—he had to get to Lauren.

He slid around a corner onto his street.

Three blocks left.

Two hundred yards from his apartment, he saw two men running from the building.

They had guns.

Then he saw her.

To his left, less than a block away, Lauren was running down the sidewalk. Scott grabbed his Beretta and stuck it out the window. He slowed as he came even with her pursuers and fired three shots.

One of the men dove for cover, the other returned fire. Bullets tore into the side of his car. He looked ahead and saw that a third gunman had come from the side of the building and had stopped on the sidewalk. The man raised his pistol and aimed at Lauren.

Scott swerved across the street, cut his speed, and maneuvered the tires on the left side of his car onto the sidewalk.

The startled man spun and pointed his gun toward the car.

Scott shoved down on the gas pedal and opened his door. The panel caught the gunman flush in the chest, lifting him into the air. The buckled door slammed back against the car but did not shut. Scott steered back onto the street and honked the horn.

Lauren turned and saw him.

He skidded to a stop and yelled, "Get in!" Scott reached back with his left hand and unlocked the rear door. "Hurry!"

A bullet sliced through the rear window and struck the front windshield on the passenger's side. As soon as she got in, Scott slammed his foot on the accelerator and yelled for her to get down. He glanced in the rearview mirror as the car picked up speed. Another man had come from the right side of the street and began firing at them. Scott was not sure, but it looked like Victor Merrick.

More bullets crashed through the rear window.

Scott heard what sounded like a tire blowing and the car swerved uncontrollably.

Lauren yelled, "What's wrong?"

"Hold on." He slammed on the brakes and had almost come to a stop when he struck a parked car.

He turned toward the back seat. "Are you all right?"

"Y—yes. I'm okay."

"Where's your gun?"

"On the floor."

"Grab it. We've got to get out of here."

Lauren picked up her pistol and tried the door handle. "It won't open."

Scott was going to follow her out that side but the impact with the gunman had jammed the door. He motioned with his hand. "This side. Come on." He got out and looked back. A car stopped, and the man who had been running after them got in. Scott helped Lauren, and then shoved her toward the sidewalk. "Run!"

When they reached the corner, two shots rang out. One bullet whizzed by Scott's head, the other dug into a wall to his right. He yelled, "Turn right and keep going." He went around the corner and ran a hundred feet to a large truck. He got behind the vehicle, turned, and raised his pistol. When the gunmen's car skidded around the corner, Scott fired five shots at the window. He could not tell if he hit anyone, but the car careened to the left and slammed into the side of a delivery van.

Scott turned to look for Lauren and saw that she had stopped near the end of the street. He started running and waved at her to keep going. He did not think the gunmen's car was going fast enough to cause the occupants serious injury, which meant they would pursue Lauren on foot. He shoved the gun into his coat pocket and ran toward her. He was twenty feet behind when she reached the next intersection.

He caught her, grabbed her hand and ran to the next street. Just before they turned, Scott glanced over his shoulder. Three men were running up the sidewalk less than a block away. When he turned the corner, Scott remembered that a hotel took up most of this block, and there were usually several taxis parked at the curb. He looked ahead and saw three. One was just pulling away from the taxi zone to pick up passengers in front of the hotel, but there were still two waiting at the curb.

Scott ran to the first car, opened the door, and shoved Lauren inside. He yelled at the driver. "I'll give you three hundred bucks to get us out of here *fast*."

The cab driver shoved the gas pedal down so hard that Scott felt himself propelled backward against the seat. He turned to look out the rear window and saw the men come around the corner. They stopped, searched the street, and then continued running.

He turned to Lauren. "Are you all right?"

She nodded. "I did exactly what you told me to do. I—I think I killed a man."

"You had no choice." He slid next to her, put his arm around her, and held tight. Scott started to give the cabby Jason's address, but changed his mind and told him to go to an intersection about five blocks from Jason's apartment building. He turned his attention back to Lauren. "We may have lucked out. I don't think they saw us get into the cab."

Scott spent the next few minutes looking out the back window. All he remembered about the gunmen's car was that it was dark blue. There was no way of knowing if it was still serviceable, but he studied the vehicles behind them just in case.

The taxi approached the designated intersection and Scott told the driver to slow and go around the block a few times. When he felt sure no cars followed them he instructed the driver to stop. Scott pulled four bills from his wallet. "Here's twenty for the fare, and the three hundred I promised you. And, thanks. You did a hell of a job."

"Heck, mister. That's the most fun I've had in a long time."

Scott opened the door and helped Lauren out.

The driver yelled out the window. "Take good care of that young lady."

Scott put his arm around Lauren. They walked two blocks and stopped in front of a library. He removed his arm and stood in front of her. "I need to talk to Jason, but he might not have gone straight home. He may have checked my place to see if we were all right."

"Let's try to call him."

"We'll go into the library, and I'll phone every fifteen minutes until I reach him. We'll borrow his car and try to get out of town."

"But they'll just keep looking for us. I know they will."

"We'll figure something out." Scott tried to convey confidence but knew his attempt was feeble. It was impossible to hide the fact he had no idea what they should do next.

Jason answered on Scott's fifth attempt.

"It's me."

"Thank God, are you all right? Where's Lauren?"

"She's with me and we're safe. At least for now."

"I went by your apartment after the shooting. There were cops all over the place, but I couldn't find out anything. What are you going to do?"

"We obviously need to get out of town. I need to borrow your car."

"You got it. Where are you?"

"We're at that library about three blocks from your place. You know the one?"

"Sure. I'll be there in five minutes."

"Hold on," Scott said. "They probably don't know about you, but we'd better be careful just in case. Drive around for a while and make sure no one is following you."

Thirty-five minutes later, Jason's black Porsche stopped in front of the library. Scott checked the street and walked Lauren to the car.

Jason got out and motioned toward the car. "It's all yours."

Scott took a deep breath. "I really appreciate this. Get a rental and I'll cover it later."

"Nonsense. My dad has two cars. I know I can borrow one of his."

"Thanks."

"If there's anything else I can do, just call. And be careful." Jason hugged him, then went to the other side of the car and kissed Lauren on the cheek.

Scott slid into the driver's seat. "How are you holding up?"

"Okay, I think," she said, shaking her head. My God, what an experience."

"How would you like to go to Colorado?"

"Colorado?"

"I think we'll be safe there." He paused, his mind replaying the attack on Lauren. "It bothers me to see you living in fear all the time. Today was just too much. I almost lost you." He leaned over. "I love you."

They clung to each other for a moment, then Lauren said, "If we're safe and we're together, I'll go anywhere." She cast her gaze downward. "But I know they're never going to give up."

Scott could think of nothing to say. He worried about the same thing, but he was not going to let her know. He decided to change the subject. "First things first. We're going to need some money; so we'll go by my bank and I'll draw out some cash. Then we'll head straight for the tollway."

Scott drove to a branch where he was known and drew out $25,000. He told the manager he might require money to be wired to him at various locations in the near future. The manager promised discretion and quick response to his needs.

Scott left the bank and drove to the Tri-State Tollway, which he followed to Interstate 55. After twenty-five miles, he turned west on Interstate 80. They began the thousand-mile journey with Scott watching the rearview mirror almost as much as he watched the road. He considered their future and his mind kept going back to what Lauren had said about the killers not giving up. He knew she was right.

284

CHAPTER 39

After Merrick had sent his gunmen chasing after Scott and Lauren, he immediately went back to his car and left the area to avoid the imminent swarm of police. He went back to Burgess Grain and awaited news. Since the fleeing pair's head start had been less than a block, he expected that his men would be able to overtake them.

He went into his inner office and sat at his desk overlooking the train layout. As the minutes ticked by, his optimism faded with frightening speed. He had too much riding on the outcome, and he began to worry. He focused on his problems and a cobweb of emotions engulfed him. He felt a strange sensation of being outside his body, watching himself. The mood disturbed him.

The phone jolted him back to reality. It was Mac Hammitt.

"What happened?"

"They got away."

Merrick threw the phone off his desk. He was so enraged he could not talk. He stepped off the platform and paced rapidly for a moment, full of anger. He finally reached down and picked up the receiver. "You still there?"

"Yeah."

"Get over here right away." Merrick slammed down the phone.

Hammitt knocked on his door forty minutes later.

Merrick yelled, "Get in here."

Hammitt walked in looking like a child who had been caught stealing candy.

Merrick had been pacing the floor, but he moved to his chair. "What happened in the apartment?"

Hammitt went over the details.

The words fueled Merrick's contempt. Two of his men had let a trapped woman get away. He simply could not tolerate such ineptitude. He flipped a switch on his desk that sent a long train in motion. It wound its way down the track and into a tunnel. When the locomotive reached the other side, he looked at Hammitt and motioned toward the end of the layout. "You see that red caboose on the sidetrack?"

"Sure, but—"

"Pick it up and bring it to me."

Hammitt cocked his head as if he did not understand the strange request.

"I told you to bring me the damn caboose."

Hammitt walked over and reached for the small red model. When his hand touched the caboose, Merrick reached under his desk and pulled a lever. The connection sent a deadly surge of electricity through the caboose.

Hammitt's eyes bulged and he shook violently.

Merrick watched a moment, then he switched off the power.

Mac Hammitt collapsed to the floor. Death throes sent spasms through his body.

Merrick sat quietly, his eyes dark and empty, watching the train maneuver its way through a forest before entering a tunnel. He loathed incompetence.

CHAPTER 40

When Michael Tucker reached his twenty-fifth birthday, he knew he would probably be bald by the age of thirty. All the signs were there: family history, thinning hair, and the alarmingly early retreat of his hairline. His fellow officers, in the San Francisco Police Department, frequently teased Tuck about of his hairless destiny.

On a foggy July morning, Tuck decided to help Mother Nature by speeding up the clock. He shaved his entire head, becoming the youngest baldheaded police officer in department history—at least as far as anyone knew. The first few days brought an onslaught of verbal abuse, but after the sun changed the pale white scalp to a rich golden tone, one thing became obvious; Tuck was one of those rare and fortunate men who actually looked better with a completely baldhead. No one was sure what caused it, but women began complimenting him on his looks—especially his eyes. The lack of hair seemed to bring out their depth and intensity. Many said he had the look of a young Yul Brenner.

During the next few years, the pressures of being a cop gradually began to alter Tuck's view of the world around him. The brutality of the crimes committed in the streets and alleys wore on his resolve, and his attitude toward his fellow man became more pessimistic. He began to lose his distinctive sense of humor, and his propensity for playing creative practical jokes all but disappeared.

Eventually, Tuck realized that the negative aspects of his job were altering his personality.

On a cool night in October, he had responded to a 911 call in a particularly troublesome neighborhood. The report said shots and screams had been heard from inside a residence. Tuck and his partner burst into a scene of blood and death. Someone had broken into the home, murdered the mother and father with an axe, then shot and mutilated their two children, aged two and five. Tuck had seen atrocities before, but the brutality inflicted on the small children proved to be too much, and it took only one glance at the horrible scene for him to realize he'd had enough. He resigned the next morning, moved to Colorado, and opened a small backpacking business.

Motivated by his desire to get away from people, Tuck bought a house nestled halfway up the slope of a stunning alluvial fan. The tree-covered site was about ten miles from town, and he could mark his nearest neighbor at a distance of over two miles.

Scott Quinn had moved to Chicago long before Tuck left the department, but the two had kept in close contact and Scott had visited his friend on two occasions. A relationship that had started on school playgrounds had evolved to a level that epitomized the meaning of the word friendship—true and unconditional.

———

Tuck had just returned from a pack trip and he was tired. He put away his gear, got a cold beer, and checked his answering machine. There were the usual array of messages, but when he heard his friend's strained voice, he listened intently. Scott said he had a serious problem and that he would keep calling.

Tuck waited next to the phone, sipping his beer, but there were no calls. He finally got up and went into the kitchen to fix a late dinner, but he could not get the message out of his mind. He had worried about Scott ever since he had sent the gun to Chicago. Something was wrong, and the more Tuck thought about it, the more he worried. He ate his meal in a house full of silence and presentiment.

———

Scott stopped at a gas station off Interstate 80 and filled the tank while Lauren went to the rest room. Although there had been no sign of anyone following them, he watched intently when she left the lady's room and entered a small store. He paid for the gas, then drove across the lot and parked next to a phone booth. He dialed Jason McDonald's home number, got his answering machine, and left a brief message, saying they were safe and that they would be staying at Tuck's house after Monday night. He started to give the phone number but caution held him back. Jason could get it through directory assistance.

He tried Tuck's number again. Scott had been unsuccessful in several attempts to reach his friend, and he was about to hang up when Tuck answered.

"It's Scott."

"I've been worried. Everything okay?"

"Yes and no. I'm going to take you up on that offer to stay at your place for a while."

"No problem. Where are you?"

"We're on Interstate 80 about seventy miles west of Des Moines. We should be there sometime tomorrow night."

"We?"

"Lauren's with me. You're really going to like her."

"I'm sure I will." Tuck paused. "Since you're already on your way, I take it you're into some serious shit."

"That description fits." Scott explained what happened in Chicago, but he became increasingly nervous as the minutes ticked by. "Listen, Tuck, I think we should keep moving. I'll fill you in on the rest when we get there."

"All right, but keep in mind what I told you before. You're obviously dealing with professionals. Don't *ever* underestimate them."

He got back in the Porsche, took the soft drink Lauren offered, and pulled onto the interstate. An hour later, they stopped at a small motel well off the highway. Scott followed Tuck's warning and told Lauren to get some sleep while he stayed on watch. He woke her at three and traded places. Lauren woke him at seven o'clock. They ate breakfast and returned to the freeway. Scott glanced at the rearview mirror throughout the long drive, but he became more relaxed as they distanced themselves from Chicago.

They drove all day and entered the small town of Little River, Colorado just before midnight. Even in the darkness, Scott could easily picture the beauty of the surrounding area. He especially enjoyed a large stand of Aspen that extended several hundred yards up the slope behind Tuck's house. They reached the turnoff, and Scott drove under a small sign that read Tucker Pack Trips. He took Lauren's hand. "This is it. Wait until you see this place in the morning. Beauty and solitude in every direction."

It turned unusually dark as a cluster of clouds scudded across the sky, blotting out the stars. Trees that grew right to the edge of the road suddenly teemed with menacing shadows. A pair of eyes from a forest creature caught the light from the car and flung it back. Lauren tightened her grip on Scott's hand.

Their tension eased when the lane widened and the trees fell away from the edge of the road. After a quarter of a mile, they pulled up in front of the house. Tuck stood on the porch wearing a sidearm in a holster. A rifle leaned against the wall behind him.

———

The two men were extremely vigilant the first few days, staying near the house and rotating watch at night. They kept a shotgun and rifle nearby, and Tuck fitted Scott with a holster for his pistol. At night, they placed the guns within easy reach of their beds.

Because Scott had not done any shooting in several years, he gathered both pistols and took Lauren to a spot behind the house. They shot at targets for over an hour, and decided to practice every day until they became proficient with their weapons. They reduced their vigilance on the fourth day. It seemed likely that Scott and Lauren had managed to escape to Colorado without anyone knowing their whereabouts—at least for now.

———

Tuck went to town Thursday and came home with a truck full of groceries. He pulled up in front of the house and waved. A woman with short, brown hair, a tanned face, and a bright smile sat next to him.

Scott and Lauren stepped off the porch to help with the bags.

Tuck went around the front of the pickup and opened the door for the woman. "I'd like you to meet Debbie Holloway."

Scott and Lauren stepped forward and greeted her warmly.

Tuck picked up a bag of groceries and put his other arm around Debbie. "She's the best thing that's ever happened to me. If I hadn't moved out here, I never would have met her. Life's funny that way." He smiled broadly, then added, "She's the best damn cook hereabouts, and she's dead set on preparing a special supper for you folks."

"She doesn't have to do that," Scott said.

"That's what I told her," Tuck replied, "but she insisted. I've known her long enough to accept that when she sets her mind on something, it's best to back off."

"Actually," Debbie said, "It's something I want to do. It's my way of making you feel at home."

Tuck reached into the bag and withdrew two bottles of wine. "These are for the table."

That evening, good food mixed with conversation and laughter brought a relaxed mood to the secluded house. Lauren felt more at ease than she had for some time, but she could not completely unburden herself from the sense of danger lodged in her soul. Though the men had not commented on their actions, she knew why they took turns excusing themselves to walk around the outside of the house.

After a time, the wine and the remarkable compatibility of those at the table allowed her to enjoy the evening. She particularly liked Tuck's storytelling abilities. He delighted in recalling experiences the two men had shared years ago, many of which brought groans of remembrance from Scott.

Lauren laughed at one of Tuck's anecdotes and turned to Scott. "You two certainly got into your share of trouble."

"You have no idea," Scott said. After several more stories, he leaned over to Lauren and whispered, "Ask him how he went bald."

She looked surprised. "I can't do that."

Scott leaned over again. "It's okay, really. He loves it."

Lauren refused until Scott repeatedly nudged her under the table. She looked over her glass, hesitated, then said, "Tuck, I was wondering how you lost all that hair?"

Tuck smiled broadly, then replied in a ringing voice, "Too many U-turns under the sheets."

Everyone burst into laughter except Debbie. She blushed at first but quickly joined the fun.

After dinner, Tuck winked at Scott and nodded toward the next room. When they were out of hearing range, Tuck said, "I'm going to make some of my special pancakes for Lauren in the morning. What do you think?"

Scott suppressed a laugh. "Absolutely. I can't wait."

Evening ran to night and a rich, comfortable aura of friendship drifted outward from the small dining room table, spreading its warmth through the house.

———

Tuck rose early the next morning, prepared coffee, made a large bowl of pancake batter, then went to his bedroom and retrieved a new handkerchief. He cut two round pieces out of the white cloth that were slightly smaller than the size of his pancakes. When he had finished preparations, he knocked on Scott and Lauren's bedroom door. "Breakfast is ready."

Scott took the cue and rolled over. "Honey, wake up. Tuck's made some of his famous pancakes."

A few minutes later Lauren padded into the kitchen, sat down at the table and reached for her coffee. She took a sip, and then glanced toward the stove. "This is awfully nice of you, Tuck."

He turned away from his griddle. "Aw, it's nothing really."

Scott walked across the kitchen and stood between Lauren and the cook so she could not see the unique ingredient added to her pancakes.

Tuck poured batter onto the griddle. When he had just the right amount, he placed a thin circle of cloth in the middle of two of the pancakes, then he poured on enough batter to conceal the cloth. The two men struggled to suppress laughter.

A few minutes after Scott seated himself, Tuck came to the table with a platter of pancakes. He put two on Lauren's plate and two on Scott's.

Scott prepared his food and covertly watched Lauren.

She spread butter over the cakes and poured maple syrup on top. Scott glanced at Tuck, who was grinning widely. Lauren picked up her fork and tried to cut into the pancakes, but she stopped suddenly and a peculiar expression spread across her face.

Scott immediately used his fork to cut into his pancakes, took a bite, and looked at Tuck. "Boy, these are great. Just great."

Lauren again took her fork to the pancakes, this time using a sawing action. No help. She glanced up, sheepishly, then picked up her knife and tried to cut the pancakes. Her face displayed bewilderment at her failed attempt. When she glanced up with a suspicious look, Scott and Tuck burst into laughter.

Lauren used a knife to scrape off the top part of the pancake, then she tilted her head back and laughed. After a moment, she wiped tears of laughter from her eyes and said, "I see some definite payback in the future for *both* of you."

Scott feigned terror.

The following days brought an increasingly relaxed atmosphere. Because an attack seemed unlikely, Scott allowed Lauren to venture outside the house but only with an armed escort.

———

Two days later, Tuck left for a pack trip, and the lovers found themselves alone in a beautiful setting. They began taking horseback rides through the countryside behind Tuck's house. They enjoyed the excursions tremendously, and reveled in the feeling of peace so different from Chicago.

They decided to try a longer trip and had prepared a picnic complete with wine. They left the house and headed toward a small meadow on the up-slope edge of the aspen grove. They rode, side by side, enjoying the smattering of wild flowers lining their route. The mixed fragrances of trees, blossoms, and grasses filled the air.

They reached the meadow and selected a spot adjacent to several aspens. Lauren placed a white tablecloth on the ground and laid out food. They sipped a Ridge zinfandel and ate slowly. When they finished, Lauren snuggled next to Scott and they sat in silence, looking into the distance.

Their vantage point offered a sweeping view of the surrounding area. To their left, and extending far down the slope were the aspens, thick as stars, their leaves orchestrating a dulcet, swishing sound with each stir of the breeze. Straight across from them stood a mountain range. Distance softened the peaks and made them appear smooth and sweeping with velvety purple slopes. The mountains, directly behind them, offered a sharp contrast of rocky cliffs dotted with jagged outcroppings.

A skein of geese crossed the distant sky.

The combination of the wine, the natural beauty, and their feelings for each other were strong potions. Soft kisses turned passionate, and they began to make love. They moved together as the breeze moaned through the treetops.

Vibrant rays of sunlight streamed through the fluttering aspen leaves and danced among the shadows on their skin.

CHAPTER 41

Zina Martell sat stoically in front of Victor Merrick's desk, relaying details of how the pigeons had blurred Cade's vision through the riflescope. The bullet had fallen short of its mark, saving Scott Quinn's life.

Merrick leaned back and shook his head. "On top of that the Chandler woman escaped. Hell, I emptied my gun on the car, but they still got away."

"It'll take a little longer," Zina replied, "but Cade will find them."

"How in the hell is he going to do that? I'm sure they've left town."

"People like that always go to friends or relatives for help. It takes more time and manpower, but there are ways to find them." Zina looked out the window. "If you want this done quickly, we'll need to have some of your men watch the more obvious places they might go."

Merrick rose and paced the room, gesturing with his arms as he talked. "I've had a man watching her parent's house in Idaho. Now we know why he hasn't seen anything. They were right here in Chicago all the time."

"Keep him there." She jotted a note. "There are ways of finding them through their friends. I'll go to work on that."

Merrick stepped away from the window. "I want you to keep me informed so I can coordinate things with my men." He walked back to his desk. "I can't afford any more mistakes."

"Fine. We'll use the same arrangement as before. We'll find them and kill the man. You and your people take out the woman."

Merrick lit a cigarette. "All right, but I can't overemphasize how—"

Zina interrupted, her voice charged with determination. "I give you my word we'll find them. I guarantee it." She leaned back. "There is one more thing. Since we know they aren't in the Washington area, you might want to bring some of your men back to Chicago."

"I was thinking the same thing. I'll leave one there to watch over things." Merrick paused, and then said, "I'd still like to meet Cade."

"I've told you before; it doesn't work that way—and it never will." Zina got up and walked toward the door. "I'm very confident. We should have something in a few days."

Merrick followed and spoke in a softer tone, "Here, let me get that door." He stepped closer. "You're an intriguing woman. Have dinner with me this evening."

Zina walked through the door and spoke without looking back, "You're not my type."

———

Each time her target had left the Chicago Board of Trade, Zina noted that the same man had accompanied him. Judging from the way the two men had interacted she knew their relationship went beyond that of business associates. She would concentrate her immediate efforts on Scott's friend. If this failed, she would change her strategy.

Her first priority was to learn the man's identity and find out where he lived. Zina walked into the Chicago Board of Trade Monday morning and went straight to the visitor's gallery. She scanned the various pits until she spotted her subject, then she took out a small pair of binoculars and focused on the ID badge on the man's jacket. Three large initials spelled out MCD. Twenty minutes later, she had learned that the man's name was Jason McDonald. Zina waited near the parking garage, then followed him to his apartment. It had taken only a few hours to learn his name and where he lived.

She intended to monitor his movements for two or three days to see if he would lead her to Scott and Lauren. The next morning she followed Jason and was surprised when he drove to O'Hare Field instead of the Chicago Board of Trade. She thought he might be leaving town to meet her targets, and she decided to buy a ticket on the same flight if necessary.

She followed McDonald into the terminal and watched him stop at a gate for an incoming flight. She began to worry that he was simply going about his business and that his immediate actions would not lead her to Quinn. Ten minutes later, Jason McDonald met a young woman who came off an arriving flight. Immediately, Zina knew it was not Lauren Chandler. She followed the pair and heard enough of their conversation to learn they were on their way to New York to see a Broadway show, and they would be gone for three days.

She left the airport and decided to use the next two days to research Scott Quinn's other friends and relatives. She also intended to search Jason's apartment while he was away because she felt certain he knew where Quinn and the Chandler woman were hiding. It might take several days, but she knew she would locate her target—she always did.

CHAPTER 42

Scott saddled two horses and walked the animals out of the barn. After Tuck had left, he and Lauren made daily rides to the front gate to check the lock and inspect the area. Though he still believed their whereabouts were unknown, he felt acutely responsible for Lauren's welfare.

Scott felt an inner warmth as he thought about the change he had seen in Lauren. She was more relaxed and her full personality had emerged from the constraints imposed by desperation and fear. He also felt good about his own changes, including his disposition, and his bouts with insomnia had tapered off to an occasional, minor problem. He realized all of the improvements occurred after he had fallen in love with Lauren. He knew this was the woman he had waited for all of his life.

They mounted and had gone only a few yards when he saw Tuck coming up the road. Scott waited until the truck stopped. "I was just going down to check the lock."

"Everything looks okay," Tuck replied. "How have you two been getting by?"

"Quite well, thank you very much," Lauren said.

Tuck laughed. "I don't doubt that."

Scott followed Tuck to the barn, helped him unload his gear, then the two men talked until Lauren called from the porch. "Jason's on the phone from New York."

Scott entered the house and picked up the receiver. "Jason, how's your trip going?"

"Great, but that's not why I called. I figured you were safe but I wanted to make sure."

"We're fine now but it was touch and go for a while." Scott gave further details of their narrow escape from Chicago.

"That's scary as hell," Jason said. "I'm just glad you're both okay. Listen, there's another reason I wanted to talk to you. I think something big is happening in cash gold."

"Why?"

"No international news, or anything like that, but I had lunch with an old friend today. You've heard me mention John Goodman. Well, he's a trader at the Comex, and he thinks the Russian's are starting to unload gold. He's convinced they're selling mixed lots at various locations to disguise their actions. What do you make of it?"

"Give me a second." As Scott ran through the possibilities, one thing stood out—he had always believed the Russians did not have enough grain stocks to meet demand over the winter. When the Russians canceled their grain negotiations with the United States, world opinion had shifted to the belief that recent harvests were better than expected and the Russians did have enough stocks. Scott never subscribed to that theory. He thought they would eventually have to import large quantities of grain—especially wheat, soybeans, and soybean meal.

After a long silence, Jason asked, "You still there?"

"Yeah. How long are you going to be in New York?"

"Another day but I can change my plans."

"No need to do that. I'm going to make a call to a friend of mine in London. He follows gold and he has excellent contacts in Zurich and the Mideast."

Scott hung up and paced the floor, considering the implications. He was convinced the Russians had to sell gold to raise hard currency because of the recent weakness in the price of oil, which was a major source of revenue for Russia. If they came to the cash market for grain, futures prices would soar. He sat down and scribbled notes on a yellow pad. His first priority was to call London. Next, he outlined a trading strategy. Because the latest USDA report indicated a substantial increase in the U. S. soybean harvest, he would concentrate his buying elsewhere. Small carry-over stocks had already given wheat better relative strength than the other grains, and any large purchases by Russia would only increase this tendency.

At the bottom of the page, Scott circled wheat as his major purchase, but he also listed soybean meal because the Russian's needed the by-product to provide high protein feed for livestock. If he did enter the market, he intended to put 70 percent of his commitment into wheat futures and the remainder in soybean meal.

Before calling London, Scott walked out to the porch and found Lauren curled up on a chair, reading a novel. He held out his hand. "Let's go for a walk."

They held hands and strolled to the aspen grove behind the house. They said very little until Lauren rested her back against a tree. "Is there something wrong?"

"Not at all." Scott replied, looking into her eyes. "Jason and I are working on something that might turn into a major opportunity in the futures market. Because of our situation, I wanted to talk to you before I got involved."

"I don't understand."

"Your safety should come before anything else. I wouldn't want to get heavily involved in the market and not be ready if something should happen."

"Scott, I appreciate your reasoning, but I thought you said we were safe here."

"I think we are, but I wanted to talk it over with you."

"This is your decision. You don't need to ask me."

Scott stepped closer. "I believe my wife should have a say in every important decision."

"Y—your wife? Are you asking me to marry you?"

Scott stepped around the tree and bent down to pick up a small jewelry box he had hidden earlier. He opened the box and looked into her eyes. "Lauren, will you be my wife?"

"Oh, Scott. Yes!" Tears streamed down her cheek as she threw her arms around him.

Scott held her for a long moment, and then he wiped the moisture from her face and kissed her. He felt her tremble with emotion as they embraced.

When they separated, Lauren asked, "Where on earth did you get the ring?"

"I had Tuck pick it up when he was in town, and I put it here while you were in the house. They didn't have much in such a small town, but we can get another one later."

She looked from Scott to the ring on her finger. "Believe me, this will do just fine."

They talked for several minutes and decided to wait until after the next crop report to get married. Hopefully, Merrick's scheme would be uncovered, and Lauren would be cleared of any wrong-doing. They went back to the house and broke the news.

————

An hour later, Scott phoned Latham Clifford in London. Clifford said there were a few signs the Russians might be selling gold, but he needed to make several phone calls to verify his assumptions. He would check his sources and get back to Scott by 8:00 a.m., Mountain Time.

After the call, Scott went to the kitchen and talked with Lauren until dinnertime.

The phone rang while they were eating. Tuck answered, then motioned to Scott. "It's for you."

He took the handset. "Jason?"

"Yeah, what did you find out?"

"Clifford's going to do some checking and call me early tomorrow. If it goes as planned, we should have about thirty-minutes before the market opens."

"What's your thinking on this?"

Scott had analyzed the possibilities and answered quickly. "If Clifford thinks the Russians are selling large quantities of gold, my gut tells me to buy grains, especially wheat." He paused a moment, then asked, "Where are you going to be in the morning?"

"I'll stay in the hotel until you call. I can watch the market from here and then fly home after the close."

Scott jotted down Jason's phone number before hanging up. While looking over his notes, he remembered seeing a few charts and a copy of the *Wall Street Journal* in Jason's car. If the charts were not too old, he could easily update them. He went outside and walked toward the car, scanning his surroundings as he went. He looked over the Porsche's roof as he approached the driver's side.

In the trees behind the house—something moved.

He narrowed his eyes, squinting, concentrating on the spot. Again, he saw movement. Scott reached for his holster, hesitated, then spun and ran to the house. He burst through the door, grabbed a shotgun and yelled, "Lauren!"

"I'm in the kitchen."

Scott ran toward her voice. "Lock the door behind me, then get your pistol and hide."

"What? What is it?"

"Somebody in the trees."

"I'm going with you."

"No." Scott ran toward the backdoor, yelling as he went, "Get your gun and stay put."

He opened the door, his gaze searching for obvious points of ambush; then he ran across the small clearing and dove behind a stand of thick brush.

No shots.

Scott crawled several feet to his right and peered toward the trees. Nothing. He waited a few seconds, calculating his safest route; then, he rose to a crouching position and ran into the timber. He stopped behind a large tree and listened as he looked back toward the house. He estimated his position to be about fifty yards from where he had seen the movement. He moved forward in a crouch, making sure he maintained visual contact with the house.

Scott closed on the target area, his shotgun poised.

Ten more yards.

He heard movement to his right and swung his gun around, bracing for the jolt of a bullet. Two deer bounded across a clearing and disappeared into the aspen. Scott leaned against a spruce and wiped his forehead. He rested the back of his head on the tree, his mind processing the transition from vigilance to relief. He listened for a few minutes, scouted the area, and went back to the house. Though it had been a false alarm, Scott felt a strong need to spend time with Lauren before making another trip to Jason's car. He also reminded himself that they were in constant danger, and he had to remain vigilant.

An hour later, he retrieved the items from the Porsche and entered the house. The price charts were two weeks old, but they would still help him monitor trading activity. He made a phone call, updated recent price movements, and then plotted resistance and support areas. A small, downward sloping trend-channel had formed for most grains with soybeans showing the sharpest angle of decline. As expected, wheat had maintained its positive relative strength and appeared poised for a rally. The wheat chart reinforced his trading strategy.

With his mind overflowing with thoughts of the day's events, Scott got little sleep that night. The combination of his proposal to Lauren, the incident with the deer, and a possible big play in grain futures made it impossible for his mind to shut down. After only three hours of sleep, he got up at five thirty and turned on the TV. Fortunately, Tuck had a satellite dish that picked up CNBC. The network provided current financial news and ran a ticker tape on the bottom of the screen. He watched for an hour but heard nothing significant. Gold, however, was down again. Europe had led the way.

The phone rang a few minutes before eight.

"It's Clifford. I've talked to four of my contacts, and I think you're onto something. I'm eighty percent certain the Russians are systematically unloading a large supply of the metal. They're being very careful how and where they do their selling, but certain things point to them. It's bloody incredible."

"Are there any rumors on the trading floor?"

"There's been little talk so far. You've probably got a day or two before the word is out."

Scott told him about his theory on the grains, but he did not have to worry about Clifford as they had an understanding about such things. Scott knew his words would not go beyond Clifford's ears. He thanked his friend, hung up, and checked his charts. Fifteen minutes before the opening, Scott phoned the floor and got a pre-call on the grains. Soybeans and corn were called steady; wheat was expected to open one to two cents higher.

He called New York.

Jason answered on the first ring. "Scott?"

"You must be sitting on the phone."

"Hell, I knew it was you. What did you find out?"

Scott relayed the information he had obtained from Clifford, and mentioned the pre-call for the grains. He glanced back at his charts. "Jason, I've got a good feeling on this one. I think we should go in right after the opening. I'm going seventy-thirty in wheat and meal."

"Let's do it. Shit, this could really work."

"Yeah," Scott said, "but since we're not on the floor, we'd better protect part of our position with stops."

Scott waited until the market opened before calling the floor. Wheat had gained two cents and soybean meal was unchanged. Trading activity was moderately heavy, but there was no news of interest on the wires. His initial strategy had been to purchase half of his position at the market, then place orders for the other half a few cents under current prices. Intuition combined with what

Clifford had said changed his mind. He placed market orders for the entire position.

After early strength, grains softened and traded lower for most of the day; wheat enjoyed a late rally and moved up four cents a bushel from the previous session. There had been no announcements regarding a potential Russian grain purchase, but he knew it could come at any time—if he was right.

———

Scott spent the remainder of the day horseback riding with Lauren. They decided to call Angela Williams to see if plans to catch Hayden Benson were in place. The next crop report was twelve days away. The rest of the day was uneventful.

They went to bed, and Lauren fell asleep with her head on his shoulder. Scott lay awake, enjoying the immense pleasure he always felt when she slept in his arms. He smelled her scent and felt the heat radiating from her body. He gently ran his fingers through her hair as he listened to her breathe. He felt an intense moment of bliss he wanted to capture and hold on to forever.

After a time, his thoughts turned to his father, and his mind spun slowly over memories of his past and of his childhood home. He became aware of a deep undercurrent of pain fracturing and breaking apart. He felt a sudden warmth and a strange sense of release so profound it startled him, though he could not interpret its exact meaning.

He stroked Lauren's hair and went to sleep with love in his heart.

———

Jason phoned early the next morning and said there was no overnight news. They planned a strategy for the day and agreed to keep in close contact. Wheat opened down three cents and spent most of the day backing and filling, buy orders again came into the pit at the close. Wheat settled with a two-cent gain on the day. The action on the close was favorable, but Scott worried that a major announcement might not be forthcoming. Gold had also stabilized over the last two days—a bad sign.

Lauren rose early the next morning and prepared breakfast. Scott pulled out his chair just as the phone rang. Jason's voice was full of excitement. "Scott, have you seen the news?"

"Not yet."

"The Russians just signed a big grain deal with the United States."

CHAPTER 43

Whenever Zina Martell changed her identity to Cade, she became relentless in her attention to details. She had developed a long, meticulous checklist of techniques to insure that she missed nothing during a search. She spent two days gathering information on Scott Quinn and learned he had numerous friends in the Chicago area, his parents were deceased, and that most of his other relatives lived in California. After researching Scott, she would concentrate on Lauren Chandler. Zina was convinced they were still together, and she suspected they would initially hide with friends or relatives.

On the morning of the third day, Zina drove past Jason McDonald's apartment and parked two blocks away. She opened the trunk and retrieved a large handbag containing several electronic devices. She walked to the apartment, obtained the room number from the mailbox, went to the second floor, waited until the hallway cleared, picked the lock and went inside.

Zina made a cursory check of the front room and then went directly to the master bedroom. After a thorough search produced nothing of interest, she went down the hall to the next bedroom. The room had been converted to an office and it contained the normal equipment including a computer. She went to the desk, turned on the answering machine, and began a thorough search of the drawers. She heard a variety of calls but nothing of interest. Zina started to jot down a number from Jason's address book when the last message came across. It was from Scott Quinn. She replayed the tape and listened carefully: "Jason, this is Scott. I wanted to let you know we're safe, and that we'll be staying with Tuck for a while. We should be there late Monday. Call me when you get back."

She flipped through Jason's address book, stopping at the letter T. There were four listings but none could be associated with Tuck. She leaned back and thought for a moment. Her targets had obviously left town, but if she could get Tuck's phone number, she knew she could easily locate them. She rummaged through her bag, then crawled under a table and followed the phone line to the wall outlet. The line plugged in behind a two-drawer, wooden file cabinet. She slid the file out and attached a pen register to the line. The device would analyze the dial tones for each outgoing call, storing the numbers in memory for later retrieval.

She moved the cabinet back in place and checked to make sure no one could see the device with a casual glance. She then recorded Jason's phone number, made a quick inspection of the rest of the office, and left the apartment. Zina walked to her car, uplifted by a sense of excitement she always felt when tracking her quarry. The pursuit was an intense game, a complex puzzle, and she was the master. She went back to her hotel and thought about her strategy. If Jason kept to his schedule, he would return late today, and he would probably return Scott's call immediately. All she had to do was wait.

She spent the afternoon visiting two art galleries, followed by an early dinner. It was a little before nine when she picked up the phone and punched in Jason's number. A man answered. She apologized for dialing the wrong number and hung up.

The next morning she waited in front of Jason's building until he left for work, then she went to his second floor apartment and retrieved the pen register. Though she took a chance by removing the device after such a short time, it seemed likely that Jason would have called his friend as soon as he got the message. If not, she would repeat the process and leave the unit connected for a longer period.

She returned to her hotel and made a log of Jason's outgoing phone calls. There were four. Two local and two long distance. Zina dialed the number in the 212 area code, which she knew to be in Manhattan. No answer. She tried the next number. She did not recognize the 303 area code but she thought it might be in a Western state.

She got an answering machine: "Tucker Pack Trips. Please leave—"

She hung up and leaned back against the headboard of the bed, pleased with herself. Pinpointing the geographical location of the area code and the prefix would be a simple matter. She opened the phone book and flipped through the pages until she found a map of the United States depicting area codes. Her finger skimmed across the page and stopped on the outline of Colorado. The state was divided into two area codes, with 303 covering most of the northern and western sections.

She reached into her briefcase and pulled out a map of the United States. Zina looked at the outline of Colorado, her mind running ahead, developing a plan. She would rent a car, drive to Denver, and then locate the specific area for the telephone prefix. This strategy allowed her to take the rifle and other equipment necessary for the job. She packed, checked out, and was on the highway within an hour and a half.

———

Zina spent the first night in Des Moines. She checked into a motel and immediately dialed the unlisted number for Merrick's home. No answer.

She tried again before going to bed. Merrick picked up.

"The people you're interested in are in Colorado."

"Colorado? Jesus, how do you know that?"

"That doesn't matter. We don't have their exact location yet, but we should have it in three or four days."

"Listen," Merrick said, "I've got a place in Aspen. We'll fly out late tomorrow so we can be close by when you call. I'll give you my number. When you find them, I want you to call me right away."

"No problem."

"Three or four days, you said?"

"Maybe sooner."

"Good work." He gave her his Colorado phone number. "When this is wrapped up, I'm going to throw a big party at my place in Aspen, and you and Cade are invited. You won't want to miss it."

"We don't socialize with our clients." Zina hung up and went to her room, smiling at a vision of Merrick staring at a dead phone. She studied a map of Colorado, read a fine art magazine while she took a bath, then she went to bed.

The next morning she ate, filled the gas tank, and was on the road by six-thirty. When she drove across the state line separating Iowa and Nebraska, she felt certain she would not only find the couple, but also that it would be exceedingly easy. The telephone number was as good as a homing beacon.

CHAPTER 44

Scott listened intently while Jason read the bulletin announcing the agreement between the United States and Russia. Full details of the pact were not yet available, but the statement indicated that substantial amounts of wheat, corn, and soybean meal were involved. Options to take smaller amounts of other grains and seed oils were also included.

"I'm sure I don't have to ask," Scott said, "but what's the reaction on the floor?"

"Hell, you ought to be here. The traders with big short positions are in total shock. They can't figure out why the Russians canceled the earlier agreement when they needed so much grain."

"That's easy," Scott replied. "They didn't have enough hard currency."

"I've gotta hand it to you, Scott. You were spot-on with this one. It looks like the grains will be limit up across the board this morning."

"I'd be shocked if they weren't." Scott thought about his strategy. "The only thing we need to watch for is if soybeans weaken and that causes some kind of weird reversal in the rest of the grains. It's not likely, but keep your eye on it just in case. Otherwise, we'll just sit tight and enjoy the ride."

Scott spent the morning watching the business channel, which provided substantial coverage of the new agreement. Grains opened up the limit and remained there for the entire session. Jason called three times, but only to talk as there was little else to do with the market locked limit up. They were on the right side of an explosive situation.

After the market closed, Scott and Lauren took one of their few trips to town. Lauren called her parents once a week to let them know she was all right. Though it was probably safe to call from Tuck's, Scott thought it prudent to continue using a pay phone. Lauren completed the call and expressed concern about her father. He was ill and had taken several tests, but the results had been inconclusive. His condition did not appear to be serious, but they decided Lauren should call frequently over the next two weeks to check his progress. They shopped for an hour before returning to the house.

Tuck was preparing for a trip and said that he would be gone only a few days. Scott helped him with his gear, then he and Lauren waved as Tuck drove out of sight.

———

Jason called the next morning. He said that wheat and corn had opened up the limit, but beans were only up eight cents. Soybean oil provided a drag on the market, and after opening slightly higher, oil closed unchanged on the day. Beans held only slight gains at the end of the day. Despite the weakness in the soybean complex, wheat and corn maintained their strength for the entire session and again closed up the limit.

Scott was delighted with the strength in wheat, but he felt uneasy about the weakness in soybeans. The recent predictions of record yields continued to act as a drag on the bean complex. He calculated his gains and determined his combined position of wheat and soybean meal gave him paper profits of nearly $3 million. Normal procedure would have called for Scott to trade aggressively to obtain maximum profits. Because their situation dictated a more judicious approach, he decided to sell half of his position on any strength the next day. His last two trades had earned more than he had lost on the original Russian grain cancellation. It was not a time to be greedy.

Lauren treated him to a candlelight dinner that night. The evening turned cool, and they decided to burn a few logs. After Scott lit the fire, they settled on the couch and talked while sipping wine. The firelight caused tiny reflections to flicker on Lauren's face, and Scott thought he had never seen her look more beautiful. He leaned over and kissed her with a depth of feeling that blocked out all other sensation. He then ran his hand under Lauren's blouse and caressed her. Her moan vibrated softly in his mouth. They made love to the sound of logs popping and hissing in the background.

———

Scott was still in bed when Jason called the next morning. He glanced at the clock as he picked up the phone.

"Hey, Scott. You sound like you've got a hangover."

"Late night. What's up?"

"Cash grains are strong this morning. Wheat looks to be up four to six cents, and beans look steady."

"I want you to sell all of my meal and two hundred contracts of Dec wheat on the opening. Transfer the funds to T-Bills."

"Do you think the rally's over?"

"No, but I'm not in a position to trade properly." They discussed the technical aspects of the market before Scott hung up.

Jason called back and confirmed Scott's sale of Dec wheat and all of his soybean meal. After trading higher most of the day, a late round of profit taking pushed most of the grains slightly lower for the day.

Freed from concern about the market, Scott decided to take Lauren to their favorite meadow. He walked out of the house and searched the sky as he headed toward the barn, paying particular attention to a layer of dark clouds threatening in the western sky. It smelled of rain. He had been in the barn for only a few minutes when thunder rumbled over the mountains. Within minutes, light rain began to patter on the roof. He stepped outside and inspected the sky. The worst of the storm appeared to be moving to the south, but he thought it best to postpone their ride until the next day.

Scott walked a short distance from the barn and stood, staring toward the charcoal gray clouds billowing to his south. He watched for a long moment and then let his gaze sweep across the land, settling on the aspen grove. He loved the trees; yet he suddenly felt as if an unknown menace lurked there, waiting to destroy everything precious to him. He stood for a long while, oblivious of the growing breeze and the raindrops striking his body. He tried to shake off the ominous feeling but could not.

CHAPTER 45

Zina had car trouble ninety miles west of Des Moines and had to stay over a day while the repair shop obtained parts. The next morning she resumed her journey to Colorado. She pushed hard and arrived in Denver late that night. The next morning she contacted the phone company and learned the prefix she was interested in covered a rural area around the small town of Little River. It took a bit of searching until she found the town on the state map. It was located in the mountains northwest of Denver.

She went to a sporting goods store and bought several items of clothing suitable for mountain terrain including boots and a pair of binoculars. Experience had taught her to prepare for every possibility. She left for Little River at eleven-thirty. Later that day Zina, followed a narrow, twisting mountain road, and after an hour of climbing, she dropped into a small valley cradled between rugged mountains, crossed a bridge, and entered Little River.

She stopped at a gas station, went directly to a telephone booth, and picked up the phone book. She looked under the letter T and found a listing for Tucker Pack Trips. She pulled out the number she had obtained from the pen register on Jason's line and compared it with the number in the book. They matched.

There was a small motel in town, but she did not want to stay that close to her target. She remembered seeing two motels in the last town about thirty miles from Little River. She drove back the way she had come and checked into one of the motels.

———

The next morning, Zina drove to Little River, stopped at the same gas station, filled her tank, and asked the attendant where Tucker Pack Trips was located. He told her it was about ten miles up the road and to look for a sign over the gate.

She spent most of the morning getting acquainted with the valley, giving special attention to the back roads. Before completing a contract, she always checked every possible escape route. As usual, she was meticulous in her attention to details. When she drove by the sign indicating the turnoff for Tucker Pack Trips, she noticed the gate was locked and thought it odd because all of the other gates in the area were wide open. That single clue reinforced her belief that Scott Quinn and Lauren Chandler were somewhere on the property.

Zina made a U-turn and drove a short distance before turning onto a narrow dirt road on the other side of the highway. She parked the car behind some brush, retrieved her binoculars, and walked back to the road. If she met anyone, she would simply act the part of a bird watcher on vacation. No one would ever imagine she had a 9mm pistol under her jacket. She crossed the highway and made her way through the shrubs before entering a stand of trees. When she could no longer see the highway, she turned and headed toward the dirt road to Tucker Pack Trips. She followed the private drive, being careful to stay far enough into the wooded area to remain out of sight. She located a house, crept up to a small knoll, sat behind a clump of brush, pulled out her binoculars and waited.

Two hours passed before she saw Scott walk out of the house and enter the barn. After several minutes, he came out of the barn with two saddled horses and led them to the house. A woman with short, blonde hair came outside. She mounted and the two rode toward the rear of the house, then they cut across an open area to a trail that passed by a grove of aspen trees. Zina watched until they were out of sight; then, she went back the way she had come.

Zina's pattern dictated that she always stalked her victims carefully before making a kill. It usually took only a few days, but she occasionally found it necessary to watch for as long as a month before striking. Hasty actions increased the chances of things going wrong. Her methods had worked well in the past, and she would continue using them for this contract. She was surprised she had seen no sign of other people around the house. Following her rigid rule of never assuming anything, she would check again tomorrow.

———

The next morning, Zina packed a lunch and drove to the same dirt road she had used the previous day. She took a slightly different route to the small knoll and settled down for a long watch. She knew such a remote location was an ideal spot for her and Merrick to make the kill, but she wanted to know how many others were on the premises, or if there were any particular daily routine. It seemed obvious that at least a man named Tucker resided there, but what about a wife, children, or frequent visitors?

She waited for three hours before she saw anyone. Just after one o'clock, Scott Quinn came out of the house and crossed to the barn. A few minutes later, he led two horses to the house and the blonde came out. They mounted and left in the same direction they had gone the day before. Zina rolled over and sat up. It was the same pattern as the previous day—almost to the minute.

She watched the house for another thirty minutes, but there were no signs of movement. She rose and made her way through the trees, but instead of heading back to her car, she climbed a ridge and stopped on a small ledge that offered a sweeping view of the area. Zina made mental notes of important landmarks and drew a rough map of the surrounding region. She then took out the binoculars and made several sweeps up and down the entire area, paying particular attention to the terrain that lay in the direction her target had taken.

She scanned across a meadow, stopping suddenly to focus on two riders who had entered an open area below the meadow. From their attire, she knew it was Scott and Lauren. Zina watched them and felt surprised by a feeling of jealousy that swept through her. Even at this distance, she could sense the strong bond between the pair. She had never experienced a relationship with such obvious depth. When it came to men, she thought life had parceled out assorted misfits just for her. She forced the thoughts from her mind. This was business.

The sky darkened and she heard the faint rumblings of thunder. Though it appeared the storm would stay to the south, she headed back through the trees to her car. She stopped at the edge of town, grabbed her notebook, entered a phone booth, and flipped the pages, stopping at a particular entry: V. M. - Aspen. She dialed the number and asked for Victor Merrick.

"We found them," she said. "I think they're about three or four hours from where you are, but I'm not sure."

"I'm impressed. Cade is every bit as good as I've heard."

"Yes," Zina replied flatly. "There's no one better."

"I want to get this over with quickly," Merrick said. "Where are they?"

"Just outside a small town called Little River. They're way back off the road with no other houses around. It's an ideal situation."

"Perfect."

"How soon can you leave?" Zina asked.

"I was just waiting for your call. We can leave in thirty minutes."

"How many men did you bring?"

"Seven, including myself. There's not a chance in hell of them getting away again."

"One more thing: I suggest you stay in the same town I'm in. Cade is nearby, but we never stay in the same motel."

She gave Merrick directions, then hung up and drove to her motel. After dinner, she took out her map and made another copy, then she outlined two options for making the kill. Her first choice depended on the targets following the same pattern they had used the last two days. The alternate plan was to kill them at the house, but that obviously involved more risk. Satisfied with her preparation, she put down her pencil and stared at a barren wall. If Scott and Lauren went for another horseback ride, it would be their last.

———

A little after ten-thirty, Zina heard two cars stop in front of her room. She grabbed her pistol and went to the window. The light was not good, but she recognized one of Merrick's men. She opened the door and saw several men carrying bags toward rooms farther down the walkway. She motioned for Merrick to come inside.

He made no attempt at small talk. "What's Cade's plan? I want this whole thing laid out for me."

Zina gave him details about the location of the house and showed him a map of the surrounding area. "They apparently go horseback riding several days a week. There's an open area a little over a mile from the house that has good cover. It's ideal for an ambush. We think you should put men on both sides of the trail and wait for them to show. Cade will use a rifle with a scope to take out Quinn. As soon as he fires, I'll shoot the horses. After that, the woman is yours."

"Hell, that sounds easy enough."

"Isn't that what you want?"

Merrick ignored her question. "Are you a good enough shot?"

"Deadly," Zina replied sharply, her dislike for Merrick ticking up another notch. "One more thing. It would be best if you took the bodies a mile or so into the woods and buried them."

"Good idea. What time do we start?"

"It's imperative to Cade that no one ever sees him, so he'll leave early. He wants you to meet me at eleven o'clock." She gave him a map and pointed at her markings. "There's a dirt road right here. I'll be standing behind cover. When I see you, I'll step out and direct you so your cars can't be seen from the road; then I'll guide you to the ambush site."

"Cade's a real careful fellow."

"You expected something different?"

CHAPTER 46

Scott slept in Friday morning and awoke to the smell of fresh coffee, birds chirping outside his window, and Lauren humming in the kitchen. Pleasant sounds. Tuck usually rose with the sun, but he had not returned from his trip. Scott expected him later in the day. Normally, he would have been up early to check market news and prepare his strategy for the day, but this morning, he had a leisurely attitude. He felt little pressure as he had liquidated seventy percent of his position, and he had given Jason stop orders to protect the remaining contracts. He had also managed to push aside the ominous feeling that had gripped him the previous day.

Lauren came into the room with a breakfast tray. She smiled and seemed in high spirits. She kissed Scott on the forehead. "Okay, Mr. Lazy Bones. Breakfast is served."

He smelled the coffee's aroma and reached for the cup.

Lauren wiggled her index finger. "Ah, ah . . . not yet. You only get to eat if you take me riding this afternoon like you promised."

Scott smiled at her playfulness. He looked toward the window and said, "Well, I don't know. Last night's weather report said there may be thunder storms in the area today."

"I don't mind."

Scott hesitated, stalling.

Lauren picked up the tray. "All right, no breakfast for you."

He knew his empty stomach had dealt him a losing hand. He looked at the steaming food. "Okay, okay."

He finished his breakfast and then checked the market. The grains had been open for fifteen minutes when he got the first quotes. Another round of profit taking had pushed prices down a few cents. Scott considered the action normal, and he suspected that wheat had entered a support zone. He periodically checked prices and was pleased to see a late rally push wheat to a four-cent gain on the day. He knew this type of action favored a resumption of the rally. He held his position and decided to liquidate the remaining contracts during periods of strength over the next few sessions; then he would wait for the USDA crop report. Scott talked to Jason and raised his stop orders. Just as he hung up, Lauren came into the room wearing her riding clothes.

Scott tried to look serious. "You know, there are some really nasty looking clouds out there today. I'm not sure we should go riding."

"Scott Quinn, you'd better stop teasing me and get out to that barn right now." She walked toward the door with a decided bounce to her step, turning back to grin just before she went out of sight.

Scott changed clothes, strapped on his holster and went outside. He noticed a darkening sky to the west but felt little concern. If they did encounter bad weather, they could seek shelter under one of the many overhangs nature had carved in the side of a nearby cliff. On his way to the barn, he stopped next to an old horse trailer. Tuck had mentioned the need for replacing the trailer, but an addition to his house had left him short on cash. Scott thought of his recent gains and decided to buy Tuck a new trailer. It was the least he could do for a friend who had taken them in without hesitation. The thought gave him a feeling of satisfaction as he saddled the horses.

When he returned to the house, Lauren stood on the porch with a daypack and a blanket.

"I've got our lunch. Guess what else I packed?"

Scott noticed the look in her eyes. "It wouldn't happen to be wine, would it?"

"Do you remember what happened the last time we took a bottle of wine?"

"No, not really."

She put down the pack and chased him around the horses. After a several minutes of mutual teasing and laughter, Scott helped her gather their gear. After mounting, they started up the path toward the meadow. Scott thought that he could not possibly love her more than he did at that moment.

When they could no longer see the house, he took the lead, his eyes searching the trees as they rode.

CHAPTER 47

After a light breakfast, Zina left the motel a little before nine-thirty, drove to the designated meeting site, inspected the area, checked her rifle, and then sat down and watched the road. She occasionally glanced at the darkening sky, hoping the threatening weather did not cause her targets to stay inside today.

A few minutes after eleven, two cars came around a bend and slowed as they approached the turnoff. Zina stepped into view and motioned for them to pull onto the dirt road. Fifteen minutes later, she led Merrick and six of his men across the highway and into the cover of the woods. She followed a twisting route through rough terrain for nearly two miles before stopping on a tree-covered ridge that offered a good view of the clearing below.

Merrick approached her, wiping sweat from his forehead. "Damn, I didn't think you were ever going to stop. Why did we have to come so far?"

"Pretty simple, really. There's no chance anyone will see anything this far from the road." She gestured toward the surroundings with a sweep of her arm as she spoke. We've got a perfect line of fire, and it's an ideal location for disposing of the bodies."

Merrick nodded and looked at the sky. "It looks bad over there. I hope a storm doesn't screw things up."

"If they don't go riding today, we can wait until tomorrow or take them in the house. It's up to you, but it'd be a lot cleaner if we could do it up here."

"Yeah," Merrick said. "It would be better here. We'll just have to wait and see."

Zina pointed toward the open area. "If they follow their regular pattern, they'll come up that trail next to the gully. Have some of your men take cover to my left and send three or four into the trees on the other side. We're quite a bit higher on this side, so crossfire won't be a problem. Make sure they don't fire a shot until we've taken out Quinn. The woman is your responsibility."

Merrick scanned the area. "This is perfect. It should be easy." He told Billy to take three men and station them behind cover on the other side of the clearing. He then told Lisowski and two others to follow him. He looked back at Zina. "Where the hell is Cade?"

"A little farther up."

Merrick shrugged, and then led his men several yards to the left where they took cover in the trees.

They waited.

At 12:55, two riders came into view near the bottom of the clearing, moving up the trail at a walk, her target leading the way. Zina moved a few yards to her left and spoke quietly, "It's them. Get ready." She went back to her original position, checked her weapon and waited.

When Scott pulled even with Zina, she raised her rifle with a sense of mission. This time she would not miss.

———

Michael Tucker was tired. Though his trip had been shorter than most, the long hours still took a toll on a man's body. He looked forward to a shower, a beer, and an early supper. The thought reinforced his belief in the value of simple pleasures.

He negotiated the last curve before his turnoff. Two hundred yards from the gate, Tuck thought he saw a glint of reflection coming from the trees. He slowed, concentrating on the spot. Nothing. He turned and stopped in front of his gate. He sat in the idling truck for a moment, then moved the gearshift to reverse and swung back onto the highway. The instincts he had learned as a cop had taken over, pushing fatigue aside. Experience told him to check the site and make sure.

Tuck pulled to the side of the road, opened the glove compartment, grabbed his pistol, got out, and moved cautiously toward the trees. He stopped at the edge of the timber and waited a few seconds before moving forward with his gun ready. He had gone about ten yards when he saw the rear bumper of a car. He took cover and scanned the area carefully. Satisfied, he crept forward and found three cars. It looked as if the vehicles had been parked to conceal them from the road.

He checked the ground and found several sets of footprints leading back toward the highway. Tuck moved quickly along their trail. When the prints stopped at the edge of the pavement, he ran across the road and searched the ground. He spotted the footprints. When he saw the direction they had taken, distress gripped his soul.

"Shit!"

He began to run.

There were at least six or seven sets of prints. They were probably professionals, and they were obviously here to make a kill.

His concern grew with each passing yard. He was surprised when their route took him deep into the woods. Had he misjudged the clues? Assassins surely would have turned toward the house. Tuck stopped and considered veering from the trail and racing to the house. It was a tough choice, but he decided there had to be a reason they were going in this direction. He maintained his pace and stayed on their trail.

A few minutes later, the tracks angled to his left and went up a slope. He climbed rapidly until the trees became dense. He slowed and grew cautious. A cloud darkened sky and thick timber made the trail almost impossible to see. He crept forward, stopping every few feet to search the ground and listen. It was quiet except for the occasional sound of thunder rumbling overhead.

He topped a ridge and saw a woman crouched next to a tree. She was twenty feet in front of him, and she had just raised her rifle to sight on the clearing below. Tuck's position, above her, allowed him to look toward the clearing to locate her target.

The sight of Scott and Lauren sent him into action. Just as Tuck brought up his gun, his foot snapped a twig. He saw movement to his left at the same instant the woman in front of him turned in his direction.

CHAPTER 48

Scott had been watching the darkening sky and became concerned that he and Lauren would be caught in the open by the approaching storm. The increasing wind had caused the black clouds to move swiftly during the last few minutes, and the thunder had intensified dramatically. He suspected they would have to ride to one of the nearby alcoves to seek shelter. When they moved into an open area, he checked the sky again.

They were halfway across the clearing when gunshots rang out from the wooded area above them and to their right. Fear for Lauren swept through Scott's mind as he looked to see if she was all right. The sound of two more shots roared across the clearing. Someone was firing, but nothing seemed to have come in their direction.

He yelled at Lauren. "In the gully. Quick!" He slapped her horse on the rump.

More shots sounded from the slope. Bullets whined over Scott's head, sending a rush of adrenalin through his body. A few seconds after they reached the bottom of the ravine, the sky unleashed a tremendous hailstorm against the earth. Huge stones began crashing into the ground all around the gully.

Lauren's horse reared.

She held on.

Several bullets dug into the bank to Scott's right. To his dismay, he realized the shots had come from the other side. They were in a crossfire.

The hail quickly increased in size and intensity, so much so that ice missiles had now become a serious threat. A hailstone nearly the size of a tennis ball struck his horse on the head sending the animal crashing to the ground. Scott barely managed to jump clear.

He got to his feet and yelled at Lauren. "Get down! Get down!" He grabbed the reins while she jumped off, then handed them to her. In swift movements, he took the saddle off Lauren's horse, thrust it over his head, and slammed it against the side of the gully wall.

He yelled, "Under here. Quick," His voice ringing with intensity.

They huddled beneath the heavy leather. The combination of the saddle and a slight overhang protected their heads and most of their bodies from the storm's vicious onslaught. When the huge hailstones began pummeling the earth, the shooting came to a sudden halt. The gunmen were obviously under the same terrifying rain of stones.

Scott turned his attention to Lauren. Feeling a need to reassure her, he said, "We're going to be all right. Do you hear me?"

"Yes, but—"

"We've got to stay sharp. When this hail stops, they're going to come after us." Scott looked around. "Where's your gun?"

"It's in the backpack."

"Okay." Before Scott could continue, several huge hailstones struck the saddle nearly toppling them. They clung to each other.

"We'll be okay."

She nodded.

"Our lives depend on us working together." He glanced at the sky. "The hail's easing some. As soon as it stops, I'm going to grab your backpack and get your gun. When the time comes, use it." He looked at the sky. "If we can get your horse saddled, we'll lead him up the gully, then climb up and make a run for the trees. If not, we'll have to go on foot."

"I'll be ready."

While Scott gave final instructions, his horse suddenly rolled over and struggled to get up. The animal was dazed, but the instinct to get to its feet prevailed. Scott grabbed the reins. The horse still had its saddle on, and if the animal were strong enough, they might be able to ride up the gully without having to saddle Lauren's horse while under attack, a task he desperately wanted to avoid.

The sudden cessation of hailstones gave way to heavy gunfire. Scott tossed the saddle to one side and grabbed Lauren's backpack. He retrieved the pistol, chambered a shell, and handed it to her. He looked over the edge and saw three men running toward them from the trees to their left. When he raised his gun, crossfire from his backside sent bullets digging into the dirt next to him. Somewhere in his mind, distress notched up to desperation.

Scott fired three shots. The man in front took a bullet in the throat and collapsed. The others took cover.

More bullets whined over the gully.

Scott dove to the ground and crawled toward Lauren. "We're going to make a run for it."

He grabbed the reins and led the horse to the lowest part of the ravine, putting them temporarily out of vision.

The gunfire eased.

After twenty yards, the gully veered to the left and narrowed. He made the turn and looked ahead. The ditch split in two and became very shallow.

He looked back.

No sign of anyone.

He glanced at Lauren. "Okay, we've going to try it right here. Ready?"

"Yes."

Scott jumped onto the saddle and held out his hand. Lauren climbed up as a barrage of shots rang out. He jabbed his heel into the horse's flank. The animal started to run but faltered after a few yards. More shots sounded from both sides. Bullets whizzed all around.

Scott pulled on the reins and yelled, "It's not going to work. Get down."

After she dismounted, he jumped off just as the horse started falling. The animal's dazed condition combined with the extra weight had proved too heavy a burden. He grabbed Lauren's hand and ran up the gully until they came to the fork. Since most of the shots had come from their right, Scott took the left branch.

He thought about the ambush while they ran and found it odd that the first shots did not seem to come near them. One other thing was significant, and it had probably saved their lives—at least for now. Most of the shots sounded like they had come from pistols. He was surprised but grateful. Rifles were far more accurate at anything over twenty yards. If the majority of the gunmen had used the superior weapon, Scott thought he and Lauren would surely be dead.

The gully took another turn and angled toward the trees. It also became shallower and was now only about four feet deep. He stopped and looked over the edge. He caught a glimpse of men running through the woods about sixty yards away.

"They're trying to cut us off. Head for the trees. Quick!"

They bent as low as possible and ran up the narrowing gully. The walls began to close in and they were soon hitting the muddy edges with their shoulders. At one point, they had to stand up to get by. This brought a barrage of shots from the side and from their rear. They slid through the gap and ducked. Bullets whined overhead.

When they had nearly reached the trees, Scott saw movement to his left. He spun around just as a man took aim. Scott fired twice. The gunman got off one shot and then crumpled to the ground, but Scott had seen at least three on that side. Where were the others?

Bullets smashed into the bark as they ran by the first trees. Scott's instincts told him to keep running, but he became increasingly worried about the other men on this side.

Where were they?

He motioned for Lauren to stop and, quickly, he scanned the trees. Nothing. He looked behind them and saw two men running across the clearing toward the gully. They had obviously come from the high ground on the other side. When Scott turned back toward the trees, a gunshot roared in his ear. He looked to his right and saw a man slump to his knees. The gunman started to raise his pistol, but Lauren fired again. The bullet struck him in the chest, propelling him over backwards. His legs twisted in a peculiar fashion, and he lay still.

"Go through the trees," Scott yelled as he wiped his brow. "I'll be right there." As soon as she left, he turned and fired two shots at the men running along the gully behind them. They dove for cover, and he ran after Lauren.

He looked ahead and saw her darting among the closely set trees. He had nearly caught her when a man suddenly came through the trees on his left on a dead run.

Neither had time to react.

Scott crashed into the right side of the man's body sending them both sprawling. The hard fall jarred the gun from Scott's hand. He rolled over expecting a bullet to tear through his body.

With a glance, he saw that the gunman had also lost his weapon. Scott searched frantically through the matted leaves and branches. *The gun. Where's the damn gun?*

As his hands moved over the ground, he looked to his left and saw the man suddenly leap toward the base of a tree. He had found his gun. Scott turned to his right and saw the butt of his pistol five feet away. He lunged forward, grabbed the weapon, and rolled over in one swift action. Just as he raised his arm, the gunman's pistol roared. Once—twice.

Bullets bit into the ground where Scott had been a split second before. His own gun sounded.

Lauren ran toward him, screaming, "Scott! Scott!"

He crawled to his feet and motioned with his hand. "I'm okay, but we've got to keep moving." He looked at the man to make sure he was no longer a threat and realized it was the same man he had collided with in the storeroom at the department store.

Billy Barker sat against the base of a small tree, blood oozing from a hole in his chest, his gaunt face portending death. He spit up blood and uttered three words. "Bad f—fucking karma." His head tilted to one side.

Scott shoved Lauren ahead of him. "Run. We've got to keep going." They veered to the right and dodged in and out among the thick trees. Branches swatted their faces, and shrubs tore at their legs. His mind whirled in turmoil as they ran. What should they do? How many men were still out there? He had no answers; yet, one thing was clear: somehow, Victor Merrick had found them and his only goal was to end their lives.

After running three hundred yards, Scott stopped and looked back, but he could neither hear nor see anything. He made a quick decision to make a wide loop and try to get back to the house. Obviously, they could not stay there, but they might be able to grab his cash and make it to the car. It was then that he thought of Tuck and became worried. Had the men gone to the house first? Was Tuck even back yet? He grabbed Lauren's hand and turned to their right. She sucked in air, but she had a determined look on her face.

They raced through another thick stand of trees. He let Lauren move ahead of him, but she was having trouble maneuvering among the low boughs that extended out at angles from the trunks. She fell twice, splattering herself with mud. Scott helped her up and pushed her forward. The trees grew increasingly dense and blotted out much of the light.

Lauren turned and grabbed his arm, panting heavily. "I've got to rest."

He stopped, his chest heaving and looked back. "Just for a minute."

While she rested, he searched several yards in each direction, trying to get his bearings. They had continually moved to the right in an attempt to circle, and he thought they should have come to the slope near the aspen grove. Where was it? He went back to Lauren. She was bent over with her hand against a tree, breathing heavily. He took her hand. "We'll go on at a walk for a few minutes. We can catch our breath while I reload and try to figure out where we are."

Scott decided they had not angled far enough to the right. He turned in that direction and walked at a fast pace, stopping often to look and listen. After five minutes they started climbing, and he began to feel hopeful until he heard shouts from below and off to their right. He quickened the pace. After ten minutes, they came to a small opening on a narrow ridge. Scott looked to his right and saw the meadow. He knew where they were.

As they worked down the slope, he thought about how to approach the house, which was still over a mile away. He knew they had to use extreme caution as they got closer, and there was a good chance some of Merrick's men watched the house. They were half-way down when they came even with the clearing where they had been ambushed. Scott started to cut back through the trees when Lauren suddenly stopped. He looked back. "What's wrong?"

"There's a woman over there with a bullet hole in her chest."

He started toward Lauren. He was looking at her and saw a sudden, dreadful change in her expression—a look of horror spread across her face. She lifted a limp arm and pointed to their left, then sank to her knees and put a hand over her mouth.

Scott ran to her. "What? What's wrong?" He swung his head in the direction she pointed and saw Tuck's blood-soaked body sprawled on the ground. A terrible agony swept through him as he rushed to his friend. He bent over to check Tuck's pulse and heard a hollow gasp. Tuck's eyes opened slightly, and he attempted to say something. Scott put his ear closer and listened.

"R—raise me up. I want one last look at the land."

Scott helped him to a sitting position against a tree. "It's okay, Tuck. You'll pull through."

Tuck smiled weakly. "Don't bullshit me. . . . Come closer." His voice weakened and tailed off as he spoke.

Scott sank to his knees.

Tuck whispered, "I—I love you, pal." He coughed up blood, then continued, "I want you to do something for me."

"Anything."

Tuck whispered his final wish to Scott, then his head slumped to one side, and he took a last, poignant breath. Scott put his arms around Tuck and pulled his dead friend's face against his chest. Tears ran down his cheek and mixed with Tuck's blood. Sepulchral thoughts took possession of his mind and a feeling of grief—pure, elemental, and raw roamed through his soul.

He did not know how long he held his friend, but it just did not seem right to let go. After a long moment, he became aware of Lauren's hand on his shoulder.

"I'm sorry," she said softly.

He held Tuck a few more seconds, then gently lowered him to the ground.

The shouts from behind grew louder. Scott hesitated, his eyes riveted on Tuck, and then he rose and looked through the trees. He heard men thrashing about in the timber. He glanced at Tuck's body, then at Lauren. He did not want to leave his friend this way, but he had no choice. He grabbed her hand and started down the slope in the direction of the house, his sadness giving way to hatred as he went.

They alternated running, walking, and hiding for fifteen minutes and finally stopped at the edge of the trees. There was no sign of anyone around the house, and there were no cars visible. Where was Tuck's pickup? Scott decided to take a chance. If the gunmen had come up the road to the house, he might be able to see their cars. Since the truck was not here, Tuck must have seen something on the highway and cut across country on foot instead of coming up the drive. That meant there was a reasonable chance there was no one at the house.

He turned to Lauren. "We're going to make a run for the back door." With his gun ready, Scott took the lead. When they reached the back wall, he waited a moment and then opened the door with his pistol raised. The house was empty, but he estimated they had only a few minutes before the gunmen caught up with them. He yelled instructions for Lauren to get only the things she needed most; then he went to the bedroom and got his money. He grabbed two boxes of cartridges and headed for the front door. "Let's go."

They stepped outside and looked toward the trees. No sign of anyone yet. He ran across the clearing, opened the door to the Porsche, and glanced back.

Two men ran out of the trees.

He yelled at Lauren, "Hurry!"

Though the distance was too great to shoot accurately, the gunmen opened fire.

Scott snapped off four rounds, then jumped in and fumbled with the ignition, missing the keyhole. "Come on. Come on."

He tried again.

A bullet slammed into the rear of the car just as the engine turned over. Scott shoved the pedal to the floor. The tires spun in the mud, then caught hold, and the Porsche roared down the drive. He slowed to negotiate a turn before speeding up again. The car's tires gained traction, and spit up mud and gravel as the car sped away from the house.

———

Victor Merrick stood in the middle of the road, his arm hanging at his side, his hand clutching a pistol. Exhaustion held his rage in check, but it did not temper his disgust. After his men had shot the man who killed Zina Martell, he knew Cade should have opened fire on Scott, but all Merrick had heard was silence. He had often wondered about the mysterious Cade, and the truth struck him like a thunderbolt—it was the woman. As he thought about it, everything fell into place. Zina Martell was Cade, and she was dead. He shook his head, wondering why he had missed the signs until now.

The grueling chase had left Merrick's men scattered through the forest. He had no idea how many were killed, wounded, or lost, and it was of little concern. His mind revolved around one thought; his targets had escaped. If the stranger had not interfered, they would have been dead.

Because of his huge bulk, Ray Lisowski was not exactly a cross-country runner. Six minutes after Merrick had reached the house, Lisowski lumbered up and stopped. He leaned over, red faced, panting, his body awash with sweat. He spoke between breaths. "Did they get away?"

"What the fuck do you think?" Merrick paced back and forth before turning to Lisowski. "Yeah, they got away, but it'll be the last time that happens. There's one sure way to catch them, and we're going to use it. I'm putting an end to this shit once and for all."

CHAPTER 49

The burden of Tuck's death weighed heavily on Lauren. He had given his life for them, and she felt that another innocent person had been killed because of her. She felt especially disturbed when Scott had phoned Debbie Holloway to tell her the news and ask her to call the authorities. Lauren saw the pain in Scott's eyes when he got back in the car. Her guilt and sadness deepened.

When they left Little River, she knew they had to put as much distance between themselves and the gunmen as possible. They cut over to highway 40 and headed west. They reached Craig, Colorado and turned north, drove into Wyoming, then turned west on Interstate 80 and headed for Rock Springs.

After a brilliant, orange sun slid between distant cloudbanks and dropped below the horizon, Lauren stared at the road ahead. She sat motionless, watching mile after mile of white stripes race toward the headlights as she continually replayed the horror of what had happened. If only she had not heard Hayden Benson make that single phone call, none of this would have ever happened.

Scott had given most of his attention to traffic and the rear-view mirror. When they were thirty miles from Rock Springs, he reached over and touched her arm. "I love you, and it's forever."

Lauren felt a surge of emotion. She put her hand on his, feeling the warmth of his skin, linking to him.

———

They spent the next two days hiding in a motel on the outskirts of Rock Springs, Wyoming. Scott went out once a day to get food, but he would not let Lauren leave the room. They carried their pistols constantly and placed them on the table when they reviewed the map and discussed their plans.

After only twenty minutes, they decided to leave for California in a day or two. They would also call Angela Williams for an update. Lauren prayed that Benson and Merrick would be caught, and the terror that haunted them would end. On the second night, she worried about another problem. It had been over a week since she had called home, and she had become increasingly concerned about her father's health. She convinced Scott to let her use a phone booth inside a nearby store while he kept watch outside.

The phone rang four times before an answering machine came on. Lauren listened to her mother's monotone message and became concerned. Her parents had always hated answering machines, and her father had said he would never own one of the contraptions. She paid particular attention to her mother's voice as the message ended. It sounded strained, unnatural. She worried that her father's illness had deteriorated and that he might be in the hospital—or worse.

Lauren hesitated, then said, "Mother, pick up if you're there . . . Mother?" Several seconds went by without a response. She started to hang up when she heard a male voice.

"If you want your mother and father to live, don't hang up."

Instantly, she knew what was wrong—the killers had her parents. She shut the door and yelled into the phone. "Don't hurt them, damn you. Don't you dare hurt them."

"As soon as you calm down we'll talk about it. In the meantime, listen closely. If you tell anyone about this, I'll kill your parents. That includes Scott Quinn and the police. The instant someone comes toward this house, they're dead. Is that clear?"

She put her hand to her face in horror.

"Did you hear me?"

"I—I heard you."

"Good. The next part is very important so listen carefully." He paused for a moment as the boom of a thunderclap echoed in the background, then he continued. "If I don't see you walk into this house, alone, by four o'clock tomorrow afternoon, your parents will die. It's that simple."

"And if I do?"

"I'll let them go free. That's a promise."

"What good is your promise?"

"Lauren, you don't have any other choice, and remember; if you tell anyone—they're dead. And it won't be pretty."

She hung up and slammed her hand against the phone but her anger quickly gave way to distress. The thought of Merrick harming her parents was too much to comprehend. She rubbed her forehead and tried to think of a way out, but there seemed to be no answers—no hope. Despair filled her heart. She glanced around to make sure Scott was still outside. When she thought of him, she realized she only had one choice. Innocent people had died because of her but it was not going to happen again—especially to those she loved so deeply. She pictured Scott in her mind, then she opened her wallet and looked at a picture of her parents. Thinking she had only one option, she made her decision.

Lauren had two immediate problems. She had to hide her emotions from Scott and she had to find a way to get away alone. She thought her first dilemma might not be as hard as it seemed because they were still suffering from the tragic events of the past few days, and she had not been her usual self. The second problem would be more difficult. Because of Scott's concern for her safety, he would not let her out of his sight. Even if she did manage to get away, she would need a substantial head start. Lauren's mind searched for possibilities, settling on what seemed to be her only option. She would have to sneak out while he was asleep. The more she thought about her plan, the more confident she became. Because Scott had been keeping watch for such long hours, he slept very soundly once he finally went to sleep. Lauren knew he was exhausted.

She fought to control her emotions, and she had just opened the phone booth door when Scott stuck his head in the store and looked around.

He came up to her. "I was starting to worry."

"My father's not doing so well, and with all the other things going on—"

He put his arm around her. "I understand. Let's go back to the room."

"Scott, can we get a nice takeout dinner and have some wine tonight?"

"Sure, we could both use it."

Scott bought Chinese food and one bottle of Chardonnay, but Lauren insisted on a second. She wanted the wine for two reasons. She would never see Scott again, and she wanted to make love to him one last time. She also knew the wine would intensify his exhaustion, causing him to sleep soundly. They drank a full bottle of wine and talked for nearly an hour before they ate. After dinner, Lauren made sure Scott's glass was never empty, and she was careful to control her own intake of wine. She felt guilty, but she thought she had no other choice.

They had not made love since Tuck's death, but Lauren hoped the wine would temporarily remove their pain. After the second bottle was half finished, she got up and began taking off her clothes. She knew it aroused Scott when she undressed slowly—it worked every time.

She lay on the bed and held out her arms.

He moved next to her and kissed her for several minutes, then moved his lips to her breasts.

A single tear rolled from the corner of her eye as they made love for what she knew would be the last time.

———

The combination of the wine, the late hour, and exhaustion produced the anticipated effect on Scott. After he had fallen into a deep sleep, Lauren waited an hour to be sure. It was two-thirty when she quietly gathered a few items and walked toward the door. She stopped when she realized she had forgotten to write a note. She went to the desk, took out a sheet of paper and quickly sketched a picture of a single rose. Below that, she wrote:

> They have my parents, and there is only one choice I can live with. I have to go to them. Though it will be too late when you read this note, don't try to follow me because they will kill Mom and Dad. I love you more than anything in this world.
> Please forgive me.
> Lauren.

She left the note on the table and turned to look at Scott one last time. After a long moment, she wiped her eyes and left the room.

When she pulled out of the parking lot, a dreadful sorrow engulfed her. Her choice seemed too much to ask of anyone; yet there was no other way.

A little before seven o'clock, her black Porsche crossed the Utah state line and entered Idaho. Lauren was careful to follow all traffic laws and kept the speedometer pegged on the posted limit. She looked at her watch and estimated she would arrive in Pilot Hill around noon.

She stared ahead mournfully as mile after mile slid by. There was a great ache in her breast and she found it difficult to swallow. She felt as though she was passing through a narrowing tunnel with no exit, but she knew it was a journey she had to take. There would be no other innocent people killed because of her. "Except for one," she said softly.

CHAPTER 50

A wine induced headache woke Scott at 6:52 a.m. He reached for Lauren but the bed was empty. In his somnolent state, he assumed she was in the bathroom and he rolled over. Seconds later his eyelids blinked open and he sat up. He looked toward the bathroom and saw that the door was open and the room was dark. He bounded out of bed and flipped on the light.

Lauren was gone.

He was halfway to the front door when he saw the note. Even before reading it, he knew the sketch of a rose had a profound significance. Lauren would not have done that if she were coming right back. He read the note, then slammed his fist on the desk. "No, dammit. No!"

He ran to the side of the bed and slipped on his pants and a shirt. He moved swiftly until he thought of the Porsche. He ran to the window and looked out. A pickup truck now occupied the space where he had parked the car.

"Shit."

Scott paced while he tried to think. His immediate concern was that he had no way of knowing when she left. Had it been thirty minutes or five hours? He did not know how much of a head start she had, but one thing was obvious—he needed a car. He had enough money, but he could not wait for a dealer to open. The town seemed large enough to have car rental agencies. But where?

"The airport."

As he spoke the words, he thought about taking a plane to Boise and renting a car. He picked up his watch and knew he did not have enough time. He walked toward the window, opened the curtains and looked out. He stared at nothing in particular, his mind processing his dilemma. He spoke aloud. "There's got to be a way. There's just got to."

Then it struck him.

He could go to the airport and try to book a charter. Hell, he had enough money to get the fastest airplane they had. He finished dressing, checked his gun, and stuffed extra cartridges in his jacket. He opened the phone book to Aircraft Charter and Rental Services and jotted down three numbers. No one responded at the first number and machines answered the other two. *Too early.*

Scott went outside and ran to the street. He had no idea how far the airport was, or whether there was a taxi service in town; he knew only that he had to hurry. He saw a coffee shop and ran toward it. Dust flew up from under a car as it skidded a stop, nearly hitting him. He dodged sideways, ran to the building, and opened the door.

Several men were eating breakfast at the counter and talking to a waitress. Three or four groups of people occupied nearby booths. The smell of coffee and bacon permeated the air. Scott burst into the cafe in a manner that caused several people to turn in his direction. He spoke loudly. "I'll give three hundred dollars to anyone who'll drive me to the airport."

The sudden pronouncement caused a grizzled looking old man with a gray beard to spit out a mouthful of coffee. He raised his hand. "You're on, mister." He took a quick gulp of coffee and spun on the stool.

Two minutes later, Scott sat in a dilapidated, rust-covered pickup with a hole in the floorboard. The truck did not start on the first try. He figured the truck obviously had to run better than it looked, or it would not have made it to the coffee shop. The engine turned over on the next try.

The old man's name was Floyd, and he talked constantly. He especially wanted to know where Scott was off to in such a rush. His questions seemed to stem from natural curiosity. Scott gave evasive answers, but he took a liking to Floyd. Any other time he would have enjoyed talking to the old man.

Floyd soon had the truck moving at its maximum speed— fifty-two miles an hour. They arrived at the airport and Scott gave him the promised money and thanked him.

The old man smiled through his beard. "Good luck, pardner."

Scott saw there were not many charters, but one was all he needed. Two hanger doors were open. He inquired in the first building only to learn their two planes were booked and out of the area. He went into the next building. The smell of brewing coffee filled the small, empty room. He went outside and found another charter service but was disappointed when told they had only a single engine plane, and the pilot was not due for two hours. He went back to the second hanger and waited. Someone would obviously be back for the coffee. He paced the floor until a smiling man of about forty came through the door.

"Good morning," the man said. "There's fresh coffee if you'd like some."

"Thanks, but what I really need is a two-engine charter, and I need it right now."

"Big hurry, huh? Well, I'm afraid you're out of luck. I've got one but it's scheduled for service this morning."

"I'll double your regular fee."

The man's eyebrows shot up. "Cash?"

"Yeah."

"Where to?"

"Pilot Hill, Idaho. It's north of Boise, don't know how far."

The man shook his hand. "Ramsey Mortenson. We'll be in the air in thirty minutes."

As soon as they reached cruising altitude, Scott asked Ramsey for a map of Idaho. He found Pilot Hill and estimated the route Lauren would have taken. They could follow the highways, but that would take more time than flying in a straight line.

Scott felt frustrated because he had no idea when Lauren had left. He finally decided he had to plan on a worst-case scenario, which he estimated to have been between one and two o'clock. That gave her a substantial head start. If, however, they took a straight route and got to Pilot Hill before she did, he could try to locate her parent's house and intercept her before she got there.

He marked Lauren's probable route for the last hundred miles of her journey, then instructed Ramsey to go the fastest way possible until they reached the spot Scott had marked on the map. When they reached that point, they could drop altitude and follow the highway hoping to locate her car.

They headed northwest and soon crossed into Idaho. It was ten after eleven when they reached the designated spot on route 55. A few minutes later, they turned right and followed another highway. They gained altitude to cross a series of ridges, then dropped into a small valley surrounded by tree-covered hills.

Scott was staring at the thin line of highway when Ramsey spoke, "You'd better have a look up ahead of us. I've been watching that smoke for some time and I think it's pretty close to Pilot Hill."

Scott looked toward the smoke and was surprised he had not seen it before, but he had been concentrating on one thing—finding a black Porsche on the highway below. He studied the smoke. "That looks too big to be anything but a forest fire."

"I'm afraid so. There have been a lot of thunderstorms in the area recently, and I've heard of two fires caused by lightning strikes." Ramsey squinted as he looked toward the smoke. "If it's as close to Pilot Hill as I think, I won't be able to land there. They'll have tankers in the air."

"Can you check it on the radio?"

"Yeah, I should be able to find out what's going on."

A few minutes later, Ramsey informed Scott that Pilot Hill's landing strip and the nearby airspace were restricted.

"Get me as close as possible."

"I've got no place to land now."

"Is there another airport in the area?"

"Well, there is a small town about twenty miles to the west I could use."

"All right. Take me as close to Pilot Hill as you can. At the last minute, we'll head for the other airport. I'll just have to get a ride somehow." The unexpected detour dealt a severe blow to his chances of finding Lauren in time. His distress increased but he had to maintain focus.

They flew over a small range of hills and dropped into another valley. Ramsey glanced at Scott. "That fire's coming from the northeastern section of Pilot Hill. I can't go in much farther."

"Just a few more miles."

Ramsey hesitated at first, then he agreed after being reminded of the double fee. Scott concentrated on the road below, and then he searched in the distance. He squinted and saw a small black dot. He pointed toward the car. "Take her down a little so I can get a better look at that car."

Ramsey seemed reluctant but he dropped two hundred feet and headed toward the highway.

A moment later, Scott yelled out, "That's her! It's her."

"It doesn't matter now," Ramsey replied. "I've got to pull up and turn west."

Scott looked toward the end of the valley. There wasn't much time before she would enter the last stretch of timber before reaching Pilot Hill. "I want you to fly ahead of her and land in the field next to the road."

"Christ, man. I can't do that."

Scott reached into his pocket and pulled out a banded stack of hundred dollar bills. "Five thousand dollars says you will."

Ramsey grabbed the money and sent the plane into a dive in the same motion. "Hang on."

Scott felt his stomach summersault.

They passed the Porsche and Scott looked again, concentrating. No doubt about it—it was Lauren. His attention went back to the field below, which suddenly looked shorter and much rougher than it had from a distance. He glanced at Ramsey and saw that he was lost in concentration. The plane lurched up and down.

Forty seconds later the wheels touched down, hit a small rut, and the plane bounced into the air again.

Ramsey yelled out, "Wahoo! Hang on to your ass."

The landing was much rougher than Scott had expected. Fear welled up inside him as he looked ahead and saw the trees, rushing toward them, growing larger by the second. With a final lurch, the plane's wheels came to rest in a small ditch a few feet short of the trees.

Scott took a deep breath, unbuckled himself, jumped out, thanked Ramsey over his shoulder, and headed toward the highway at full speed. If he did not get there before she passed, all was lost.

Run.

He came to a barbed wire fence and crawled through. The wire ripped his shirt and scratched his back but he hardly noticed. He ran to the edge of the road. The Porsche was less than three hundred yards away and closing fast. Scott ran onto the highway and waved his arms.

A pair of long, black tire marks played out behind the car as it slid to a screeching stop.

He saw the look of astonishment on Lauren's face, her expression that of a person in complete and total disbelief. He saw another car coming and waved her to the side of the road.

Lauren got out and threw her arms around him.

He held her close. "Don't say anything. I understand." He stroked her hair. "It's okay. . . . It's okay."

Scott held her for a long moment and then kissed her tenderly. Separating from her, he said, "We're in this together until the very end. No matter what. Do you understand?"

She wiped her eyes and nodded. "I love you."

"I love you too. More than you know." He walked her to the other side of the car. "Now comes the hard part. Let's get at it." Fifteen minutes later, they were on the edge of Pilot Hill. The fire had grown substantially and dense columns of smoke billowed over the town.

"Where do your parents live?"

"They're in those hills to the east."

"That's in the direction of the fire," Scott replied.

Furrows lined her brow. "I know."

He started to ask for directions when he saw a roadblock. The local officials were obviously trying to evacuate residents and seal off the town. "They won't let us go through," he said. "Is there a back way?"

"Yes, but it's a bit rough."

"Which way?"

"Back up and turn right on that last street."

They twisted and turned along back roads for several minutes but stopped suddenly when they saw another roadblock. Scott looked at Lauren. "Where to?"

"Turn around and take that dirt road we just passed. It won't take us all the way but we can get close."

He started up the narrow road and saw they were going straight toward the fire. "Jesus, Lauren. I don't think we can go much farther."

"We'll turn to the left in a minute. It looks a little better in that direction."

Scott turned onto another dirt road and climbed a steep hill. There was less smoke in this area; yet he knew how fast fires could travel. They were still dangerously close to the blaze. They drove past a house and watched as people frantically carried personal items to a truck before fleeing. When the road came to a dead end, he turned to Lauren. "What now?"

"Our house is right over that hill. We'll have to go on foot."

Scott checked his gun. "All right, let's have a look." When they reached the top of the hill, he was awestruck by the size and intensity of the fire. The most dangerous areas were still on their right, but his concern increased as he viewed the spectacle.

Lauren pointed toward the bottom of the hill. "That's our house."

Scott looked down and saw an open space surrounded by timber. A grassy area dotted with trees lay between the bottom of the slope and a swimming pool. The house was just beyond. A small ridge covered with pine ran along the other side of the house. He studied the surroundings, but he had no idea how to approach the house or what to do once they got there. He did not know how many men Merrick might have or whether they had fled because of the fire.

They were in a tough spot but they had to try something. He was surveying the area when he noticed that the wind had changed. Earlier, there had been a light breeze in their face, but stronger gusts now swirled behind them. He turned and looked back and was surprised to see the house they had gone by minutes before engulfed in flames.

He touched Lauren's shoulder and pointed behind them. "It's turned this way. We'd better get the hell out of here."

She looked at Scott, trepidation showing from her eyes. "I can't go without knowing if my parents are still in there. I just can't."

A gust of hot air blew across their backs. The fire was moving rapidly, and the heat intensified by the second. Scott grabbed her hand. "We'll work down to the left side of the house and see if we can get in. If Merrick's in there, it's going to be dangerous as hell."

Lauren nodded, her expression determined. "I know."

CHAPTER 51

They were halfway down the hill when the noise from the advancing fire became deafening. Scott looked back and saw that the wind change had fueled the fire and sent it rushing up the hill so quickly that it had already reached the crest. The blaze had developed into a firestorm with enough power to create its own winds, and the temperature had risen to an almost unbearable level.

He looked about and changed his priorities. The fire raged fiercely on all sides, and was now threatening the Chandler home from the opposite ridge. Any attempt to get to the house would probably be suicidal. Though they appeared to be trapped, he decided to move to their left and hope for a break in the flames.

They had nearly reached the bottom of the hill when several nearby trees exploded in flames. A tree off to their right suddenly crashed to the ground sending burning branches and a shower of sparks into the eerie, reddish-orange sky. The smoke roiled and thickened, diminishing their vision with frightening speed.

Terrible, heat-bred images ricocheted in Scott's mind, and he knew the fiery air was now more than a concern—it was life threatening. Their predicament took on exigent proportions, propelling Scott to desperation in his search for a way out. He grabbed Lauren's hand and ran toward the bottom of the slope. They reached the grassy area, dodged around a large burning tree, and headed for the swimming pool. Thick, turbulent smoke obscured most of the house.

He stopped at the edge of the pool. "Jump in! I'll be right there."

She looked toward the house and hesitated.

He pushed her off the edge.

Scott ran to the rear of the house and grabbed a blanket that was folded over a bench. He ran back to the pool, jumped in and soaked the blanket. He then swam to the corner farthest from the fire and motioned for Lauren to get under the wet blanket.

They could not see, but heat from the roaring inferno seemed to come from every direction, seeking them out. They repeatedly ducked under the water to soak the blanket and gain relief from the intense firestorm. They had just come up for air when Scott thought he heard shouting. He maneuvered to the edge of the blanket and heard a loud crash that sent huge waves surging through the pool. He thought the house had collapsed, but realized it was not close enough to have had such a drastic effect on the water in the pool.

Again, he heard shouting.

Scott looked out from under the blanket and saw that the top of a large tree had fallen into the other end of the pool. The portion of the trunk that stuck out of the water flamed brightly. Curls of blue smoke rose from the water line around the trunk.

He started to duck under the blanket when he saw several people jump into the pool. They had to have come from the house. Scott reached for his gun but it was not there. He checked again. The Beretta was gone. Where in the hell was it? He thought it must have fallen out when he jumped into the pool. He got under the blanket and tugged on Lauren's arm. "I lost the gun, and I think it's on the bottom. I'm going down to get it."

He took a deep breath and swam toward the bottom. He was halfway down when he looked up and saw two men swimming toward Lauren. The hell with the gun. *Help her.*

He swam upward, targeting the man in front. A few seconds later, he surfaced next to the startled swimmer. Before the man could react, Scott sent a vicious right-handed punch to the man's face. Because his momentum had lifted his upper body slightly above the water line, he was able to put considerable power into the blow. The tremendous force of the punch stunned the man, causing him to flounder.

Scott looked toward the second attacker.

Victor Merrick, his face contorted in rage, raised his gun.

Scott dove under him, grabbed his foot, and twisted hard. When Merrick flinched, Scott shot up out of the water and delivered a solid right hand to the jaw. He grasped Merrick's right arm and smashed his fist down on the weapon, jarring the pistol loose. Scott sent several hard punches at the gunman's face. His blows stunned Merrick, sending him in retreat to the side of the pool.

He had started to swim after Merrick when the other man grabbed him from behind and applied a vicious chokehold. Scott submerged with the man's hands still around his neck and struggled to free himself, but the outsized man had exceptional power.

He was running out of breath when his attacker abruptly released his grip and went up for air. Scott moved to his right and surfaced next to his attacker. He gasped for air as he realized he was now face to face with the gunman he had hit with the baseball bat and the tree limb. The man's eyes blazed with revenge.

Lisowski unleashed his fury in a violent rage. The big man's first blow landed with such power that Scott nearly blacked out.

More punches landed in a flurry. Scott dove to get free and resurfaced nearby.

Lisowski came at him again.

Scott remembered that his attacker had surfaced before he did when they were previously under water, and he thought his best chance was to dive again. Just as Lisowski reached him, Scott took a deep breath and went under.

Lisowski followed him to the bottom, but Scott swam out of his grasp at each attack. He waited until the big man started to surface, then Scott swam over and grabbed him from behind. He put his arm around the gunman's neck and channeled every ounce of strength toward a single purpose. He tightened his grip.

Lisowski panicked. He was obviously badly in need of air, and began thrashing about in a desperate attempt to get free.

Scott's own lungs screamed for air, yet he held on.

Lisowski's violent efforts increased his consumption of oxygen. He thrashed again but with less vigor. He continued to struggle, but Scott was now the stronger of the two men, and he again tightened his hold around the man's neck.

Scott felt the struggling man gasp and suck water into his lungs. The instant Ray Lisowski went limp, Scott propelled himself to the surface and gulped for air. On his second breath, he heard Lauren yell but it was too late.

Merrick had regained his strength and lashed out.

A fierce blow struck Scott above the eye.

Blood spurted into the water.

Scott gasped for air and tried to clear his vision. Another fist caught him on the right temple. He reeled under the punch and fought to keep from going under. Blow after blow rained upon him. Punishment and exhaustion weakened Scott to a point of desperation.

His vision narrowed and blurred.

When the last fragment of Scott's strength crumbled, his resolve gave way to a numbing weakness.

———

Lauren felt horrified as she watched the vicious struggle. Scott fought with fiery determination, but the battle against two larger men made the odds greater than he could possibly overcome. When Scott had surfaced and been attacked by Merrick, Lauren's distress turned to anger. Her mind searched for a way to help, but there did not seem to be anything she could do. She looked about and saw that the worst of the fire's intensity had swept by, but the house was now ablaze. She swam to the edge of the pool, pulled the blanket over her head and climbed out. She looked about frantically but found nothing she could use to help Scott. She had decided to dive in and fight Merrick with her bare hands when she saw a long, nylon cord at the end of the pool. Her father often used ropes to hang flags and other decorations in the back yard for small gatherings. She rushed over, grabbed the cord and dove in.

Lauren swam toward the two men, took a deep breath, and dove under the water. She maneuvered directly under Merrick and wrapped one end of the cord around his ankle. She tied knots until she ran out of breath. She surfaced, sucked in air, and submerged once more. She grabbed the cord, wrapped it around his leg again, and tied several more knots. She had to secure enough knots to insure that removal would be difficult and time-consuming.

Lauren surfaced, took a huge breath, then she dove toward the bottom with the other end of the cord. She reached the fallen tree and barely managed to swim under a narrow space near the bottom. She came through on the other side and grabbed the underwater ladder at the edge of the pool, then she struggled upward, pulling on the rope as hard she could.

She reached the surface and saw that the taunt cord had pulled Merrick directly over the fallen tree but he was still above water. She looped the end of the cord around the ladder and dove again. When she came to where the cord went under the tree trunk she put her feet against the bottom of the pool for leverage and then pulled hard on the cord. When she had taken up two feet of rope, she swam to the ladder and pulled up the slack. She ran out of air and had to surface.

Lauren looked across the pool and saw that she had succeeded in pulling Merrick under water. That was what she wanted, but she had not sufficiently secured the cord. She dove again and wrapped the end through the loop she had made on the ladder, and then she tied several knots as tight as possible.

Just as she was running out of air, she saw Merrick swim lower and disappear on the other side of the submerged part of the tree. There were too many knots on his leg to untangle, and he obviously realized his only chance was to free the other end of the cord.

She surfaced, inhaled deeply, and quickly submerged. She went lower and watched his frantic search for the end of the rope. Merrick found where the cord ran under the fallen tree and tried to swim under the massive trunk, but his bulk proved too large to fit through the narrow space.

Lauren swam to the surface and looked for Scott. She saw him clinging to the side gasping for air. Blood streamed down his face, curling around large welts, but he was alive. She swam toward him and yelled, "Are you all right?"

He nodded weakly and looked back across the pool. "Merrick? Where's Merrick?"

"I tied a rope around his ankle and fastened the other end to the ladder, but I don't know if it will hold." She reached him. "Let me help you."

They climbed out and scanned the water.

Unable to free the cord from the bottom, Merrick tried to surface. His arms, visible from his elbows up, waved frantically back and forth. The top of his head stuck out about an inch but not far enough for him to breathe. Merrick struggled desperately, but he was unable to get his nose above the water line.

They watched as his arms thrashed less violently, then his water-slicked, black hair disappeared. Victor Merrick floated to the bottom amid a tangle of cord and tree branches.

Lauren turned her attention to the burning house. "My parents—" She started toward the house.

Scott yelled out. "Wait. Over there."

Lauren turned and saw him pointing toward the far corner of the pool. An elderly man and woman were climbing out of the water.

Relief washed the concern from Lauren's face. She yelled and rushed toward them. "Mom! . . . Dad!" She threw her arms around them, and they clung to each other. After a moment, they turned and watched the house burn.

Scott went over and put his arm around Lauren. He wiped blood away from his eyes and said, "We'll build another one."

CHAPTER 52

They tended Scott's cuts using a compression technique, then watched the firestorm move to the west on its search for new fuel. When the fury had passed, Scott, Lauren, and her parents walked through a world of ash and destruction. They eventually found an operable phone, and Lauren's father called friends who came and picked them up.

Scott explained what had happened, and said he was concerned because Lauren was still considered a fugitive. They decided that Scott and Lauren would use the friend's car and immediately leave the area. Two hours after their departure, Lauren's father would phone the police and explain what happened at the house.

———

A hundred miles from Pilot Hill, Scott stopped at a phone booth and called Hayden Benson. The phone rang several times until a man answered.

Scott spoke firmly, "Listen carefully, and don't hang up."

"Who is this?"

"You know me as Jim Carpenter, but that's not my real name."

Benson responded nervously, "I won't talk to you."

"Victor Merrick is dead."

"W—What?"

"It's all over. Merrick's dead, and you have only one choice left."

"What do you mean?"

"I was watching when you retrieved the crop report data from the men's bathroom. I know the information was sent down the pipe on an eraser."

"Dear God."

"I also know about you and the woman at the apartment."

Silence.

"Benson?"

"What are you going to do?"

"I'll give you forty-eight hours to confess everything. If you don't, this will all be released to the press. Everything. Do you understand?"

"I—I can't talk now."

Scott pressed him. "I'll check back in two days. If you haven't done exactly what I told you to do, I'll go straight to the newspapers."

After the phone call, they drove to Boise, checked into a hotel and waited.

———

On the morning of the second day, Scott ordered breakfast and a newspaper from room service. He had just taken a sip of coffee when Lauren unfolded the newspaper and gasped, "My God. Look." She spun the paper around and showed Scott the headline.

AG OFFICIAL COMMITS MURDER, SUICIDE
USDA crop reporting procedures under review.

The article stated that Hayden Benson had apparently murdered his mistress, Shannon Peterson, and then turned the gun on himself. The incident occurred in the woman's apartment the previous day. Benson recorded a full confession and an apology on a camera he said was hidden to take pictures of him and the woman for use as blackmail.

When Scott approached the end of the article, he jumped up and grabbed Lauren's hand. "Listen to this." He looked at the paper and read aloud, "Benson further disclosed that a former Agriculture Department employee, Lauren Chandler, had no part in the scheme and that she was not involved in the murder of her roommate." He put his arms around her. It's over! It's all over." They embraced, engulfed in emotion.

An hour later, they called Angela Williams and arranged for her and government authorities to meet them the following day at National Airport in Washington. That night they had dinner in the most expensive restaurant in Boise. When they got back to the hotel, they did not make love; they simply held each other, shared the closeness, and enjoyed their newfound freedom.

———

Scott and Lauren remained in Washington, D.C. for three days. They were allowed to leave, with the understanding they would have to return at least one more time. They flew to Chicago and were met by a smiling, Jason McDonald.

A few days later Scott told Lauren to pack for a trip of several days. They flew to Colorado, rented a car and drove to Debbie Holloway's home in Little River. On the evening of their visit, they held hands, laughed, cried, and shared stories about Tuck.

The next morning, Scott and Lauren rose with the sun and drove to Tucker Pack Trips. While Lauren waited at the house, he hiked to the site where Tuck had died. He stood in front of the tree for a long moment, then he pulled out a pocketknife and cut Tuck's name into the bark. Below the name, he added the dates of his birth and death.

Scott moved back several steps, sat cross-legged on the ground, and looked at the tree. He knew his gesture might appear as a mere token to some, but to him it was a solemn dedication to a fallen friend that he hoped would remain long after his own departure from this earth. He sat motionless, staring, his thoughts spiraling through the years. It was a moment in time unlike any he had ever felt, and he sat silently, taking in the enormity of his emotions.

It took nearly an hour to assuage his feelings. He finally rose, stepped up to the tree, and moved his fingers slowly along the fresh grooves, tracing Tuck's name. He knew he would return to touch the memorial, and he knew he would again shed tears for his friend.

He let his hand drop, turned, and walked through the forest, wondering why a good man had been taken so young. It seemed to Scott that death was life's evil companion. He pushed the notion aside as he came out of the trees.

When he saw Lauren standing outside the house, he thought about their future together. From deep in his soul, he made an oath to extract as much from life's journey as humanly possible, and he would do it with the only woman he had ever loved.

AUTHOR'S NOTES

1) This novel is set in 1991. At that time, the USDA issued the monthly Crop Production Report after the grain markets closed. The release time was changed in 1994, and again at a later date. The report is currently released during market hours.

2) An end of an era took place in July of 2015. Because of the overwhelming use of electronics, trading in open-outcry trading pits ended for many commodities. Open-outcry volume had steadily declined because of the increase of electronic trading. A vibrant, long-standing tradition has come to an end.

Made in the USA
Columbia, SC
06 November 2024

45790345R00228